W9-BXY-731

The Glendower Conspiracy

A M E M O I R

of Sherlock Holmes

from the Papers of Edward Porter Jones, His Late Assistant

LLOYD BIGGLE, JR.

COUNCIL OAK BOOKS, TULSA

Council Oak Books
Tulsa, Oklahoma 74120

Published 1990
Printed in the United States of America

Library of Congress Catalog Card Number 90-80355
ISBN Number 933031-25-4

Designed by Carol Haralson

Grateful acknowledgement is made to Dame Jean Conan Doyle for permission to use the Sherlock Holmes characters created by Sir Arthur Conan Doyle.

To Maurice Richards
Historian of Newton, Powys, Wales
whose generous assistance
made this book possible

to my daughter, Donna Emerson
Chauffeur and Fellow-Explorer
who discovered Wales with me

and to the memory of
Sir Arthur Conan Doyle,
creator of Sherlock Holmes.

I

On a warm Saturday evening in early June, 1904, I heard a flurry of footsteps on the stairs, the door to the rooms at 221B Baker Street opened abruptly, and — to my complete astonishment — I found myself face to face with a spectral figure: Sherlock Holmes, who was supposed to be in Scotland with his long-time friend and associate, Dr. John Watson. His unusually tall, gaunt form was intimidating to a man of my stature in the best of circumstances, and it seemed gigantic when he confronted me suddenly. He was paler than usual — there had been no sun at all in Scotland — but his sharp, penetrating eyes had lost none of their disquieting effect.

A dramatic entrance that totally surprised his audience always delighted him. He faced me with a taut smile on his lips — an unmistakable sign of good health and restless expectation. Obviously he was eager to slough off his idleness and resume work.

He pointed his thin nose into the room, sniffed deeply, and announced, "So you've been attending to the scrapbooks." Then, before I could respond, he continued, "Why hasn't Lestrade stopped by recently? Is he taking his holidays?" His eyes continued to dart about the room. "I see that Radbert hasn't returned yet. How is the new maid working out?"

My mind was still whirling in an effort to take all of this in when he set his valise down and said sternly, "Well, Porter?"

It was always thus when he had been away. The remark about the new maid, for example. The old one had been called home unexpectedly by the illness of her mother, and Mrs. Hudson had to replace her, but all of that happened several days after he left for Scotland. There was no ordinary way that he could have known about it. He hadn't met the new maid on the stairs — she was out for the evening. I could only assume that his remarkably quick perception had discovered an object — any object — out of place. The old maid had learned to leave everything untouched; hence there had to be a new maid in the house.

He performed such feats of logic brilliantly throughout his waking hours and with such a dazzling swiftness that even those closely associated with him found his reasoning difficult to follow. Dazed strangers thought him a wizard — until they prevailed upon him to explain his methods, which were firmly grounded in the humdrum but meticulous observation of trivia.

The scent of paste informed him that I had been at work on the scrapbooks — I never used it for anything else; the absence of the peculiarly lingering odour of Turkish tobacco indicated no recent visit from Lestrade, the Scotland Yard inspector, who was addicted to Turkish cigarettes; Rabby, the ragged street Arab who was Sherlock Holmes's favourite member of his Baker Street Irregulars, wore heavy boots that invariably put scuff marks upon the legs of any chair he sat in, much to Mrs. Hudson's distress, and our unscuffed chairs were incontestable proof of his continued absence. Thus baldly explained, Sherlock Holmes's remarkable deductions lost all of their magic. As he himself remarked ruefully on more than one occasion, *Omne ignotum pro magnifico,* "Everything unknown is considered admirable." The most complicated problem could seem childishly simple after he had explained it.

It was his "Well, Porter?" that totally deflated me. I was too dumbfounded to say anything. He was supposed to be in Scotland for at least another month. Nothing was ready for his return. Of course he deduced that, also, and the result was as sharp a display of temper as I had ever witnessed from him.

He had cause for it. We hadn't had an interesting case during the three months prior to his departure, and Rabby, who frequently enlivened our evenings with descriptions of the strange events he observed in the London streets, had inexplicably disappeared. Rabby carried messages and ran errands from one end of metropolitan London to the other, and no one knew what went on there better than he or observed it more sharply. Sherlock Holmes had given him a roving assignment: Whenever he saw anything unusual, he was to come to Baker Street at his first opportunity and tell us about it.

His strange disappearance had been the most perplexing of the frustrations Sherlock Holmes suffered during this period of stagnation. Rabby's descriptions of the oddities he had seen relieved the day's tedium for us even when the events that produced them were trivial. When the third week passed without his calling, Sherlock Holmes became concerned about him and sent me to find him; and I turned up the astonishing information that he had gone to Eastbourne for early holidays.

Work never seemed to tire Sherlock Holmes, no matter how long the hours or how little sleep he got, but idleness quickly exhausted him. A lengthy spell of enforced inactivity actually threatened his health and left Mrs. Hudson worried that she would soon have an invalid on her hands.

Then Dr. Watson enticed him to Scotland with the combined offer of a remarkable puzzle about a missing will and a charming country inn that was the centre of delightful walks. Unfortunately, an absent-minded solicitor discovered the will in his safe before Sherlock Holmes reached Edinburgh, and the delightful walks dissolved in the buffeting of a chill, persistent rain.

Sherlock Holmes gave up and returned to London, fully expectant that I would have honoured the request he flung at me like a Parthian shot on his departure: Have a case — any case — ready for him when he returned. I had failed miserably.

It was not for want of trying. Sherlock Holmes could not have tolerated an assistant who vacillated or procrastinated, and whenever he left me to my own devices, I gave myself the most exacting tasks that I was capable of inventing. I worked diligently on his files and scrapbooks during the two weeks that he was away and got them fully organized and current for the first time in years. I devoted my evenings to studying them, along with records of his past cases, in the hope that they might furnish a clue that could be developed into a new case.

I also made the rounds of the police stations daily and searched the newspapers for oddities of the kind that he delighted in. I consulted every informant I could think of. There simply were no crimes in London worthy of even a casual glance from Sherlock Holmes. In actual fact, the police calendar had been so dull that both Lestrade and our friend Stanley Hopkins, the Scotland Yard detective, were taking early holidays.

I didn't have Rabby's knack for discovering bizarre events that Sherlock Holmes would find intriguing. Ferreting these out required more leisure and patience than I could devote to such a project. Rabby prowled the streets of London from dawn until midnight in search of chores and commissions that would bring him a few pence or even the odd shilling or two. He was certain to encounter an occasional interesting occurrence.

That was the situation Sherlock Holmes found waiting for him on his return, and it had been severely aggravated by a blunder Mrs. Hudson made that very morning. She confessed her error tearfully a few minutes after his arrival. There actually had been a caller asking for Sherlock Holmes — from her description, an extremely interesting potential client. "He was a foreigner," she said. "Leastways, he talked like one." She had told him that Sherlock Holmes was in Scotland, and she allowed him to depart without so much as taking his name. She didn't even think to inquire as to whether he might be willing to discuss his business with Sherlock Holmes's assistant, Mr. Jones, who was available.

She had been unusually flustered. Cook had allowed the roast to burn, and the maid had just dropped her largest tureen — but these excuses did nothing to assuage Sherlock Holmes's frustration. He threatened to throw his valise, and Mrs. Hudson fled.

She returned a short time later with a telegram that had arrived, reply prepaid, asking whether the sender might call upon Sherlock Holmes for a consultation at nine the next morning. He scribbled his assent and handed it to Mrs. Hudson to dispatch.

"It is signed 'Arthur Saunders,'" he said. "The name means nothing to me. Does it to you?"

I shook my head.

"The reply was addressed to the Euston Hotel. Very likely he is a visitor to London from the West or North by way of Euston Station."

"Could he be our foreign-sounding caller of this morning?" I asked.

"Surely you haven't forgotten everything I taught you in a mere two weeks," Sherlock Holmes said testily. "Mrs. Hudson chased him away with the information that I was in Scotland. He wouldn't be sending me a telegram eight hours later requesting an appointment."

The possibility that two new clients had appeared on the same day dispelled his gloom completely. The telegram seemed promising to him — a visitor to London willing to get out of bed to consult a private investigator at nine o'clock on a Sunday morning was not likely to present a trivial problem, and there remained the possibility that the foreign-sounding gentleman would return later. His homecoming was a success after all, and he was able to relax and entertain me with an account of Dr. Watson's clumsy efforts to add a veneer of interest to a rainy Scotland. He actually seemed in a cheerful mood when we retired.

Sunday at 221B Baker Street was Mrs. Hudson's day of approximate leisure. After superintending the preparation of the most elaborate breakfast that the boundaries of her imagination could encompass, she carefully arrayed herself for church, to which she escorted the servants with proper ceremony. Any necessary preparations for Sunday's cold supper had been made the day before. She served no Sunday dinner except by special order, and then the cooked food was prepared in the home of a neighbour with whom she had "arrangements" or brought in from a nearby restaurant.

Sunday was not a day of leisure in Sherlock Holmes's rooms, but some semblance of the mood of the vast city around us penetrated there, and everything was done more leisurely. Unless there were urgent errands, we breakfasted at a later hour. The Sunday papers arrived along with our food, and we immersed ourselves in them immediately, absently eating while we read.

The remarkable thing about 221B Baker Street when we arose on a Sunday morning was the stillness that surrounded us. Outside our windows, pavements and street were empty. The neighbourhood had the air of a vast cemetery of mausoleums, unattended and unvisited. The interminable rumble of commercial wagons, of butchers', or bakers', or greengrocers', or fishmongers', or other delivery carts and vans, of four-wheelers, of hansom cabs, of broughams and landaus and drays and wagonettes and coaches, all of them built with iron-rimmed wheels that ground and rattled and reverberated over London's paving stones in an unending procession on weekdays, was miraculously stilled. There were no cries or bells of street traders, no shouts from drivers of vehicles contending for rights of way, no cracking of whips, no whistling from errand boys or blasts on whistles from pedestrians hailing cabs, no turmoil and clamour from dray drivers who had clumsily managed to lock wheels with each other. The only sound that intruded was the rustle of stiff petticoats as the maid passed our door, already clothed in her Sunday best; or, if we opened the door, we might hear subdued voices floating up to us from the kitchen far below along with the enticing aroma of coffee and savoury indications of frying bacon and fish and sausages.

On the Sunday that followed Sherlock Holmes's return, I sat waiting for breakfast at an earlier hour than usual because of the nine o'clock appointment. Sherlock Holmes had not yet appeared, but he was awake and dressing. I heard the muffled sounds of wardrobe doors and drawers in his room as he opened and closed them. There were footsteps on the stairs — announcing, I thought, the coming of breakfast — and I opened the door to assist the maid.

It was Mrs. Hudson. She said excitedly, "Here's Rabby!" She had been fully as concerned as Sherlock Holmes had about the boy's disappearance.

"Rabby!" I exclaimed. "Come in. Join us for breakfast. I've never seen a more welcome face!"

The grinning Rabby stepped around Mrs. Hudson and slipped into the room. He had been transformed during his absence. He wore a new coat, waistcoat, and long trousers of quality worsted, and he carried a cap in his hands.

"It isn't Rabby!" I protested. "This is the newly found missing heir!"

He burst into laughter.

I got him seated at the table and sat down beside him. "I hope you have brought us something," I told him. "This place has been in the doldrums for weeks. Mr. Holmes has been frantic. I heard you had gone to Eastbourne, and now you walk in looking like a swell. What happened?"

"I went to Eastbourne with Doctor Tilbury," Rabby said proudly. "His page got sick just before he left, and Mr. Mullens recommended me."

Mr. Mullens was an ostler who let Rabby sleep in his stables and occasionally employed him to look after the horses. I had never heard of Dr. Tilbury, but doubtless he was well-known in Harley Street.

"Was it Doctor Tilbury who outfitted you?" I asked.

Rabby nodded. "He's rich. He and Mrs. Tilbury were nice to me. There wasn't much to do so I had good holidays."

"You had a marvellous time, I'm sure. I've always wanted to go to Eastbourne. But you should have let us know you were going. When did you get back?"

"Wednesday," Rabby said. "Since then I been catching up."

He had a clientele of business and professional men who made regular use of his services. No doubt some of them missed him as much as we had.

Sherlock Holmes appeared, greeted Rabby with amazement, and made him prance about the room to show off his clothing. "But it won't do, Radbert," he said, shaking his head severely. He always insisted on calling Rabby by his proper name. "No one took notice of you in your old clothing. You could go almost anywhere. Now you look like a barrister's clerk."

"I saved my old things," Rabby said, stroking his sleeve. He was enjoying being dressed up for the first time in his life. "I can wear them if I need to."

Our breakfast arrived. Mrs. Hudson supervised from the doorway while the new maid and a kitchen helper served us. Rabby watched with sparkling eyes as the dishes were uncovered. When we began to eat, his performance surpassed both of ours. He ate with such a robust appetite whenever free food was offered to him that I couldn't understand how he managed to eat so little at other times.

When Rabby had taken the edge from his hunger, I asked him hopefully, "Do you have something for Mr. Holmes?"

"Yes and no," Rabby said.

"What do you mean, yes and no?" Sherlock Holmes demanded with mock sternness. "Surely during your long holiday fling at Eastbourne, you noticed *something* of interest."

Rabby shook his head. "I didn't bring anything. I didn't plan to stop. I took a bottle of medicine to a customer in Henrietta Mansions for Mr. Onslow —

he's the chemist in Marylebone Road — and I chanced to come back this way. As I passed here, I noticed something you should know about."

We waited. There was no hurrying Rabby. He had an innate sense of the dramatic, and he told a story in his own good time.

"I was walking along looking in shop windows," he said, "and suddenly I glanced straight ahead and saw a nose."

"A nose?" I repeated blankly.

Rabby nodded. He took a bite of sausage, chewed solemnly, and swallowed it with evident relish. "It disappeared. Then it stuck out again, and that time there was a chin with it. A toff peeped around the corner, took a quick look down the street, and ducked back out of sight. He was in the doorway of the bank opposite the Bazaar. He made me curious."

It took very little to make Rabby curious. A well-dressed man peeping out of a doorway would occupy him until he got the mystery solved.

Sherlock Holmes was listening with delight. "Your curiosity is always well-founded, Radbert," he said. "What did you do?"

"I went on up the street. When I got to Dorset Street, I saw something else that seemed curious. There was a boy standing at the corner and not doing anything."

A boy who had nothing to do but idle at a street corner at that hour of a Sunday morning was even more of an anomaly than a skulking toff. Two such phenomena encountered in a short stretch of Baker Street had turned Rabby's curiosity on end. He wondered whether the events might be connected. Then he turned the corner into Dorset Street and discovered a third phenomenon.

"There was a hansom at the kerb, and the driver was doing nothing," Rabby said. "When a gentleman tried to hail him, he shook his head. I went back to Baker Street and found my own doorway where I could watch all three of them."

"How long ago was this?" I asked.

A timepiece would have been a nuisance to Rabby; he had no need of one. Church bells and the clocks displayed by business establishments provided as much indication as he required of the passage of time, though they often left him vague as to its more precise details.

He shrugged. "I watched them for a bit more than an hour. Until just before I came here."

"Then you had an early start this morning," Sherlock Holmes observed.

Rabby nodded. "Mr. Onslow's customer was sick. He wanted the medicine right away. I took a cab."

"And then you walked back to pocket the return fare," Sherlock Holmes said with a smile.

Rabby nodded unblushingly.

"The toff had a much earlier start than Rabby if he was doing a spying act in Baker Street at that hour," I remarked. "Were you able to find out what he was watching?"

Rabby's grin broadened. He was delighted at having worked out this puzzle by himself, and he refused to be hurried. "The boy — that was easy. He was watching the toff. He almost never took his eyes off him. The cab driver was harder. He just sat there. But now and then the boy tossed half a glance that way. I worked it out like this. If the toff wanted a cab in a hurry, all he had to do was signal. The boy would signal to the cabby, and the cabby would be around the corner and down the street in a jiffy. They had it all arranged."

"Then the toff was waiting to follow someone," I said.

"He was," Rabby agreed. "The problem was to figure out what house he was watching. That's what took me an hour. Finally I got it."

"What house was it?" I asked.

"This one."

I stared at him. "It couldn't be! Mr. Holmes has just returned from Scotland. We haven't had a case for months. Why would anyone be watching this house?"

"Don't know," Rabby said, "but someone was. And is."

Sherlock Holmes and I exchanged glances.

"Describe this toff," Sherlock Holmes said.

"Red-faced and heavy-set, no whiskers, dressed to kill with a gold chain, and a gold-handled cane, and all. He's wearing a boater."

I looked questioningly at Sherlock Holmes. I was as eager for action as he was. The toff presented a mediocre challenge, at best, but following him would give me something to do.

He shook his head. "I may need you," he said, referring to the nine o'clock appointment.

I turned to Rabby. "Could you follow him and find out who he is?"

"I might need help."

"Hold a moment. He saw you come in here — "

Rabby shook his head. "Not me. I circled around by the back door."

I looked again at Sherlock Holmes. He gave me an approving nod.

I supplied Rabby with a handful of coins. "You'll need a cab of your own," I said. "A couple of your chums might come in useful, too. Can you manage it?"

"Of course," Rabby said. He was grinning happily. It would be a fun-filled Sunday for him.

The clatter on the stairway outside our rooms sounded like a procession. Sherlock Holmes always referred to such approaching footsteps as the summons of fate. We never knew what high drama — or sordid melodrama — might enter our lives when the door was opened. The only thing we could be certain of was that someone needed a specialist in crime.

There was a sharp rap on the door. Mrs. Hudson, displaying none of the ill temper she must have felt at having her Sunday disrupted, announced pompously, "Two gentlemen to see Mr. Holmes."

It was nine o'clock and time for the appointment.

Rabby slipped out when I opened the door. I waved him on his way and turned to make our visitors welcome; but Sherlock Holmes was already attending to that, so I assisted the maid with getting the breakfast things cleared away. I heard the preliminary conversation over my shoulder. Arthur Saunders, after introducing himself as a solicitor from Newtown, Montgomeryshire, Wales, presented his companion, Mr. Bryn Huws, and Huws said something that I didn't understand. I learned only much later that he had said, "Sut mae?" which was reason enough for my not understanding it. I paid little attention to them until I heard my name mentioned.

Arthur Saunders said, "To be truthful, it isn't you that we have called to see, Mr. Holmes. Is this Mr. Jones, your assistant? We wish to engage his professional services."

2

I TURNED IN BEWILDERMENT. THERE WAS A LOOK of blank astonishment on Sherlock Holmes's face such as I had never seen before, and my own expression certainly matched it. I possibly had a modest reputation among our friends and clients as a capable assistant, but this is not the kind of fame that attracts commissions from well-to-do strangers. I had never achieved anything in my profession without the guidance of my employer.

Sherlock Holmes was highly sensitive to professional slights, and to have a supposed client prefer his assistant to himself, for any reason, was a monumental affront to him. I spoke quickly, hoping to smooth the waters before Arthur Saunders troubled them further. "I'm only Mr. Holmes's employee," I protested. "I couldn't accept any kind of commission without his permission and approval."

"We'll make it right with him," Saunders said confidently. He was tall, stout, bald, and plushly dressed, with the air of a man accustomed to getting what he wanted. Bryn Huws, his companion, was lean, taciturn, and clipped in speech. His dark hair was long and shaggy. He was plainly dressed and carried a gloomy, foreboding expression as though it were a burden life had imposed on him.

"Why are you so intent on engaging me?" I asked. "I'm a mere journeyman. I've never undertaken any kind of an investigation without Mr. Holmes's supervision."

"But you are *Welsh,*" Saunders said.

Huws was nodding emphatically.

Sherlock Holmes chuckled. He could be charmingly affable when he chose, and he was so now. "All of us should be reminded occasionally that we have ancestors," he said. "I gravely fear that Porter has forgotten his. Pray make yourselves comfortable and tell us about your problem."

Arthur Saunders took the chair that once had been Dr. Watson's. The doctor still used it on his occasional visits; otherwise, it was reserved for clients. It was an elaborate, lavishly upholstered monstrosity known as a library chair. The front rail pulled forward to form a foot rest, and the back reclined. Sherlock Holmes, who thought that comfort anaesthetized the mental processes, thoroughly disliked it.

Bryn Huws took one end of the sofa. I occupied the other. Sherlock Holmes settled himself restlessly on a mahogany armchair.

"You can't mean that Mr. Jones isn't Welsh," Saunders protested. "With a name like Jones? Impossible! He has to be Welsh!"

"My grandfather came from Wales," I told him. "He worked on a canal boat that brought slates to Paddington. He liked London, so he settled here and married an Englishwoman. That made my father only half Welsh. He also married an Englishwoman, so I'm no more than a quarter Welsh, and even that is misleading. My grandfather was thoroughly Anglicized by the time I knew him."

"Then you don't speak Welsh?" Saunders's voice was tense with disappointment.

I shook my head. "Not a word."

The two men exchanged grave looks. So depressed was their manner that one would have thought a national catastrophe had occurred. "That is most unfortunate," Saunders said. "In rural Wales, there are many people who don't speak English. It would be difficult — "

"It would be impossible," Huws said.

Saunders nodded. "We'll have to look elsewhere, and where are we likely to find a capable investigator who can even pass the time of day in Welsh? I told you when we started — it was an inconceivable stroke of luck that Sherlock Holmes had a Welsh assistant. What are we to do now?"

"Gentlemen," Sherlock Holmes said dryly. "Perhaps if you would confide in us to the extent of describing the problem, we could then consider who would be best able to deal with it."

"They may know someone," Saunders said to Huws. "They may even have a connection in Wales. It is a business with them."

Huws considered this. "All right," he said. "Tell them."

Saunders turned to us and reflected for a moment before he spoke. "Is the name Emeric Tromblay familiar to you?"

Sherlock Holmes answered instantly. "No."

They turned to me, and I shook my head.

"The man is a fiend in human form," Saunders said.

"Y Diafol! He is the Devil!" Huws muttered.

"He has committed two murders with impunity," Saunders went on. "Now he plots the ruin of a beautiful young lady."

"My niece," Huws said.

Sherlock Holmes was rubbing his hands together with satisfaction and at the same time frowning. A double murder exceeded his most sanguine expectations, but the plot against the young lady might prove to be a nuisance.

"Details, please," he said. "How is it possible in Wales to commit two murders with impunity?"

"Emeric Tromblay did it," Saunders said.

"Surely Tromblay is not a Welsh name," Sherlock Holmes observed.

"It isn't," Saunders said. "In Wales, all of our worst fiends are English. Tromblay has extensive holdings in agricultural and mining properties, and his wealth must be immense. Unfortunately, his greed is insatiable. Glyn Huws, Mr. Huws's brother, was only a hard-working farmer, but he owned one of the most prosperous farms in that part of Wales. Tromblay coveted it and offered to buy it. Glyn Huws intended the land to be the inheritance of his daughter, Meleri, his only child. His wife died when she was born, and he never remarried. When he refused to sell, Tromblay sent his son, Benton, to court Meleri."

Huws spoke up. "The worst ne'er-do-well scallywag in the kingdom."

Saunders shrugged. "I grant you that he is as useless a young man as ever squandered three years at Oxford, but he is not really all that bad. At least he has the good sense to be in a constant state of disagreement with his father, and that takes courage with the old man threatening to disinherit him. In any event, when Glyn Huws refused Tromblay's offer for the farm, Tromblay was determined to have that land by whatever means, and he sent his son to court Meleri."

I was having difficulty in attaching these odd-sounding names to real people. "What was Meleri's reaction?" I asked.

"Meleri is a well-brought-up girl," Saunders said. "She received him as politely and as formally as possible—and kept her distance. It might have been the vicar calling on her from the way she treated him. When Emeric Tromblay finally had to accept that there was no chance for his son, he changed his plans. He determined to marry the girl himself."

"How old is he?" Sherlock Holmes asked.

"Pwy a fesura oed y Diafol?" Huws muttered. "Who measures the age of the Devil?"

"Fifty-five or sixty," Saunders said.

"Is he an attractive person?"

"He is a shrivelled miser, inhuman in all of his dealings. The entire countryside detests him."

"If the girl was able to resist the son, she should have no difficulty in saying no to the father," Sherlock Holmes remarked.

"I know what you are thinking," Saunders said. "Even in the remote wastes of Wales, it should not be possible to force a girl into marriage against her wishes, especially when her family vehemently opposes the match. You are underestimating Tromblay's fiendishness. The first obstacle to the marriage was his wife of thirty years, a lovely lady distantly connected to the Earl of Powys. Eleanor Tromblay had always enjoyed excellent health. He dealt with that problem first. She died suddenly and mysteriously."

"She died suddenly and mysteriously," Sherlock Holmes mused. He paused. Then he said again, slowly, "She died suddenly and mysteriously. Porter — would you kindly find for me the third volume of Pennant's *Tours in Wales?* It may be on the bottom shelf."

It was on the bottom shelf. He invariably knew where he had last seen a book. I found it and handed it to him.

"The original was published in 1778," he explained while he flipped the pages. "This is the reprint of

1883. One moment, please." He found the passage he sought and read.

"'In a pretty park near to the town —' The reference, Gentlemen, is to your own town of New-town, in Wales. 'In a pretty park near to the town is the seat of the Pryses.' I will omit the family pedigree, which is impressive. 'It became possessed of this place about the time of Henry VI. The late owner, Sir John Pryse, was a gentleman of worth, but of strange singularities. He married three wives; and kept the two first who died, in his room, one on each side of his bed; his third declined the honor of his hand till her defunct rivals were committed to their proper place.'"

Arthur Saunders and Bryn Huws were regarding him with astonishment. I was suppressing a smile. This was the method he chose to repay them for their effrontery in making an appointment with him in order to engage his assistant.

"When Sir John's third wife died," Sherlock Holmes continued, paraphrasing Pennant, "he tried to persuade one Bridget Bostock, of Cheshire — who claimed to be able to work miracles 'by prayer, faith, and an embrocation of fasting spittle,' to come to Newtown and restore his dead wife to life. If she succeeded, he promised that 'recompence of any kind, that you could propose, would be made with the utmost gratitude.'" He closed the book. "Has

Emeric Tromblay displayed any singularities in this respect?"

The Welshmen were too stunned to reply.

"Is Tromblay's wife properly buried?" Sherlock Holmes persisted.

Saunders continued to regard him incredulously. "Of course she is. In the family vault in the church at Pentrederwydd."

"Has he conducted any occult ceremonies aimed at restoring her to life?"

"Not that I am aware of," Saunders said testily. "Nor would I expect any. I was just explaining why he wanted her dead."

"To be sure," Sherlock Holmes said meditatively. "But you also said that he murdered her. The clever murderer frequently feels compelled to act a part — in this case, that of a grieving husband. It is a nuance that the student of crime learns to watch for. Did Tromblay demonstrate more grief than you would have expected if his wife had died naturally?"

"He is not the grieving kind," Saunders said. "The demonstration of any grief at all would have been out of character. Acting a part would not have occurred to him."

Sherlock Holmes was absently tapping his fingers together. "Interesting. Pray continue."

"After his wife's death, he was able to court Meleri openly. Glyn Huws remained unalterably opposed to marriage or even to neighbourly conversation with the likes of an Emeric Tromblay. His opposition ended abruptly two months later. He was found in his summer sheep walk with his skull crushed. He had been brutally and treacherously murdered — he was attacked from behind."

"How long ago was this?" Sherlock Holmes asked.

"Three weeks," Saunders said. "Now the fiend is applying all the wiles his black soul can conceive of to force the girl into marriage."

"It still should be possible for Meleri to say no," I protested.

"Don't forget that he is a wealthy fiend," Saunders said bitterly. "He owns a splendid home. He can offer servants and jewels and magnificent gowns and trips to Paris. Sooner or later, she will succumb. His courtship must be stopped."

"If it were not for the two murders and the fact that Emeric Tromblay is a despised English fiend in rural Wales, might it not be thought that the girl had the opportunity to make a brilliant marriage?" Sherlock Holmes asked politely.

"It would not be thought that by anyone who knows Emeric Tromblay," Bryn Huws growled. His words were vibrant with hatred for the English fiend and with frustration at being unable to take the vengeance he obviously would have preferred.

"Several times in my career I have been invited to match wits with a criminal who was alleged to personify the Evil One," Sherlock Holmes remarked. "His supernatural prowess always proved to be exaggerated. I am confident that the same will be true of Emeric Tromblay — if he is indeed guilty of these crimes." He turned to Bryn Huws. "Does the girl have any relatives other than yourself?"

"None," Huws said. "I am her father's only surviving brother. Her mother also had brothers, but they left their bones in distant places — America, Africa, the Orient."

"Your case certainly merits looking into. Not only are there several points of interest, but the issues may be far graver than you are aware of. However, both Mr. Jones and I deny having any skill whatsoever in influencing the minds of young ladies when they are contemplating — or not contemplating — marriage. We would not know how to begin, and therefore we couldn't accept such a commission. The murders seem more promising. If they — or just one of them — could be brought home to Tromblay, it would permanently disrupt any marriage plans he has formed. I suggest that the best way to proceed would be to investigate the deaths of Tromblay's wife and of Glyn Huws."

Saunders nodded an emphatic agreement. "Yes. Of course that would be the best way."

"Then — since at least some of the essential witnesses speak only Welsh — the question would seem to be whether Mr. Jones and I could investigate these deaths through an interpreter. I am wondering whether it would be possible for him to visit the neighbourhood in the role of himself, a descendant of Welsh ancestors. He could be passing his holidays in Wales in order to see something of the land of his forefathers. Would he be welcome in that role?"

"But of course," Saunders said impatiently. "Everyone of Welsh descent would be hospitable toward him. But how could he investigate anything at all when he wouldn't be able to talk to people?"

"Couldn't you find a reliable young man who is fluent in both English and Welsh and who could pretend to be Mr. Jones's remote cousin? He could act as his host, and while doing so, he also could serve as his interpreter."

Saunders supposed that this could be done, but he plainly was not convinced that it would accomplish anything.

"What are your plans for London?" Sherlock Holmes asked.

"I have commissions for several clients to undertake tomorrow. These will occupy me for a full day and perhaps longer."

"I suggest, then, that you concern yourself with your clients' affairs and leave the problem of the murders and Meleri Huws's unwanted suitor in my hands. It will require reflection and perhaps a preliminary investigation. You will hear from me again either today or tomorrow."

The Welshmen were prepared to discuss the iniquities of Emeric Tromblay for the remainder of the morning, and they had to be persuaded that we now had sufficient material for a preliminary investigation. They left reluctantly.

We went to the window to watch them go. The four-wheeler they had arrived in was waiting at the kerb, and they climbed in and were driven away. Seconds later, a hansom flashed past, and immediately after it came another four-wheeler with three boys in it. Rabby grinned and waved in our direction as his cab rattled in pursuit.

I retreated to the sofa. Sherlock Holmes began to pace back and forth.

"So our mysterious toff is following the Welshmen," I said. "Were you expecting that?"

"I thought it likely. The Welsh gentlemen are the only clients we have had in months, so it seemed probable that Radbert's toff was waiting for them."

"Interesting," I mused.

"It is much more than that, Porter. The fiend in Wales not only has contrived two murders and a conspiracy against the young heiress, but he is able to manipulate events as far away as London, and that requires a long reach indeed. Has Mrs. Hudson left for church?"

She was about to leave. She looked handsome in her rustling blue satin dress, and she swept into the room like a duchess.

Sherlock Holmes said to her, "Please describe the foreign-sounding gentleman who called yesterday."

She could not have been Sherlock Holmes's landlady for so many years without developing her powers of recall, if only in self-defence. "He had a sturdy figure," she said. "He was red-faced as though he had spent time out of doors. He carried a cane with a gold handle. He was well-dressed — his suit cost him real money."

"Was he a bona fide gentleman?" I asked.

"No," she said instantly. "Perhaps a countryman or a prosperous town tradesman who has to be out in the weather."

"A village tradesman?" I suggested.

She shook her head. "He had the air of being more successful and more stylish than a village tradesman, but he lacked the manners of a city tradesman. And he was wearing a boater. A city tradesman would never make a formal call wearing a straw hat."

"Did he display a gold chain?" Sherlock Holmes asked.

"Yes. Yes, he did." She pursed her lips. "There was no cab at the kerb when he called. I didn't notice which way he walked."

Sherlock Holmes thanked her, and she hurried down the stairs in a swish of rustling skirts. The servants were waiting at the front door with their prayer books. I watched from the window while she bustled them into a four-wheeler.

When I turned away, Sherlock Holmes had already retired to the most uncomfortable chair in the room. "Without a doubt, the foreign accent was Welsh," he said.

I nodded my agreement. Mrs. Hudson's countryman with a boater and cane and gold chain certainly was identical to Rabby's toff.

"The murders — and our beautiful heiress's problem — may be only incidental to something much larger and far more sinister," Sherlock Holmes went on. "Why should our visitors be spied upon in London? Why would our fiend in Wales care how many investigators they appeal to in this remote place? The victims are safely buried. He should feel secure in his influence with the local authorities and confident that no outsider could disrupt it." He lit his pipe, leaned back, and exhaled a cloud of smoke. "This matter cuts deeply, Porter. It even could be that rare case that is worth waiting months for."

I recognized his mood. When an unsolved problem confronted him, he would work upon it tirelessly, turning it over in his mind, rearranging the facts, studying it from every point of view until he had either resolved it or convinced himself that his data were insufficient. He intended to belabour this Welsh problem until he discovered its true import or until he exhausted his tobacco.

If necessary, he would pursue a problem for days, but only rarely did one occupy him for more than an hour or two. The moment he finished, he would be asking me for my own interpretations, and I preferred to do my thinking while lying down. I also preferred to think in a clearer atmosphere. I retired to my own room.

Rabby's mysterious toff seemed less mysterious to me when I had analysed his behaviour. Someone — I called him Emeric Tromblay, though the evidence on that point was less clear than our Welsh callers seemed to believe — someone overheard or had reported to him the news that Saunders and Huws were travelling to London and intended, among other things, to consult Sherlock Holmes. In order to counter this deadly threat, he needed to know at once if they actually did so. Such was Sherlock Holmes's fame among evil-doers.

So Tromblay enlisted a friend, an associate, or perhaps an employee not known to either Saunders or Huws. "Go to London," he said. "Follow them. Find out whether they call on Sherlock Holmes."

This posed a pretty problem for his agent, who obviously didn't know the two men by sight and had no idea what hotel they would stay at. He may not have known what train they would be taking. Even if he had, a railway station would be a risky place for him to try to identify persons he had never seen before. They could slip past him unnoticed in the throng of arriving passengers. The solution he chose was to watch Sherlock Holmes's rooms.

That much was easily deduced. Why it had been done — what Tromblay expected to gain from it — was a much more difficult question.

I opened my door an hour later and found that our sitting room had been transformed into a fair imitation of a Thames-side fog-bank. In the middle of it, the dim figure of Sherlock Holmes was still perched on his uncomfortable chair. When he heard my door open, he spoke without looking up.

"Do you see the problem, Porter?" he asked.

"Yes, sir. At least — I see one problem. It's a contradiction in comparatives."

"A contradiction in comparatives?" he mused. He turned to look at me. "How do you mean that?"

"Meleri Huws is an heiress. She is now the owner of the most prosperous farm in that part of Wales. Even allowing for exaggeration, a neighbouring farmer, or a local townsman like Arthur Saunders, might consider that a sizeable patrimony. To a man like Emeric Tromblay, who is described as immensely wealthy, it would be trivial. I'm asking myself whether he would risk committing two murders in order to acquire one more farm, however prosperous, when he already owns many."

Sherlock Holmes nodded. "Very well put. That certainly delineates an important unanswered question. It is only one side of the coin, however."

"Yes, sir. The other possibility is that he is wildly in love with the beautiful Meleri, and the farm is irrelevant. From the description of him as a shrivelled miser who is inhuman in all of his dealings, I have difficulty envisaging him serenading Meleri from below her bedroom window or composing sonnets to her in the moonlight."

"I have that same difficulty," Sherlock Holmes said, "though I had not considered the serenading or the sonnets. Does a heart that is youthful and gay vibrate within that revolting husk? Is his ardour really that of a devoted lover? A much more likely alternative is that we see here the vile passion of a loathsome old lecher, but not even lechery should cause him to lose his head and commit two murders for the girl with no certainty of obtaining his desire even then. We can't resolve that without seeing the man in person and forming our own judgement of him. Did no other possibility occur to you? There is one that I consider highly important, but perhaps it's a bit obscure. I've trained myself to see what others overlook, Porter, and you must do the same. What do you make of our toff with the Welsh accent?"

"Obviously he knew our clients were coming here, but he didn't know when they would arrive. He may have watched for them all day yesterday."

Sherlock Holmes nodded. "I'm wondering whether he watched the house until late last night and witnessed my return. When we hear from Radbert, we will know more about him."

I went to change my clothing. When word did come from Rabby, it might be a call for help, and I would have to respond at once. I put on a shabby suit of the type that an ordinary labourer would wear on Sunday and sat down to wait. I had an intuitive feeling of my own that I would need both skill and determination to outwit that remote fiend in Wales.

3

RABBY'S MESSAGE WAS BROUGHT BY HIS FRIEND George, one of the street Arabs who had accompanied him. George was a snub-nosed little chap with curly hair. He would have looked like some mother's darling had he been cleaned up and dressed up; but like Rabby, he had no mother.

"The toff is at the Three Nuns Hotel in Aldgate High Street," George said breathlessly. "Rabby can't get his name. He says will you come."

Sherlock Holmes nodded at me. George and I went down to the street and hailed a passing hansom. The two of us looked so disreputable that the driver asked to see my money before we started. Aldgate High Street was a long drive from Baker Street.

In the light traffic of Sunday morning, we made a quick trip of it, rattling through vacant streets where the only obstacles were refuse and dust stirred by the gentle June breeze. All around us we saw the highly visible symbols of a London Sunday — the white sheets of newspapers. On back doorsteps, householders could be seen in shirtsleeves or in waistcoat and best trousers, restfully settled to their Sunday reading. In windows an occasional flash of white showed as a page was turned.

I stopped the driver a short distance from the hotel and paid him, and I included a tip large enough to inspire genuine respect in his voice when he thanked me. This was a practice Sherlock Holmes often indulged in when he went about in disguise. He thought that those who earned their living serving the public should be taught that appearances can be deceiving.

Rabby saw us approaching, and he popped out of the doorway where he was lounging and walked to meet us.

"Is he staying at this hotel?" I asked.

"I expect so," Rabby said. He described the toff's morning activity. After following our visitors to the Euston Hotel, he waited outside for a time. Then he dismissed his cab and entered the hotel for a talk with the clerk — presumably to satisfy himself that Saunders and Huws were actually staying there. He next took a cab to the Three Nuns Hotel and went upstairs. "Maybe he was tired from being up so early," Rabby said. "He needed to take a nap."

At that point Rabby had sent for me.

"Have you found out who he is?"

Rabby shook his head. "I don't know anyone there. The porter keeps chasing me away."

Outside porters of quality hotels tried to keep street Arabs — or any of London's enormous variety of beggars and street traders — from annoying the guests, and they tended to be suspicious of unattached boys of whatever appearance. The Three Nuns was a venerable establishment that had been completely refurbished about the time of my birth, and it was highly-regarded.

My clothing was more of a disadvantage than Rabby's age. This is a problem one must contend with in adopting a disguise. The toff would not look twice at me in the street; but I could expect no consideration whatever from any employee of a respectable business establishment, and that was a severe disadvantage. I would have been totally out of place in the public rooms of the Three Nuns Hotel — during those brief moments before I was asked to leave.

I discussed strategy with Rabby, and then we crossed the street. Rabby began to walk slowly back and forth in front of the hotel, glancing inside each time he passed it. The porter eyed him disapprovingly, but he said nothing. His attention was focussed on me, an adult loiterer, and he kept sending suspicious glances in my direction.

Finally Rabby came hurrying back to me. "He's gone to feed himself," he said.

I walked toward the porter, who watched me menacingly until I showed him my palm with a half-crown in it and offered to shake hands with him. Then he greeted me like an old friend.

"There's a toff in your dining room," I said quietly. "He's a guest of the hotel. I need to know who he is and where he comes from."

The porter frowned.

"The half-crown is for the clerk," I said. "There will be two more for you when you give me the information."

"How will I recognize him?" the porter asked.

I called Rabby over and introduced him. "Let him sweep the pavement for you," I suggested. "He'll keep an eye on the dining room and point the gentleman out to you when he leaves."

The porter produced a broom for Rabby, who proceeded to give an energetic demonstration of pavement sweeping. Finally he signalled to the porter. The porter went in to speak with the clerk. While they were talking, the toff crossed the entrance hall, paused for a moment at the door, and then walked off down Aldgate High Street, nonchalantly wearing his boater at a rakish angle and carrying his gold-handled cane under his arm. Rabby and his two friends followed him discreetly.

The porter came out and offered me a slip of paper. I exchanged two half-crowns for it. The writing, in the clerk's neat hand, read, "Mr. Evan Evans, Cardiff."

I nodded my thanks and hurried to overtake Rabby.

Mr. Evan Evans strolled along Aldgate High Street only as far as Middlesex Street, where he turned and headed straight for the maelstrom of the Petticoat Lane Sunday Market. I thought to myself, "It was bad enough having to contend with the Welsh language. If Yiddish gets mixed in with it, I'm going back to Baker Street and start looking for another case." For Middlesex Street was the centre of London's Jewish Quarter.

It was once named Petticoat Lane. Years before, its occupants had agitated to have the name changed, hoping to acquire respectability in the process. It was a vain hope. On Sundays, London's poor of every nationality — Cockneys, Turks, Lascar seamen, Chinese, Japanese, Hindus, all of the human debris that had been sucked into the swirling life force of this enormous city — descended upon it in search of penny bargains and free entertainment. Almost anything could be bought there, but it was principally a market in used clothing. Along both kerbs of Middlesex Street were long rows of stalls. Surging, eddying crowds packed the pavements and roadway. The din was tremendous as Jewish hawkers cried their wares and bartered furiously with passersby.

Evan Evans moved along slowly. I gave hurried instructions to Rabby and his friends, and the four of us spread out so we could watch him alertly from every angle. In that crowd, it would be a simple matter for him to deliver or receive a message.

He paused to study the performance of a dandified hawker who was glibly selling gimcrack jewellery for a shilling. Then he turned a puzzled gaze on a Lancashire acrobat who was performing in the mucky street for halfpennies tossed his way.

A hawker with a stentorian voice was stridently dealing in old leather: discarded engine belts, fire hose, saddlery, harnesses. He hacked off sixpennyworth at a time for amateur cobblers.

Another noisy trafficker was selling coats and vests that he modelled himself one after another. He donned a blue seaman's coat and stepped out to meet the dawdling Evan Evans. "Indigo blue!" he shrilled. "Navy blue. Bluey blue till you can't blue any more. Just your size. Come off a drowned sea captain!"

Evans stepped around him with no contact that I could discern. He also stepped around a youth who was trying on boots, and he deftly avoided a seedy old man who wanted to measure him for trousers. He stared intently at everything that went on about him, and I hoped that the melange of sights and sounds and smells was not totally occupying his attention. The Petticoat Lane Market had always been notorious for pickpockets. It was said that you could lose your watch at one end of the market and see it offered for sale before you reached the other end.

The chants of medicine hawkers caught Evans's attention. Dutch Drops did not interest him, but he heard to the end the discourse of a hawker selling an amber liquid whose name I did not catch. It was alleged to cure inward weakness, tendencies to faint, weight and pressure over the eyes, dimness of sight, nervous prostrations, cuts, burns, and old standing wounds. The next hawker, a Negro who cleaned his patrons' teeth with his fingers, was shrugged off without a second glance.

Rabby dropped back and sent me a bewildered look. I was feeling more than mildly perplexed myself. Evans was not behaving like the agent of a wealthy fiend who had sent him to London to further a dastardly conspiracy. He was gaping like the most naïve tourist. He continued to move along nonchalantly, though he was now carrying his cane by the handle and occasionally using it. He could not get through the crowds while holding it under his arm.

I maintained my watchfulness, but I was refusing to believe what I saw. Evans would not have waited for our clients at an early hour on Sunday morning — and possibly all the previous day — only to drop them almost at once and go wandering through the squalor of the Petticoat Lane Market. He was up to something.

The market spilled into the intersecting streets. It was when Evans briefly detoured into one of these and then retraced his steps that I made a stunning discovery: Rabby and his friends and I were not the only ones following him. A neatly dressed, fair-haired youth about sixteen hurried to overtake him when he wandered into the side-street and then hung back when he returned to the main market. I hung back further and watched the youth.

Evans wandered on, oblivious to the attentive parade on his heels. He picked his way among the stalls, impatiently brushing aside the coats and trousers that were thrust at him, gruffly refusing offerings of old collars, socks, studs, boots, slippers, toys, cycle horns, locks, keys, trowels, brushes, ocarinas, alarm clocks, albums, penny cameras, goldbeater's skin, violins, crockery, opera glasses, songs, old books, hats, handkerchiefs, ribbons, bead necklaces, banjos, dulcimers, knives, saws, chisels — all of the shabby clutter of civilization.

Mongers crying shellfish, or muffins, or sweets, or ice cream failed to catch his attention, but a Jewish fish merchant succeeded. That worthy wore a leather apron, and he was so plastered with shining scales from head to foot that he looked like a dingy merman. Evans paused to stare at him and then moved on. Nearby, an old woman was skewering cat's meat. An old man was whittling horseradish. A birdfancier was selling canaries and finches.

Rabby and his friends, instinctively merging with their surroundings, had purchased tricoloured bars of ice cream from an Italian barrowman, and they happily licked that delicacy from its paper as they loafed along. They were enjoying the sights as much as Evans seemed to. A performing bear, or an organ grinder with a monkey, or an energetic street musician caused them to dawdle for so long that I feared they would lose contact.

I still could not believe that Evans had no more sinister object than to enjoy the squalid sights of the market, but I had to leave him to Rabby in order to keep an eye on the fair-haired youth. Finally Evans made an abrupt turn and pushed his way into the thickening crowd that had gathered around a street musician with a gramophone. Probably the instrument was a large machine mounted on a handcart, but I couldn't see it through the crowd. It was throbbing an operatic aria. I moved quickly, trying to keep Evans in sight, but he had disappeared completely.

The behaviour of the fair-haired boy intrigued me. Instead of hurrying forward, as he had when Evans turned into the side street, he came to a stop and stood motionless, watching the crowd.

Rabby had reacted instinctively. He increased his pace and plunged recklessly into the compressed mass of people in pursuit of Evans. No sooner had Rabby disappeared than Evans emerged on the other side, hesitated for a moment, and then turned back toward Aldgate High Street, picking his way quickly through and around the shifting throngs and paying no further attention to the market's attractions. Rabby reappeared a moment later. He looked about disgustedly and then followed Evans. The fair-haired boy hung back until Evans passed him.

I did the same, trying to keep my eyes on both of them. Suddenly I gaped in astonishment. Evans was no longer carrying his gold-handled cane. Instead, he sported an umbrella.

I looked again for the fair-haired boy, but he had disappeared.

Rabby edged over to me. He noticed at once that Evans no longer had his cane, but the switch had occurred during the few seconds when Evans was lost in the crowd, and he hadn't seen it. It was too late for me to send him and his friends through the north end of the market looking for a gold-handled cane. It was also too late to start combing the market for the fair-haired boy. We'd been thoroughly flummoxed, and the only thing left for us was to continue following Evans, which we did in a mood of humiliation.

Back to the Aldgate High Street he went. He followed it to the Minories, where he turned south toward the Tower of London and the Thames. It was long after one o'clock now, and the thud of the beer engine could be heard in the taverns we passed, but Evans contained his thirst until he entered a shabby lane off the Minories and came to a drab establishment with a sign featuring a red dragon and the message, Y Llew Du. He entered it without hesitation. Rabby and his friends gathered around me, and we contemplated the sign.

"Now what could that mean?" I asked.

A passerby turned with a grin. "It means 'The Black Lion,' that's what it means. And don't ask me why the Black Lion is a red dragon. If you don't speak Welsh, don't go in. Customers that order in English don't get served."

We withdrew a few yards down the lane where a convenient doorway gave us cover for watching Y Llew Du's entrance. The Black Lion was an inn, and for all of its linguistic prejudice, it didn't lack for patrons, just as London didn't lack for Welshmen. It was enjoying a good run of business.

After a short time, to my complete amazement, the fair-haired youth appeared. He stood outside the door for several minutes as though waiting, and I had a closer and more leisurely look at him than had been possible in the market. He was a slender, good-looking youth, neatly dressed but in clothing of average quality that had a home-made look. His boots had the gleam of newness and contrasted sharply. The hair visible around his cap was so fair that it looked almost white.

A sturdy man of medium height, with dusky red hair and beard, came along and spoke to the boy for a moment, and the two of them entered Y Llew Du. I walked back to the tavern and passed it twice, peering through the windows, but I could discern very little in the dim interior. I asked Rabby whether the fair-haired boy had been following Evan Evans earlier in the day. Rabby was certain that he had not.

I needed to think, so I left Rabby in charge and went in search of another tavern. Near the end of the lane where it met Mansell Street, I found one with a solid English name and a dragon on its sign that was being properly slain by St. George. There I meditated over a half-pint of beer and a pork pie. It had been more than six hours since Mrs. Hudson's lavish breakfast, and I felt famished. By the time I finished, I had reached a decision.

There was too much Welsh in this proposition to suit me, and I needed help. I sent Rabby's friend Dick, a gawky, thin, hungry-looking lad, with a note to a friend of mine who spoke the language at home with his Welsh parents. His name, by no coincidence whatsoever — since he was Welsh — was also Jones, Fred Jones. He had once confided to me that the correct spelling was Ffred.

We continued to wait. Finally Evan Evans emerged from the tavern. The umbrella had vanished; he now carried the same gold-handled cane he had been carrying when he entered the market. Rabby and George trailed after him down the Minories toward the Tower. I waited for the fair-haired youth. I was still waiting half an hour later when Dick returned with my Welsh friend.

I thanked Dick for a good day's work, paid him, and sent him home with the suggestion that he should look up Rabby first thing in the morning to see whether he was needed again. Then I explained the situation to my amused friend.

Fred held a humdrum crib as a draper's assistant. I met him when his employer suspected him of theft and called in Sherlock Holmes, who quickly identified the employer's brother-in-law as the culprit. Fred had long envied me my romantic occupation, and my appeal for help elated him. He took enthusiastic charge of the situation. First he taught me to say "Cwrw" — beer — which he said was password enough for any Welsh public house. If I wanted to masquerade as a Welsh scholar, I could say "Cwrw da," which meant "Good beer."

The two of us entered Y Llew Du, the Black Lion.

In contrast to the dingy exterior, the large public room which served as both tavern and restaurant was clean and surprisingly well-furnished. We found a table in a dark corner. While my friend went to the bar for cwrw, I took a chair that enabled me to keep my eyes on the fair-haired youth. He was seated with the man he had met outside the door, and the remains of a heavy meal littered the table in front of them. They had managed to dispose of most of a duck with trimmings. Previously I had been unable to form any conclusions at all about the boy; now, after studying him blankly for several minutes, the only deduction that occurred to me was that he must have an adult-sized appetite.

I began to feel panicky. I knew what the reaction would be if I returned to Baker Street with nothing more than that to report.

My friend brought the beer. He was a good companion — he knew that this was no carefree Sunday outing for me, and he occupied himself with observing and overhearing as much as he could of what went on about us and leaving me to my own observations.

Suddenly he leaned toward me. "The meeting starts in half an hour," he announced quietly.

"What kind of meeting?" I asked.

He shook his head.

"Probably it has nothing to do with the boy, but keep listening," I told him.

The boy seemed to have no interest at all in his surroundings. His attention was still focussed on the remaining food. He and his companion picked in a desultory manner at the scraps and now and then exchanged a few words so quietly that no sounds reached us. I sipped my beer and continued to watch them.

Finally the landlord opened a door at the back of the room. There was a stairway beyond it. He took up his position there, and immediately several men arose as though they had been waiting impatiently. One at a time they handed something to him and went on up the stairway.

"See if you can find out what kind of meeting it is," I told my friend.

He walked over and talked briefly with the landlord. Their conversation was interrupted twice by groups of men, several accompanied by

women, whom the landlord admitted to the stairway.

My friend returned. “He says it’s a private meeting — admission only to those who have invitations. I asked him how one obtained an invitation, and he said the committee responsible for the meeting issued them. That’s all he was willing to tell me.”

“The people who go through the door are handing him something,” I said.

Fred nodded. “It’s a slip of paper with a large zero printed on it. There’s something scribbled in the middle of the zero, but I couldn’t make that out.”

It sounded suitably mysterious, but obviously it had nothing to do with Evan Evans, or he would not have left, and the boy and his companion were still toying with the remains of their dinner. More late comers arrived and were admitted to the stairway. Finally the landlord turned and squinted across the room at the clock. Then he glanced toward the table where the boy and his companion sat.

He said something; the red-bearded man nodded. The two of them got up and went up the stairway, and the landlord closed the door and locked it.

Fred, who had been watching closely, turned to me with eyebrows raised. “That’s the boy you’ve been following, isn't it?" he asked. "Don't *you* know what kind of meeting?"

I shook my head.

Stragglers arrived. The landlord had to unlock the door three times to admit them. The count I was keeping of those attending the meeting passed thirty.

"What are you going to do?" Fred asked.

"Wait until the meeting is over and follow him again," I said.

The wait proved to be far pleasanter than I had anticipated. The beer was good; a harpist arrived who accompanied himself while he sang Welsh songs in a pleasant tenor voice. Fred tried to translate the songs for me, but this brought scowls from the surrounding tables, so he desisted.

The meeting lasted all of two hours. Then someone unlocked the door from within, and those who had attended emerged in small groups, talking with animation. The patrons who were listening to the harpist tried to shush them. Some left; some found tables and settled themselves to enjoy the music.

Fred leaned over and whispered, "They were talking about someone named Robert Owen."

"Who is Robert Owen?" I whispered back.

He shook his head.

"The name sounds familiar," I mused.

"It's a familiar sounding kind of name," Fred observed cheerfully.

I listened to the music and watched the open door to the stairway. A trickle of people continued to descend. They lowered their voices as soon as they became aware of the harpist, which complicated Fred's eavesdropping.

"They were talking about Robert Owen, too," he announced finally. All that I could do was shrug.

The stairway stood empty for a time, and finally the landlord came over and locked the door again. I told Fred, "Thirty-two people went up. Only twenty-six have come down."

"Obviously there's another way out," Fred observed wisely.

"Either that, or the boy and his companion are staying here," I said.

For the second time that day, I felt completely flummoxed. There seemed to be nothing more for me to do at Y Llew Du. My Sunday's work certainly hadn't covered me with glory, and the few items of information I'd gathered seemed more likely to complicate our puzzle than resolve it, but often that is the way with investigations.

I waited for another hour. Then Fred and I strolled back to Aldgate High Street where I hailed a hansom. I dropped my friend off at his parents' home on my way back to Baker Street.

Sherlock Holmes was out, but he had left a message. It read, "Read Borrow."

I dimly remembered the name but not the book it had been attached to. What I finally located was a work entitled, *Wild Wales,* by George Borrow. I took the three stoutly bound volumes down reluctantly. They looked formidable but no more so than our case did — the investigation, in a remote place where few of the inhabitants spoke English, of the presumed murder of two persons long buried. If the murderer's guile and influence were potent enough to have his enemies watched and followed in London, how much more powerful would they be as we approached the centre of his web?

As I started to walk away with my arms full of *Wild Wales,* my eye caught a familiar name on a binding: Robert Owen. The book was entitled, *A New View of Society.* I left it in its place. The three volumes of Borrow were challenge enough for one evening. I settled myself on the sofa, put my feet up, and read.

Much later, Rabby and his friend George arrived, and I called for three servings of Mrs. Hudson's cold supper. While we ate, they described the movements of Evan Evans. They had followed him down the Minories to the Tower of London. There he gawked for a time, but he didn't enter it. Instead, he turned west and strolled along absently, taking in all of the sights, until he reached London Bridge. After some hesitation, he boarded a steamer bound for Greenwich.

They scrambled aboard just before the boat left; but Evans had nothing on his mind but a tourist excursion. Rabby was certain about that. He visited the Hospital's Painted Hall and the Naval Museum, climbed the hill in Greenwich Park to gawk at the Royal Observatory, and finally returned to the river to eat a robust whitebait dinner. When he reached London again, he took a cab directly to his hotel. The boys waited for another hour before calling off the watch and returning to Baker Street.

I told Rabby to follow Evan Evans again the next morning, warning him to be at the Three Nuns Hotel early just in case Evans made another early start. They left, and I returned my attention to *Wild Wales*. I persisted for another two hours. Sherlock Holmes still had not returned when I went to bed.

4

George Henry Borrow was a much-travelled English writer with a taste for the bizarre and a genius for languages. He mastered Welsh as a young man and developed a life-long enthusiasm for Welsh poetry. He already had achieved considerable literary success when he visited Wales in 1854. He walked throughout the country from east to west and from north to south, talking with the people, making notes on those conversations and on the grandeur of the Welsh landscape, and visiting places he already was familiar with from his reading.

Wild Wales was the account of his experiences. It was not a success when it was first published, but after Borrow's death it was rediscovered and widely read and discussed. Sherlock Holmes had scattered markings throughout the three volumes. When I noticed this, I quickly flipped the pages to find out what had caught his attention.

All of the marked passages described criminal acts: the Rebecca Riots; the adventures of Twm Siôn Catti, the Welsh Robin Hood; the red-haired banditti of Mawddwy; the wicked robber children of Devil's Bridge.

I resumed my reading at breakfast and engrossed myself in Borrow's adventures in Mona, which is Welsh for the Isle of Anglesey, until Sherlock

Holmes emerged from his room. Then I pushed the volumes aside and, while he ate his own breakfast, I gave him a summary of our meagre Sunday achievements. He listened without comment while I described the fair-haired boy; Evan Evans's sleight-of-hand with cane and umbrella; the private meeting at Y Llew Du; and the strange admission passes that had frustrated my efforts to follow the boy. It seemed to me that I had spent the day turning up questions for which there were no answers, and I said so.

"There are several noteworthy puzzles in that collection," Sherlock Holmes agreed. He gave me a searching look, and then he continued, with a twinkle in his eyes, "You didn't mention the day's most peculiar mystery, which is why you were so tardy in noticing the red-bearded man who ate dinner with the boy. He followed both of you from one end of the market to the other."

I stared at him. "How do you know that?"

"Because I was following him. I don't know whether he actually became aware of you and Radbert. He and the boy were a short distance down the street waiting for Evans when you staged your clumsy performance in front of the Three Nuns, but they paid no attention. It seems not to have occurred to them that someone else might be following Evans."

He radiated good humour. He was so pleased to have a complicated case to work on that my fumbling mismanagement of it hardly mattered. In any event, he had been on hand to retrieve the situation.

I apologized for sitting and listening to music in the inn's public room while the fair-haired boy left by the back way.

"You're apologizing for the wrong reason," he said. "Your error was in not waiting long enough. Several of those who attended the meeting, including the boy and his companion, remained behind for almost three hours. Then they left the same way the others did, through the public room. I followed the boy to Southwark. He and his companion are staying there with a Welshman named Griffiths, who keeps a dairy. As soon as I established that, I went to the Euston Hotel to call on our clients."

I raised my eyebrows. "That must have been a rather late call. Are they still our clients?"

"They were grumpy about being awakened until they learned that a spy has been following them about London. Then they were furious. They had no hesitation at all in believing that Emeric Tromblay is a fiend and a double murderer, but they never imagined that he would stoop to such a dastardly practice as spying."

"Do they know anyone named Evan Evans?"

Sherlock Holmes laughed. "You're forgetting that I hadn't heard that name until you mentioned it this morning, but I wouldn't have inquired in any case. I have no desire to insult their intelligence or to suggest that mine is deficient. They live in Wales. Of course they know someone named Evan Evans. Everyone in Wales knows someone named Evan Evans. It is a name that would naturally occur to a Welshman needing an alias.

"To return to our clients, I first wanted to know who knew that they were coming to London. Since they had made no secret of their plans, the entire town of Newtown — and environs — could have known of it and probably did.

"I next asked them who knew that they intended to consult Sherlock Holmes. They couldn't recall confiding that to anyone. When I persisted, they finally conceded that they may have mentioned to a few friends that they intended to ask Col. Edward Pryce-Jones, the M.P. for Montgomery Boroughs, to exert his influence in having Sherlock Holmes called in to investigate Glyn Huws's murder and Eleanor Tromblay's untimely death. The guilty person must have a flattering familiarity with my reputation if such a casual remark was sufficient to alert him." He spoke in the manner of a man to whom fame could be a burden. "Of course they may have said more than they chose to remember."

He had finished eating. He pushed the dishes aside, picked up his pipe, and lit it. "Did you tell Radbert to follow Evans this morning?" he asked, exhaling a cloud of smoke.

"Yes, sir. And to look for the fair-haired boy. If he sees him, he is to send George at once and follow the boy himself. Dick will whistle up one of his pals if he can and stay with Evan Evans."

"Radbert won't see the boy," Sherlock Holmes said confidently. "The boy has no interest in our two Welshmen. He and his companion were watching Evan Evans to make certain that nothing went wrong with the cane-for-umbrella switch. Then they went to Y Llew Du to watch him recover his cane. That concluded their business with him, and he probably doesn't know that they were following him. The cane is hollow, of course, and contained papers or documents of some kind. These were removed and replaced with something similar that Evans is to take back to Wales."

He sent a thick smoke ring swirling toward the ceiling before he met my astonishment with another smile. "Doesn't that interpretation appeal to you?"

"No, sir," I said.

"Why not? If you had letters or documents to exchange, would you use a different method?"

"I certainly would. I easily could devise one that would be less cumbersome and much more private."

He nodded. "So could I. Preposterous as it may seem, I feel certain that this was what they were doing. We must take it seriously if only for one reason."

"What is that?" I asked.

"They are Welshmen. A long succession of English kings learned to their great sorrow that Welshness should never be underestimated. The Welsh refuse to forget that they're a conquered people, and they've added centuries of political and economic repression to their resentment. Under the circumstances, tortuous thinking and actions may be inevitable."

He paused to puff deeply on his pipe. "I've suggested to our clients that they avoid this address for the remainder of their stay in London. After Mr. Saunders attends to his own clients' legal affairs, I want the two of them to return to Wales immediately. It is imperative that Evan Evans should take back to Wales with him the conviction that Sherlock Holmes was in Scotland and that they failed to see him. Our clients objected to cutting their stay short. They'd hoped to see something of London and do some shopping. They especially wanted to buy toys for their grandchildren. I gave them the addresses of Gamage's in Holborn, Jacques's in Hatton Garden, and Hamley's in High Holborn. They can call at one of those shops without going much out of their way as they travel between Lincoln's Inn, where Mr. Saunders must transact his legal business, and their hotel. I finally persuaded them.

"They have agreed to find a Welsh-speaking host for you. They mentioned a young poet as a possibility. You are to call on them at ten o'clock tonight to obtain such information as they can give you about the local scene. Once you reach Wales, you should avoid contacting either of them unless some emergency arises."

Mrs. Hudson arrived with the maid to clear away our breakfast dishes. Sherlock Holmes said to her, "If anyone calls asking for me, I am still in Scotland."

She nodded. "Yes, sir."

"This is extremely important. Make certain that the servants understand. They are not to mention to anyone that I have returned."

"Yes, sir."

"I am particularly concerned that the foreign-sounding not-quite gentleman who called Saturday should not know that I am in London. If he calls again, I want him assured that I am pursuing a highly involved case in Scotland and that my stay there is likely to be indefinite."

"If he calls when I am in, I will tell him that myself," she promised.

After they left, he smoked for a time without speaking. "The murder cases are feeble, Porter," he announced finally. "It would be impossible to find evidence potent enough to persuade the local authorities to exhume the body of Tromblay's wife. He is far too wealthy and too powerful a political force. Everyone concerned will go to great lengths to avoid arousing his displeasure.

"It is almost too late to be searching for clues concerning Glyn Huws's murder. He will have been dead at least a month when you finally arrive on the scene. Only an eye witness could save that case, and since none came forward when the crime occurred, either such a person does not exist, or he has his own reasons for remaining silent."

"Nevertheless, it is a case," I said cheerfully. "You remarked before you left for Scotland that anything at all is better than nothing at all."

"I was hoping for something fresher and much closer to home when I said that. This case is so distant, and the setting is so alien, and you will be so tardy in reaching the scene, that you may find nothing there for either of us to do. As soon as possible, you must interview that highly interesting young lady, the heiress."

I regarded him with astonishment. I had assumed that the young lady would be the least interesting aspect of the case to him.

"Our clients seem to have an overriding concern that she will marry an elderly suitor who has murdered both his wife and her father. That in itself is mysterious. She can hardly be unaware of their suspicions. Is she intent on accepting this offer of marriage regardless? If not, why the concern for her? What is her attitude towards her other suitors? There must be other suitors if she possesses even a hint of the beauty ascribed to her."

"Even if she possesses none of it, there will be other suitors," I said. "She is an heiress. She owns one of the most prosperous farms in that part of Wales."

Sherlock Holmes looked at me strangely. "Really, Porter, your worldly wisdom increases daily. She is an heiress. That *is* a problem for her. Only a man of resolute character is able to detect any bad qualities at all in an heiress. What should be the beginning of an emotional and spiritual relationship is transformed into a calculation of profit and loss by that one overwhelming fact. It should not doom her to marrying an elderly, wealthy murderer, however. She may prefer a younger, much more attractive man regardless of his monetary qualifications. Heiresses frequently do, as the turmoils of history amply attest.

"She is the central figure in the case as it was presented to us, and your first step will be to learn what you can about her. You may need her permission and cooperation in order to conduct an investigation into her father's death. As for the death of the wife — there is little to be done there except to obtain a reliable eyewitness description of the symptoms she displayed during her fatal illness. Surely a friend, or relative, or servant will be willing to confide in you as long as she doesn't suspect that you are an investigator. Your friendly interest should be sufficient to inspire confidence, especially if you are mourning the recent death of a mother who displayed similar symptoms. You will be in an extremely awkward position as a casual visitor with neither the excuse nor the right language for asking questions, but that will be good training for you."

"I thought my first step would be to determine whether Emeric Tromblay has an employee who matches Evan Evans's description."

He shook his head. "That might require a protracted search. Tromblay owns mines and farms. He has hundreds of employees, and they may be scattered all over Wales. If he sent one of them to follow Saunders and Huws, he certainly selected someone from a remote location who isn't known to them. We could waste weeks in attempting to identify him, and it wouldn't advance our case significantly if we succeeded. You must first investigate the scene of the crime and talk with the young lady."

He paused and thought for a moment. "If our clients succeed in finding a poet to serve as your host, you must remember to refer to him as a Bard. Bards are persons of distinction in Wales. I've observed in recent months that your observations are tending more and more toward the prosaic, and an association with a Welsh Bard should be beneficial for you." His eyes were twinkling again, and I suspected that he was suppressing a smile.

He continued, "It is unfortunate that you must undertake a lengthy journey for such an unrewarding object as the rescue of a young lady — especially when London offers quantities of attractive young ladies, even heiresses, who could have been rescued by hansom or four-wheeler. But you are right — it *is* a case, and there are strong indications that something much larger and far more sinister than murder is involved. Your task today is to finish reading Borrow."

"Should I also read Robert Owen?" I asked. "He may have had something to do with the mysterious meeting."

"Rather you should say that the mysterious meeting had something to do with him. He has been dead for almost half a century."

For some reason I found that disconcerting. I mused, "Of course, the fact that people coming from the meeting were talking about him doesn't necessarily indicate a connection."

"Porter. Those strange admission passes that were marked with a large zero. Didn't it occur to you that the zero was actually the letter O and that the reference was to Robert Owen? When we add in the facts that all of the known *dramatis personae* of this case live in or near Newtown, Wales, and that Robert Owen was born in Newtown and is buried there, surely we could not reasonably require a more explicit link with our case. This is by far the most puzzling riddle that has emerged."

"Who was Robert Owen?" I asked.

"He was one of the most remarkable men of the last century. He was a philanthropist and social reformer whose ideas were far ahead of his time. Socialism, national trade unions, and the growing cooperative movement derive from his efforts. Many of the things he advocated — shorter hours and better working conditions, special treatment for women and children employees, decent housing, compulsory education, have already come to pass, and his ideas are still vital. He has disciples around the world, but I am not familiar with the extent of his following in Wales. The question we must ask ourselves is what possible connection his ideas could have with a case involving Emeric Tromblay, a wealthy man whose philosophy is certain to be the antithesis of his." He broke off and lost himself in thought.

"Perhaps a conspiracy exists to advance Owen's ideas," I suggested.

"No, Porter. No one needs to hold secret meetings with special passes, admission by invitation only, to discuss the ideas of Robert Owen. They are debated and commented on and published with complete freedom. Their advocates try to attract the largest possible audience to any meeting that they sponsor. Secret Robert Owen meetings make no sense at all."

I spent the day reading Borrow and sifting through what I knew of our case. I was searching for the sinister implications Sherlock Holmes had mentioned. I did not find them. He was out the entire day, and shortly before ten o'clock that night, when I left to call on our clients at the Euston Hotel, he still had not returned.

It seemed unlikely that Mr. Evan Evans would be watching the hotel at an hour when the Welshmen should be preparing for bed, but I had to consider that possibility. I first strolled along Drummond Street, knowing that Rabby and his helpers would recognize me and signal in some way if they were in the vicinity. I saw no sign of them. I also took the time to make certain that Evan Evans had not given Rabby's crew the slip in order to lurk in a doorway near the hotel entrance.

The Welshmen were waiting for me impatiently. They offered me a chair, and Mr. Bryn Huws poured a small glass of golden liquid for me.

"Mead," he said. "I make it myself. From my own honey. The swill they expect a man to drink in London has no taste and less body."

I took a sip of the mead, which had a delicious taste and almost more body than I could cope with. Huws plainly expected me to finish the glass. When I had done so, I shook my head — which needed it — and asked, "How is your business going?"

"Very well," Saunders said. "We will leave tomorrow, as Mr. Holmes suggested. This afternoon we called at all three of the toy shops he told us about. As soon as we return to Wales, we will find a young man to take the part of your long-lost cousin. If he is willing, it will be a poet named Dafydd Madryn. He is intelligent and completely reliable, and his character is of the highest. Also, he was a good friend of Glyn Huws. When he was much younger, I thought that he might marry Meleri. Now — what is it you want to know?"

I wanted to know as much as possible about the place where I was going and the people who lived there. For more than an hour I asked questions and recorded the information in my notebook. Then, with both of them watching and suggesting corrections, I sketched a map of the mountain village named Pentrederwydd — "Pentre" for "village" and "derwydd" for "oak grove," Saunders explained, the whole meaning "Village of the Oak Grove" — and the surrounding country, all of which was located some fifteen miles west of Newtown. Tromblay Hall, the home of our presumed villain, occupied a prominent place in my sketch, as did Meini Mawr, "Large Stones," formerly the farm of Glyn Huws and now the patrimony of Meleri. I was especially intrigued by Llyn Tŷ-Mawr, "Lake of the Big House," which lay in the valley that separated Meini Mawr from Tromblay Hall. I wrote down several pages of descriptions of these and other locations.

When I was satisfied that I understood the situation as well as possible, we made arrangements so that I could get in touch with them secretly in an emergency — Saunders at his solicitor's office in Newtown, Huws at the small tannery that he ran, or either of them at their homes. Then I closed my notebook and shook hands with them.

"Gofal!" Bryn Huws said. "Take care! Never forget that Emeric Tromblay is y Diafol yn y cnawd — the Devil incarnate. What does Mr. Holmes think of the situation?"

"His reaction to any murder is to catch the culprit and bring him to justice."

The solicitor nodded his approval. Bryn Huws said sourly, "If you succeed in putting a rich Englishman like Emeric Tromblay in the dock in Wales, you are remarkable detectives indeed."

"Unfortunately, you are very late in asking for help," I told them. "All the trails will be cold by now, but if any scent can be picked up, Sherlock Holmes will do it. Please remember that I am only his assistant. I will collect as much information as I can. When the case is ready for him, he will take charge personally."

It was long after midnight when I returned to Baker Street. Sherlock Holmes was waiting up for me. Rabby had just left. Both Rabby and Evan Evans had suffered through a tedious day. There were long hours of waiting, first while Arthur Saunders looked after his clients' business at Lincoln's Inn, and then while Saunders and Huws shopped for toys. After seeing them back to the hotel, Evans had treated himself to a sightseeing spree. He had gone to visit Madame Tussaud's waxwork exhibition.

Rabby had not caught sight of the fair-haired boy.

I discussed my map and notes with Sherlock Holmes before I retired. Early the next morning, I joined Rabby at the Three Nuns Hotel. We followed Evan Evans to the Euston Hotel and thence to Lincoln's Inn. He — and we — waited about until the two Welshmen went to lunch. From lunch they returned to the Euston Hotel, and from the hotel the three of us followed them across to the station and saw them into a train for Wales.

I would not have expected Evans's next move, but Sherlock Holmes had. Evans took a cab directly to 221B Baker Street, where he asked Mrs. Hudson whether Sherlock Holmes had returned. According to her instructions, she assured him that Mr. Holmes was still in Scotland and planned to remain there indefinitely on a difficult case. Evans returned to the Three Nuns Hotel, collected his valise, and had himself driven to Paddington Station, where he bought a ticket for Cardiff. Rabby and I watched him board the train, and then we returned to Baker Street. Sherlock Holmes paid Rabby amply for his several days' work, and I returned to my reading — this time of Robert Owen's *A New View of Society.*

5

A PERIOD OF TEDIUM SET IN FOR ME. SHERLOCK Holmes kept himself fully occupied but without telling me what he was working on, which was often his practice. He seemed to wrap a case around himself like a cloak of invisibility. Even a trained assistant eager to help him was kept totally ignorant of what he was doing. I had learned not to ask, but I surmised that he was looking into the antecedents of the fair-haired boy. With the departure of Evan Evans and our Welsh clients, I could think of no other aspect of the case left to investigate in London.

The only contribution that occurred to me was to return several times to Y Llew Du, the Black Lion, with my Welsh friend Fred Jones. We did not see the fair-haired boy or his companion. My friend listened carefully to the conversation around us, but he never heard Robert Owen mentioned.

There was nothing else for me to do but read. I supplemented Borrow with other books about Wales and occasionally dipped into Robert Owen — with considerable wonderment. Sherlock Holmes had three of Owen's books on his shelves — in addition to *A New View of Society,* there were *Observations on the Effect of the Manufacturing System,* and *The Future of the Human Race.*

Owen wrote, ". . . every day will make it more and more evident that the character of man is, without a single exception, always formed for him; and that it may be, and is, chiefly, created by his predecessors that they give him, or may give him, his ideas and habits, which are the powers that govern and direct his conduct. Man, therefore, never did, nor is it possible that he ever can, form his own character."

After Borrow's action-filled narration, I had heavy going with Owen. The notion that character is shaped by outside forces and that the individual's own actions have little influence on that process had powerful social implications, as did much that Owen wrote, but I wondered how a man with a strong personality — an Emeric Tromblay, for example — would react to a doctrine that seemed to credit outside influences for his achievements and exempt him from responsibility for his own actions. Certainly he would consider it insolent nonsense.

Our Welsh clients left for home on Tuesday. On Friday I received a letter. It read, "Dear Cousin Jones — I have just learned of your existence and of your desire to visit the land of your ancestors. I am honoured to offer you the hospitality of my humble home, and I will receive you with pleasure. If you will advise me as to the time of your arrival, I will meet you at Newtown Station." It was signed, "Dafydd Madryn."

Sherlock Holmes's only observation was that the man sounded literate, and he considered literacy to be an excellent quality in a poet. "It is, for a poet, what a steady hand is to an artist," he said.

I suggested that a short letter in English might not be the best basis for gauging a Bard's poetic qualities in Welsh.

"So it is not," Sherlock Holmes said impatiently, "but his bardic qualifications needn't concern us as long as he has sufficient skill with English to assist in our investigation. If he didn't know Welsh adequately, our clients wouldn't have chosen him."

We conferred concerning a departure date for me, and then I sent Dafydd Madryn a telegram. The clerk at the Marylebone Station office, where I handed it in, accepted it without blinking, a reminder that even Wild Wales now had links with the twentieth century. After reading Borrow, it had seemed unlikely to me that telegrams actually got delivered there.

That night Rabby came. He was wearing his ragged clothing again. The new suit had given him an aura of dignity that seemed completely out of character for him, and we were delighted to see him looking once more like his familiar, impish self. He eagerly entered into our customary game in which we attempted to deduce what we could about his day's activities. While we scrutinized him for clues, Rabby stood motionless for all of twenty seconds, and then he burst into laughter.

I had already picked out the source of his merriment. The nose of a mouse peeped from his pocket. It was an extremely real-looking mouse. Sherlock Holmes began by identifying a yellowish mud smear from Kennington Park — a virtuoso feat because the place was so distant from the scenes of Rabby's usual rambles — and he was late in noticing the mouse.

"So you've been to Houndsditch," he remarked finally.

Houndsditch once was a real ditch just outside the London city wall. According to legend, it gained its name from the quantity of dead dogs to be found there. That was long before it became a street and the centre of the toy and cheap jewellery trade.

"I don't recall seeing that particular toy before," Sherlock Holmes went on. "Porter?"

Rabby exploded in laughter.

"I've seen it," I said. "In fact, I've owned several just like it. It's a real mouse."

And so it was. Rabby had expended considerable effort in training it to maintain a motionless pose in his pocket with its nose exposed. It had fooled Sherlock Holmes, and that made the project a huge success. The mouse's reward was a piece of cheese that it calmly munched on the table.

"But don't let Mrs. Hudson see it!" Sherlock Holmes cautioned him. "Now, then. What interesting events do you have to describe for us?"

"None," Rabby said. "I only stopped to show you my mouse."

Sherlock Holmes persisted. Rabby obviously had been rambling from one end of London to the other. He must have seen *something* that was worth describing.

Rabby shook his head. The doldrums that had afflicted London before our Welsh clients arrived were continuing. "Nothing worth money," Rabby said.

"Describe what you have seen, and I'll decide what it's worth."

After a moment of reflection, Rabby did his desperate best. "There was a man at the bottom of Regent Street in dress clothes selling newspapers. But I've seen him before."

"Any particular newspapers?" Sherlock Holmes wanted to know.

"I think they were the *Pall Mall Gazette.*"

"I know him well," Sherlock Holmes said. "And you are quite right. There is no mystery about him. Of course, beggars and street traders are often incongruously attired simply because they wear whatever comes to hand. Only this morning, I saw a chair-mender clothed in a morning coat with tails. The case of the newsvendor is different because he is so completely and fashionably togged out. It amuses men who frequent clubs in the vicinity to supply him with their discarded clothing. So he sells his papers while wearing an opera hat, frock coat, watered silk waistcoat, dress trousers, and the finest polished boots. He is also an anarchist, and his patrons find the effect of an anarchist in dress clothing selling newspapers to be irresistible. He spends his evenings copying political tracts, and he hands them out with the papers he sells. He is otherwise a mild gentleman and a conscientious citizen, polite to everyone and kind to his wife and the several grandchildren he is raising. Such oddities are common in London."

"I know a cobbler who writes poetry," I said. "He distributes his poems with the shoes he repairs."

Sherlock Holmes was interested. "Are they good poems?"

"Unfortunately, no. They are unbelievably bad."

He shook his head regretfully. "There is a chemist in Maida Vale who nurtures an ambition to be a clergyman. He ornaments his shop with exhortations from the Scriptures and passes out prayers with the ointments and pills he sells. His customers think highly of him. Then there is a fish-monger plying Threadneedle Street and Bishopsgate who is said to secrete occasional half-crowns in the fish he sells. From time to time it is reliably reported that one of his customers has actually found one, but I have no evidence as to the frequency with which he performs this largess."

"It may increase his business," I suggested.

"Perhaps so, but I doubt that this is his motive. All of these gentlemen are harmless eccentrics, Radbert. Some people call them cranks. They enrich our lives, each in his own humble way. I collect them because they brilliantly support my conviction that for the strangest effects and the most extraordinary combinations we must go to life itself, which always is far more daring than any effort of the imagination and infinitely stranger than anything that the mind of man could invent. These eccentrics have no kinship whatsoever with toffs who spy from doorways or exchange canes for umbrellas in the Petticoat Lane Market, and it pleases me that you are able to discern the difference."

After Rabby left, I gave thought to the impression I wanted to make in Wales and packed—not a valise, but a knapsack.

The following day, Sherlock Holmes confided to me what he had been able to learn about the fair-haired boy's history. "He and his companion have left, and I am unable to find out where they went. Probably they are no longer in London. At least I now know who he is. He was raised by the Welsh couple he was staying with, the dairyman Griffiths and his wife, and he is called Alban Griffiths. The Griffiths never considered him their son, though they gave him their name and always treated him kindly. They boarded him from the time he was a baby until recently, though his real father has supported him and paid him irregular visits. The boy had been living elsewhere for a number of weeks prior to this recent sojourn.

"My investigation has been severely handicapped by the fact that the non-Welsh neighbours know so little about the family. I mention this because you are certain to encounter similar difficulties in Wales. The Welsh tend to close ranks quickly against outsiders, and they are deeply suspicious of any Englishman who asks questions about a Welshman. The English neighbours assume that the boy left because he obtained employment or was apprenticed somewhere. Nothing at all is known about his companion except that the two of them appeared suddenly at the end of last week.

"We have two mysteries here, Porter. If it were not for the fact that Evan Evans was involved in both of them, it would not have occurred to us that they are connected.

"Evans was assigned the task of discovering whether our clients contacted Sherlock Holmes. He also received another, far more important, assignment for which he was supplied with meticulous instructions. At the prescribed time, he was to walk through the Petticoat Lane Market in search of a street musician with a large gramophone. There he was to meet a person described to him or who was able to give him a code word and who would exchange an umbrella for his cane. Still following detailed instructions, he next was to go to Y Llew Du where his cane would be returned to him, probably by someone who would arrive by way of a private entrance and sit at the same table with him. The papers would have been removed from the cane, and others substituted, in a back room. It is unfortunate that you were unable to observe the mechanism of the exchanges, but I have no doubt that they were managed deftly. Once Evans retrieved his cane, he was free to wander about like any other tourist until the next morning, when he resumed his surveillance of the Welshmen.

"It was an enormous stroke of luck for us that Radbert chanced to walk through Baker Street last Sunday morning. We might have discovered that our clients were being followed, but we certainly would not have known about Evan Evans's second assignment and the meeting at Y Llew Du. Do you feel that the books you have been reading about Wales have prepared you adequately?"

"I won't know that until I get there," I said, "but I have turned up one Welsh mystery that I want to investigate. A man named Robert Newton was hanged for sheep stealing in 1821. He swore that he was innocent and predicted that grass would not grow upon his grave until his memory was cleared. He was buried in Montgomery, which is not far from Newtown. I would like to visit his grave and see whether there is any grass there."

"I will save you the effort," Sherlock Holmes said. "You would find very little grass."

"Then he was innocent."

"It is much too late to determine that, but surely you don't need to see the grave to deduce its condition. Tourists have been visiting it for more than eighty years for that very purpose, to see whether grass is growing there. Even if they haven't trampled the grave completely bare, they will have noticeably discouraged the growth of grass."

I asked him whether he had detailed instructions for me.

He shook his head. "You are going to see Wales as few Englishmen are privileged to see it. Borrow glimpsed it, but I suspect that he was severely handicapped because he thought he could speak Welsh. A language known imperfectly can be more of a barrier than an interpreter. The first thing you must be aware of is that Wales is a foreign country. Sovereignty means much more than lines on a map. It is a state of mind, and the Welsh have it. Their civilization is much more ancient than that of England; their language is older — in fact, they have the oldest literature of any contemporary European country; their Royal House had a lineage far more venerable than that of the upstart English rulers until the Norman English cruelly slaughtered the tragic Llewelyn the Last and all of his kin; it has even been claimed that English law is based upon a much older Welsh law. The Welsh would be more or less than human if they didn't resent their English conquerors. They are both proud and resourceful. The mere fact that their country is still an entity after all of these centuries, and that they are a recognizable people with their own distinct language, is both a mystery and a miracle. Take great pains to conduct yourself as a guest and never fail to demonstrate in every way you can that you are proud of your Welsh ancestry.

"As for our case, you must develop your own lines of inquiry as you proceed. Whether or not our adversary is named Tromblay, he will remain a mere shadow until we collect more facts about him. We can't confront him until we have evidence that clearly establishes his connection with the crimes, and that may require prolonged investigation."

The following Monday morning, I boarded a Great Western train with a through carriage to Wales by way of Birmingham. It left Paddington at nine-fifty, and both Sherlock Holmes and Rabby came to see me off.

The railway lines from London to Birmingham have never gained plaudits for scenic interest. Even the guidebooks refer to them as somewhat monotonous. The journey was far worse than that for me. It took slightly more than three hours — the train arrived a few minutes late — and I was seething with impatience to get on to Wales and find out what awaited me there.

Beyond Birmingham the country became more interesting, and by the time we crossed the Severn and headed due west into Wales, we were threading our way through lovely hills with mountains looming ahead of us. We stopped at Welshpool and at Montgomery, and when we finally reached New-town, shortly after three-thirty in the afternoon, the perplexing preface to our case that London had supplied seemed as remote as another lifetime. I was eager to assume my own role in the investigation.

My function in any case of Sherlock Holmes's was to arrive on the scene before him and go over the ground as thoroughly as possible, collecting as much pertinent data as I could for him to make use of when he arrived to take charge. This was an aspect of Sherlock Holmes's work that Dr. Watson paid little attention to except in those rare instances when he performed some of that drudgery himself. Sherlock Holmes often criticized his friend for overdramatizing cases because the doctor's accounts of them left out much of the hard work. Before Sherlock Holmes could perform those brilliant deductions, someone had to labour tirelessly to collect information and sift out the essential facts that made deductions possible.

My work also enabled Sherlock Holmes to pursue separate lines of investigation simultaneously and thus bring a case to a conclusion much more quickly than he could have without an assistant.

According to the guidebook, Newtown, Montgomeryshire, Wales, was a flannel-manufacturing town with 6,500 inhabitants, an important weekly market, and a monthly horse fair that attracted dealers from long distances. My task was to learn whether it also possessed a sinister and highly complicated conspiracy that the guidebook did not mention.

The town stood in the valley of the River Severn between imposing hills. I had a sweeping view of its buildings and its several tall factory chimneys as the train approached. Then a steep hill to the north, with rows of houses on its lower slopes, caught my eye. As the train slowed to a stop, my view was suddenly cut off by two tall buildings that seemed totally out of character for a small Welsh town.

The train halted on an embankment beside a long brick station building. As my feet touched the platform, a bearded man stepped forward to greet me. "Edward Jones?" he asked politely. "Do you mind if I call you Iorwerth? Or Iori? I am Dafydd Madryn."

It was thoughtful of him to pronounce his name for me. I had been wondering all the way to Wales whether I had forgotten how Arthur Saunders pronounced it. He was a young man, not yet thirty, but the shaggy beard made him look middle-aged.

"It is an honour to have you here," he said.

"It is an honour to be the guest of a Welsh Bard," I returned.

He halted and looked at me. "Not *Bard,"* he said. "I do write poetry, which entitles me to the humble title of poet, but Bards are poets of high distinction — poets who win honours in an eisteddfod."

"I didn't know that," I said. I wondered whether Sherlock Holmes knew. He had played similar pranks on me before. He said it contributed to my education. I added lamely, "Your English is excellent."

"Yes," Madryn said sadly. "Perhaps that is why my Welsh poetry will always be mediocre."

I could think of no response at all to that.

We walked together to the steps that descended to the street. Newtown continued to be an enormous surprise to me. Near the station were the two tall buildings I had seen from the train. One was a handsome large brick structure some five storeys in height, and at the end of the street was a newer building that looked even taller. Either would have been a valued ornament to almost any street in London. They were connected at an upper storey by a bridge above the roadway. Directly across from the station was the County Intermediate School, a well-lit building with pleasing lines. To the left was a large church.

The bustle stirred up by the arriving and departing train was rapidly diminishing, but a small, light carriage stood waiting for us. Madryn greeted the driver with a wave and a grin.

"This is my London cousin," he told him. "Iorwerth Jones. Iori, this is Humphrey the Bear from the Bear Hotel. You are about to ride in his famous Bear Bus."

Humphrey, whose long, graying moustache was at least as distinguished looking as that of a duke, gave me a friendly nod followed by a searching glance.

"Healthy looking specimen for all that London air he has been breathing," he said to Madryn.

Since I had no luggage for Humphrey to take charge of, he mounted to the top of the carriage. Madryn and I found seats for ourselves. We were the only passengers.

"We have much to talk about," Madryn said to me quietly as the carriage got underway, "but Newtown is not the best place for it. I understand what you intend to do. I have discussed with Mr. Saunders the ways in which I may be most helpful to you. I met you here because Benton Tromblay lives in Newtown. I thought you would want to meet him."

"Is that Emeric Tromblay's son?"

He nodded.

"I very much want to meet him."

"He works at the Warehouse." We were passing the two tall buildings I had admired from the station, and Madryn gestured at one of them. "That is Sir Pryce Pryce-Jones's Royal Welsh Warehouse. The other is one of his factories."

"What does Benton Tromblay do there?" I asked.

"He works as a clerk, I expect. He desperately needed employment, and the Colonel — Sir Pryce's eldest son, who runs the business — took pity on him. The Colonel's grandmother was related to Robert Owen." He seemed to think that explained everything, whereas it raised more urgent questions than I could contemplate at that moment.

"Would you like to see Robert Owen's grave?" Madryn asked suddenly.

"Yes, I would," I said quickly. My eagerness surprised him.

He said apologetically, "I suggested it because of Benton. The first thing he likes to do is take visitors to see Robert Owen's grave. It will give us more time to talk if you've already seen it."

"What does Benton Tromblay have to do with Robert Owen?" I asked.

He looked at me blankly. "I keep forgetting that you are a complete stranger. Didn't Mr. Saunders tell you about Benton?"

"He told me that he was no longer living with his father. I didn't inquire further."

"Mr. Saunders and Bryn Huws have their prejudices," Madryn said. "You should form your own opinion of Benton." Then he added, "If we can find him."

We had passed under the bridge that connected the two large buildings. An ordinary-looking roadway stretched ahead of us with two- and three-storey buildings of timber or brick.

"I reserved a room for us at the Bear," Madryn said. "You can leave your knapsack there. Are you accustomed to walking?"

Before I could respond, he added quickly, with a grin, "Not London walking. Not short strolls of a mile or two on pavements. Real walking. Walks across country of fifteen or twenty miles or more."

If he expected to shock me, I disappointed him. I had just read Borrow, who thought nothing of thirty-mile walks through the Welsh mountains day after day. I told Madryn that I was sure I could manage, but it might be easier on my feet if I accustomed myself to it gradually.

"That's what I thought," he said. "We will ride when we can and walk when we must." He scrutinized my shoes disdainfully. "You should get yourself some walking boots."

Newtown continued to impress me. I was startled to find such a range of well-kept buildings in a Welsh country town. When I remarked on it, Madryn said indifferently, "Newtown was once considered the Leeds of Wales. It was a major centre of the weaving industry and a wealthy place. Haven't you ever heard of Welsh flannel? But now it has fallen on hard times."

Despite those hard times, we passed a splendid new red-bricked building with a domed clock tower and a new library building as we arrived at Broad Street in the centre of town. Madryn pointed out Robert Owen's birthplace, now the nondescript-looking printing and stationery shop of Park & Son, where, a hundred and thirty years earlier, Owen's father had kept a saddler's and ironmonger's business. On the ledge below the upper windows was an inscription in large black letters: **BIRTHPLACE OF ROBERT OWEN, PHILANTHROPIST.**

The Bear Hotel, located just beyond it, advertised itself as one of the largest and most comfortable hotels in North Wales, and among its amenities were hot and cold baths, a bowling green, billiard rooms, convenient access to golf links, and good fishing and shooting. Our programme called for none of those things, so I left my knapsack there, and we strolled along Broad Street and then followed Old Church Street down to the churchyard on the bank of the Severn where Robert Owen was buried. It was a pleasant walk in a pleasant town. At quarter-hour intervals, the town clock, whose tower I had just seen, sounded ding-donging, mellow chimes. They could be heard all over Newtown.

The venerable church of St. Mary's was a wreck. It had been abandoned more than fifty years earlier on the completion of the new church of Saint David's, the church I had seen from the station. The roof had fallen in and the walls were crumbling, but the squat, square tower looked almost intact. It was a sad ending for a house of worship that had stood for many hundreds of years. Madryn said it dated from the thirteenth century.

Robert Owen's tomb was located close to the south wall of the old church. As we walked towards it, Madryn told me about the recurring scandal it had caused. Owen had denounced orthodox religion — he considered all religions to be erroneous — and when he died, on a visit to the town of his birth in 1858, there had been controversy over his burial in consecrated ground. Later, when the Co-operative Union wanted to erect a monument over the grave of the man whose work had given birth to the co-operative movement, church authorities had objected. As a result, an impressive monument to Owen had been built in Kensal Green Cemetery in London, and the Newtown grave had only a low iron palisade around the tomb.

Recently there had been another attempt to honour Owen's memory appropriately in his native town, and the palisade had been replaced by taller, much more elaborate iron railings. In addition, a Robert Owen memorial section was included in the new library.

None of this offered any kind of a clue to the long-dead social reformer's connection with two Welsh murders and the surprising manoeuvres I had witnessed in London. The tomb was marked with simple tributes to Robert Owen, Philanthropist. I strolled from one side to the other, studying it intently, but its secrets, if it had any, were immune to my scrutiny. On the ironwork at one end was a metal plate erected by the Co-operative Union, reading: **TO THE MEMORY OF ROBERT OWEN, FOUNDER OF THE CO-OPERATIVE MOVEMENT.**

A plate on the other end contained a quotation from Robert Owen: "It is the one great universal interest of the human race to be cordially united and to aid each other to the full extent of their capacities." On the side was a bronze plaque showing a group of workers — no doubt to indicate the many persons whose tribulations had been eased by Owen's reforms — with the phrase, EACH FOR ALL. There also was a medallion portrait of Owen.

He had been buried in the grave of his parents, and the tomb also contained memorials to his mother and father.

The setting was wonderfully peaceful; even though there were buildings nearby, the town seemed remote and insignificant. The old churchyard was washed by the much older river, and its graves were so venerable that they no longer were marked by mounds. In that setting, the recently adorned Robert Owen tomb seemed startlingly new. I looked at it doubtfully and wondered whether the secret I sought was even newer and would have to be searched for elsewhere.

Madryn nudged me. "Here's Benton," he said quietly.

I turned. A thin, slightly built young man with spectacles was approaching us from the direction of Old Church Street. He wore no hat, and his long, straw-coloured hair drooped untidily. His dress was neat but noticeably thread-bare. He looked like a poorly paid clerk — which in actual fact he was.

Madryn greeted him affably and introduced his long-lost cousin from London.

"He has just arrived," Madryn said. "He is interested in Robert Owen, so I brought him here first."

"Indeed." Benton Tromblay turned an intense gaze upon me. His pale, watery blue eyes blinked frequently behind the thick lenses he wore. "What interests you about Robert Owen?"

"I have several of his books," I said modestly. "He was one of most remarkable men of the last century — a visionary and social reformer whose ideas may yet be realized if enlightened people everywhere will support them."

Benton stared at me. "How interesting! That's just what I would have said myself!" He turned back to Madryn. "I'm giving a lecture tonight. You must come — both of you. The Club Factory Building on New Church Street. Do you know where it is?"

Madryn nodded.

"Eight o'clock. You must come."

He took two pieces of paper from his pocket, scribbled on one and then the other, and handed one to each of us.

"Here are your passes. Present them at the door — you won't be admitted without them."

I stood staring at the slip of paper. Benton Tromblay had written his initials in the centre of a large wood block print of the letter *O*.

6

THE MOMENT WE POCKETED OUR PASSES, BENTON experienced misgivings. He said uncertainly, "It's a private meeting. I'd rather you didn't tell anyone about it. If outsiders try to attend — "

"I don't know anyone in Newtown to tell except you," I said cheerfully. I wanted to gain his confidence, and it seemed to me that the only way to do that quickly was to feed him. It was just approaching five o'clock and early for dinner, but he had a hungry look about him, as though he had been subsisting for weeks on raw cabbage and an occasional sausage roll, and I felt certain that we could find an inn or restaurant willing to serve us.

"Come and have dinner with us," I said. "I've been travelling all day, and I feel ravenous. What is the famous Welsh food? Mutton? Where can we find a good roast leg of mutton?"

Dafydd Madryn was watching with amusement, fascinated to see a detective at work. Benton Tromblay seemed embarrassed. Perhaps he feared that we would expect him, the son of a wealthy man, to pay for the dinner.

"Do come and be my guest," I said quickly before he could refuse. "You'll be doing me a favour. I like to have interesting people to talk with, and you can tell me all about Newtown and the Welsh people. Is it really true that there are towns in Wales where every family has its own church?"

Luckily that was a subject that interested him. He had Nonconformist views himself, probably because his father was so staunchly Church of England. He delivered a concise summary of the history of religion in Wales back to the Tudor monarchs — when the Welsh preferred Catholicism to Henry VIII's Reformation — with illuminating observations on Puritanism and Cromwellism, the Methodist revival, Calvinism, and Presbyterianism. He tossed in several verbal footnotes along the way regarding the Baptists. The man was a frustrated historian. He was still chattering when we turned into Broad Street from Old Church Street and Madryn led us across to the three-storeyed brick building that housed the Unicorn Hotel. While Tromblay and I seated ourselves by a window in the hotel's dining room, Madryn went to confer with the proprietor.

He came back to inform us that we were indeed fortunate. Roast mutton, though not leg of mutton, would be available in half an hour or so. We could pass the time pleasantly enough if we didn't mind drinking beer from Sam Powell's Brewery, a local concern. I tasted it apprehensively and found it a pleasant surprise. Borrow had described in great detail his frustrations with locally brewed beer and ale all across Wales, and I was prepared to be disappointed.

My first problem was to get Benton off the subject of religion. I pointed across the street at the Checkers Inn. I had noticed it on our earlier stroll along Broad Street because it presented such a dramatic contrast to the surrounding buildings. It was an old, old black and white structure with a thatched roof, and it stood almost apologetically among taller, much younger brick buildings that seemed to be looking down on it with contempt. "Is that the oldest building in Newtown?" I asked.

Both of them pondered that for a moment. "Possibly," Madryn said. "There is Tynyrhelyg, the name means 'The House in the Willows.' We passed it on our way to the Bear. It's an extremely old timber-framed building. Then there is Cwrt-Plâs-yn-dre, Owain Glyndŵr's Parliament House — "

"Just a moment," I said. "Is Owain Glyndŵr the same person as Owen Glendower?"

Madryn's body shook with laughter. "The first is Welsh and the second is English. And yes, they are the same person. This is the problem the Welsh have been racked with ever since Norman times. Is it any wonder that this is a confused country?"

"A lot more than the language is confused," I said. "I spent the past week reading about Wales, and one of the things my reading mentioned was Owen Glendower's — if you will pardon my English — Parliament House. But it wasn't in Newtown. It was in a town called — "

I broke off. I refused to try to say "Machynlleth" in the presence of a genuine Welshman.

Madryn's body shook with laughter again. He pronounced "Machynlleth" for me. After I heard it, I didn't believe it. He started to pronounce it again, one careful syllable at a time.

"Never mind that," I told him. "I'm going to learn some Welsh at the earliest opportunity, but that isn't the word I want to start with. Just tell me whether Owen Glendower had a moveable Parliament House."

My own introduction to one of the legendary national heroes of Wales had come through Borrow's accounts, and I'd been interested enough to read more about him. Owen Glendower gave the English fits for more than a decade at the beginning of the fifteenth century. In that short period of time, he did something that had never been done before — over a period of years he defeated one English army after another; and he achieved something that had never existed before — he made Wales a nation, with a red dragon flag and its own great seal featuring himself, as Prince of Wales, on its throne. He had much more than military skill. He exchanged emissaries with foreign rulers. He entered into negotiations with the Pope with the object of establishing a Church of

Wales that would be independent of Canterbury. He made pacts with English enemies of King Henry IV. He was a far-sighted leader whom some have called a statesman. He twice convened national parliaments, important steps toward giving Wales a parliamentary government, and he planned to establish two Welsh universities.

He gave Wales one of the few shining moments it has enjoyed during the past thousand years or so of its history. Then, when his luck turned and the English dealt him a series of defeats, he vanished. Wales had to wait almost five hundred more years for its universities, and their eventual establishment owed nothing to the government in London. They were financed by contributions from the Welsh people.

No one knew or yet knows what happened to Owen Glendower. Legend holds that he sleeps in a remote mountain cave with his army — just as another Welsh hero, King Arthur, is said to sleep with his knights — awaiting some future crisis when he will rouse himself to fall upon the enemies of Wales.

Dafydd Madryn described for me the antecedents of Newtown's version of Owen Glendower's Parliament House. It originally stood in the mountain town of Dolgellau, and its connection with Owen Glendower was tenuous if not actually fictitious. It really was a very old building, however, dating from the sixteenth century or even earlier, with an interesting history of its own. It didn't come to be called Owen Glendower's Parliament House until modern times. When it was doomed to demolition, Sir Pryce Pryce-Jones, owner of the Royal Welsh Warehouse and factory I had admired near the station, purchased the materials of the building, arranged to have them carefully marked and removed to Dolerw, his estate at Newtown, and the building reconstructed.

"Then Owen Glendower actually has no connection with this part of Wales," I said. Somehow that disappointed me.

"But he does," Madryn said. "His principal residence was at Sycharth, which is only twenty-five miles north of here. The mound it stood on is still there. He ranged all through the border country."

"There aren't many parts of Wales that someone didn't fight a battle over," Benton said gloomily. "We wanted to give the Robert Owen lectures at Cwrt-Plâs-yn-dre, but Sir Pryce wouldn't permit it."

"He did you a favour," Madryn said. "You should never give a lecture in a place that has no taverns nearby. Listening to lectures is a thirsty business. Also, if you're expecting a large audience, Cwrt-Plâs-yn-dre is too small."

"Owain Glyndŵr and Robert Owen were two of the greatest men of Wales," Benton said defensively. "It would be appropriate to honour one in a place associated with the other. But Sir Pryce didn't want strangers tramping about his estate at night."

The waiter served our dinner with courteous efficiency. It was not as good as I had hoped — I suspected that an elderly sheep had contributed the mutton — but it was very well prepared, and no hungry person would have despised it. The beer had begun to mellow Benton Tromblay, and he succumbed completely to the food. Watching him, I tried to think of questions that would gradually turn the conversation in a more profitable direction.

Madryn was ahead of me. He asked him, with a directness I would not have dared to use, "Why are you off work early today?"

"The Colonel gave me a leave of absence," Benton said.

The two of them continued to talk. I addressed myself to the mutton, listened attentively, and gradually began to fill in the blanks in my knowledge about Benton Tromblay.

He had left home after a long series of disagreements with his father. "More like wars, they were," Madryn told me afterward. The dissension was caused in part by Benton's persistent attempts to convince his father that the mines the family controlled should be reformed according to Robert Owen's ideas.

Benton very quickly ran out of money, and for a time he was destitute. He stubbornly refused to ask his father for assistance; probably it would not have been forthcoming. Emeric Tromblay was at least as stubborn as his son. Benton's avid interest in Robert Owen had caught the Pryce-Jones family's attention, and the Colonel, who managed the Royal Welsh Warehouse because of his father's declining health, acknowledged his distant connection with the Owen family by giving employment to Benton.

"How did you happen to become interested in Robert Owen?" I asked.

"I made friends with a Scottish student at Oxford," Benton said. "His family estate was in the neighbourhood of New Lanark, where Owen had enormous success with social reform. He knew all about Robert Owen — was a disciple, in fact. My home was near Newtown, where Owen was born and died, and I knew almost nothing about him. My friend made me feel ashamed of myself. 'You walked in the shadow of a great man and never noticed him!' he exclaimed. I quickly became fascinated with what my friend told me. Under his tutelage, I set about learning as much as I could concerning Robert Owen and his ideas. I'm still learning."

I found the Royal Welsh Warehouse and its astonishing success at least as interesting as

Robert Owen. It had been the first business of its kind in the world. Orders were taken and filled by mail. Sir Pryce Pryce-Jones began by selling Welsh flannel "direct from the looms to the customers" and expanded his offerings to include other merchandise. Now the firm had more than a quarter of a million customers all over the world and ran its own railway carriages between Newtown and Euston to speed the distribution of orders. Queen Victoria had been one of its customers, and she knighted Sir Pryce for his business achievements. It amazed me that two such notable men, Robert Owen and Sir Pryce Pryce-Jones, should come from this quiet corner of Wales.

Offering employment to Benton imposed no hardship on the Pryce-Jones family. Its Royal Welsh Warehouse employed more than three hundred persons. Perhaps the firm took pride in having a graduate of Oxford on its payroll. His leave of absence was not so easily explained, and he seemed reluctant to talk about it.

Madryn persisted. He knew that Benton was too impoverished to live without his salary. He was still repaying loans to friends who had helped him when he first left home.

"I'm going lecturing," Benton blurted finally.

"Lecturing?" Madryn echoed perplexedly.

"Lecturing about Robert Owen," Benton said. "The Robert Owen Study League pays me a salary and expenses. I'm going to travel all over Wales. Maybe England, too, but Wales to start with. But please don't tell anyone. Powerful people would try to interfere if they knew what we are doing." He added as an afterthought, "My father would blow sky high. When I tried to show him how he could increase his mining profits with Robert Owen's ideas, he ordered me to never mention Robert Owen in his presence again."

"Would Robert Owen's ideas work in mines?" I asked innocently.

That touched off a discourse that lasted almost to the end of our dinner. I listened politely. Madryn's eyes were bright with amusement. He kept directing glances at me as though he wanted to ask whether this was really what I had in mind.

It was not. I finally managed to stem the flow by mentioning Meleri Huws. Her name brought Benton's oration to an abrupt halt. "Do you know her?" he asked in surprise.

"I've never met her, but we are related on my grandfather's mother's side," I said. Surely Meleri Huws could be my cousin if Madryn could.

Benton accepted that without blinking. He was surfeited with food and in the most congenial of moods. I had fed him; I was interested in Robert Owen; I needed no further credentials. We were companions.

"Her father's death was a terrible blow to her," he said. "But she'll be all right, I'm sure. She's very capable."

"Do you still have ideas about marrying her?" Madryn asked.

Benton looked startled. "Me? Marry Meleri?" He laughed. "What made you think I had ideas about marrying Meleri? She needs a farmer for a husband."

"I heard that you were courting her," Madryn said.

Benton shook his head. "Not I. I called on her a few times. Pentrederwydd is such a God-forsaken place, and my father only entertains his own cronies. Sometimes I got lonely. But all she could talk about was sheep and cows, and shearing and threshing, and that sort of thing palls very quickly."

"Perhaps she would say that all you could talk about was Robert Owen," Madryn suggested politely.

Benton laughed. "Perhaps she would. That palled for her just as quickly. She is a lovely young woman, she is intelligent, she'll make someone a far better wife than I'll ever find, but she needs a farmer for a husband."

"Haven't you heard that your father is courting her?" Madryn asked.

That dumbfounded him. Obviously he hadn't heard it. He refused to believe it. "The governor's talk about mines and shares and dividends would bore Meleri as quickly as mine about Robert Owen, and I simply cannot see her playing hostess at Tromblay Hall. She'd want to dismiss all the servants and do everything herself. She grew up delivering lambs and milking cows and baking bread and bara ceirch. She bakes delicious bara ceirch."

"Oatcakes," Madryn said in an aside to me.

"I couldn't imagine Meleri married to the governor any more than to me," Benton went on. "Anyway, she's Welsh. She's fiercely Welsh. She would never be so unpatriotic as to marry an Englishman. Never!"

"Then you haven't heard the rumours," Madryn said.

"What rumours?"

"That your father killed Glyn Huws, or had him killed, because Glyn opposed his courtship of Meleri."

Tromblay was flabbergasted. Moments later, when he had managed to grasp the full implications of that, he was furiously angry. "Don't tell me anyone actually believes that silliness!" he exclaimed.

"It is being repeated," Madryn said.

"It is rank calumny and an insult to the intelligence of anyone it is told to. The governor and I disagree on almost everything, but that doesn't mean he isn't a decent man, and a law-abiding man, and a just man. Ask anyone who has been taken poaching at Tromblay Hall. He wouldn't commit murder for any reason. He loathes violence."

The town clock chimed four ding-dongs to denote the hour. The pause that followed became an agonizing suspense before the first of seven strokes was heard. Benton took out his watch and glanced at it in alarm. "Have we been here that long? What a pleasant dinner!" He got to his feet. "I must hurry. I have to review my lecture notes. You are coming to the lecture, aren't you?"

He shook my hand warmly, thanked me for the dinner, thanked Madryn for introducing me, and rushed off.

Madryn's beard seemed to be concealing a smile. "Does he have a guilty connection with your case?" he asked quietly.

"I doubt that he is guilty of anything but naïvety," I said. "Anyone who would try to convince Emeric Tromblay that he could increase his profits by improving the wages and working conditions of his miners surely has led a sheltered life. A man ought to know his own father better than that. But Benton certainly has a connection with the case. I don't know what it is, but he has it. I can guarantee that." I had not told Madryn about the meeting at Y Llew Du in London with passes identical to those Benton had given us. "What is the Robert Owen Study League?" I asked him.

"I don't know," Madryn said. "I've never heard of it. There was a meeting here last winter that had something to do with Robert Owen, but I didn't hear any mention of the Robert Owen Study League. I'll have to ask someone."

We both were luxuriously stuffed with mutton and trimmings, and the Unicorn's cherry tarts balanced on that precariously. I paid the bill, adding a London-sized tip that astonished the waiter, congratulated all concerned on the delicious meal, and left behind me an enormous friendliness for persons of Welsh descent who returned, with ample funds, to seek the land of their ancestors.

We walked along Broad Street, stopping in at the Bear Hotel so that Madryn could ask the proprietor about the Robert Owen Study League.

Mr. H.E. Breese was as much of a surprise as his hotel had been. He was a fine figure of a man, stocky, of medium height, about fifty years old, with a splendid bushy moustache. He possessed neither the jollity nor the gloom that so often, one or the other, mark the characters of small town innkeepers. He was a highly successful business man with his own distinctively grave sense of humour, proud of his fine hotel and the roles he and his lovely wife played in Newtown's business and social circles.

His attitude toward Dafydd Madryn also was a surprise. Perhaps Madryn had not attained the lofty rank of Welsh Bard, but it was obvious that even a very ordinary poet could command considerable respect in Wales.

The meeting that Madryn remembered had taken place the previous February. It was one of a series held all over Britain under the sponsorship of the education departments of local Co-operative Societies, and it had featured Mr. Philip Snowden, a nationally known politician, as speaker. Snowden's speech, on the subject of "Co-operation: Its relation to other reforms," had only incidentally concerned Robert Owen, who was honoured as the founder of Co-operation. It was evident that this event had no connection with Benton Tromblay's lecture series.

Mr. Breese had never heard of the Robert Owen Study League. "Newtown has at least four literary societies, including a Welsh Literary Society," he said. There was resignation in his voice but twinkling good humour in his eyes. "It has two bands, a Harmonic and Orchestral Society, a branch of the Guild of Church Bellringers, and the Newtown Eisteddfod. It has more political, religious, recreational, temperance, and friendly associations than I have ever been able to keep track of. It even has two mutual improvement societies. It only stands to reason that sooner or later someone would start a study league. I can't see that it makes much difference whether the group purports to study Robert Owen or David Lloyd George."

"It may not be a public organization," Madryn said quickly. He didn't want to start rumours that would disconcert Benton Tromblay. "Probably a few friends are meeting to improve one another's minds."

Mr. Breese nodded wisely.

Leaving the Bear, we walked along Broad Street to the Cross, where the building with the domed clock tower stood and where several streets intersected. I stopped to admire the handsome new brick and frame building of the Newtown Free Library and read the plaque on the Robert Owen memorial section: "This portion of the building was erected by the Co-operative Union acting on behalf of the Co-operators of the United Kingdom to the memory of Robert Owen, Founder of Co-operation."

"The town seems properly proud of its famous native son," I remarked.

Madryn responded with a shrug. "I told you about the religious controversy. The plaque is here because of a gift to the library in Robert Owen's name. Perhaps the gift was really a bribe — in return for money given to the library, permission was granted to Owen's followers to erect the new decorative railings around his grave. Many of his beliefs are still highly controversial, and the Church of England authorities — who conveniently forget each Monday the forgiveness they preached on Sunday — never forgave him for some of the things he said about religion. The rector who permitted the burial of Owen in St. Mary's churchyard was severely criticized. He responded by preventing the erection of a monument over Owen's grave."

"But that was almost fifty years ago," I protested.

"That isn't very long for a religious controversy," Madryn said. "It was clever of you to invite Benton to dinner. I was wondering how to get him to talk freely. But he talked mostly on the wrong subjects, didn't he? Did you get what you wanted?"

"Yes. I got almost everything I wanted, and I'm convinced that he really doesn't know any more than he let on. How does he feel about the alleged murder of his mother?"

"He would have jumped straight through the ceiling if either of us had suggested such a thing. He really thinks his father is a decent chap who always does right according to his lights. Eventually they'll be reconciled, and Benton will put the wild ideas of his youth behind him and take over his inheritance as a proper squire." He added thoughtfully, "In justice to him, he may be completely unaware of some of his father's more vicious business practices."

Across the street from the library was the shop of Park & Son, which occupied the premises where Robert Owen had been born. I stepped inside to select a few picture postcards of Newtown. The town continued to surprise me, but I also found it vaguely disappointing. The people seemed more English than Welsh. I heard English spoken everywhere and only rarely the incomprehensible lilt of another language. Obviously Newtown was a border community, and for the moment it seemed to rest on the English side.

We turned into the High Street, which was unusually wide because of verges between the street and the pavements where stalls were erected on market days. The buildings — including a handsome Market Hall — continued to impress me. At the end of the street I managed a historical note for Sherlock Holmes: Beyond, set in spacious grounds, was the sprawling but drab-looking Newtown Hall, where Charles I had once slept. In the eighteenth century, it had been the home of Sir John Pryse, that gentleman of worth but strange singularities who made such original arrangements for two dead wives and then tried to purchase a miracle to restore the third to life.

We returned along Ladywell Street, and Madryn explained the peculiarities of Newtown's architecture. When the town had been the Leeds of Wales, these tall brick buildings, which dated from early in the nineteenth century, contained cottages for workers on the lower storeys while those above served as weaving factories. Newtown had been filled with the clacking of hand looms. Buildings erected later were larger and contained an additional feature. At the end of each row of cottages there had been a "truck shop," owned by the proprietor of the factory, where the workers were required to purchase food and necessities for themselves and their families at the proprietor's prices. Factory owners were careful to hire weavers with large families so as to guarantee a maximum amount of indebtedness.

Newtown had indeed fallen on hard times when its weaving industry lost out to more efficient factories in England. Behind the impressive buildings were old courts and alleys where the poor and the unemployed were crowded into filthy and insanitary quarters with — on the average — only two water closets for five houses.

I had the feeling that I should be looking for something, but I couldn't think what it might be. I had no way of knowing — yet — whether the town of Newtown was a part of the mystery that had brought me to Wales or only a backdrop. Madryn kept sending side glances at me as though he found the ways of a detective to be exceedingly strange.

When eight o'clock approached, we abandoned our walking tour and turned from Market Street into New Church Street, which ran down to St. David's. The Club Factory Building was one of a block of buildings very like those we had already seen. The cottages were still occupied as dwellings. The club, a workers' benefit group, occupied a former factory room above them. No doubt Robert Owen would have approved of offering a lecture dedicated to his teachings in such surroundings. It was a far more appropriate setting than even a genuine Owen Glendower's Parliament House could have provided.

We climbed a long, winding staircase to the upper floor, where our passes admitted us to a large, bare, dimly-lit room with a low ceiling. Chairs were arranged in rows with a table and two chairs at the front. We selected seats in the centre of the room and settled ourselves to wait. The place gradually filled up, which surprised me. So did the number of women who had accompanied their husbands. I was curious to see whether any of Newtown's elite would patronize the Robert Owen Study League — Sir Pryce Pryce-Jones and his family, for example — but there were very few well-dressed people in attendance. Most of those present had the shabby, defeated look of the unemployed.

Shortly after I heard the town clock distantly chiming eight, Benton Tromblay entered accompanied by an elderly, bearded man, and the two seated themselves at the table. The elderly man opened his watch ceremoniously, snapped it shut, glanced at Benton — who nodded — and then arose and began an introductory address, eulogizing Robert Owen and almost incidentally introducing Benton.

As Benton got to his feet, I glanced over my shoulder. I was curious as to whether the back of the room was as full as the front. It was — and seated two rows behind me, I saw, in the dim light, a slender, good-looking, neatly-dressed, fair-haired boy of about sixteen. He was wearing the same clothing he had worn in London. Seated next to him was the sturdily-built man of medium height with dusky red hair and beard who had enjoyed a leisurely Sunday dinner with the boy at London's Y Llew Du, the Black Lion.

I began composing in my mind the letter I would write to Sherlock Holmes before I retired. Benton Tromblay, Robert Owen, the peaceful town of Newtown, and perhaps even Owen Glendower and Sir Pryce Pryce-Jones's Royal Welsh Warehouse, were, all of them, in some way intertwined with this baffling mystery.

7

I NUDGED MADRYN AND WHISPERED TO HIM ABOUT the boy and his companion. "In London, he is called Alban Griffiths," I said. "I need to know what names they are using here and where they live."

Madryn nodded. He glanced back casually. A few minutes later, he took a searching look. Then he whispered to me, "I don't know them. I'll try to find out who they are."

I gave my attention to Benton Tromblay.

To my surprise, he was an effective speaker. He began by presenting a detailed biography of Robert Owen. Owen had been a precocious youth. He read voraciously, and at school he was so advanced for his age that he became a "pupil-teacher" when he was only seven. He left school at the age of nine to work in a local haberdasher shop.

At ten he was sent to London to join an older brother. Apprenticeship to a draper followed. When he finished his apprenticeship, he went to Manchester looking for employment, and at the youthful age of eighteen, he was already a partner in a firm that manufactured spinning machines for the rapidly expanding cotton industry.

He next set up his own business as a cotton spinner and so prospered that at the age of twenty he was managing a modern steam-powered mill employing five hundred people. He quickly acquired a reputation as a producer of fine cotton cloth. In 1799, at the age of twenty-eight, he formed a partnership to buy the large cotton mills at New Lanark, Lanarkshire, Scotland, from a wealthy Scottish businessman whose daughter Owen married.

His ideas on social reform developed simultaneously with his business success. At the beginning of the nineteenth century, working conditions in factories were appalling. Workers laboured for fourteen or more hours a day in dark, poorly ventilated mills. Their wages were meagre. Large numbers of children worked in the mills as apprentices. They were taken from parish workhouses and virtually became the property of the mill owners, who were supposed to feed, clothe, house, and educate them. These children, some as young as five years old, worked the same hours as the adults. They were severely beaten by their employers to keep them at their tasks. Safety standards were non-existent, and many children were killed or maimed at work. Their food was often inadequate; their living conditions miserable. At the end of their long day's work, the exhausted children were hustled off to school where it was expected that the crude but stern methods of the day would educate them.

Factory towns were notorious for low moral standards and drunkenness. Owen felt that the working conditions had an injurious influence upon the entire population, and he began to put his ideas for reform into practice.

He improved the housing and paved the streets at New Lanark. He opened a company store where, unlike the notorious truck shops Madryn had told me about, quality goods were sold at prices only slightly above cost. He controlled the sale of alcoholic beverages. He attempted to shorten the working day, but his partners opposed this. Eventually he bought them out and was able to institute the reforms he wanted. He set a minimum age of ten for apprentices and reduced their working day to twelve hours.

He lobbied for new laws that would improve working conditions. Parliament gave him much less than he asked for, and even those inadequate laws were ignored by far too many employers. Owen advocated a system of inspection to enforce the laws, but it was not adopted for many years. When Parliament failed, he attempted to achieve reforms by shaping public opinion and by increasing the power of the workers with a new Grand National Consolidated Trades Union. Public opinion changed very slowly, and the government combined with employers to smash the union.

He had his greatest success with education. He admitted children as young as two years old to his schools, and he maintained that the object of education should not be to cram the child with facts but to prepare it for life by developing its character and personality. He wanted children surrounded with love and understanding and given encouragement that would make them desire knowledge. He introduced dancing and music as important subjects. His schools were a phenomenal success and attracted visitors from all over Europe. He declared that "the best governed State will be that which shall possess the best national system of education."

From time to time I looked around at the other members of the audience. The sturdy Welshmen were at first politely interested, and then, as Benton began to detail Owen's ideas, they became engrossed. Owen had maintained that labour was the source of all wealth. It represented a natural standard of value that should replace gold and silver. Competition between men and machines was the permanent cause of distress and unemployment, and the only effective remedy for that was the united action of men and the subordination of machinery to men. At the time that Benton was speaking, machines had caused wide-spread unemployment, and trade unions were being severely repressed in the courts. The bitterness that I knew existed all across Britain was intense in that severely stricken centre of Welsh textile manufacturing. Owen had harsh words for those mill owners who gave more money and concern to the development and maintenance of their machines than to the welfare of their human employees.

As Newtown's unemployed listened eagerly to the words Robert Owen had written and spoken seventy-five or more years earlier, Benton must have felt that the time for his master's teachings had finally come.

"We must study Robert Owen's ideas," he said. "We must learn. We must work together to bring about the utopia he envisaged. In my next lecture, I will give you the details of his plan for the future."

As he seated himself, I joined in the enthusiastic applause. He had added considerably to my knowledge of Robert Owen. Unfortunately, he had provided no discernible clue as to what the Newtown philanthropist had to do with our two murders and a conspiracy that stretched from Wales to London.

The chairman announced the next meeting for Wednesday night and offered passes to all those present who desired them. A younger man moved through the audience handing them out. Madryn and I each took one though we hadn't yet considered how long we would remain in Newtown. I was mildly surprised that there was no appeal for money to finance the lectures.

When the audience began to leave, I gave Madryn a meaningful look. He nodded and pushed his way towards the exit. I moved in the opposite direction and joined the crowd that already surrounded the speaker's table. It was several minutes before Benton noticed me.

"You are an excellent speaker," I told him. "I enjoyed it very much. Robert Owen was even more remarkable than I had thought."

He smiled his pleasure. "Will you come Wednesday?"

"If I am still in Newtown, I certainly shall come."

I stepped aside to make room for others and turned to look about the room. Alban Griffiths and his companion had disappeared. So had Dafydd Madryn.

I hurried down the stairs to the exit. Night had settled on the town, and Newtown's streets were somewhat less brightly lit than Piccadilly. Peering into the dimness, I saw Madryn waiting for me. Members of Benton's audience had gathered into small groups and were talking enthusiastically in Welsh — probably about Robert Owen, as those who left the meeting at Y Llew Du in London had been talking about him. Other groups headed north towards the Green Tavern. Madryn took my arm and guided me in the opposite direction towards New Road and St. David's Church.

As soon as we could talk without being overheard, he said disgustedly, "They vanished. I was hanging back so they wouldn't notice me, and when I got to the street, they were nowhere to be seen."

"They must have entered a neighbouring building," I said.

"True, but there is no way of telling which one. They may have had time to cross the street. There are at least five possibilities and more if they moved quickly."

"They had no need to hurry," I said. "They didn't know you were trying to follow them. There is only one way to find out where they went."

"What is that?"

"Watch all of the doors until they come out," I said grimly. I was not about to invite another reprimand for giving up too soon.

Madryn peered at my face in the dim light. "So that is how detectives work. Mr. Saunders says that your employer achieves remarkable results. He uses remarkable methods."

"Did you ask whether anyone recognized them?"

"I asked several people when we were coming down the stairs. No one knew who they were."

"Why don't you go on to the tavern? Half of Benton's audience went in that direction. Someone should have noticed the boy. Ask about him.

Then find yourself some hot coffee. This may be a long wait."

Madryn went to the Green Tavern, stopping to talk with people along the way. He was gone for some time. He came back to report that a number of those present had noticed the fair-haired boy and the red-bearded man and had been curious about them, but no one knew who they were. No one remembered seeing them before.

I took my own turn — not in the tavern, but in the Newtown Coffee and Cocoa House just around the corner on Market Street, where I drank two cups of hot coffee. Then I returned to Madryn, and we waited together.

By the time the town clock struck eleven, Madryn was convinced that the pair had left by a rear entrance. I thought it more likely that they were staying somewhere near the Club Factory and had simply gone home. Even if they were habitually cautious, there was no reason at this stage for them to be practising deviousness. Madryn had not even started to follow them.

At eleven-thirty Madryn returned to the Bear to warn Mr. Breese that we would be late — possibly even very late. "I told him we were carousing with old friends," he said when he returned. "He gave me a key so he wouldn't have to wait up for us."

"I thought people didn't bother to lock doors in an innocent small town," I said.

"A town with as many unemployed as Newtown has is no longer innocent. Prudent people lock up everything."

It was after one o'clock when I finally gave up and we trudged back to the Bear through deserted and very badly lit streets.

From the moment I met him, Madryn had demonstrated a surprising perceptiveness about our case and the problems of investigating it. Now he asked me, "There's much more to this than the murders, isn't there?"

"There is," I said. "But I don't know how much more."

"Mr. Saunders didn't let on about anything else. Maybe he doesn't know. But I thought there had to be something."

"Why?" I asked.

"Because the murders make no sense. That is — the murder of Glyn Huws makes no sense. I'm not convinced that Eleanor Tromblay was murdered. Mr. Saunders and Bryn Huws have decided she was, but their only reason seems to be that a very wicked man murdered Glyn, and he would be as likely to murder two people as one. Do you think she was murdered?"

"I don't know," I said. "That's one of the questions I will be trying to answer."

"I can't think of any reason why anyone would murder her. Everyone loved and respected her.

But then — everyone respected Glyn Huws, too. So there has to be much more to this than the murders."

Before I went to bed, I wrote my report for Sherlock Holmes and enclosed one of the passes for the Wednesday Robert Owen meeting. I also wrote postcards to Rabby and to Fred Jones.

I slept well and was awakened by a cow lowing outside my window. That seemed preposterous — Newtown wasn't that small a town — so I went to the window and looked out.

There was a cow lowing outside my window. There were several cows and horses there, and a small flock of sleep was being driven past.

"It's Tuesday," Madryn said sleepily when I asked what was happening. "Tuesday is market day."

"It is a strange day for a market," I complained.

Madryn sat up and looked at me. "Why is it strange? Tuesday has been markct day in Newtown ever since the thirteenth century."

"In that case, perhaps we shouldn't change it," I told him.

By the time we dressed and went down to the dining room, I had formed my plans for the day. We would make one more attempt to get on the trail of the fair-haired Alban Griffiths. If it failed, we would move on. Our case certainly involved much more than the murders, but the murders were my assignment, and they might be the key that would unlock the rest. Madryn could ask a friend to continue the search for Griffiths after we left.

We ate our breakfast amidst the bustle of the Bear's dining room — a market town bustle, because tradesmen, dealers, farmers, and the families of all of them were converging on Newtown, and many of them arrived hungry. We had almost finished when a pleasant-looking, heavy-set, dark-haired man of about forty entered. He noticed Madryn and came directly to our table.

"Sut ydych chi, Dafydd?" he said warmly.

Madryn got to his feet and shook hands with him. "This is my cousin, Iorwerth Jones," he told him. "Iori, this is Wain Welling."

I also stood up and shook his hand.

Welling cocked his head at Madryn. "Where is he from?"

"London," Madryn said with a grin.

"Ah! I wondered why you were speaking English. One of our renegade Welsh, is he?"

"His grandparents were the guilty ones," Madryn said, still grinning.

Welling rubbed his hands delightedly. "But he has come back! That is splendid!" He turned a warm smile on me. "This is the best thing you could possibly have done for yourself. I'm the child of renegades myself. Born in Liverpool, moved God knows where — my childhood was a blur of new places — ended up in Newcastle by which time I had totally forgotten my Welsh if I ever knew any. But I came back, learned Welsh, and once I knew the language, I knew I belonged here. Come and see me when you can. There are excellent positions open to you here. Mr. Tromblay is very partial to Welshmen who have had an English upbringing. But start learning Welsh as soon as you can!"

He turned back to Madryn. "What brings you to Newtown?"

"I came to meet Iori. What brings you?"

"Sheep," Welling said. "Mr. Tromblay has bought a new farm. Plâs Morris, west of Rhyd. Do you know it?"

Madryn shook his head.

"It is understocked, so I'm buying sheep today if I find any that look likely." He turned to me again. "Don't forget — come and see me. I'll introduce you to Mr. Tromblay."

"I certainly will do that," I said enthusiastically.

He nodded to both of us and walked on. He greeted people in friendly fashion and was greeted by them at every table he passed.

We sat down again. "Who is he?" I asked Madryn.

"He calls himself Emeric Tromblay's secretary. I don't know what Tromblay calls him. He functions as a steward and chief assistant. He is very capable, and Tromblay relies heavily on him."

"He seems like a pleasant-enough person," I said.

"He is. Now that Eleanor Tromblay is dead, he is the one remaining kindly influence at Tromblay Hall. He is able to offset many of Tromblay's harsh actions. Tromblay will take a sudden dislike to one of his tenants and evict him. No special reason. Maybe he suspects him of voting for a Liberal candidate. He rides up, asks a few questions, and orders him to pack and leave. Can you imagine what that means to a man with a family? Suddenly he has lost not only his home but all means of livelihood. Where is he to go? What is he to do?

"Welling will find a place for him to live temporarily. He will try to find another farm for him — which is a genuine problem, there simply aren't enough farms to go around — or some other kind of employment. Normally the assistant to a man like Tromblay would be hated from one end of the shire to the other, but people have a rare kind of affection for Welling. They know he will do what he can for them. He has to be extremely circumspect, of course. He wouldn't last long if he went against Tromblay's direct orders, but he finds a way around them if he can or handles the problem in such a way that Tromblay isn't likely to hear about it. What will you do if Tromblay offers you employment?"

"Welling implied that I have to learn Welsh first, and I sincerely hope that this case will be finished in less time than that would take!"

I tried to envisage a universally hated squire with a universally liked steward and failed. Either Tromblay had to be much better than represented or Welling had to be worse.

I settled our hotel bill, and we left. Madryn carried a small bag, and I had my knapsack. Outside, the market had already taken shape in Broad Street. Stalls had been erected, and tradesmen were arranging displays of clothing, blankets, cloth, and household accessories. The flavour of Newtown had changed overnight. It still had the atmosphere of a border town, but Welsh was heard much more frequently.

We went first to the post office, which was located in a large building near the river. Broad Street crossed the Severn there on a bridge called the Long Bridge, and after posting my letter and the cards, I walked to the bridge's centre to study the town from a different vantage point. There was a splendid view of the venerable St. Mary's Church, where Robert Owen was buried. We walked back to the Cross and turned up the High Street, which was cluttered with market activity. There were cattle everywhere, and crowds of small boys — who should have been in school — were dashing about in the hope of earning a penny or two looking after animals or running errands.

We walked through the Market Hall with Madryn introducing me to friends along the way. Tradesmen offered their goods from stalls, but the farmers' wives sat on benches with the items they were attempting to sell. Some had elaborate displays of dressed poultry and rabbits, but I was surprised at the small quantities many of them had to offer — a few eggs, a bit of butter. The pennies that these would bring them were critically important, Madryn explained, and they often came long distances to try to convert the meagre results of a week's work into cash.

"They must have cash to pay the landlord," Madryn said.

By the time we emerged in the next street, I had abandoned any thought of tracking down Alban Griffiths. The chaos of the market spilled all over Newtown. Even the more remote streets were filled with pens from which sheep and pigs were sold. We located a friend of Madryn's, an unemployed weaver named John Davies, who lived in New Church Street near the Club Factory. Madryn mentioned Mr. Saunders's name to him, and he was delighted at the prospect of earning a few shillings.

We gave him the remaining pass for the next meeting of the Robert Owen Study League, and I described Alban Griffiths and his companion. Davies was to attend the meeting, arriving early enough to be the first one admitted. He was to sit at the back of the room, identify the pair as they arrived, and — if they did attend — leave the moment the meeting was over, wait for them in the street, and follow them wherever they went. He was to try to find out what he could about them.

He also was to start inquiries at once among his friends to see whether anyone knew anything about the pair.

When we finished our business with John Davies, we were halfway to the station. We forwent the pleasure of another ride with Humphrey the Bear and walked the remainder of the way, cutting through the County Intermediate School grounds.

We caught the morning train headed west, and when we finally settled into a third-class carriage, I had the feeling that at last I was putting England behind me. Our case had its roots in rural Wales. I didn't yet know whether it would become more intelligible to me on its native soil, but I looked forward to seeing it without the confusion that had cluttered it in London and in Newtown.

8

We left the train at Groesffordd Halt. I stepped onto the small platform pondering the word "groesffordd," which was supposed to mean "crossroad." Since the one road in sight intersected nothing but the railway, I asked Madryn to explain the name. He said the village of Groesffordd — and its crossroad — were invisible behind a hill. When the railway was built, the two had not seemed important enough to justify even a feeble detour in their behalf. They still were unimportant. In all of the time that I spent in that part of Wales, I never saw them.

I could see no visible justification for placing a railway halt on such a bleak stretch of line. Two scruffy stone buildings stood by the road, one of them a small inn — named, oddly enough, Y Llew Côch. The other was a dilapidated house. Both were very old and looked as though they had been built by piling up flat stones haphazardly in an enormous hurry.

Behind the inn was a combination barn and stable, a surprisingly large structure for such a barren location. It was in a better state of repair than the inn. The explanation was simple enough. The Master of Tromblay Hall and his servants sometimes left carriages and horses at the inn when they made short trips by train; and visitors to the Hall sometimes hired horses or traps when they arrived unexpectedly or when there was no one available to meet them.

In that small corner of Wales, the magic words "Tromblay Hall" explained everything: Y Llew Côch's large stable, the existence of a railway halt at Groesffordd, and — as I learned later — the unusual size and prosperity of a remote mountain village called Pentrederwydd.

I asked Madryn about the difference between the "Du" in London's Y Llew Du, the Black Lion, and the "Côch" in Groesffordd's Y Llew Côch. As far as the names were concerned, it was a distinction of color only. The Groesffordd lion was red.

The train wound out of sight, and Madryn led me toward Y Llew Côch. A short time later, mounted upon sturdy ponies — with a saddle for me but none for him — we were following the single road into the mountains. The scenery, once we left the blight of the railway stop behind us, was beautiful.

The modest heights that now surrounded us were mere hills compared with the towering Welsh mountains to be found farther north-west, in Snowdonia, but to a Londoner such as myself, they looked formidable. The road was narrow but unexpectedly good. The words "Tromblay Hall" also accounted for that — it was the Hall's only link with civilization, and all of the residents of those valleys benefited from it, but its quality lasted only until it reached the turnoff to the Hall and Emeric Tromblay's farms. Then it became very bad indeed, diminishing in rapid stages to a rutted wagon track and then to an animal track.

We followed the narrow road up a broad valley with the low mountains piled steeply on either side. A swift mountain stream paralleled the road. At intervals, splashes of whitewash or pinkwash marked the locations of farm buildings on the slopes. Far above them, the white dabs of fluff scattered widely about the landscape were slow-moving sheep, intent on their business of grazing. Many were followed by smaller dabs, their lambs. Overhead, large white woollen fluffs of cloud drifted aimlessly against the bluest of blue skies. The tops of the mountains had a bare, rocky look; the valley also showed its bones in rocky outcrops, in stone walls, and in the smaller stones piled along the edges of fields that generations of farmers had worked to make productive.

Madryn was trying to remember the last time he had ridden a horse between Groesffordd and Pentrederwydd. Ordinary persons such as himself never hired ponies or horses to travel those few miles. He had done so now only because it would enable me to become familiar with all of the places I wanted to visit much more quickly.

I volunteered to pay for them. I didn't know what his source of income was — certainly not poetry — and Sherlock Holmes had been emphatic in his instructions: Any local people from whom I received hospitality and assistance were to be generously reimbursed.

"Some of them will be extremely poor," he had said. "They will be far more hospitable than they can afford to be, and they will neither expect nor want payment. Your problem will be to find ways to compensate them without offending."

I was relieved to learn that this would not be a problem with Madryn. Mr. Saunders had amply supplied him with money for any expenses he might incur on my behalf.

It was an old land that we rode through, wrinkled and twisted with age, and there was a grotesqueness in the beauties it displayed, as though a graying, bent man or woman should make a ludicrous appearance spiffed out in the gay attire of youth. The venerable valley had clothed itself in youthful green with sprinklings of wild flowers that were unfamiliar to me. Sometimes far up the mountain I glimpsed a flash of silver where a tiny stream leaped in its eagerness to reach the lower slopes. By the time it arrived at the road, it was a brook rushing between verdant banks, and we crossed it on a sturdy stone bridge old enough to have been ordained by a much earlier master of Tromblay Hall than the one suspected of murder. It flowed on to join the broader stream that coursed swiftly down the centre of the valley.

Madryn kept up a friendly, enthusiastic commentary. He named trees and flowers and birds in English and Welsh. He pointed out the rabbit run along the hedge and the tangle of shrubbery where a house had once stood. When the walls collapsed, he said, William Williams's grandfather had hauled away the stones to build a barn, and the only trace remaining of the dwelling where generations had been born and lived and died was the bruised earth that the shrubbery concealed and a few straggling descendants of flowers once hopefully cultivated by long-dead farmers' wives. Hadn't I noticed the roses?

It was my first intimation that I might have problems with him. As Sherlock Holmes would have remarked, such insights were an excellent thing in a poet, but they could dangerously obscure a detective's landscape.

When I asked why William Williams's grandfather had gone to the trouble of hauling stones from that particular location when there must have been many scattered about the site of his proposed barn, Madryn gave me more information than I ever expected to need regarding different kinds of stones and how and why they were or were not used for building.

The mountains became more menacing in appearance as we rode toward Pentrederwydd. They were not higher, but their upper reaches seemed steeper and more jagged. The road was climbing as well, and I received a sudden chill whenever a cloud obscured the sun. There was nothing sinister or even unpleasant about that lovely valley, but a feeling of remoteness, of an indefinable strangeness, grew upon me. It was as though we had taken a wrong turning at the railway and passed to the far side of the moon, and it seemed peculiar that a crime committed in such an alien landscape should have a familiar label, "murder."

We met no one on this ride until we actually approached the village, but we did see a number of the valley's inhabitants. Farm women paused in their work, curious about these ordinary-looking men who rode ponies. Children halted what they were doing to stare. Solitary men at work in distant fields, who should have been too far away to recognize Madryn, waved greetings. Madryn knew them all, waved, called out to them.

Then the valley took a gentle curve, and we came in sight of Pentrederwydd.

The road veered toward the mountain slope and became the village's high street, and the village lay along and above it in charmingly disorganized tiers. The first structures we encountered were dwellings widely separated by gardens, barns, stables. Further along the road, at the centre of the village, the buildings were grouped more closely together, and they climbed the mountainside in irregular short rows until they reached the church, a low stone building with a high tower but no steeple. Nearby was a school. Above the church, houses and barns were widely scattered about the mountainside.

I halted my pony and stared. "How do all of these people earn a living?" I asked.

"Many of them work at the Hall or on Tromblay's farms," Madryn said. "The rest work for the people who work at the Hall or on the farms — except for a few who work for themselves."

"If Tromblay and his Hall and farms vanished suddenly, what would be left in Pentrederwydd?" I asked.

Madryn smiled. "A few farmers and one poet. We will turn off here. If we go through the village, everyone will want to meet you. It might take the remainder of the day. I suggest that we leave that for tonight when there will be nothing else to do."

We followed a path that climbed diagonally and looped above the village. When we left it, we were able to descend a steep slope to Madryn's own back yard.

"Pay attention to the paths," he told me. "If you want to come and go without having everyone in the village know about it, you must know which paths to use."

He lived in a small stone house with a slated roof. On the slope above it was a large kitchen garden. Behind that was a small barn.

As Madryn swung to the ground, a child called out, the rear door of the house was flung open, and a young woman leaped into his arms. She was small, plump, dark-haired, and very pretty. Three children followed her closely. I dismounted and waited with mild embarrassment while Madryn tried to cope with the problem of not having enough arms to return all of their embraces.

When the children had welcomed him, and his wife had embraced him a second time, affectionately rubbing her forehead against his beard, he spoke a sharp word, and the four of them took their first notice of me. He introduced me to his wife, Mairwen, and his children, Dafi — or young Dafydd — eight years old, who was the eldest, and the two girls, Megan, who was six, and Gwenda, who was four.

"What would you like to do first?" he asked me.

"I would like to meet Meleri Huws," I said, "and I would like to visit the place where Glyn Huws was murdered."

He turned to his wife. "We should take food with us. Have we bread and cheese?"

She darted back into the house. Madryn took my knapsack and handed it to Dafi. "Put it in Mr. Jones's room," he said.

Mairwen returned with a bag, and Madryn slung it around his shoulder. Mairwen smiled shyly at me. "Won't you drink first?" she asked.

"Please do," Madryn said. "Before we leave, I must write a note to Meleri and ask her to meet us."

He went to write the note, and I sipped buttermilk from a large mug while I waited. When he returned, he spoke to Dafi in Welsh, and Dafi agilely climbed up in front of him when we remounted our ponies.

"I should have asked you whether you wanted to visit Meini Mawr openly," he said apologetically.

"Isn't that the Huws farm?"

"Yes. There are two megalithic monuments — standing stones, the scientists call them — in the farmyard. They're enormous. Their height above the ground is eight or ten feet. The farm takes its name from them — Large Stones. At this point you really would gain nothing by going there, so I've asked Meleri to meet us at Llangelyn. Dafi will ride with us as far as the turning to Meini Mawr. Then he can go on foot the rest of the way and deliver the message. That will save time for us."

"But he will have to walk back," I objected.

Madryn smiled. "It is only a few miles."

The eight-year-old Dafi grinned at me. He looked like a miniature of his father — without the beard — and he was ecstatic at being able to share in one of his father's enterprises.

In its loop around the village, the path passed above the church and churchyard. Madryn hesitated when we reached them. "Would you like to see where Eleanor Tromblay and Glyn Huws are buried?" he asked.

"Yes, I would," I said.

We dismounted at the lych-gate, and Dafi held the ponies. From the outside, the Church of St. Peter, Pentrederwydd, seemed large for the village; when we entered it, I decided that this was fortunate. The interior was almost austere except for the north side of the nave, which was cluttered with memorials to various deceased members of the Tromblay family, dating back to the eighteenth century. These varied greatly in style, in execution, and in elaboration. Earlier Tromblays had been accorded simple, unadorned tombs. With the passage of time, the monuments grew more complex. For several decades in the mid-nineteenth century, they erupted into ornate statuary. I remarked on this to Madryn.

He laughed. "The Johnes family at Hafod — near Devil's Bridge — had a monument sculpted to their daughter, who died young. They hired a famous sculptor, and it got talked about, and people travelled long distances to see it. They still do. The Tromblays tried to immortalize themselves in the same way. Then they tired of it or decided it was too expensive."

"Or perhaps it wasn't working," I suggested. "It would be rank flattery to call any of this statuary mediocre. The Tromblays impress me as the sort of family that would hire third-rate sculptors and expect to achieve their immortality at reduced prices."

Emeric Tromblay certainly had economized with Eleanor Tromblay's memorial. It was a simple slab in the church floor, but I took it as ample proof that she actually had been buried.

I looked at the sturdy but unadorned benches used by the congregation. "Don't the Tromblays have a family pew?" I asked.

"They don't attend church here," Madryn said. "They have a chapel at the Hall. But they do their burying here. They got started with that before they built their own chapel, so they keep up the tradition."

I asked about the church's dedication to St. Peter. I wondered whether there was a Welsh tradition associated with that saint.

"There was an earlier church here, and it almost certainly was dedicated to a Welsh saint," Madryn said. "When the Normans took over the Welsh churches, they evicted the Welsh saints and replaced them with their own favourites. Many of us believe that this church was originally dedicated to St. Celyn. Perhaps someday it will be again."

"Who was St. Celyn?" I asked.

"A saint who is never heard of outside these valleys."

We visited the grave of Glyn Huws in the churchyard. It had no tombstone as yet, but the ground was covered with flowers. A month after his murder, everyone in the village still mourned him.

We remounted our ponies and rode on.

The well-worn path circled the village and finally descended to the road again. Far ahead of us, the valley was intersected by lateral valleys on either side. The one to the west was part of the Tromblay estate, and the improved road turned in that direction on its way to Tromblay Hall. Meini Mawr, the Huws farm, was situated in the valley to the east. We paused there to let Dafi scramble down, and he headed up that valley's deeply rutted road at top speed to deliver Madryn's letter to Meleri Huws.

Straight ahead, the valley narrowed to a pass through which rushed the stream we had been following since we left the railway line. When it emerged from the pass, it immediately slowed its pace and flowed down the valley to collect, on its way to join the Severn, the waters of all of the brooks that we had crossed. Smaller streams from the other two valleys also joined it. The road, which became noticeably poorer the moment we passed the turning to Tromblay Hall, crossed the stream from the Meini Mawr valley by way of a shallow ford — there were stepping stones for pedestrians — and threaded through the narrow gap ahead of us on the bank of the larger stream that foamed there. The road remained passable as far as a farm called Tynewydd, Madryn told me.

Beyond the gap, the valley widened again in breathtaking beauty. At its lower end, where we stood, a sheet of water filled it almost from side to side. The lake narrowed toward the upper end, finally diminishing to the stream that fed it, and against the height beyond was suspended a long silver ribbon where a waterfall fell to the valley floor to disappear in churning foam. The water collected in a series of pools and then ran placidly down to the lake.

"Llyn Tŷ-mawr," Madryn said. "Lake of the Big House."

I looked from one side of the valley to the other. "Where is the big house?"

"There." He pointed. I could discern some kind of mound. "It fell into ruins long ago. Or perhaps it was destroyed. It wasn't really a big house although it may have seemed so in olden times. The mound it left isn't very large."

Tynewydd, which simply meant "New House," was actually an old, old farmstead, a cluster of pinkwashed buildings that stood close to the lake at its widest point. There was a pleasant-looking stretch of lawn between the house and the lake. I remarked upon it. In that harsh land, where farmers had difficulty in growing anything at all, it seemed remarkable that one of them would devote his attention to cultivating grass.

"Lawns only mean that someone is rich," Madryn said with a shrug. "You will see another at

Tromblay Hall — along with fountains and a formal garden. Kyle Connor lives at Tynewydd. An Irishman, people say. No one knows much about him. He is an invalid — he lost the use of his legs in an accident — and he came here in search of peaceful surroundings and an invigorating climate."

"He certainly found both," I said. "Also solitude and great natural beauty."

Except for a few tiny farmsteads high on the mountain slopes, he had the entire valley to himself.

Madryn nodded. "He swims in the lake — he says it is good for his health. Perhaps it is for an Irishman. Local people won't go near it. There are legends and tales about that water."

"I am sure that there are," I said. Legends and tales about Kyle Connor would have interested me more. I had an instant, intense curiosity about anyone with a blank past who lived close to the scene of two murders. "Does Kyle Connor have any friends in Pentrederwydd?"

"A few," Madryn said. "There is nothing mysterious about him. Because he is unable to walk, he rarely leaves home, but he does entertain local people who share his interests — the vicar calls on him regularly, and he has a few friends in Newtown and Llanidloes who pay him overnight visits. Emeric Tromblay seems to like him — he rides over to see him occasionally and invites him to the Hall, and I hear that some of the regular guests at the Hall are much impressed with him and make a point of visiting him at Tynewydd each time they come. His farm-hands and servants call him the best employer in Wales."

"How long has he lived here?" I asked.

"Just since last autumn."

The testimonial sounded much too flattering to be believed. I wanted to know a great deal more about Mr. Kyle Connor.

The road turned east and followed the lake shore toward Tynewydd. We kept to the faint path on the western side of the lake. The shore there was completely overgrown with thick shrubs and even young trees. The water was almost inaccessible. Across the lake, where the farm was located, there was a narrow beach and a small jetty to which a boat was moored.

The beauty of the day was reflected in the still beauty of the water. It was the deepest of velvety blues, as deep as blue could be without becoming purple. The vibrant colour hinted of mysterics concealed. I wanted to fit a piece of it into one of the windows of the Pentrederwydd church and cut out holes that could be leaded with other colours: reds, yellows, greens, whites, oranges. I could envisage a complete representation of our case in stained glass, but I quickly abandoned it. I was committing what Sherlock Holmes considered a cardinal offence — reasoning from insufficient data. Any picture that I created would have disfiguring patches of plain glass, and every suspect would have a blank face.

I wondered how anyone could possibly concoct an evil legend about that lovely water. Sheep grazed high above us; clouds floated serenely overhead, and their reflections lay just as serenely on the lake. The scene was altogether beautiful.

The path threaded its way through humped and rocky ground as we followed the overgrown lake shore back to the stream I had seen descending from the waterfall. We rode along the stream to the base of the hills that blocked the far end of the valley.

I would have been delighted to stop and enjoy the view of the fall and perhaps eat our lunch there, but the setting was no novelty to Madryn. He pushed ahead, leading the way up the steep slope along a time-worn crease in the ageless hill down which a small stream trickled. He rode up easily on his bare-backed pony. I clung to my saddle and was grateful for it. We emerged in a level area that the shoulders of the hill curled around almost completely. There was a breathtaking view of the lake behind us and crumbling, overgrown stone walls just ahead. A chill wind blew up out of the valley with surprising force.

Madryn halted his pony. In the background, I heard the subdued murmur of the waterfall. "This is the place," he said.

It seemed like an excellent setting for a murder but a wretched one for a murder investigation. The ground was rough and stony with a hardness suggesting that nefarious forces had packed it down for centuries to prepare it for whatever dastardly crimes might occur there. Our ponies' hoofs left only faint depressions in the turf; a man would leave no traces at all. "Exactly where was Huws's body found?" I asked.

"I don't know," Madryn said. "That's one reason I asked Meleri to meet us here."

"What did you call this place?"

"Llangelyn."

"What does that mean?"

"'Church of Holly.' That may mean that there once was a holly tree here, or trees, but 'Holly,' — 'Celyn' in Welsh — is found in very old manuscripts as a name. Our local tradition holds that one of the old Celtic saints built a chapel here, and that the place is named after him — St. Celyn."

"Meaning — St. Holly?"

He nodded.

"How long ago was that?"

"No one knows. The ninth century at the latest. Perhaps as early as the sixth."

"Then those walls are more than a thousand years old?"

"That's the local tradition. A learned visitor — I don't know how learned — inspected the place many years ago and offered the opinion that the walls were the remnants of an old sheep-fold. Seventeenth century, he thought. He was made to feel extremely unwelcome, and he soon decided to pursue his studies elsewhere."

"You don't agree that it was a sheep-fold?"

"I do not."

"Why not?"

"The gods would not have permitted that. And no one would have dared to keep sheep here, ever."

I stared at him. It was not what he said that startled me but the vehement seriousness with which he said it.

"The further we go into the mountains of Wales, the more aware we become of the ancient Celtic gods," he said. "We are very close to them here. See that stone?"

It was partially overgrown, but it loomed up out of the surrounding bushes — a stone that rose about six feet above the ground. Apart from its partially rounded top, it was singularly devoid of distinction, even for a stone.

"What about it?" I asked.

"There is another." He pointed. "And another."

He showed me four of them. A fifth was invisible beyond one of the crumbling walls. "A stone circle?" I asked. "A Druidic circle?"

"Not Druidic, though the Druids may have used it. Something much older. Those stones prove that this has been holy ground for four or five thousand years — or more. The old saints often built their churches in what was already a community place of worship."

"There certainly is something uncanny about this place," I agreed. I suddenly became aware that I no longer heard the cries of birds. The distant bleating of sheep had been with us throughout our ride; in this small depression in the mountain-side, we were mysteriously cut off from it. Sitting there on my pony, with my arms clasped for protection against the chill wind and with the relentless murmur of the fall in the background, I understood how one might feel close to supernatural forces in such a place.

"Do sheep graze here?" I asked.

"Never," he said.

"Do you believe in the ancient gods?"

"Of course. In Wales, it is always unwise to ignore them."

"You really are serious," I said wonderingly.

"I am," he said. "Consider this. To the ancients, one of the most holy places in Wales was Mount Snowdon — Eryri, or the High Land, they called it. They also called it Yr Wyddfa Fawr, the Great Tomb, because of the legend that on its summit is the grave of the giant, Rhita Fawr, slain by King Arthur. The entire region figures importantly in Welsh legend. Surely you have heard something of it."

"A little," I admitted.

"Not long ago, it was decided to build a railway line to the top of Snowdon for tourists — an act of enormous sacrilege. The builders irrationally ignored every sign of warning. They built the railway; they ran the first engine to the top. There were no problems." He paused. "On the way down, the engine suddenly leaped off the rails and over a precipice. Engineers studied the place of the accident, but they never were able to explain why or how it happened."

"Have there been other accidents?" I asked.

"None. The outraged deities were propitiated by the sacrifice of one locomotive. This happened only eight years ago. Never blaspheme the ancient gods."

"In that case, whoever committed a murder in this sacred place perpetrated a very considerable act of blasphemy."

Madryn nodded. "That's why I think Mr. Saunders's concern is unnecessary. He has asked for my help, so I am bound to give it to him, but I know that when a murderous act is so evil that human justice is incapable of comprehending it, let alone punishing it, the gods will render their own judgement in due course. They are very old gods, and vengeful gods, and the punishment they exact is certain to be far more horrible than anything that mere humans could devise."

9

WE GAVE THE RUINS AS WIDE A BERTH AS POSSIBLE and made our way to the foot of the steep slope beyond. There we dismounted, tied the ponies, and seated ourselves beside a pool of water from which a tiny stream trickled. It passed close to the ruins and ran down the slope we had climbed from the valley.

We ate our bread and cheese while we waited. The bread was newly baked and fragrantly delicious; the cheese strongly flavoured and very good. I had never eaten a better casual meal in gloomier surroundings. I like to divide saints into two categories — those who praise God, and those who contend with the Devil. Obviously St. Celyn's attention had been fixed on the Evil One when he chose this strange setting for his church.

I already had the answer to one important question. Only the most fantastic coincidence could have provided a witness to a crime committed in this desolate spot.

Madryn bent low to drink from the pool of water. I cupped some in my hands and drank. It was cold and wonderfully refreshing.

"It is fed by a spring at the bottom," Madryn said. "Local people consider this a holy well."

"Does that mean that the water cures sickness?" I asked.

"That is the belief. It is supposed to be especially efficacious with eye and skin problems."

"What does one do? Pray to the saint and then splash the water on?"

"Follow one's own inclinations, I suppose," Madryn said. "Only those with true faith are cured. Some holy wells have astonishing histories. That of St. Winifred, at Holywell in North Wales, resulted when an angry suitor she had repulsed cut her head off. A new spring broke from the ground where the head lay, and that became the holy well."

I asked lightly, "Did the water cure her?"

"She was a relative of St. Beuno, who happened to be nearby. The saint restored her head to her body."

"And she recovered?"

Madryn nodded. "She became a nun and an abbess and lived for many years."

"That is an astonishing history," I agreed.

I wondered whether anyone had thought to sprinkle water from this holy well on the battered body of Glyn Huws.

Meleri Huws finally arrived, riding down the steep slope, and neither she nor her horse seemed disconcerted by it. She wore a man's clothing, and she rode bare-back with the easy manner of someone accustomed to long hours on a horse. She dismounted with a graceful motion and tied her horse to the stunted tree where we had tied our ponies.

She studied me gravely while Madryn introduced me.

"Mr. Saunders and my uncle told me about meeting you in London," she said. "I fear that you come much too late, but since you are here, you might as well do what you can. I will gladly give you any assistance in my power."

In a flowing gown, dancing at a brilliant ball, she would have possessed a stunning beauty. There in that wild place, with the cold wind whipping at her hair and her masculine clothing, there was something decidedly unreal about her, as though she were neither man nor woman. She might have been mistaken for one of the Tylwyth Têg, the strange Welsh fairies that are so unpredictable in their actions toward humans, had she not been unusually tall. She had raven-black hair, black eyes, and a comely face, but there was a hardness in her expression, a bitterness, suggesting that everything feminine in her nature had been thrust aside.

I was surprised that she spoke English so well. Madryn told me afterward that her father had put on airs where his daughter was concerned. He insisted on her learning English, and he even sent her to school in Shrewsbury for a year. I was equally surprised at the frank interest in the gaze she turned upon me. There was no shyness in her manner, no softness, none of the feminine modesty that English society prized. I could see how a man accustomed to the traditional womanly traits might misunderstand her nature with embarrassing consequences. No doubt she had looked at Benton Tromblay — another male from the romantic outside — with the same frank interest, and he had responded at first and then felt repelled when he became better acquainted with her. I read it as nothing more than an open curiosity that is often encountered in men but which most women learn to modestly conceal.

"What do you want to know?" she asked.

"Did anyone know that your father was coming here?"

She shook her head.

"Do you know why he came here?"

She shook her head again. "He said nothing about it to anyone. He took his dog with him, but that meant nothing. His dog went everywhere with him."

"Did he ride a horse?"

"No. He walked."

"There was no farm work — " I hesitated because I knew so little about farming. " — no missing sheep, for example, that might have brought him to this place?"

"Sheep never come here. No one comes here except strangers who are curious about old ruins and visitors to the holy well."

"Is this place part of your farm?"

"No," she said. "My farm is in the next valley." She placed an unmistakable emphasis on the my. "My summer sheepwalks are on the mountain slopes beyond." She pointed.

"Then you can't think of any reason at all for your father to come here?"

"None," she said firmly.

"Would you show me exactly where he was found?"

He had lain within the crumbling walls where his body could not be seen unless the ruins were approached closely, but this didn't seem to indicate a deliberate attempt at concealment. He simply lay where he had fallen. His dog had led one of the shepherds to him.

Meleri believed that the dog witnessed the murder, which had been the result of a sudden, cowardly assault on Huws when his back was turned. The murderer may have tried to kill the dog as well, but the dog had been too quick for him. It limped badly afterwards as though it had received a blow on its haunch. If it had not escaped and attracted the shepherd's attention, Huws's body might not have been found for days.

Meleri showed me the exact place and described how the body had lain. I then asked her and Madryn to wait some distance away until I had searched the ground carefully. It was extremely unlikely that any traces had survived a month of weather in that harsh locale, but the search had to be made.

They watched intently while I moved at a crouch on a wide circuit around the ruins, occasionally dropping to my knees and exploring the coarse turf with my hands. It was a long and strenuous ordeal for me, and the waiting should have been tedious for them, but they continued to watch with interest. They did not speak, even to each other, as I slowly inched toward the ruins.

I found nothing. A cigar stump or even a piece of cheese rind might have told volumes — or might have told nothing at all, of course. But smoking was far too expensive an addiction for the impoverished Welsh peasantry, and cheese rinds were more likely to be eaten than thrown away. I would have welcomed any sign at all that the place had an occasional human visitor, murderer or not, but I found nothing.

Within the walls there were a few bare spots that would have taken footprints, but no one had stepped there. The rains had obliterated all traces of blood and also any marks left by those who carried the body away. I straightened up, finally, and moved off a short distance to rest my back and survey the scene.

Glyn Huws had lain on his face with his body pointed in the direction he was facing when the first blow crushed the back of his skull. Obviously his murderer had known that he was coming to that lonely place and had lain in wait for him. That was how I read the riddle. The murderer bided his time until Huws turned his back. Then he made a stealthy rush, and the sound of his footsteps was concealed by the incessantly moaning wind and the distant, muted roar of the waterfall. The first brutal blow crushed Huws's skull before he became aware of the murderer's presence. He was then clubbed repeatedly while he lay on the ground. Probably the dog tried to protect its master and was clubbed at the same time.

I rejected the possibility that Huws met someone, had an altercation with him, fought, and was killed. The few available facts made Huws a victim taken unawares.

The murderer had been hidden. Therefore the murderer had a hiding place. It had to be close enough to an opening into the ruins to enable him to reach Huws quickly but remote enough for him to avoid arousing the dog's suspicion until he was ready to strike.

I surveyed the possibilities. Then I went to one of the shrubs growing at one side of a break in the ruins and carefully raised the heavily leafed branches.

Underneath, in the soft, moist earth, was a muddle of footprints. Someone had crouched there for some time and moved his feet repeatedly. Several impressions were almost intact.

I backed away, surveyed the possibilities once more, and tried another shrub. There I found another set of footprints — similar and yet distinctively different. There were other shrubs nearby, but the ground under their branches was undisturbed.

I called Madryn and Meleri and showed them the two sets of footprints.

"But what does it mean?" Meleri asked wonderingly.

"It means that we have found the murderers," I said. "There were two of them. They hid here while waiting for the best opportunity to attack your father."

"Those are clogprints," Madryn said. "Clogs are very common in Wales — and in parts of rural England, too, I understand. They are wooden shoes with leather uppers. Those deeper indentations are made by iron loops nailed to the bottom of the sole to make the clogs wear longer."

"I know about clogs," I said. "I was wondering whether there is any significance in the fact that these two pairs have different shapes. One has rounded toes. The other's toes are square."

Madryn went to look again at the other set of prints. "Clogs aren't as popular here as in some other parts of Wales," he said, "but many people wear them. I do myself for outside work. They are warm in cold weather and keep the feet dry when it rains. All the clogs worn in these valleys have rounded toes, including mine. Ifan Vaughan can tell you whether the square toes mean anything."

"Who is he?"

"Shoe and clogmaker in Pentrederwydd."

"Then we must see him next," I said.

I took measurements of both sets of clogprints. Then I got out my notebook and made careful drawings, showing the shapes of the wood soles and the position of the irons as accurately as I could. In those days before photography was common, sketches were a valuable method of preserving clues, and often they served as important evidence. Early in my apprenticeship, Sherlock Holmes sent me to an artist for lessons so I could be as proficient as possible in situations such as this one.

I noted that the irons on the square-toed clogs were badly worn but those on the round-toed clogs left crisp impressions with sharp edges.

When I had finished, Meleri Huws asked impatiently, "But what good are they?"

"Someday, these drawings may help us to identify the men who murdered your father. We no longer have a case that is totally without clues."

Meleri said bewilderedly, "Then — there were two murderers, and they wore clogs?"

"That is what the clogprints tell us."

"And they hid here waiting for father? But that is miraculous! You have proved that two men did it and that they wore clogs! How astonishing!" Her gloomy countenance was transformed by a smile of delight. It was more than a transformation. Her face was suddenly, radiantly illuminated. "No one else thought to look," she said wonderingly. "For all anyone knew, the Tylwyth Têg or the Devil himself might have done it. But you knew exactly what you wanted to find, and what sort of place it would be found in, and you looked, and there it was. I never realized what it meant when Mr. Saunders said you had uncommon skill. I must tell him!"

I asked both of them to please tell no one. The fewer people discussing my prowess — and this particular discovery — the better.

We walked back to her horse and the ponies, and she made ready to remount. Since her mood had changed, and since she now seemed favourably disposed toward me — I had been uncertain about that before — I risked more questions.

"Did you give any thought at all to marrying Benton Tromblay?" I asked.

She laughed. "Dear Benton. He seemed so amusing at first, but after one has laughed at him, what could one do with a man like that? Except for reading, he was the most helpless person I have ever met. No, I never gave any thought at all to marrying Benton Tromblay."

"And — what about his father, Emeric Tromblay? Have you given any thought to marrying him?"

She turned toward me. Her smile froze on her face. "Mr. Jones," she said with cold bitterness. "I have my farm, which I love. I have my work. I have employees who are dependent on me. I have no intention of marrying anyone — now or ever."

She mounted her horse and rode quickly up the slope. We watched her until she disappeared over the distant crest.

"You made an impression on her," Madryn said. "I have never seen her respond that enthusiastically to anyone. As a farm girl, she has grown up admiring men who can do things. It is easy to see what went wrong between her and Benton. While he was away at Oxford, he seemed to be doing something. He was full of the gospel of Robert Owen and he was going to change the world with it. But she quickly found out that the world changes very slowly, and the changes are never made by men like Benton Tromblay. Almost anyone she knows can do almost anything better than Benton can do it. As she said herself, what could one do with a man like that? Certainly not make a farmer of him.

"But you are a detective. Obviously you do things and do them very well. You have uncommon skill and you are able to demonstrate it. And then — you come from London, which may seem like the most romantic place on the globe to a farm girl who has never been further from Wales than Shrewsbury. If you aren't careful, you may suddenly find yourself thinking that Meleri Huws is more interesting than the murderers' footprints. She can be a beautiful woman when she chooses to dress the part."

I smiled and shook my head. "Many years ago, a friend who was assisting Sherlock Holmes became romantically interested in a young lady whose case they were working on. Mr. Holmes says his friend was never the same man after that. I've had a severe indoctrination concerning romantic involvements with clients."

Madryn laughed merrily. "Your employer might as well indoctrinate you against being struck by lightning. When it happens, it will happen."

I joined in his laughter, but I didn't feel greatly at risk where Meleri Huws was concerned. I had no interest whatsoever in sharing the heritage of a Welsh farm, no matter how prosperous. At the same time, although Meleri had much more than her beauty to commend her — she was intelligent and very capable — she would have been no happier living permanently in London than I could be in Wales.

"Mr. Saunders mentioned that you once had a romantic interest in Meleri," I said to Madryn. "What happened?"

This time his laughter was bitter. "We were both young," he said. "But she was a highly practical person even then. Does she impress you as the kind of woman who marries a poet?"

"No," I said thoughtfully. "She certainly doesn't impress me in that way."

We mounted our ponies and rode back down the steep slope to the valley. I was more grateful for the saddle on the descent than I had been on the climb.

For a time Madryn seemed lost in deep thought. Finally he said, "It was difficult enough trying to think of one man who would hate Glyn Huws enough to murder him. There couldn't be two."

"We will find them," I said confidently. "As an English Bard wrote, 'Other sins only speak; murder shrieks out.'"

"There is a Welsh proverb, 'Nid ymgel drwg lle y bo,' evil will not be concealed. There is another, 'Nid cyfrinach ond rhwng dau,' it is no secret except it be between two. If the murderers were acting on their own, you may never catch them. If there is more to this than the murders, sooner or later someone will whisper."

Madryn pulled his pony to a halt when we reached the lake. "I thought we might call on Kyle Connor," he said. "But perhaps it would be best to wait for an invitation."

"Perhaps so," I agreed. I was in a hurry to talk with Ifan Vaughan, the clogmaker.

We turned to the right and circled around the lake the way we had come. When we reached a point opposite the buildings of Connor's farm, I noticed a commotion on the jetty. Several people seemed to be struggling there. Finally they threw or pushed something into the water — and that something immediately swam toward the centre of the lake.

"Kyle Connor," Madryn said. "His servants help him down to the water for his daily swim."

"Isn't that water rather cold?" I asked.

"I would think so. Connor is accustomed to it."

"Probably the surface warms during the day," I suggested. "Let's try it sometime."

Madryn looked horrified. "No Welshman would swim in this lake!"

"Why not?"

His shrug was almost a shudder. "The Ceffyl-y-dŵr, the water horse."

The sun-filled valley was pleasant; the lake sparkled. Connor seemed to be enjoying himself. He swam far out into the lake before he turned back.

"The water horse, whatever that is, doesn't seem to be bothering him," I said.

Madryn muttered something in Welsh.

We rode through the gap beside the rushing stream. The turning to Tromblay Hall was just beyond it, and from that point we had the advantage of Emeric Tromblay's road. We rode quickly back to Pentrederwydd.

Ifan Vaughan's shop was at the edge of the village. Like most of the buildings, it was an old stone structure, and he lived above his shop. He was at work in his kitchen garden when we arrived. The shopkeepers and craftsmen of Pentrederwydd were, almost all of them, involved in more than one endeavour. They closed their shops in order to milk cows or plant potatoes or till their gardens, and no one thought anything of it.

Vaughan was an elderly man with a carefully cultivated graying moustache and a completely bald head. His muscular arms belied his age. He had been a friend of Glyn Huws, and Madryn thought our best course would be to confide in him. If we told him something in confidence, he would never reveal it to anyone; if we aroused his curiosity by attempting to obtain information without telling him why we wanted it, everyone in the village would know about it before bedtime.

He spoke English correctly but rather slowly. Madryn introduced me; Vaughan would have questioned me at length about my reactions to the home of my ancestors, but Madryn intercepted his first question, stated matter-of-factly that we had gone to see the place where Glyn Huws had been murdered, and told him what we had found.

Vaughan was tremendously interested and excited. He scrutinized my sketches, darted a glance at Madryn, and then turned back to me as though he guessed what I was about. He pointed at the sketch of the clogprints with rounded toes.

"This pattern is very common here," he said. "These clogs could be mine."

"To my uneducated eye, the prints they left looked as though they had been made by new clogs," I said. "The irons didn't seem to be worn at all — the impressions showed sharp edges. The irons on the other pair were badly worn. Who has bought clogs in the last two or three months?"

Vaughan threw up his hands. "But I sell clogs all the time, and there are clogmakers in other places. Groesffordd, Llanidloes — "

"There are clogmakers everywhere," Madrum said. "I know of at least two in Newtown."

It was the square-toed sketch that intrigued Vaughan. "We don't often see clogs like this," he said. "They are usually worn by men who have to kneel when they work."

"Kneel?" I echoed blankly.

"Miners," he said. "Sometimes factory workers. Anyone who has to kneel. Square toes are more comfortable than the common round style for kneeling."

"Then squared-toed clogs ought to be highly conspicuous in Pentrederwydd," I suggested.

"Most people wouldn't notice them," Vaughan said. "But I would. I always look at shoes."

I asked politely, "Did you see any square-toed clogs in Pentrederwydd about the time that Glyn Huws was murdered?"

"Matter of fact, I did."

I managed to contain my excitement. To embark on the hopeless investigation of a clueless murder and secure a detailed description of one of the murderers, plus the footprints of both of them, in the first few hours, was the kind of rare good fortune I had never experienced. "What did the man look like?" I asked.

"Well, now." Vaughan scratched fretfully at his bald head. "It was his clogs I was attending to. They had square toes." He nodded at my sketch. "They looked just like those except I was seeing them from the other side, of course, from the top down instead of from the bottom up. As for what *he* looked like, by which I suppose you mean his face, I don't exactly remember that. I suppose I didn't attend much to his face. I do know that his clogs had square toes, though. I had a real good look at them, and I always remember clogs and shoes."

IO

VAUGHAN HAD SEEN THE SQUARE-TOED CLOGS AT the village tavern, but he had no recollection of the man who wore them. My attempts to jog his memory proved futile because he had none to jog. His avid interest in footwear was counterbalanced by a total lack of interest in faces. The sudden encounter with a style of clogs rarely seen in that part of Wales had engrossed him in technical matters having to do with stitching and nailing, the style of cut, the crimping, and the kind of clasp used. Probably he hadn't looked above the man's ankles.

"Would you recognize those clogs if you saw them again?" I asked.

"That I would," he said calmly. "The crimping was very unusual. Fish, they were. I'd recognize them anywhere."

Questioned, he admitted that it was the craftsmanship of the clogmaker that he would recognize. He guaranteed that he could instantly pick out any pair of clogs made by that person. Crimping, which was the name for the stylish patterns cut in the leather of the uppers, was a clogmaker's way of signing his work. Each had his own designs and guarded them jealously. But Vaughan said emphatically that he wouldn't need to see this particular clogmaker's crimping, which often was omitted from cheap clogs, in order to identify his handiwork. The cut of both soles and uppers had been distinctive.

I extracted a solemn promise that the next time he saw square-toed clogs, in the village tavern or anywhere else, he would raise his eyes, take a good look at the owner, and try to engage him in conversation and find out who he was.

Madryn pledged him to secrecy. Then I ordered a pair of walking boots, which elated him. He measured my feet at least as meticulously as I had measured the clogprints, and he promised to start work on the new boots at once.

Pentrederwydd's shops were spread out along the road surrounded by the owners' gardens and animal pens. We called at each in turn, and Madryn introduced me as his cousin visiting from London. It was almost a disappointment to me that all of the tradesmen spoke English.

Madryn explained that life in Pentrederwydd revolved around Tromblay Hall, its English master, and a succession of English-speaking guests who came and went throughout the year. A shopkeeper who couldn't speak English wouldn't be patronized. Further, many of them were Tromblay's tenants — he owned much of the village — and he preferred that they speak English. His tenants sent their children to the church school as a matter of course, and the teacher there taught only English and ridiculed children whom he caught speaking Welsh. There was a board school that was enthusiastically supported by parents who were not Emeric Tromblay's tenants, and the conflict between the two schools and their supporters sometimes waxed furiously — especially at the moment, when the Education Act of 1902 had several of the Welsh County Councils in a state of rebellion, including that of Montgomeryshire.

"The Education Act requires districts to support church schools from the rates, does it not?" I asked.

"It does worse than that," Madryn said gloomily. "It also sets up religious requirements for teachers in private schools, and it lets the Church of England administer them."

I pursed my lips thoughtfully. Our case was suddenly taking on new complexities. "I suppose, since Emeric Tromblay is fervently Church of England, that he favours the new law emphatically."

"That he does."

"What about his tenants and employees?"

"They have to pretend to favour the new law. Otherwise, Tromblay would evict or discharge them. I don't know how many of them actually do favour it."

"And I suppose that Glyn Huws, an ardent Welsh patriot, was strongly opposed to the new law."

"He was indignant about it," Madryn said.

"Then Meleri was not the only cause for dissension between Huws and Tromblay."

"They disagreed about almost everything. Glyn was the leader in opposing Tromblay. He was well off, and he owned his own farm. There wasn't anything that Tromblay could do about him — or to him."

"Except have him murdered?" I suggested.

Madryn frowned. "I always thought that Tromblay had a grudging respect for Glyn Huws that was almost a liking."

"If Tromblay is so opposed to the Welsh language, why did Welling tell me that I had to learn Welsh in order to be employed by him?"

"If his employees in positions of responsibility, like Welling, couldn't speak Welsh, they would be frightfully handicapped. Many of the small farmers and farm hands don't speak English. I suppose the same is true of the mine workers. Tromblay needs Welsh-speaking people to run his businesses. But he also looks to the future when he expects everyone in Wales to speak English, so he wants English stressed in the schools. Paradoxically, he is immensely proud of the fact that he speaks a little Welsh himself. He wanted to change the name of Tromblay Hall to Plâs Tromblay, which would have offended every Welshman who heard about it. Welling talked him out of it."

I was introduced to Evan Jones, the baker, who was delighted to meet a Jones from London; and

David Bevan, the blacksmith, who was attacking a glowing piece of iron with indescribable violence when we entered his shop. When the blows ceased, he proved to be surprisingly gentle and soft-spoken.

Arthur Pritchard, the carpenter, was making a hay rake when we visited him. It was fashioned with remarkable precision, and he proudly handed it over for my inspection. His workshop was crowded with the things he made to sell — milking stools; bellows; wood tools; hay rakes and scythe cradles; axe hafts; bowls, plates, and spoons. The latter were made of sycamore, which, he explained, does not taint food and will not split if washed frequently. There were finely crafted oak dressers and cupboards, several of them beautifully carved. There was even a coffin, for Pritchard was also the village undertaker. His shop was filled with the marvellous fragrance of freshly worked wood.

Next door was the grocery shop and post office of Mrs. Adwen Edwards. The postmistress was a large, friendly woman with whom I expected to become well acquainted as I posted daily reports to London. I wondered whether she would talk about the addresses she read.

The sign above the door of the village tavern, Ceffyl-y-dŵr, looked vaguely familiar to me. Madryn reminded me that it stood for the dreaded water horse. I questioned its appropriateness as a name for a tavern.

Madryn thought it sacrilegious. "That was Eleanor Tromblay's doing," he said gloomily. "She was trying to eliminate drunkenness."

"She thought that naming the tavern Ceffyl-y-dŵr would eliminate — "

"There used to be four taverns in Pentrederwydd. Each had its small group of regular patrons, men who liked to get together and talk of an evening. And of course there were a few who drifted from one to the other and sometimes got drunk. Eleanor Tromblay used her influence and got three of the licences dropped to cut down on the drinking."

He explained that Emeric Tromblay owned all three of the taverns, so she could do that without any appearance of impropriety. If she had tried to eliminate the licence of the remaining tavern, which her husband did not own, a scandal would have ensued. At that time the tavern went by the uncomplicated name of Yr Hen Dafarn, or the Old Tavern, and after its three competitors closed, it had to be enlarged to accommodate the increased business. The result was more drinking and drunkenness than the village had ever known before. The problem was that most of the farmhands in the area had nowhere to go of an evening. Farm houses were often too tiny to accommodate the farmers' own families. Their employees had no place to spend their free time except in their sleeping quarters, which too often were located in unheated lofts and barns and always were cramped and uncomfortable and sparsely furnished. So they went to whatever taverns were available. At least they could sit down there, and be comfortable, and talk with friends. For some reason Madryn couldn't comprehend, they drank much more when they were crowded into one tavern than they had with a choice of four.

"Eleanor Tromblay finally realized that she had made a mistake," Madryn said. "She reopened one of the closed taverns as a temperance house and café. It immediately became very popular. It gives the village another place where people can go in the evening. Even some of the women servants go there. It costs less than the tavern, and of course its customers don't get drunk. Mrs. Tromblay put a reading room in it, too. The only problem now is that she insisted on naming it Y Fuwch Frêch, which means the Fairy Cow, after a Welsh legend about a fairy cow that kept the whole countryside supplied with milk. Having done that, she pestered the landlord of Yr Hen Dafarn to change the name to Ceffyl-y-dŵr. I'm not sure that there weren't threats made about his licence. Finally he put up the sign, but almost everyone still calls it Yr Hen Dafarn."

"The Fairy Cow and the Water Horse. She probably thought that was clever."

"That's one of the problems with the English," Madryn said bitterly. "They're clever. They are at their absolute worst when they are being clever for the benefit of the Welsh. She was trying to cure us of our superstitions. She thought we would be less likely to believe in water horses and fairy cows if taverns and temperance houses were named after them."

"What *is* the water horse?" I asked.

"It looks like an ordinary horse, but if anyone is foolish enough to try to ride it, he can't get off. The water horse plunges into the lake, takes him to his home at the bottom, and eats him."

"I see. It does seem like inappropriate symbolism for a tavern name."

"Very much so."

The main parlour of Ceffyl-y-dŵr, which everyone still called Yr Hen Dafarn, was a long room with a low ceiling. Its fresh whitewash pleasantly set off the rich colour of the old brown beams. There was a large stone fireplace with a small fire burning in it. Such a venerable stone building had extremely thick walls, and these could be chill and damp even on a day in June, but the fire made the room comfortable. Old brass utensils and pewter pots were arranged in orderly fashion above the fireplace, and they were polished to glow like gold and silver. There was a remarkable display of hams hanging from the beams.

We drank mediocre beer, which unfortunately had not come from Sam Powell's Brewery in Newtown. I met Lloyd Hughes, the landlord — he was no relation to Glyn and Bryn Huws — and told him, in response to his questions, that I liked what I had seen of Wales very much, but it was a bit early for me to think of settling there permanently since I had no notion of how I could earn a living.

We continued to move from place to place, and I felt increasingly frustrated. It was obvious that these good people of Pentrederwydd could cast no light at all on the murders. None of them would have dared to venture past the lake where the dangerous water horse lived or visit the gloomy ruins of St. Celyn's church except to make use of the holy well, and they would have done that only in numerous company.

Further, all of them were dependent on the Master of Tromblay Hall in one way or another — even those who were not his tenants. If against all odds one of them did know something, would he have the courage to give evidence against Emeric Tromblay and face financial ruin?

We moved on. "What next?" I asked Madryn.

"Mrs. Williams," he said. "Iola Williams. She's a midwife."

I thought he was joking. I asked, "Is that really necessary? I know that this case is extremely complicated. I anticipate much hard labour before we solve it, but I honestly do not believe that a midwife — "

"You will find Mrs. Williams interesting," he said. "She predicted Glyn Huws's death."

"I already find her interesting. When did she do that?"

"A week before he died."

"What did she use? Tea leaves or an embrocation of fasting spittle?"

Madryn looked at me strangely. I hadn't yet related to him Sherlock Holmes's tale of the peculiarities of Sir John Pryse and his three wives; nor that of Bridget Bostock, of Cheshire, and her miracle working.

"I will let her tell you about it," Madryn said.

We remounted our ponies and followed a path that led to buildings farther up the hillside. Mrs. Williams lived in a tiny cottage located at the rear of a larger house. Her wrinkled face looked infinitely old, but her frame was wiry, and there was a sprightliness in her manner and a bright twinkle in her eyes.

Her English was uncertain and severely limited, and she obviously preferred to speak Welsh. When Madryn explained to her that his cousin from London wanted to hear about the cannwyll gorff, the corpse candle she had seen, she ceremoniously got the two of us seated in the sparsely furnished room that functioned as both kitchen and parlour. She quickly and expertly made tea for us and served it with small bara ceirch, oat cakes, after which she perched on the edge of a chair and began to relate her experience while Madryn translated.

I already knew about corpse candles. Borrow recorded several accounts by people who had seen them. A corpse candle is usually described as a pale, bluish light that travels a short distance above the ground. It not only predicts a death, but it is said to mark the route that will be followed later with the corpse. Corpse candles are extremely dangerous to meet with; anyone who carelessly allows one to brush against him is stricken dead on the spot.

Mrs. Williams had been called to a difficult delivery. The place — and Madryn made certain that the geography was clear to me before he allowed her to continue — was a tiny cottage high on the mountainside and overlooking the valley where the Huws farm, Meini Mawr, was located.

The pregnant girl was only sixteen and having her first child, and the labour was a long and hard one. The girl's husband had walked to Carno that morning hoping to sell the bit of butter that the girl had made and a few eggs, and he intended to visit his parents on his way back. She had gone into labour shortly after he left, but hours went by before she was able to attract the attention of some passing children, who finally brought word to Mrs. Williams. Labour continued all through the day and into the night, and the girl was in a mental state and becoming dangerously weak. Mrs. Williams thought that her husband's presence would calm her, and she was anxiously awaiting his return. She went to the door several times to look for him, and that was how she happened to see the corpse candle.

It had just come over the mountain at the head of the valley where Meleri Huws had ridden to meet us earlier that day. *Now* Mrs. Williams knew that it had come from Llangelyn, St. Celyn's church, where Glyn Huws was to be murdered, but at the time she had no premonition at all about that. She immediately feared for the girl who was having such a difficult time giving birth.

"If it had been the girl's corpse candle, why would it have come from such an out-of-the-way place?" I asked.

She didn't know. When one saw a corpse candle, one asked no questions about where it came from or where it was going. One simply prayed.

But this corpse candle had remained down in the valley, moving its slow but relentless way to Meini Mawr, the Huws farmhouse. She saw it enter the house. The next morning, having delivered the girl of a healthy baby boy, she went home and told her neighbours that there would soon be a death at Meini Mawr. Glyn Huws's body was found a week later, and it was brought home by a route identical to the one that the corpse candle had followed.

"Why didn't you warn him?" I asked.

She threw up her hands in dismay. Who was she to warn? The candle could have meant anyone living in the house, or a visitor, or just anyone at all who might be brought there on the way to somewhere else. It was best not to talk about corpse candles until long after the death happened. Anyway, what good would it have done?

"You told your neighbours," I said. "Did they tell anyone?"

The neighbours could talk as freely as they chose. They hadn't seen it.

I turned questioningly to Madryn. He told me that the rumour of an approaching death at Meini Mawr had been all over Pentrederwydd, but of course no one had mentioned it to any member of the Huws household. "What good would it have done if they had?" Mrs. Williams demanded. Once the corpse candle had been seen, Glyn Huws was foredoomed, even though no one knew for another week that the predicted death was his.

We thanked Mrs. Williams and returned to our ponies. "What are you suggesting?" I asked Madryn. "That the murderers took advantage of the rumour?"

"You are collecting facts. The rumour was a fact."

"Was Mrs. Williams's corpse candle a fact?"

"Of course it was."

"Yes," I mused. "Whatever it was she saw, she must have seen *something.* But what did it have to do with Huws's death?"

"Just deal with it as a fact," Madryn said impatiently. Facts looked much simpler to one who didn't have to report them to Sherlock Holmes.

We passed the church on our way back to Madryn's home. Tied up at the fence by the lych-gate was as handsome a bay horse as I had ever seen. It was splendidly groomed — there was even a ribbon in its tail — and it had a silk saddlecloth monogrammed with the letter *T* and also a saddle monogrammed with a gold inlaid *T*. Even the bridle was ornamented with a *T* on either side of the bit. Madryn rode past indifferently, but I pulled up my pony and turned to admire this phenomenon.

At that moment the church door swung open. A small man strode out. He was impeccably attired in black, and he carried his black hat under his arm. His face had the tentative wrinkles of advanced middle age, and his light hair was thinning and showed premature touches of gray. The bulge of his stomach suggested that he would eventually become a fat old man. He had an incisiveness of manner that is frequently encountered in the immediate vicinity of the House of Lords or the Royal Courts of Justice but seemed misplaced in a remote Welsh village. He looked up at me and nodded politely when he reached his horse, but he didn't notice Madryn until he had mounted. He swung gracefully into his saddle, turned the horse, and then halted.

"Hello, Dafydd. I was about to stop at your house. I'm resuming my Saturdays. Could you write a memorial for Eleanor?"

"Of course," Madryn said. Then he introduced me — but I already knew that this was the fiend, Bryn Huws's Diafol, Emeric Tromblay.

His eyes were intelligent, his voice pleasantly soft, his attitude toward both of us polite and gentle. He looked at me with interest. "From London? You grew up there? What is your occupation, Mr. Jones?"

"I'm a confidential clerk in a solicitor's office," I said. Sherlock Holmes had arranged this. If challenged, I could supply the name of my employer, and an inquiry addressed to him not only would bring confirmation of my credentials but also a glowing testimonial if one were called for.

"Do you speak Welsh, Mr. Jones?"

I smiled. "A few words, but I have a slight problem in remembering what they are. I only arrived here today."

"If you can manage to learn Welsh adequately, come and see me," he said. "A Welshman with training in English law would be extremely valuable to me."

"I'm aware of that, sir," I said boldly. "We met Mr. Welling in Newtown, and he told me the same thing."

"Did he?" Tromblay looked pleased. "If you talked with Wain, then of course you know. Wain is a splendid example of how extremely capable you Welsh can be. The best kind of Welshman has no equal — in England or anywhere else. Learn Welsh, and then come and see me. You won't regret it." He turned back to Madryn. "I'll expect you on Saturday, Dafydd. The usual time. Bring your cousin."

He rode away.

We looked after him until the curving path took him out of sight. Then I dismounted.

"Where are you going?" Madryn asked.

"I'm indulging my curiosity," I said.

I tied my pony at the gate and started for the church. Madryn dismounted and followed me.

If Tromblay was indeed y Diafol, it behooved me to learn as much about him as I could. I wanted to know whether there was anyone in the church who could tell me what he had been doing there. Had he prayed? Had he visited the grave of Glyn Huws, the man he was suspected of murdering, and then prayed? Was he looking for the vicar — perhaps to discuss wedding arrangements or to enlist an ally in his pursuit of Meleri Huws?

Sometimes such touches loom largely in the unravelling of a crime.

I entered the Church of St. Peter for the second time that day. There was no one there. I walked slowly toward the Tromblay monuments.

On the slab that marked the grave of Eleanor Tromblay, someone had left a small bouquet of wild flowers.

II

I ASKED MADRYN WHETHER TROMBLAY AND HIS wife had been an affectionate couple.

"I only saw them together on their Saturdays when their attention was on their guests. I would have said that they treated each other very politely."

"What were their Saturdays?"

Twice monthly the Tromblays had held formal Saturday dinners for guests staying at the Hall and for the few available local people of the Tromblay's own social class. Madryn often attended to recite his poetry. Some of the English landowners, descendants of families that had lived in Wales for generations, had never bothered to learn Welsh, and Tromblay liked to flaunt what he presumed to be his own fluency in the language. He frequently invited Welsh poets or musicians to perform.

Tromblay's wife had been dead for only three months. Certainly Arthur Saunders was prejudiced against him, but he had spoken the truth when he said Tromblay was not the grieving kind. Saunders also said Tromblay began courting Meleri Huws shortly after his wife died. Was the resumption of formal entertaining an announcement to the world that the Master of Tromblay Hall intended to marry again? Perhaps Tromblay thought to silence criticism by commissioning Madryn to recite a memorial poem.

I said with a frown, "This doesn't sound like a sincere obeisance to the muse, Dafydd. Does he pay you?"

"Yes," Madryn said. "He pays me well. In ancient times, the Bardd Teulu, the Bard of the Household, was an extremely important servant in every nobleman's retinue, and I suppose Tromblay pictures himself as carrying on a venerable tradition. I don't enjoy reciting poetry in Welsh for a group of condescending Saxons, most of whom don't understand it, but patrons for poets are very rare and must be accepted as they are found."

"Or as they find you," I suggested.

He nodded grimly.

"In any case, I'm pleased to hear that you are Bardd Teulu at Tromblay Hall. I have been wondering what I would have to do to obtain entry there. We will go together on Saturday. How formal is the occasion? Will I need dress clothing?"

Madryn shook his head. "Tromblay isn't aware that he is being condescending, and he would feel offended if anyone suggested that his tributes to Welshmen are insincere. However, if you were to arrive at his Saturday wearing what you call dress clothing, he would be both astonished and resentful—and he is going to seat you at a separate table with his Welsh retainers regardless of what you wear."

Mairwen Madryn greeted her husband affectionately for the second time that day. The two girls, Megan and Gwenda, hurled themselves at their father as though he had been missing for weeks. Dafi promised to take good care of our ponies and proudly led them to the barn. Madryn asked his wife what had been happening during his absence.

He spoke English with her — for my benefit, I was certain. She was not as fluent as her husband, but I had no difficulty in understanding her. She said, "Cadan Morgan thinks he saw the Rebeccas again."

Madryn laughed. Then he frowned. "Where?" he asked.

"He met them on the road when he was walking back from Carno last night. He says there were five of them."

Madryn turned to me. "Have you ever heard of Rebecca?"

I had, thanks to Borrow. Wales had been cursed with a stupidly organized and managed road system. Under it, sections of roads were owned privately, and each owner set the tolls for the roads under his proprietorship. A farmer on his way to market had to pay each time he passed from one sector to another, and that could involve a bankrupting series of tolls for a short journey. Rich and poor alike were plagued by the exorbitant tolls, and the economy of the whole country was placed in jeopardy. Finally the people revolted. Men donned women's clothing and roamed the countryside at night, smashing toll gates and toll houses. London had to take notice of this, and the roads were removed from private ownership.

Borrow's account of the Rebecca Riots was one of the items marked by Sherlock Holmes, but all of this had happened some sixty years before. "I've heard of Rebecca," I said, "but I didn't know she was still active."

"Cadan Morgan thinks she is. I don't know of anyone else who claims to have seen her. On the other hand, Cadan is the only person I know who travels about much at night. He works in a tavern in Carno — his uncle owns it — and he walks home afterward."

"How many times has he seen the Rebeccas?" I asked.

"Several. I don't know exactly how many."

"And — how long has this been going on?"

Madryn pursed his lips and thought for a moment. Then he turned to his wife, who shook her head.

"Were they first seen before or after Glyn Huws was murdered?" I asked.

Madryn looked at me wide-eyed. "Do you think the Rebeccas — "

"We are collecting facts," I said. "I would like to know when it was that Cadan Morgan first thought he saw them."

"I'll ask him," Madryn said. "I haven't paid much attention to what he says about them. I don't think anyone really believes him. He has a reputation for taking liberal samples of his uncle's beer."

Mairwen offered tea to us. Since we had just had tea, Madryn looked at me questioningly. I deferred to the girls, who were delighted to take part in an adult tea party. We sat around the table in the big kitchen and drank tea and munched on bara ceirch, the crisp oak cakes. The girls had only a few words of English, but their smiles needed no translation.

Suddenly Mairwen burst excitedly into Welsh. While she was speaking, I mentally compared her with Meleri Huws. Mairwen was as dark as Meleri but a striking opposite to her: Small and slightly plump where Meleri was tall and muscular, pretty in her rough woollen dress but offering no hint at all that stylish clothing would have made her look beautiful. She was a feminine woman where Meleri had seemed masculine. She obviously delighted in her role as wife of a poet and mother of these charming children. She and Madryn had married young, and there was not the slightest indication that either of them had ever regretted it or that Madryn would have preferred the heiress for a wife.

Mairwen halted suddenly in mid-sentence, appalled by her own discourtesy in speaking Welsh before their guest, and wrenched herself back into English.

"— an old friend of the vicar's," she said. "Uncle Tomos is delighted."

Madryn explained to me, "Mairwen's aunt and uncle — really her mother's aunt and uncle — have been very badly off. They are too old to run their little farm effectively, but they insist upon trying. We've been worried about them. Now a horse dealer, an old friend of the vicar's, has rented a bit of pasture that they weren't using anyway and is paying them to look after his horses. They're delighted. The extra money will keep them very comfortably for a long time."

"A horse dealer," I mused. "When did this happen?"

"Yesterday."

"Has it ever happened before?"

Madryn looked at me curiously. "Do you mean — has anyone rented their pasture before?"

"Anyone's pasture. Pentrederwydd isn't exactly on the main road to the horse fairs. Why would a horse dealer go this far out of his way to find a pasture for his horses?"

Madryn smiled. "We aren't so isolated as all that. The railway and also the main road from Newtown to Machynlleth and Aberystwyth are only a few miles away. And as Mairwen said, this horse dealer is an old friend of the vicar's. He is staying with him. It is convenient for him to have a place nearby where he can leave his horses. The vicar recommended Uncle Tomos and Aunt Hafina to him."

"Has this horse dealer ever visited his good friend the vicar before?"

"I don't know," Madryn said. He regarded me with amusement. "You detectives certainly are suspicious people. Why would the vicar say it was an old friend if it wasn't?"

"This case has had far too many coincidences already." I turned to Mairwen. "Are there any other strangers renting pastures and visiting in the district?"

"There is a boy staying at the Parry farm. His health has been poor, and his doctor thought the mountain air would be good for him — or so Gwen Parry said."

"Is he an English boy?"

Gwen Parry hadn't said much about him, but Mairwen supposed he was Welsh. The Parrys spoke very little English.

"How long has he been here?"

Several weeks, she thought. She couldn't remember exactly when he arrived.

"How old is he?"

She gestured vaguely. She had no idea how old he was. All she knew was that Gwen had called him a boy. She hadn't seen him in Pentrederwydd — perhaps his health didn't permit him to travel about. She added as an afterthought that shortly after he arrived she had seen him at the farm once, from a distance, when she went to visit Eira Evans, a neighbour of the Parry's.

"What did he look like?"

My persistent questioning was confusing her. She protested that she had only seen the boy that one time, from a long way off, and anyway she hadn't paid much attention to him. "All I noticed was that his hair looked white," she said. She stared open-mouthed when her husband and I scrambled to our feet.

"I knew about this boy, but I never heard what he looked like," Madryn said to me. "Do you suppose it's the same one?"

"I'm positive it's the same one. The horse dealer may be the man who accompanied him in Newtown and also in London. Where is the Parry farm? If it is the same boy, and if the vicar's friend is the same man, I must verify that as quickly as possible."

Mairwen was still looking from one of us to the other in amazement.

"I understand your haste," Madryn said, "but it may be too late to visit the Parry farm tonight. We passed it twice earlier today, but it is high up the mountain near the head of the valley and a long climb to undertake with darkness coming on. What did you intend to do — ride up and ask to see the boy?"

"It would be better if we could arrange to see him without his knowledge."

"That will take some thought. The vicar poses no problem at all. If I tell him I have a cousin visiting from London who prefers the English church, he will make us welcome at any time. Perhaps we will catch a glimpse of the old friend who is staying with him. Is there anything else that you must do quickly?"

"Talk to a servant at the Hall — preferably one who nursed Eleanor Tromblay."

Madryn turned to his wife. "Letty Howell?" he suggested.

She nodded.

"Is she coming home nights?"

"She's still staying with her daughter."

"We will go at once to see the vicar, and then we will see Letty Howell," Madrun told me. "First I will show you where you're to sleep."

This involved us in a discussion that quickly became an argument. I was a guest. The small house had only one bedroom, their own, and both Madryn and his wife were intent on surrendering it to me. They would have had to sleep in an unfinished loft with their children.

I already had selected my quarters. There was a loft in the small barn that stood higher up the mountain some distance behind the house. Sleeping there, I could come and go unobserved and without disturbing the family. Madryn protested that Mr. Saunders was paying well for the most comfortable accommodation that they could provide. I answered that I was not there for comfort. I had to have sleeping quarters that enabled me to work effectively.

I had my way, finally, and Madryn and I made an extremely comfortable bed for me in the loft, using straw and heavy woollen blankets. I hung my few possessions on pegs in the rafters and declared myself at home.

As soon as my sleeping quarters were arranged, we went to the vicarage, a large house located just below the church. Like all of the other structures in the village, it was built of stone and looked very old. Unfortunately the vicar, the Reverend Ezekiel Browne, was not at home. Madryn deftly turned the conversation to the vicar's old friend, the horse dealer, and his gaunt, elderly housekeeper informed us that the guest was a fine gentleman with very genteel habits. This had surprised her — she hadn't expected it of a horse dealer. His name was Mr. Batt, and he had left early that morning on another round of horse buying, but he would return in a day or two.

We had better luck with Letty Howell. She had worn herself out during Eleanor Tromblay's fatal illness. For days at a time she hardly slept, and she had been in a state of collapse herself when her darling mistress finally died. Now she was staying with her daughter because Emeric Tromblay had told her to take a rest — as long as she wanted. He continued to pay her wages.

It was not necessary to turn the conversation to her mistress's illness. Three months after Eleanor Tromblay's death, she still was unable to talk about anything else. When I mentioned my mother's lingering illness, she was immediately interested in all of the details, and we compared symptoms and treatments and weighed the relative competence of the two doctors.

My mother's fictitious ailment, which I fabricated from all of the descriptions of arsenic poisoning that I could remember, bore a striking resemblance to that of Eleanor Tromblay: the wracking stomach pains — the mere recollection of her mistress's suffering brought tears to Letty Howell's eyes — the vomiting, the diarrhoea.

"My mother also had a terrible rash from lying in bed for so long," I said.

Letty Howell nodded and wiped her eyes again. "Just dreadful, it was. Having to itch like that in addition to everything else."

Arthur Saunders had been wrong in one respect. He said that Eleanor Tromblay had died suddenly and mysteriously. She died a prolonged, agonizing, and messy death. There certainly had been nothing sudden about it; but her fatal illness, in one who had enjoyed life-long good health, could properly be called mysterious.

When we left a short time later, I knew all that I needed to know about Eleanor Tromblay's death except what had caused it. Unfortunately, the common symptoms of arsenic poisoning are also the common symptoms of several ordinary illnesses that also can be fatal, which is why doctors are far less suspicious of this type of ailment than they should be.

The only thing inconsistent with the conclusion that Eleanor Tromblay had been murdered was Letty Howell's description of Emeric Tromblay's conduct — his worry and concern, his efforts to make certain that his wife had the best possible care, and, finally, his grief at her death.

If Emeric Tromblay did not murder his wife, certainly no one else had reason to do so. She was as universally well-liked as her husband was despised.

Dafydd Madryn was finding murder investigations to be a shocking business. He knew that I had an invalid mother — in good health except for her inability to walk — in London, and my heart-rending description of her fatal illness left him open-mouthed. As we walked toward Yr Hen Dafarn, the Old Tavern, he said, shaking his head, "I don't believe I could do it. You have to be an actor, don't you? And tell lies and pretend to all kinds of things?"

"You have to do whatever is necessary to encourage people to talk," I said. "If I were to move to Pentrederwydd, and become the friend of all of these people, perhaps in a year or two they would have sufficient confidence in me to tell me what I need to know — if they still remembered. By that time, it would be too late to track down the murderers. I must have that information now. So I pretend, and tell lies, and use whatever guile occurs to me. If necessary, I will burgle houses and commit fraud and extortion — in search of the truth. None of these activities could possibly harm anyone except the murderers."

"I understand that. Was Eleanor Tromblay murdered?"

"All of her symptoms are consistent with a verdict of death from arsenic poisoning. Unfortunately, those symptoms could have other causes, and only exhumation and scientific tests on her body would provide the necessary proof. Until that is done, I am inclined to believe that Emeric Tromblay poisoned his wife while giving a masterful performance as a loving, caring husband."

We drank our half-pints of ale at the tavern, and I was introduced to those present, most of whom were local residents. It was too early for the influx of farm workers, some of whom had long distances to walk. We returned home to a plain but delicious supper. I was surprised at the robust appetites of the Madryn children until I discovered that they rarely enjoyed such a lavish meal. Both the quantity and variety of food and the large platter of meat — the delicious roast leg of lamb I had been unable to find in Newtown — were novelties to them. Especially the meat. On the tables of rural Wales, meat was uncommon. So was butter, even though the Welsh farmers produced both butter and meat in quantity. Anything that could be exchanged for cash had to be sold in order to pay the rent. Arthur Saunders had been aware of this, and he provided sufficient funds so that the Madryn family could eat well as long as I stayed there.

I spent the remainder of the evening writing a long report to Sherlock Holmes. When I finished, I addressed it to the firm of solicitors that was my alleged employer. It would be sent around to Baker Street by messenger the moment it arrived. Madryn's son, Dafi, took it to the postmistress. There were no formal hours at the post office in Pentrederwydd.

I went to bed early in my rough loft and fell asleep at once.

I was awakened by voices and the snort of a horse. Bright moonlight made me think for a dazed moment that it was morning. I went to the window at the end of the loft and looked out. Horses and riders were moving along the path above the darkened and sleeping village. I suddenly found myself wide awake and staring. It had been a man's voice that I heard, but the silhouettes of the riders were those of women.

I dressed quickly, leaped down the ladder, and saddled and bridled my pony. By the time I gained the path, the Rebeccas were no longer in sight. They had moved beyond the village and taken a turning that led down to the road.

I cursed myself for a fool, but I followed as quickly as I could until I reached the turning. There I hesitated. If I descended to the road, they would see me the first time they looked back. They would have no reason to think that I was following them, but I would be in an awkward position regardless — and these Rebeccas might prove to be far rougher customers than their namesakes who had smashed the toll gates.

If I tried to follow by keeping to the mountain-side above them, travelling across an unfamiliar country at night, I would be frustrated by the first hedge, or fence, or wall I encountered. I decided to follow the mountain path as long as I could. I urged my pony forward, and I soon overtook them. They moved along the road below me in leisurely fashion, and I was able to dismount and lead my pony and still keep pace with them. I could see the path more easily on foot. It took me across rough pasture land, through gates, and — once — through the yard of a tiny farmhouse. There was no sign from the road below that the riders were aware of me. They walked their horses and now and again called something to one another.

I moved forward without incident until I approached the eastward curve of the Meini Mawr valley where the Huws farm was located. There I had a choice between two paths, one turning upward and the other down. I took the downward path and discovered that I had moved some distance ahead of the Rebeccas. I halted in the shelter of a cluster of trees and waited.

Then I saw that I was not the only one waiting. Down by the road, a man was seated on a large boulder. As the Rebeccas approached, he slipped to the ground and stepped forward to meet them.

The Rebeccas halted. After a brief conversation, the man who had been waiting mounted behind one of the riders. The Rebeccas moved on.

I made a quick decision. As long as they continued at a walk, I could follow them on foot with far less likelihood of detection. I tied my pony to a small tree, making certain that there was grass for it, and then I hurried after them, keeping under cover as much as possible and avoiding the open road.

They passed the turn offs to Tromblay Hall and to Meini Mawr. I had to give them a long lead when they moved through the narrow gap beside the rushing stream on the road that led to Tynewydd and the lake that concealed the horrible Ceffyl-y-dŵr, but as soon as they passed out of sight, I crossed the Meini Mawr stream on stepping stones and broke into a run. When I reached the other side of the gap, the Rebeccas were headed toward a grove of trees to the west of the lake. A solitary figure, probably the man who had met them, was walking toward Tynewydd, the home of the invalid, Kyle Connor.

I waited until the Rebeccas disappeared into the trees. Then I started in pursuit of the man on foot. He approached the farm along the lake shore and finally took cover at the end of a stone wall that marked the edge of the farmyard. I retreated a short distance and found a comfortable seat amidst some bushes. I could watch the man by the wall as well as the silent and dark farmhouse and also keep an eye on the distant grove where the Rebeccas were lurking.

The night passed tediously because nothing at all happened. The man by the wall changed his position several times, probably in an attempt to find a soft spot in the stone he was sitting on and also to keep himself awake. I had some difficulty myself in keeping awake. There was no sign of movement from the Rebeccas, and the farmhouse remained dark.

Dawn was finally approaching when I was startled into alertness by a strange cry. It was a signal; the Rebeccas were leaving. The moon had long since set. In the thin light of early dawn it was harder to see them than it had been when we arrived, but I thought they had removed their dresses.

The man by the wall had heard the signal. He stood up. The horsemen waved to him; he waved back and hurried toward them.

I felt totally mystified. These men must have ridden a considerable distance wearing dresses and watched Tynewydd all night for some other object than to enjoy the mountain vapours. Were the Rebeccas involved in a plot against the invalid, Kyle Connor? There were more sinister undercurrents in Wild Wales than I felt able to cope with.

Then the man who had been watching by the wall passed quite close to me, and I abandoned my speculations. It was Alban Griffiths, the fair-haired boy I had seen previously in London and in Newtown.

One of the horsemen waited for him. The boy leaped up behind the rider, and they moved off toward the gap. I followed as rapidly and as silently as I could. They were far ahead of me when they separated, with a quick exchange of farewells, and the boy started quickly up the mountainside. He followed a path that was invisible to me. I watched his receding figure from the cover of a clump of bushes until he finally vanished into a tiny farmhouse high on the mountain. Probably he told Jac and Gwen Parry, with whom he was staying, that he had enjoyed his early-morning walk and worked up a splendid appetite for breakfast.

I walked back to the place I had left my pony and took the road to Pentrederwydd, returning to the Madryn barn by way of the path that looped above the village. One of the children chanced to see my arrival, and the entire family rushed out in astonishment. I told them I had enjoyed my early-morning ride and worked up a splendid appetite for breakfast. Dafi took charge of my pony.

Later, after we had eaten, I spoke with Madryn privately. "I followed a group of Rebeccas that rode past shortly after midnight," I told him. "I don't understand all that I saw, but I can tell you one thing for certain. The fair-haired boy is indeed the boy we saw in Newtown, and he has some connection with the Rebeccas — and I very much want to meet Mr. Kyle Connor."

12

I RETURNED TO MY BED IN THE LOFT AND SLEPT. IT was late morning when I awoke, and Wales had been transformed. The bright sunny weather was gone; rain was rattling against the window and dripping through the roof in several places, fortunately none of them near my bed. I went to the window and looked out into the thickest gloom I had ever experienced. Swift moving, black clouds impinged upon the mountain tops.

Dafi, looking like a very wet puppy in a cloak that was far too large for him, was walking toward the house. He looked up and saw me, waved, and broke into a run. A few minutes later he was back, carrying a wooden bucket. He adroitly scaled the ladder with it and poured hot water into a basin that he placed on a small table. I had acquired the table the night before, along with an odd-looking three-legged chair, for my letter writing.

I thanked Dafi for the water. The day seemed less gloomy after I had performed my ablutions and shaved. I climbed down the ladder and hurried through the rain to the house.

Mairwen had food ready. She said her husband had already eaten and gone out and we were not to wait for him, so I sat down with her and the children. I thought it odd that Dafi was not in school, but the practice in rural Wales was to keep children home whenever they were needed. In the case of Dafi, his father taught him in the evening, and he was far ahead of his classmates.

Mairwen asked suddenly, "Were you up all night?"

I nodded.

She shook her head sadly. "Such happenings. A murder, and now the night riders. It worries me."

It worried me, too — the more so because the one had left so few clues and the other made no sense.

Mairwen's Uncle Tomos, who had rented his unused pasture to the horse dealer, stopped by while we were eating. He had come down to the village to purchase a few necessities, a chore left for a rainy day when he couldn't work in his fields. I had the amusing experience of attempting to make sense of a totally unintelligible conversation in Welsh between him and Mairwen. She invited him to eat with us, I thought; he protested that he'd already eaten; she waved aside his excuses and finally got him seated at the table with us where he ate with a robust appetite. He was a kindly looking man, extremely old, extremely grey, extremely wrinkled, and shy in the presence of a stranger.

He spoke no English at all.

The day before, I had committed a blunder that Sherlock Holmes would have taken me sharply to task for. It was critically important to learn whether the horse dealer, the vicar's friend, was indeed the blond boy's red-bearded companion. If I'd had my wits about me, I would have extracted an adequate description of the man from the vicar's housekeeper.

I tried to make amends for that with Uncle Tomos. "I do believe I know this man who rented your uncle's pasture," I told Mairwen. "Would you ask him whether the horse dealer has a reddish beard?"

Mairwen translated that into Welsh. Uncle Tomos answered hesitantly. Mairwen persisted. I caught the words "barf côch" and remembered that "Y Llew Côch" had been "The Red Lion."

"The horse dealer has a beard," Mairwen said to me finally. "Uncle Tomos says it may have been red, but he doesn't exactly remember. His eyesight is poor, and he forgets easily. He and Auntie shouldn't be living up there all by themselves."

For the moment, a man with a beard that may have been red was confirmation enough. The horse dealer had adroitly established the boy with the Parry family weeks before, and now he had found a place for himself nearby that enabled him to come and go as he chose.

It was his friendship with the vicar that troubled me. I was not disturbed by the notion of a vicar having an unsavoury friend, but it did seem odd that one would have an "old friend," with all that implied, from the wrong social class.

Then it occurred to me that this particular vicar had obtained his living — and kept it — through the favour of Emeric Tromblay, whom he also served as chaplain at the Hall. Any henchman of Tromblay's would automatically become an "old friend" of the vicar's if Tromblay requested it.

When we finished eating, I returned to my loft and paced about impatiently, waiting for Madryn. I had tentatively identified the horse dealer, but there was still one person in the neighbourhood who posed a large question mark — Mr. Kyle Connor.

I learned afterward that Madryn was visiting Pentrederwydd's shopkeepers at that moment in search of an excuse for calling on Connor. If one of them had a package for Tynewydd, or even a message, we could pretend to make a slight detour on our way to the Hall or to Meini Mawr and deliver it as a favour.

This was well conceived, and it dramatically illustrated the difference between Madryn's thinking and mine. He knew Connor only very casually, having met him several times at the Tromblays' Saturdays, and no Welshman would ride several miles in a driving rain to call upon a virtual stranger — especially a stranger who was not Welsh — without a good excuse.

But I was three-quarters English, and ordinary restraints didn't apply to a holiday-making Englishman. I also was gaining confidence rapidly. The conversation with Mairwen's uncle convinced me that my ignorance of Welsh was not the handicap I had expected it to be. In the village, at least, there always would be someone near by who spoke both Welsh and English and could translate.

Connor certainly would speak English, and in that remote valley he would not have many callers. I reasoned that an unexpected call by a visitor from London would brighten a rainy day for an invalid. If he refused to see me, I would have wasted my time and drenched myself to no purpose, but I had dry clothing in my knapsack and nothing else to do anyway.

I told Mairwen that I had an errand of my own to perform. A look of concern crossed her face, but she said nothing. The rain had not diminished, and I resigned myself to arriving at Tynewydd in a thoroughly soaked condition.

She came running after me and gave me a heavy cloak. I thanked her. "If I get too wet," I told her, "I'll hurry back to your kitchen fire." I mounted my pony and started out.

I wanted to see by daylight the path I had followed the previous night. I had a presentiment that I would be using it again. I let the pony slosh along at its own pace, and my cloak got extremely wet, but it kept me dry except for the bottoms of my trouser legs.

I studied the lay of the land all the way, cutting through the farmyard again and passing close to the house. There was no one about. Finally I descended to the road near the large stone where the fair-haired boy had sat waiting for the horsemen. There I paused to look up at the tiny farmhouse high on the mountainside where he was staying. The murky sky hung low over it, and there was no sign either of him or of the farmer. If the boy had been in Wales for as long as Mairwen thought, he certainly would have learned enough about Welsh weather to stay in out of the rain. The natives would nod wisely and remark that I had not.

I followed the road past the two valleys that led to the Hall and to Meini Mawr, forded a swollen stream — the stepping stones were under water — and passed quickly through the narrow gap beyond, where the rushing stream from the lake was foaming violently. The lake, a beautiful calm, blue sheet of water the day before, was showing the ugly side of its character. It was grey and storm-tossed. On such a day I would have feared the dreaded Ceffyl-y-dŵr myself. I urged the pony forward, rode past my hiding place of the night before, rode past the wall where the boy had sat, and arrived at the door of Tynewydd, the "New House."

As with so many things called "new," it looked extremely old — several hundred years, at least. House and barns, which formed a rectangle around the farmyard, were of rough stone but very well-kept. Their pink wash had looked beautiful from across the lake the previous day, and the sculpted design of the house's thatched roof had made a handsome effect. Now the house looked as dull and dingy as the weather.

I dismounted boldly in a small paved court before the entrance. My arrival had been observed; a woman swung open the heavy door as I approached and looked in astonishment at the dripping form that confronted her. "Is Mr. Connor in?" I asked. It was the wrong question to pose concerning an invalid. She drew herself up indignantly.

"Of course," she said. "Mr. Connor is always in. May I ask who is calling?"

"Edward Jones," I said. "From London."

"From *London?*"

I nodded.

She called over her shoulder, "Mr. Edward Jones. From London." Then she added, as though she didn't believe a word of it, "He says."

"Send him up," a deep voice called back.

A farm-hand hurried out to take charge of my pony. I descended a short ramp to the flags of a low-beamed kitchen, where the housekeeper took my dripping cloak and distastefully set about hanging it near the fire. There was a splendid array of old oak furniture: an elaborately carved dresser several tiers high and also a huge cupboard, both displaying large pewter dishes; low three-legged chairs similar to the one that had been placed in my loft — they were called "Cardiganshire chairs" and were much favoured for rooms with rough stone floors because they didn't teeter on an uneven surface; a handsome clock with a carving of "The Death of Gelert," a famous Welsh historical legend — of doubtful authenticity — about a faithful dog; an enormous table that had been formed of one thick slab of oak.

There was a shelf with bright copper teakettles, skillets, and pans. There were wood bowls and dishes that looked like those I had seen in the carpenter's shop at Pentrederwydd except that these were well-seasoned with use. The immense fireplace had a bread oven built into its side, and it projected into the room as though demanding attention. A fire burned merrily. The ceiling was adorned with ropes of onions, assorted herbs, flitches of bacon, hams, pieces of beef. It was such a pleasant room, warm, comfortable, filled with enticing aromas of food and sights to delight the appetite, that I would have enjoyed sitting there to dry my trouser legs.

The housekeeper pointed to a broad stairway, and I climbed it with squishing shoes. At the top, a man of middle age sat waiting for me. The first thing I noticed about him was his head — it was unusually large, as though designed to compensate for the shrivelled lower part of his body — and his large, good-natured face. He was clean-shaven, but his hair was thick and shaggy. The upper part of his body also appeared to be unusually large, and even beneath the heavy woollen sweater that he wore, his arms looked muscular.

I took in all of that with my first glance, and then I gave my attention to his chair. I had never seen one like it. On either side it had one large central wheel, with small, swivelling wheels in front and in back. There was an adjustable support for his shrunken legs, and the whole appeared to be extravagantly padded.

He spun the chair around and rolled it to one side as I reached the top of the stairway. "Mr. Jones?" he asked, extending his hand.

I shook it warmly. "I'm very pleased to make your acquaintance, and I offer my sincere apologies for this unwarranted intrusion."

He laughed. "A call on an invalid is never to be considered an intrusion. What brings you to this out-of-the-way corner on such an unruly day?"

"Now that I'm actually here, I feel embarrassed. I had nothing else to do. I'm visiting my cousin in Pentrederwydd for my holidays and also to familiarize myself with this land of my ancestors. It's a beautiful land — in the sunlight. I expected to find some charming walks and enjoy riding about the countryside. Until today, all of my expectations were realized, but Pentrederwydd is not the most interesting place in which to pass a rainstorm."

"Indeed it is not," he agreed, laughing.

"The residents are charming people, but my interest in conversation about sheep and cows is limited. I feel like an outsider, and I heard that you, also, are an outsider. Frankly, I came here looking for someone to talk with."

He tilted his head back and laughed resoundingly. "I know exactly how you feel. As you say, the good citizens of Pentrederwydd are charming people with unfortunately narrow interests. I have few close friends among them for that very reason. The vicar is kind enough to give me a game of chess occasionally, but he is a busy man with many demands on his time. The doctor has the excuse of calling on me professionally, and he extends his visits as much as he can, but his conversation — apart from medical matters — is restricted to the subjects of fishing and hunting, and I have never followed either. Emeric Tromblay rides over occasionally and has the kindness to invite me to his Saturdays, but he is a business man, and I am no more interested in mining shares and profits than in hunting and fishing. And of course his Saturdays have been suspended since his wife died, though he is about to resume them. The only friends I can depend upon are my books. If one of them proves faithless or boring, it can be sent packing with no offence to anyone but the author, who needn't know about it. Don't just stand there dripping, man! Take that chair by the fire and tell me about yourself."

He wanted to know all about me. He was not put off by my casual remark that I was a confidential clerk with a firm of solicitors. He asked the name of the firm and what sort of confidential work I did. He also asked highly technical questions about London.

Fortunately, my investigative work kept me as well informed about the metropolis as anyone living there except my employer. In addition, Sherlock Holmes had a special interest of his own in transport developments, and he frequently discussed these with me. For this reason, I was able to handle Connor's query about the electrification of the Kennington-Streatham cable tramway — it had been shut down early in April for the conversion and hadn't yet reopened — with an ease that astonished him. I also had no difficulty in answering his questions concerning the progress of electrification on the London County Council tramways — it was proceeding slowly — or in describing the growing competition between the new cabs with petrol engines and the traditional hansoms and four-wheelers.

On the pretense of wanting to order merchandise, he tested my knowledge of various shops in London. To his immense amusement, I had no recollection at all of the Leadenhall Street branch of John Pound, the leather merchant, though I knew the Pound shops in Piccadilly, Regent Street, and Tottenham Court Road. He outstripped me easily in his recitation of tobacconists and wine merchants, but I knew more booksellers than he did, and I matched him fairly well on the principal chemists.

From the moment of my arrival, it had been obvious that he was deeply suspicious of me. He frankly didn't believe I was what I said I was, and he was resolved to test me. As I answered his questions in great detail, the test quickly became a contest that both of us enjoyed and then a friendly discussion. We exchanged impressions on such varied subjects as holiday time on Hampstead Heath, the music hall stars Little Tich and Marie Lloyd, the aftermath of the Oscar Wilde scandal, and fog on the River Thames.

"You are an extraordinarily well-informed young man," he said finally. "You should be of immense value to your employers."

"It is a great pleasure to talk with someone who knows London better than I do. You must have lived there for many years."

"I did. I was an engineer until an accident cost me the use of my legs. I lived on in London for several years — which was a mistake. A large city is not designed for invalids. Even the most lavish city home becomes a prison cell. I decided to live where I could design my own home. I settled in Shrewsbury and spent a year in profitless and uncomfortable excursions until I finally found this place. The original house was a tŷ hir or long-house. The farmer and his family lived in one end of it, the animals lived in the other, and they shared a central entrance. As the farmer prospered, he built other quarters for his animals and remodelled the combined house and barn for more comfortable family living.

"When I bought it, I had suitable accommodation built for myself on this level — it is the former loft — with wide stairs that have tracks for my chair. I am extremely comfortable here. This is a rather poor farm, and the income from it barely covers expenses, but it provides me with food throughout the year, and I can derive some entertainment from watching the farm-hands at work. My servants consider me an ideal employer because I interfere very little with the running of the place and make as few demands on them as possible."

"When did you come here?" I asked.

"I moved in late last autumn. I bought Tynewydd early last year, but the remodelling took time. Would you like to see the place?"

He had indeed made a comfortable home for himself. He had a large, book-lined study, bedroom, bathroom, guest rooms, the living-room at the head of the stairs, a small dining room, and — at the south end of the house — a room with large windows to catch the warmth every moment the sun penetrated the valley. This room opened onto a porch above the lower level's kitchen. He was able to move swiftly from room to room in his wheeled chair, which he handled with surprising adroitness.

Our conversation extended through most of the afternoon. He was delighted to meet someone who could talk about London. Finally he rang for tea and served it himself, playing the host with great pleasure and urging a variety of cakes and sandwiches on me.

"Mr. Jones is not only a Londoner but an unusually well-informed one," he told Mrs. Pugh, the housekeeper. "I hope he will be calling often."

Finally I said that I really must go. My cousin would be worried that his clumsy city relative had managed to lose himself. Connor said, "I will see you to the door, then."

He rang for Mrs. Pugh, who came and pulled a rope from a large box at the head of the stairway. Connor invited me to go first, and then he boldly rolled his chair down the stairs after me. Turning, I saw that the wheels fitted neatly into grooves on either side of the stairway. At the top of the stairs, a stanchion folded out with a pulley at the end; the rope fed around that, and the mechanism in the box let the rope out slowly and gave him a comfortable ride down the slope.

"Is there a motor to pull you back up?" I asked when he reached the bottom.

"Not exactly a motor," he said. "There is a system of gears with a handle that turns very easily. I invented it myself. Mrs. Pugh manages it without difficulty."

"You should put a motor in the chair," I suggested.

"I would if there were anywhere to go. It's hardly worth the trouble just to travel from the house to the lake."

"My cousin and I saw you swimming yesterday. The lake looked so lovely that I felt tempted to join you. Today it is less attractive."

"Come and swim any time you like. I'll warn you, though, that the water is extremely cold. I'm accustomed to it."

We shook hands again. Mrs. Pugh brought me my cloak, which now was almost dry, and I took my leave of him, promising to come again soon.

The farm-hand had taken my pony to the barn, and it, too, was almost dry when we started the return trip, but the rain quickly drenched both of us. I gave the pony its head so I could devote all of my thoughts to Kyle Connor.

The man seemed like an open book — frank and confiding about any subject our conversation touched. It was difficult to see how an invalid, which he assuredly was, could be involved in murders or conspiracies.

But involved he had to be. The boy and his confederates had not watched Tynewydd for most of a night out of casual curiosity or a fondness for viewing the lake by moonlight.

The Madryn family was becoming accustomed to the eccentric behaviour of its guest. Dafi hurried out to take charge of the pony; none of the others appeared. I climbed the ladder to my loft and changed to dry clothing. Madryn came out a short time later and joined me.

"Bring your wet clothes into the house, and Mairwen will dry them by the fire," he said. "I was afraid you wouldn't return in time. The vicar has invited us to tea."

I groaned. My wet ride back to Pentrederwydd had done nothing at all to settle the lavish tea that Kyle Connor inflicted upon me.

"I thought that was what you wanted," Madryn said reproachfully. "The horse dealer has returned, and this is an opportunity to meet him."

"I was only wishing that it could have been arranged without the tea," I explained. "I just had tea."

"Come along. We're almost late."

Along the way, I described my meeting with Kyle Connor.

"His inability to walk doesn't seem to affect his swimming," Madryn said.

"Swimming is probably the only exercise he can take. He does swim extremely fast. On the other hand, if someone threw me into that cold lake, I would swim fast, too."

We arrived at the vicarage damply out of breath. The vicar's housekeeper took our cloaks and escorted us into the parlour, where the Reverend Ezekiel Browne, a large, portly man with bristling whiskers, was talking jovially with several guests.

I picked out the horse dealer at once. To my enormous disappointment, he bore no resemblance at all to the fair-haired boy's companion. He had a neatly trimmed black beard; otherwise, he looked completely nondescript.

Madryn introduced me to the vicar, and the vicar introduced both of us to his guests. There was nothing nondescript about the horse dealer's name. "Mr. Haggart Batt," the vicar said and remarked vaguely about Batt being an old friend from his Oxford days. Batt responded with a joking reference to a youthful adventure they'd had with a pig, which the vicar listened to with a pained expression.

I reminded myself that Mr. Haggart Batt's arrival in Pentrederwydd still seemed suspiciously opportune, and I took a chair near him, determined to learn what I could about him.

"How long have you lived in Wales?" I asked him.

"I've never lived in Wales," he said. He spoke with a twanging accent that I couldn't place. "I come here now and again in hope of acquiring a few sound horses, but too often it's a forlorn hope."

"I've seen at least one good horse since I arrived here," I said. "Emeric Tromblay owns it."

He shook his head. "I've seen it, too. I call it a sham horse—all show and no substance. It may look good with ribbons on it, but only an idiot would try to plough with it. No one but a wealthy man can afford a horse or a wife like that."

"What breed of horse do you prefer?" I asked.

"Clydesdale or Shire," he said. "Those are horses that can do an honest day's work. There are precious few of them in Wales, though. You have to go somewhere like Lanarkshire to see real horses."

"Lanarkshire," I repeated. "Isn't that where Robert Owen started his reforms?"

"Who's Robert Owen?" he demanded. Then he winked at me.

It was Sherlock Holmes.

13

LATER THAT NIGHT HE VISITED ME, AND HE WAS highly complimentary about my choice of quarters. Not only could I come and go unobserved at any time of day or night, but the barn, damp and draughty though it was, gave us a place to meet privately.

I lit candles for us; he settled himself on the low three-legged Welsh chair, stretching his own long legs out uncomfortably, and I sat on the pile of straw I used for a bed. He seemed distraught, and I concluded that his researches had not advanced our case any further than mine had.

He began his arrangements for the role he was playing as soon as the Welshmen called on us. He left London on Monday, shortly after I did, and came directly to Pentrederwydd, pausing only to take possession of a few horses he had arranged to have waiting for him at Groesffordd so he could properly present himself as a horse dealer. The vicar, who had never heard of him, was delighted to accord him the status of "old friend." The Dean of St. Paul's had written to him requesting the favour. Now everyone in the valley knew that Mairwen Madryn's Uncle Tomos and Aunt Hafina were renting their pasture to the vicar's horse-dealing friend, and there were half a dozen horses of fair quality in the pasture to prove that. The friendly Mr. Haggart Batt had no need of further credentials.

There hadn't been time for either of my letters to be forwarded to him, so I started at the beginning and reported in full: The meeting with Benton Tromblay, the Robert Owen Study League, Benton's lecture with the fair-haired boy and his companion in attendance, my failure to follow them. Then came my arrival in Pentrederwydd, the scene of the murder, Meleri Huws, the clogprints, the Rebeccas and their meeting with the boy, their watch on Tynewydd, and finally my afternoon with Kyle Connor. Along the way, I paraded everyone I had met.

When I finished, Sherlock Holmes shook his head in mock disapproval. "Really, Porter — you seem to have abandoned yourself to the Powers of Darkness. Celtic gods; corpse candles; that most unusual clan of fairies, the Tylwyth Têg; water horses; fairy cows." He shook his head again. "Even without that, we have a rare confusion of characters to contend with. We may waste valuable time eliminating those who have no roles to play. Is Kyle Connor what he claims to be?"

"No, sir," I said.

"Why do you say that?"

"For one thing, because he went to such lengths to make certain that I was what I claimed to be."

"Then you hold that a person who is overtly suspicious of others must have guilty secrets of his own. It's an ingenuous doctrine, Porter, but there are certain to be countless exceptions. A principle loses its effectiveness when the exclusions outnumber the inclusions."

"Yes, sir. But I can't think of any exclusions that would apply here. For another thing, there was the night watch on his farm. I can't imagine what the Rebeccas were looking for, because I'm convinced that Connor genuinely is an invalid. I studied his movements as carefully as I could all the time we were talking. He kept shifting his position to make himself comfortable. His legs really are shrivelled and he has no strength in them. There can be no question of his roaming about at night. The Rebeccas must have been expecting someone to call on him."

"It would seem so," Sherlock Holmes mused. "Thus far our investigation has turned up no answers at all and provided us with an unconscionable number of new questions. Even if the clogprints you found are those of the murderers, narrowing the list of suspects to men who wear clogs is not really helpful in rural Wales no matter what style the clogs may be. Is Benton Tromblay genuine?"

"Yes, sir. He is completely sincere and disconcertingly naïve."

"Something similar was said of Robert Owen," Sherlock Holmes said.

"I don't agree with Madryn that this is just a phase Benton is passing through and eventually he'll turn out to be his father's son. I think the alteration is permanent. He is deriving enormous pleasure from blasting away at his father's principles."

Sherlock Holmes got to his feet. "Tomorrow we will go together to Llangelyn. I must see these clogprints myself. Then I will make the acquaintance of Kyle Connor. Did Emeric Tromblay impress you as a man dedicated to evil?"

I said slowly, "He impressed me as a man who might do an enormous amount of evil without being aware of it."

"Many wealthy men are like that, and the behaviour of the most wicked of them can be a disconcerting blend of good and evil."

"Yes, sir," I agreed. "The most wicked of all may even take flowers to the grave of the wife he murdered."

Sherlock Holmes nodded solemnly. "He may even do that. Do you breakfast early?"

"As early as I choose — or as late."

"Unfortunately, the vicar is a late sleeper. I will come as early as I can."

"Shall we take Madryn with us?"

"Of course. We may need him."

I followed him down the ladder. He strode off into the rainy night, and I dashed to the house to tell Madryn our plans.

"What excuse will he use for calling on Kyle Connor?" Madryn wanted to know.

"He is a horse dealer," I said. "When did a horse dealer ever need an excuse for calling on a farmer?"

When I awoke the next morning, the rain had stopped. I went to the window — and saw nothing. The famous Welsh mist, the niwl, had descended on us. George Borrow quoted a celebration of it by the great fourteenth century Welsh poet, Dafydd ap Gwilym:

Thou exhalation from the deep
Unknown, where ugly spirits keep!

Thou smoke from hellish stews uphurl'd
To mock and mortify the world!

Avaunt, thou filthy, clammy thing
Of sorry rain the source and spring!

Moist blanket dripping misery down,
Loathed alike by land and town!

It was as though an enormous cloud, heavy with rain, had sunk to the valley floor. Things close at hand could be seen dimly; more remote things became shadows that the mist devoured. This was indeed the watery monster, the "wild of vapour, vast, o'ergrown, huge as the ocean of unknown," of the poet's description.

There was no longer a mark of delineation in those Welsh mountains between Earth and sky. I suddenly understood Madryn's remark that sometimes the old Celtic gods were very close at hand. Earth and a hellish kind of heaven were blended at such a time; the gods could poke into human affairs without even leaving their abodes, and a careless human might wander into a weird Celtic limbo unawares.

I dressed, climbed down to the stable, and gave our ponies a friendly greeting. Madryn's two cows were left in his bit of pasture during the summer and milked there by Mairwen or young Dafi.

I stood in the door of the stable looking out uncertainly, and a shadow suddenly loomed up before me — formidable, mysterious, threatening. "Parent of thieves," Dafydd ap Gwilym had called the mist, because the flight of a thief was so easily concealed by it. Surely this was the proper season for "crimes, follies, and misfortunes."

But the shadow was only Madryn, come to see whether I was awake yet.

All was cheerful within the house. The smiling Mairwen was preparing breakfast, and the weather in no way dampened the spirits of the children. When Sherlock Holmes arrived, we climbed through the mist to the farm of Mairwen's Uncle Tomos and Aunt Hafina, where he selected three of his horses for our day's outing. He and Madryn rode bare-back, but they matter-of-factly placed a saddle on my horse. I remembered the difficulty I had on my previous experience of the climb to St. Celyn's church and made no protest. We rode slowly along an invisible path with Madryn leading the way, and the mist that surrounded us was so thick that I wanted to push it aside with my hands. We were a procession of misshapen spectres, unreal even to ourselves. The invisible village below us was like one of the famous lost Welsh villages that the sea had claimed, with church bells sounding ghost-like in the depths.

When we made our way back to the valley, we were able to move faster on the road. We were perhaps half-way to the intersection with the Tromblay Hall and the Meini Mawr valleys when I heard the sound of a trotting horse approaching. The blended shadow of horse and rider loomed up suddenly, and my horse reared in alarm. Then the shadow veered around us and was gone. In that brief moment, Madryn called, "Bore da, Wain."

The shadow responded, "Bore da, Dafydd." It was Wain Welling, off on another journey to tend to his master's business. Emeric Tromblay would not permit a small thing like mist to keep his employees from their labours.

The mist thickened over the lake, and the silence there was uncanny. At first I thought the water was churning invisibly with the sound of the waves strangely muted. Then I discovered that the lake lay completely still under the mist's sodden touch. We took the sketchy road past Tynewydd and saw no sign of activity there. Kyle Connor, the best employer in Wales, didn't expect his farm-hands to work on such a day.

The road diminished to a sheep track. We continued to move in single file with Madryn in the lead. The sound of the waterfall grew, but it remained invisible. Finally we made the climb to Llangelyn, and the horses had far more difficulty than our ponies had in scrambling up the steep slope beside a stream that now was swollen by the previous day's rain.

Madryn and I waited at the top of the incline with the horses while the shadowy, elongated figure of Sherlock Holmes moved methodically about the crumbling ruins. On this day, at least, the most skilled archaeologist would have had difficulty in distinguishing between St. Celyn's venerable church and the anonymous sheep-fold.

At the scene of a crime, any crime, Sherlock Holmes became a man transformed. The usual marks of his intense concentration — flushed face, compressed lips, dilated nostrils — were invisible to us, but the distorted shadow that ranged through that setting sacred to forgotten ancient gods was charged with energy. It stooped, knelt, crouched, and crawled on hands and knees to peruse the soggy ground. It underwent sudden magnification as it approached us, and it disappeared completely when it moved to the far side of the ruins. Objects a foot from the nose could be seen well enough, and Sherlock Holmes investigated all of the ground within the sacred stone circle from that distance. He moved swiftly and silently, turning abruptly, halting, starting again, muttering an uninterrupted monologue that the mist blanketed.

The rain hadn't affected the sheltered footprints. He examined them with care and performed his own meticulous inspection of the ground nearby. Then he broke a twig from the bush, prodded with it, and picked up something that he brought to show me after he had washed it off in the stream: a shining new florin.

"Your murderers must have had a long wait, Porter," he said. "They had to arrive very early so Glyn Huws wouldn't see their approach. The one with the round-toed clogs was nervous. He shifted his position frequently and played with the coins in his pocket. He dropped this one. Then he stepped on it and almost buried it. Who in Wales could lose two shillings without noticing?"

"Only an Englishman," Madryn said bitterly.

"You were right about his clogs being new," Sherlock Holmes went on. "The irons aren't worn at all."

He followed me about while I described for him the features of that gloomy hollow that the mist was obscuring. "Everyone agrees that Glyn Huws had no reason to come here," I said.

Sherlock Holmes shook his head. "That logic is faulty, Porter. Rather you should say he wouldn't have come here without a reason. Since he did come, he must have had one. The most likely explanation is that he came to meet someone. In this barren country, the ruins of St. Celyn's church provide one of the few places for a rendezvous that is readily identifiable. It is also a place of concealment. That is extremely suggestive. A meeting in the open could have been spied upon from miles away. Huws, or the other party — or both of them — wanted to meet secretly. Of course that suited the murderers' purpose, also."

"Wasn't his rendezvous with the murderers?" I asked.

"Either that, or the person he planned to meet with was in league with them. They certainly knew in advance that he was coming." There were times when my mind didn't function alertly enough for him, and he resorted to his own form of catechism to guide me. "Now we must ask ourselves why Glyn Huws would consent to come to this desolate and remote place for a secret meeting."

"Not for idle chatter about the market price of sheep," I said. "The reason must have seemed important to him."

"Exactly. Let's assume that someone offered to tell him something he wanted to know. What kind of information would have been important enough to entice him here?"

I shook my head.

"What was the one matter that concerned him above all others at that moment?" Sherlock Holmes persisted.

"Emeric Tromblay's courtship of his daughter."

"Then it is possible, even probable, that someone offered to tell him something about Meleri — or, more likely, about Emeric Tromblay's plot against her. Who would be in a position to do that? Surely not one of the villagers. If a villager could have offered such information, Huws wouldn't have come here to meet him. They could have talked confidentially in a back room of a shop. It had to be someone he wouldn't normally be meeting. Very likely it was someone who didn't dare to be seen with him."

"One of Tromblay's employees," I suggested.

Sherlock Holmes nodded. "Perhaps a farmhand who had seen or overheard something or could reasonably claim to have done so. Huws would accept the necessity to meet him as secretly as possible. He even walked to this meeting because a horse would have made it difficult to arrive here unseen. No doubt he chose a path that was as secure as possible from prying eyes — and thus neatly played into the hands of the murderers."

"Then it must have been a trap from the beginning," I said.

"I fear so, Porter. The murderers took advantage of his concern for his daughter to lure him to this evil place. Why he came here, and how he was killed, are clear enough. Why the murderers wanted him dead is another matter entirely. That is the key to our puzzle, but no amount of conjecture will illuminate it until we accumulate more data."

Madryn sputtered an objection. He didn't like to hear St. Celyn's church called evil.

"It certainly was an evil place for Glyn Huws," Sherlock Holmes said, smiling at him. "How would St. Celyn react to the profaning of his holy church with a murder?"

"He would invoke a terrible retribution."

"Let's hope he has done so. A crime committed secretly in this desolate place may be beyond the reach of any human agency."

Sherlock Holmes dipped a handful of water from the Holy Well and tasted it thoughtfully. Then he tidied his clothing, removing the mud stains he had acquired during his investigation.

We remounted and made our way back down the steep slope to the valley, one shadowy figure on a horse following another, and we rode slowly toward Tynewydd. Somewhere far above the mist, the sun was ascending toward noon, but no evidence of its progress reached us.

I expected Sherlock Holmes to call on Kyle Connor in his character of Haggart Batt, the wandering horse dealer. Instead, he sent in a note from the vicar, and a moment later Connor met us at the head of the stairs in his wheeled chair, cheerfully shook hands with us, and made us welcome.

"So you're a chess player," he said to Sherlock Holmes. "Are you a Londoner, too?"

"Never been near the place," Sherlock Holmes said glibly. "Cardiff and Bristol are my main orbits, but I range through the west country as far north as Scotland. Not *into* Scotland, mind you. I learned early that dealing in anything at all is a waste of time in Scotland. The only loose shillings a man finds there are the ones he carries with him."

"Haggart Batt — that's certainly a strange name."

"A remote ancestor of mine was a cudgel maker," Sherlock Holmes said. "We've been handy men in a brawl ever since."

"I can believe that," Connor said with an appraising look at his sinewy form. "Are you part Welsh?"

"Not in any noticeable amount. Just a bit here and there for leavening."

Connor tilted his head back and laughed heartily. "A horse dealer and a chess player. That's a combination I've never encountered. Do you object to a game before lunch?"

"There's nothing else going in this mist," Sherlock Holmes said. "And there's no better way to pass the time."

Connor nodded approvingly. "Very true. Would you young gentlemen care to watch, or would you prefer to make use of my library?"

We chose the library. Connor had a fascinating collection of books, but the chess game went on for more than two hours, and as midday approached and passed, the library failed to divert our attention from the fact that we were hungry. Enthusiastic sounds from the chess table suggested that the game might continue all afternoon.

Suddenly there was a crash followed by Connor's resounding laughter. "Marvellous! Marvellous!" he exclaimed. Then he said soberly, "I will trade no horses with you, my friend. You have the Devil's touch!"

He insisted that we stay for lunch, and he and Sherlock Holmes held a lengthy discourse on breeds of horses while we ate. He was testing the alleged horse dealer in the same way he had tested me the day before.

Suddenly he turned to me. "You're very quiet today. Don't horses interest you?"

"The only ones I have dealings with are on the front ends of hansoms or four-wheelers," I said. "I suspect that most of them are rather sorry crocks, but I really don't know enough about horses to say."

"Mr. Batt knows a great deal about horses," Connor said. "How long have you known him?"

"We met for the first time last evening at the vicar's, and he invited Dafydd and me to try out two of his horses today. I almost called it off when I saw the weather, but Dafydd insists that no respectable Welshman would change his plans for a touch of mist, and here we are."

"I'm grateful to Dafydd for that insistence, but if this is only a touch of mist, I'll be able to swim from my bedroom window when one arrives in earnest."

We finished a most amicable luncheon and prepared to depart. Connor wanted to know how long the horse dealer would be staying in this part of the country, and Sherlock Holmes answered that it depended entirely on his trade. He was attempting to put a string together to sell at the Newtown Fair the last Tuesday in the month. Connor expressed the hope that this would allow him ample time to revenge that day's chess game, and he received a promise that it would.

The invalid again demonstrated his ingenious mechanism for descending and ascending the stairs, and we took our leave of him at the door.

An elderly man brought our horses. As we prepared to mount, he introduced himself as Gerwyn Pugh, the housekeeper's husband and the manager of Connor's farm, and he said apologetically, "Mrs. Pugh suggested that I speak with you gentlemen."

"Please do," Sherlock Holmes said. "If anyone asks, we can say we were talking about the horses. What is it?"

"We're worried, and we don't know what to do. Last night someone tried to break into the house."

"Indeed. Have you told Mr. Connor?"

"He laughed about it. But we're worried — someone was trying to climb up to his rooms. He's a wonderful man to work for. None of us has ever seen his like. We just don't know what to do."

Holmes told Madryn to hold our horses. "Quickly! Show us where it happened."

Mr. Pugh led us around the corner of the house and pointed. "There. He was climbing up the ivy. I sleep here." He pointed. "I thought I heard something, and with the mist so heavy I was worried about thieves, so I came down to do a turn around the house. And I saw him climbing up. I ran to warn Mr. Connor, but by the time I knocked him up, the thief was gone. Mr. Connor said I was seeing things and anyway all the windows were fastened and no one could get in. But I wasn't seeing things, sir. What are we to do?"

The mist was heavier near the lake, and trying to work in it was like performing an investigation in congealed soup. We scrutinized the ivy, which grew thickly up the side of the house to the first storey windows, and then Sherlock Holmes knelt to perform his customary search for footprints. There was nothing to see in the grass, but in the soft earth close to the foundation, he showed me a complete hand print, as though someone had knelt or crouched there to look into a low window — except that there was no window.

"You have good cause for alarm," Sherlock Holmes told Mr. Pugh soberly. "Say nothing at all to Mr. Connor, but you can reassure Mrs. Pugh. I will have someone watch the house tonight to see whether the thief returns."

The old man brightened. "I'll tell her. Thank you."

"By the by — do you remember the day Glyn Huws was murdered.

"I'll never forget that day," Mr. Pugh said darkly.

"Did you or any of your help see anyone going in the direction of Llangelyn on that day or coming from there?"

"No, sir. The police asked us that. We saw nothing." He added apologetically, "People rarely come to this valley. We weren't looking for anything."

"It is sometimes difficult to see something one isn't looking for," Sherlock Holmes agreed. "You'll have help tonight."

We mounted and rode away.

"What do you make of it, Porter?" Sherlock Holmes asked.

"There was no one climbing on that ivy," I said. "It wouldn't hold a man."

"Someone was climbing, nevertheless. You were standing on the wrong side of the window. There is an iron bar affixed to the house. The ivy conceals it."

"I saw it," I said. "I couldn't imagine anyone climbing it."

"I couldn't imagine an ordinary thief climbing it, but there is much about this case that is extraordinary. We are dealing with a monstrous conspiracy, Porter. It is putting out tentacles all over Wales and even into England. It is managed so cleverly that whenever it is scrutinized, it takes on an innocuous guise like the Robert Owen Study League. I still have no clue as to what is planned, but the head of it is here — I am certain of that."

"Here — at Tynewydd?"

"Here in this part of Wales — at Newtown, or Tregynon, or Llanfair or Carno or Caersws or Llanidloes or Pentrederwydd. Draw a circle enclosing all of those places. Somewhere inside it the master conspirator lurks."

"Isn't this an odd location for him — a quiet mountain area and remote country towns and villages?"

"This quiet area has a most unquiet history, Porter. It was the centre of one of the Chartist riots. The Chartists were demanding governmental reforms shortly before the middle of the last century. There was much discontent among unemployed textile workers in Newtown and Llanidloes — just as there is today. At one point the protests changed to open revolt, and the Chartists took over the town of Llanidloes. They held it for a week, and the army had to send infantry to restore order."

"What about the Rebeccas?" I asked.

He shook his head. "Your Rebeccas are almost an incongruity. Most of that activity took place in the south — in Carmarthenshire and Pembrokeshire."

"If Connor is the head of the conspiracy, how do you account for the Rebeccas watching his house and perhaps trying to break in?"

"I don't. I couldn't attempt it without knowing what role Connor is playing and what role the Rebeccas are playing. The possibility remains that both are pursuing private ends and neither has any connection with our case. Try to get some sleep as soon as we reach Pentrederwydd. You two will have to watch Tynewydd together tonight. I must catch the late afternoon train to Barmouth, but I'll return tomorrow, and then perhaps we can plan."

Madryn said gloomily, "I must write a poem. A tribute to Eleanor Tromblay. I wonder what Emeric Tromblay's guests would say if I informed them in

Welsh that she was murdered. Probably the few who understood me would think they'd misunderstood."

"I have no doubt that an announcement of murder in Welsh would make a full-throated proclamation," Sherlock Holmes said. "How would you say it?"

"Cafodd ei llofruddio."

Sherlock Holmes beamed at him. "Splendid! But it would be premature to make use of it on Saturday. Save it for another occasion. It will be much more effective later on."

14

THE THICK MIST SWIRLED AROUND US ALL THE WAY back to Pentrederwydd. I remarked that we would have to find a place close to the farmhouse to watch from if we were to surprise the thief in another attempt at Tynewydd.

"Very close," Sherlock Holmes agreed. "You must concentrate on the west side, the lake side of the house. I promise you that no attempt will be made from the road or the farmyard. If you do see something, don't interfere immediately. Watch until you know for certain what is happening."

He rode with us as far as Madryn's house. Dafi was given the proud responsibility, along with sixpence for wages, for returning Madryn's and my horses to their pasture. Sherlock Holmes started at once for the railway halt. He planned to leave his horse at Y Llew Côch until he returned.

I climbed up to my loft and tried to sleep. Madryn went to the house to work on his poem. The next two hours were unproductive for both of us. I finally gave up and returned to the house where I found Madryn pacing fretfully. His problem was not due to any unworthiness on the part of Eleanor Tromblay, he hurried to explain. She had been a thoroughly good woman. Not only did she help the unfortunate, but she often attempted to mitigate the harm that her husband had done.

Sometimes she even succeeded. It was the idea of a tribute in Welsh for an English audience that frustrated him.

"But you shouldn't write your Welsh tribute for an English audience," I protested. "You should write it for an unfortunate Welsh family that Eleanor Tromblay helped. It is people like that who have lost the most."

"Emeric Tromblay wouldn't care for that. He likes the fanciest of languages and metres."

"That explains your difficulty. You're trying to write for someone who is more interested in form than content. Write it for that unfortunate Welsh family and make certain that it expresses what they would like to hear. You may find that this is also what Emeric Tromblay would like to hear."

He doubtfully made a renewed effort. I sat in the kitchen with the two Madryn daughters and tried to learn Welsh words for the various objects we could see there. "Beth ydy hwn, what is this? Cadair ydy hwn, this is a chair. Llyfr ydy hwn, this is a book. Cannwyll ydy hwn, this is a candle. Llwy ydy hwn, this is a spoon." It kept them highly entertained and actually taught me a few words.

We were in no hurry to reach Tynewydd that night. We were confident that any intruder would have the good sense to wait until the entire household was asleep. When darkness came on, we went together to Yr Hen Dafarn, the Old Tavern, to see whether anything could be learned there. I was surprised to find the place crowded. A thick mist couldn't keep these Welshmen from beer and good company.

The moment we stepped inside the door, Ifan Vaughan raised a hand and waved to us. We joined him; he jerked his head in the direction of the far corner of the room and announced, "That's him."

"That's who?" I asked, turning to look.

"The one I told you about. His clogs have square toes. And fish crimped on them. He says his name is Rhys Parry. He is Jac Parry's cousin."

It was the man with the reddish hair and beard.

"Where does he come from?" I asked.

"Don't know," Vaughan said. "He don't talk much."

"I'll try to find out," Madryn said.

He joined the group at Rhys Parry's table, leaving me with Vaughan. I listened absently to what the shoe and clogmaker was saying and kept my eyes on Rhys Parry. His companions were talking in Welsh, which he certainly understood, but he took no part in the conversation. He morosely sipped his beer and let his gaze wander from one end of the ceiling to the other as though he found the hams dangling there more interesting than the talk.

Vaughan said to me proudly, "Your boots are finished."

"Wonderful! I need them."

"You do," he agreed, looking scornfully at my wet city shoes.

"I'll pick them up tomorrow."

"Better take them tonight," he said. "When you're ready to leave, I'll come with you."

Out of the welter of conversation in the corner, I caught the mention of my name, Iorwerth Jones. Madryn turned and called, "Join us, Iori." Others motioned to me or said in English, "Join us." I took my leave of Vaughan — quietly thanking him for his detective work — and then, because there were no more chairs at that table, I took my chair with me. Room was made for me.

"We were talking about the places we were born," Madryn said to me. "In Wales, many people live close to their birthplaces all of their lives. Does that happen in London?"

"I'm sure it does for a great many people," I said. "A man is born in a certain district, he attends school there, he finds a job nearby, he meets his wife there, they're married there, and all of his children are born there. If he moves, it will be to a similar dwelling three streets away."

"The same applies to me. I was born in Pentrederwydd, I met my wife here, we were married here, and all of our children were born here." Madryn said suddenly to Rhys Parry. "Where were you born?"

"Bangor," Parry said.

That caused a murmur of surprise around the table. I turned to Parry with frank interest. "That's on the Menai Strait, isn't it? I've heard that it's a beautiful city. I'd like to visit it. It has both a cathedral and a university."

Parry shrugged indifferently. "The university is a piddling thing. In a hotel, they keep it. Bangor isn't much of a city, either. It's more like a big town, but the sea air makes it a healthy place to live."

He lapsed into silence, and we got nothing more from him but monosyllables. He and his companions, a group of farm-hands, had walked all the way from the head of the valley to have their beer. At intervals they good-naturedly damned the mist. Eventually he left with them.

We left immediately afterward. Vaughan fitted me with my new boots, which felt superbly comfortable. Then we went for our ponies, and I took my city shoes, which had been uncomfortably wet, up to the loft to dry when I went there to change my socks. Madryn knew of a convenient grove of trees just past the turning to Meini Mawr, the Huws farm, where we could leave the ponies, and this made it possible for us to ride most of the way. The mist remained heavy, and we didn't have to worry about prying eyes.

Gerwyn Pugh was watching for us. As we crept and fumbled about looking for a hiding place close to the house, he came out and showed us a shed where he had already placed straw to make us comfortable. By merely sticking our heads out, we could view the narrow stretch of ground between house and lake and see the entire side of the house that the intruder had attempted the night before.

In a niwl such as this one, the words "view" and "see" were exaggerations. The "smoke from hellish stews" produced the blackest of black nights. An army could have paraded between the lake and the house unseen — but not unheard. Sounds seemed distorted and yet peculiarly amplified. If anyone tried to approach the house, I was convinced that I would hear him.

The chill, damp night of waiting that I anticipated had become one of unexpected cosiness. We settled ourselves in the shed and took turns sleeping and — since there could be no watching — listening alertly.

Nothing happened. We would have passed a comfortable, peaceful night had it not been for an owl that hooted regularly somewhere nearby. Its cry resembled the signal used by the Rebeccas two nights before, and when I first heard it, I thought they had returned. Madryn assured me that it was genuine, and he stirred uneasily each time that strange, unearthly cry sounded. To the Welsh, the persistent screeching of an owl near a house foretold the death of someone living there.

When I protested to Madryn that he was slandering a useful bird that helped farmers by catching harmful rodents, he quoted a poem by Dafydd ap Gwilym: "'Large-headed, wide-browed, berry-bellied, hag-eyed old mouse-catcher.' It is a bird of evil omen."

But it brought no evil on that night. During my watches, I gazed into the blackness and thought about the fair-haired boy, Alban Griffiths. I wondered if he were hiding somewhere nearby and trying to peer through that same thick mist. Unless he had a vantage point closer to the house than ours — in which case either we or Mr. Pugh would have heard him arrive — he was doomed to see nothing at all. What was he doing when he wasn't watching Tynewydd? He certainly had a role to play in this mystery. I wanted to find out how he spent his time in that lonely roost high above the valley.

Then there was his companion, Rhys Parry. No court would convict the red-bearded man merely because his clogs chanced to be the same shape as those of a murderer, and yet I felt certain that he had killed Glyn Huws. What conceivable motive could he have had for brutally crushing the skull of that worthy citizen unless Emeric Tromblay had hired him to do it?

But if Tromblay had hired him, why was Parry still here? A stranger who commits a murder for pay can be depended upon to leave the moment the deed is done. He doesn't linger in the vicinity for weeks to excite curiosity and suspicion.

Finally dawn came, bringing the promise of a much brighter day. The mist seemed to be breaking up; the glow in the east actually suggested the sun. Mrs. Pugh sent us her thanks along with a lavish breakfast. We gave her elderly husband the welcome news that we would be back again that night, probably, and we left without Connor knowing that his house had been guarded.

On our ride back to Pentrederwydd, I spoke to Madryn about Alban Griffiths and Rhys Parry. "Are they both staying with Jac Parry?" I asked.

"I don't know," Madryn said. "Since Rhys is Jac's cousin, I would expect him to stay there."

"Do Jac and Gwen talk freely about their guests?"

"I don't recall either of them saying anything at all except for a few remarks Gwen made when the boy first came here."

"They may have been asked — or told — not to say anything," I said. "I don't remember seeing another farm nearby. Is there one?"

"There are two, but they aren't very near." Madryn described them. One was much farther down the slope, and the other was a considerable distance toward Pentrederwydd. In that part of Wales, however, they were close enough to be considered neighbours. "Why do you ask?"

For one thing, I was curious to know how the boy spent his time. For another, I wanted to know what Rhys Parry's presence implied. Was he a regular visitor? Was he employed somewhere in the area or was he looking for work? Did anyone except the Parrys know him or know anything about him?

Madryn pondered all of this with a frown. I told him I was aware that watching an isolated house on a mountainside surrounded only by pasture and a bit of farmland would be a difficult proposition. "Not really," he said. "Just to start with, we'll have a talk with one of the neighbours."

We did that on our way back to Pentrederwydd. Charles Evans, who had the farm below the Parrys, was in his pasture milking his cows when we arrived. The mist had thinned somewhat, but we still had difficulty in finding him. Madryn introduced me and then spoke with him at length in Welsh. Finally they shook hands.

Evans came over and shook hands with me. He said in English, speaking slowly and fumbling for the words, "Glyn Huws my good friend."

Glyn Huws had been his life-long friend. The mere suggestion that Rhys Parry had been involved in Huws's murder was enough to make him watch the activity around the Parry farm relentlessly.

"And he'll hold his tongue," Madryn said as we rode away. "His three farm-hands have been with him for years, and they're reliable, too. He was already curious about the Parrys' guests. Now he and his men will keep as close a watch as they can, and they'll try to pump Jac Parry for information. Jac has never been one to hold his tongue. And Evans will have one of his men watch the Parry farm at night a few times just to see whether there are any peculiar comings and goings."

I glanced up the slope toward the distant, tiny house. It was still lost in the mist, but I knew how far away it was. "I am afraid that their close watch will be rather remote," I said.

"Not as remote as you would think. Very little happens in this valley that Evans and his men aren't aware of."

Madryn was not on the friendliest of terms with the other neighbour, so he'd asked Evans to find out whether the man knew anything. We returned to Pentrederwydd, had another breakfast, and went to bed.

When I awoke, Madryn showed me a note he had received from his friend John Davies, whom we had commissioned to search Newtown for traces of Alban Griffiths and Rhys Parry. Davies had not seen either of them at the Wednesday Robert Owen meeting or anywhere else, and no one had been able to tell him anything about them.

Their only public appearance seemed to have been at the meeting we attended.

I was hoping that Davies might supply a clue in another puzzle that was bothering me — the Robert Owen Study League's connection with Pentrederwydd. Alban Griffiths and Rhys Parry formed a link; Benton Tromblay formed a link. Neither link told me anything at all.

Madryn and I went down to Yr Hen Dafarn, drank beer, and listened to the local gossip in Welsh with him whispering translations for me. It was not even titillating gossip. The carpenter's wife had refused to serve on a church committee with the baker's wife; two village feuds had been caused by barking dogs; and a major scandal had erupted around Edwyn Thomas, the landlord of the temperance house, Y Fuwch Frêch. He'd lost a new rake. He said it was stolen, and he accused his neighbour, Dafydd Bevan, the blacksmith. The blacksmith told Thomas he was welcome to any new rake he could find on his premises and added that if Thomas stopped carelessly leaving his property lying about, he would experience fewer thefts. This had seemed like a promising squabble until Thomas's wife heard about it. She'd lent the rake to another neighbour. Now Thomas wasn't speaking to his wife, and he'd refused to apologize to Bevan because, he said bitterly, the blacksmith certainly would have stolen the rake if given half a chance.

I'd heard enough, and so had Madryn. Obviously Pentrederwydd was an unnaturally moral village. I'd never imagined that an hour of gossip could be so devoid of interest.

Sherlock Holmes returned on the afternoon train. As befitted a horse dealer, he arrived riding his own horse and leading two more that he had acquired somewhere along the way. He listened attentively while I told him about the appearance of Rhys Parry and his square-toed clogs at Yr Hen Dafarn. Then he asked me to repeat it, and he wanted to know the exact words Parry used in describing his birthplace.

I asked him whether he'd found anything interesting in Barmouth.

"Another Friendly Society," he said. He turned to Madryn with a smile. "I do declare, Dafydd, that Wales is the world's most fertile soil for societies and clubs."

"The Friendly Societies couldn't have anything to do with this," Madryn said. "All of the groups I know about are old and highly respectable."

"They are that," Sherlock Holmes agreed. "Many of them date back to the early years of the last century. Some call themselves Friendly Societies. Some have fancy names like 'Grand Select Lodge of Druids.'"

Madryn nodded. "Cyfrinfa Fawr Dethol y Derwyddon."

"They seem to function principally as temperance and mutual assistance associations, but most of them also provide social and educational activities for their members."

Madryn nodded again. "They couldn't have anything to do with this."

"Perhaps not," Sherlock Holmes said. "But all across Wales, Friendly Societies are arranging to sponsor meetings of the Robert Owen Study League."

"Why not?" Madryn asked. "It would be a worth-while activity."

"On the basis of your own experience, would you be willing to testify that the Robert Owen Study League is concerned with nothing more sinister than the sponsorship of innocuous educational lectures?"

"Of course."

"That," Sherlock Holmes said, "is the problem. Every witness I've been able to interview says the same thing. Every piece of evidence I can collect is a testimonial to the virtues of the Robert Owen Study League. And yet — I'm convinced that there is something wrong here. Our antagonist has an astonishing resourcefulness, Porter. I haven't been able to decide whether he possesses a powerful intellect or merely a crafty one."

"Crafty," I said. "And given to unnecessary elaboration."

Sherlock Holmes shook his head. "You're thinking about the manoeuvre in the Petticoat Lane Market. It seemed unnecessary, but it may have been a rehearsal, a preparation for a time when elaborate subterfuge will be essential to his survival. Whatever our adversary's intellect, he certainly has a profound genius for organization and planning."

"Another Moriarty," I suggested.

Sherlock Holmes shook his head soberly. "This man plots goals that Moriarty wouldn't have dreamed of." He turned to Madryn. "Who in your neighbourhood has the intellect and the resourcefulness to organize a massive conspiracy that extends throughout Wales? He also has the money to finance it. Who could it be? My friend, the vicar?"

"The vicar isn't rich, and he's a muddled organizer," Madryn said. "He has difficulty keeping track of his church agenda."

"Emeric Tromblay?"

"If money is involved, he has it," Madryn said. "But a conspiracy wouldn't interest him unless it had something to do with business. He has no concern at all for politics. His friends urged him to stand for Col. Pryce-Jones's seat in Parliament. He refused. All he wants to do is run his mines and farms."

"His assistant, Wain Welling?"

"Too busy," Madryn said. "He's the one who actually runs Tromblay's farms and keeps an eye on the mine managers. He is on the move all the time dealing with one problem after another. Anyway, you said this man has money. Welling doesn't. I suspect that he's rather poorly paid. That may be why Tromblay prizes him so highly — he does excellent work for low wages. English landlords prefer Welsh farmers for the same reason. They are hardier, and they are accustomed to harsher living conditions. They can work harder and eat less without complaining."

"What about Kyle Connor?"

Madryn hesitated. "He seems to have money, and he certainly has plenty of time, but he's an invalid. Organizing a massive conspiracy that extends throughout Wales would require considerable travel, wouldn't it?"

"Surely there are other wealthy men — property owners, entrepreneurs. The Pryce-Joneses in Newtown, for example. The Royal Welsh Warehouse has made the family rich. Can you see them organizing a conspiracy?"

Madryn shook his head. "Sir Pryce was an excellent organizer. He started with a draper's shop and built an international business, but now he is elderly and in poor health. It's rumoured that his mind is affected. The Colonel is extremely busy. He's an M.P., and he manages his father's business. The other sons are also very much involved in the business, and their leisure time is taken up with sport — cricket in the summer and football in the winter. One is an officer in the regular army — he's rarely at home."

"Who else?" Sherlock Holmes persisted.

"There are wealthy landowners scattered through these parts, but none of them is as rich as Emeric Tromblay."

"Are any of them as wicked as Emeric Tromblay?" Sherlock Holmes persisted.

Madryn smiled. "Only when the opportunity presents itself."

"Think about it," Sherlock Holmes said. "Somewhere in this quiet part of Wales, there's a master conspirator."

By late afternoon, the niwl, the evil Welsh mist, had dispersed. The day became sunny with a scattering of white clouds in the radiant blue Welsh sky. It was difficult to believe that we'd spent the previous day and night straining to see our hands in front of our faces. I asked Sherlock Holmes if he wanted Tynewydd watched again.

"Of course," he said. "When we have so few clues, we must take advantage of every opportunity."

We went to Yr Hen Dafarn in the evening and wasted two hours there in the hope that Rhys Parry would return, but he did not. Then we left for Tynewydd with Sherlock Holmes on his favourite horse and Madryn and I riding our ponies. We left our mounts in the same grove we had used before and walked to the farm. Gerwyn Pugh was waiting for us. He again offered the use of the shed; but there was a moon with only a few scattered clouds in the night sky, and Sherlock Holmes preferred a more distant vantage point. We compromised — I used the shed, which meant that I had a close view of everything that happened between the house and the lake and could be on the scene in a few strides if quick action were called for. Madryn was placed just beyond the farm buildings, and Sherlock Holmes took up a remote post that gave him a sweeping view of the farm and also the lake shore.

There was very little wind, and the lake was quiet. The owl that disturbed us the night before had taken its haunting cry elsewhere. As the candles in the farmhouse were snuffed out one by one, and the residents retired, I thought I'd never seen a more peaceful scene.

Once the house was darkened, the watching became tedious because there was nothing to watch. Midnight approached. I stopped trying to keep track of the time because the minutes went so slowly. I may have been on the verge of dozing off when the nearby cry of an owl brought me to instant wakefulness.

I was willing to swear that no one had approached the house, but a figure clung to the bar beside the upper storey window. There was no mistaking that large head and muscular upper body. It was Kyle Connor, in his bathing dress, and he was descending. He lowered himself quickly, collapsed into an untidy heap on the grass, and then swung himself erect — with his feet in the air. He walked on his hands with amazing agility across the stretch of grass to the lake and out onto the jetty.

The boat was still moored there, and I expected him to make use of it. Instead, he lowered himself into the water without making a sound and swam away with powerful, silent strokes.

He headed directly across the lake. For a short time his head bobbed into view occasionally; for a little longer I saw the moon-flecked ripples that marked his passage; and then he was swallowed up by the darkness. I remained motionless and attempted to contend with my astonishment. I refused to believe that the master of Tynewydd had slipped out of the house in the middle of the night with no object in mind other than an innocent swim in the lake. But where could he go on his hands once he reached that desolate and overgrown shore on the far side? Would he simply turn and come back?

I watched and waited.

Suddenly I became aware of a darker shadow on the dark water. It was moving swiftly far out on the lake. There was a flash of flame followed by the sharp report of a pistol.

I sprang out of the shed and was on my way to the lake shore before the second round was fired. The report came again and again. The flashes blinded me, and for crucial seconds I could see nothing at all. Madryn also had dashed to the shore. He stood a short distance away from me on my left, and the two of us strained impotently to see through the darkness.

Farther along the shore, another gun flashed, and I knew that Sherlock Holmes was making his presence known. He fired twice more. From the lake came a loud splash and then silence. Madryn, Sherlock Holmes and I drifted together, and we continued to stare helplessly across the water.

Finally Madryn suggested that we take the boat.

"To go where?" Sherlock Holmes demanded bitterly. "To do what? If he is alive, he will have drowned or saved himself before we could locate him."

"Now we have three murders to investigate," I said. I felt angry, frustrated, despondent.

"Someone certainly made a murderous attack on Connor," Sherlock Holmes said. "As soon as he appeared outside his window, a confederate signalled with the cry of an owl. The boat set out from the opposite shore, perhaps far up the lake, and waited to ambush him."

"Are you sure it was a signal?" I asked. "Last night we heard a real owl."

"There were no feathers on the one you heard tonight," Sherlock Holmes said dryly, and Madryn agreed.

"Isn't there anything we can do?" I asked.

"Yes. We can listen — and respond to a call for help if we hear one. Otherwise, we can wait to see whether Connor returns — but that is all we can do. The boat would be useless in the darkness, and with the shore as overgrown as it is, we can do nothing on land until morning. If he doesn't come back, we'll look for him as soon as it is light."

The pistol shots had alarmed the house. Candles were lit, and faces appeared in the windows, but both lake and shore must have looked peaceful. Suddenly there was a scream. "Y tylluan! Y tylluan! The owl! The owl!" Mrs. Pugh had discovered that Connor was missing, and she remembered the warning cries of the owl the night before.

There was no further sleep at Tynewydd that night. While we maintained a vigil on the shore, the entire household waited anxiously inside. Finally dawn came with no sign of the master's return.

When there was light enough to satisfy Sherlock Holmes, he said grimly, "Now we must make an attempt to decipher last night's events. They seemed dramatic enough at the time — but were they high tragedy or low farce?"

15

MADRYN HAD NEVER SET FOOT IN ANY KIND OF water craft smaller than a canal boat, on the Montgomeryshire Canal that ran down to Newtown from Llangollen, so I did the sculling, Sherlock Holmes sat in the bow and directed me, and Madryn perched in the stern and waited uneasily for someone to tell him what to do. We moved slowly, circling the lake shore so closely that I often scraped bottom and had to punt with one of the sculls while Sherlock Holmes scrutinized the tangled thicket and looked for any evidence at all that Kyle Connor had dragged himself from the lake.

All of our movements could be watched from the heights around us and studied in detail with a telescope. My detective sagacity had been developed on the London streets, and I knew to a fine hair how best to conceal myself there and avoid being observed. I felt strangely exposed and uneasy moving about a Welsh valley where unseen observation posts spanned the horizon and nothing could be done about them.

We began our search at the south end of the lake just beyond the place where Sherlock Holmes had positioned himself the night before. When anything looked the least irregular, I grounded the boat in my attempt to force it as close to the overgrown shore as possible — and had considerable difficulty in freeing it afterward.

We progressed in this manner until we reached a point almost opposite Connor's jetty. There we found unmistakable indications that someone had pushed through the thick brush. On several leaves there were smears of blood that still looked moist in the early morning dew.

We landed some distance away and forced a passage through the thicket to the shore side, and Sherlock Holmes performed his usual meticulous search over a wide area along the lake. He moved swiftly and silently, his face distorted with concentration. Sometimes he halted and cast about like a dog searching for a scent. I followed at a distance to perform my own search. Madryn hung back to keep out of our way.

Close to the point where we found blood marks, there were horse droppings — evidence of a lengthy wait.

"Did either of you hear horses last night?" Sherlock Holmes asked us.

"Not I," I said, and Madryn shook his head.

"Nor did I, but we should have heard them easily across the water. Did you notice that there are no hoofprints, not even where the ground is soft?"

"Muffled hoofs," I suggested.

"That's how I read it. Someone was waiting for Connor with horses. Because of the quantity of droppings, I make it at least two people with three horses. After Connor was attacked, he reached the shore wounded, and his friends helped him onto a horse and carried him away."

I pushed into the thicket and tried to make my own reconstruction of what had happened at the water's edge. I found footprints at the rim of the lake — shoeprints rather than clogprints, which seemed significant to me. Two men had been waiting for Connor, and they waded into the water to assist the wounded man when he reached shore. Connor had been barefoot, and he dragged his shrivelled legs when his friends pulled him to safety.

"How badly was he wounded?" Sherlock Holmes asked.

"According to the amount of blood, not seriously," I said. "That seems surprising considering the number of shots fired. Of course, he may have lost a deal of blood in the lake."

"It isn't that easy to hit a man in the water, Porter. He was a strong swimmer, and he probably dived the moment he sensed danger. That saved his life. In any event, he was able to reach his friends, and they took him away. Now let's see whether the attacker has left us any clues."

We continued our search of the lake shore, looking for evidence that a boat had been beached or hidden. We would have overlooked it completely had it not been for Sherlock Holmes's sharp eyes, and so cleverly was it concealed that he almost missed it. We had passed the place, and he chanced to see the dim outline of a dark object when he looked back. I pushed the bow close to the bank, and he reached into the thicket and hauled out the strangest looking craft I had ever seen.

"A coracle!" Sherlock Holmes exclaimed. "Of course — it would be a coracle. Are they much in use on the lakes of mid-Wales?"

"I've never seen one here," Madryn said. "I don't understand how it could have been brought here without causing comment."

"It was made somewhere nearby," Sherlock Holmes said. "Its wood is new."

The craft was constructed of pitch-soaked canvas stretched over a wood frame. It was not circular but had an oddly fluctuating shape: One end almost blunt, the other rounded, the sides slightly indented. There was a border of wickerwork around the top. Woven laths of willow and hazel formed sides and bottom, and there was a single seat. Despite the overwhelming contempt that I felt for a would-be murderer who had ambushed an unarmed swimmer, I nevertheless experienced a grudging admiration for the man who ventured onto a dark lake in that frail craft and fired a pistol from it. I told Madryn I would feel safer riding in a boat made of egg shells.

"This type of craft has a venerable history," Sherlock Holmes said. "Its design hasn't changed since the ancient Britons used it. Look!"

One of Sherlock Holmes's bullets had cut through the end of the coracle, leaving two holes. "Probably my other shots missed completely," he said regretfully. "But this one chased him overboard. It may have saved Connor's life. Do you have your notebook, Porter?"

He wanted a careful sketch made of the coracle. While I measured and drew it to scale, he and Madryn discussed what to do with it. An observer on the western rim of the valley might not be able to see us along the western shore because of the thicket. We would be invisible as long as we towed the coracle close to shore, but if we moved out into the lake, we would be observed at once.

I said impatiently, "What difference does it make? He'll know we took it the moment he discovers it's gone."

"I'm doubtful that anyone will return for it," Sherlock Holmes said. "It's served its murderous purpose. If someone does come, he won't know for certain that *we* took it. He may think Connor's friends returned. Any element of uncertainty will work to our advantage."

When I finished my sketch, we towed the coracle for some distance along the shore and concealed it in the thicket a short distance from the place where

Kyle Connor's friends had waited. Only a meticulous search with a boat could have located it.

We returned to Tynewydd, where we found Mrs. Pugh waiting for us triumphantly. "The master has sent a note," she announced.

She showed it to us. Connor had written, in an odd, sprawling hand, "Friends brought a message late last night, and I had to leave at once because of a business emergency. I didn't want to disturb you. I'm confident that you and your husband will have no difficulty in managing the farm during my absence. I'll write again as soon as I know how long I'll be gone."

"Is this his handwriting?" Sherlock Holmes asked.

"Certainly," Mrs. Pugh said. "I should know it. I have seen it often enough."

Sherlock Holmes returned the note to her. "I'm pleased that we are able to write a pleasant ending to last night's adventure."

Mrs. Pugh was radiantly pleased. The gunshots, the cries of the owl were forgotten. She returned to the house. Mr. Pugh had brought our horse and ponies to the farm. We mounted them and started for Pentrederwydd.

"Connor must have found a refuge close at hand," Sherlock Holmes said as we rode along. "I wonder whether he'll stay there or travel farther. A question or two at Y Llew Côch would be in order."

"Did you suspect that Mr. Pugh's supposed burglar was Connor returning home after a night's outing?" I asked him.

"I *knew* that it was Connor," Sherlock Holmes said. He pulled his horse to a sudden halt and turned to me. Madryn and I also halted. "Don't tell me that you didn't!" he exclaimed.

I gazed at him blankly.

"Porter!" he said sternly. "You shook Connor's hand twice in my presence — when we arrived at Tynewydd and when we left. Probably you shook it twice more when you visited him the day before. Do you mean to tell me you didn't notice how unusually callused it was?"

"Oh, that," I said. "I thought that propelling his chair — "

"You did *not* think. That chair is a marvel of engineering. He can propel it with his fingers. Only strenuous labour involving long periods of friction would toughen the skin of his hands to that extent, and where would an invalid be performing strenuous labour? And what did you make of the hand print? Only a person walking on his hands could have left it there."

"I didn't think," I agreed.

Sherlock Holmes snorted.

We separated in Pentrederwydd, and Sherlock Holmes rode on to Groesffordd. When he returned, he stopped on his way to the vicarage to tell us what he had learned. The crippled Connor would have been highly conspicuous, but no one of his description had been seen boarding a train.

Madryn had completed his poetic tribute to Eleanor Tromblay. He asked if he could borrow my loft to rehearse his performance. I said in surprise, "I've lost track of the days. Today *is* Saturday, is it not? And tonight you have to perform."

I strolled down to the centre of the village, where I decided to try the temperance house, Y Fuwch Frêch, instead of Yr Hen Dafarn. The venture was not a success. Without Madryn, I was an unknown stranger. The other patrons spoke only Welsh and that in hushed voices as though they suspected me of eavesdropping. They kept directing suspicious glances at me.

I returned to Madryn's home. Mairwen and the children had gone to work in a field they rented higher up the mountain. I had the house to myself. I tried to learn some Welsh from a Welsh-English dictionary and found it difficult going. I abandoned that, finally, and considered the various pieces of the puzzle we were working on and how they might fit together — which seemed even more difficult than Welsh. I couldn't work Kyle Connor into our puzzle at all, but someone had considered him important enough to murder.

Madryn came and recited his poem. He delivered it very well, but it was all Welsh to me. "I took your advice," he said. "I described the simple goodness of Eleanor Tromblay. She did kind things. She helped people. There was no one like her. Now there is no one."

"Excellent," I said. "Even if Tromblay would prefer something more ornate, he won't dare to complain."

At a quarter after seven we left for Tromblay Hall on our ponies, timing ourselves to arrive about eight. Two carriages and several traps passed us as we plodded along. We took the turning that led to the Hall and rode through the long shadows of a pleasant valley to reach a gate house and then a cluster of farm buildings. Finally, after skirting a large pond, we came first to a formal garden and then to a sprawling black and white mansion.

A groom took our ponies. An English butler greeted us by name and welcomed us. Several familiar faces were already present in the library where the guests were gathering: Emeric Tromblay, whose stylish brown suit proclaimed the end of his formal mourning; the Reverend Ezekiel Browne, along with his old friend and house guest, Haggart Batt; and Pentrederwydd's doctor.

I had caught occasional glimpses of Dr. Davis Morrow, a wizened, spry little man, as he flitted about Pentrederwydd visiting patients. He lived in Groesffordd. His professional visits to Kyle Connor and the residents of the Hall brought him down the valley regularly, and the people of Pentrederwydd benefited greatly from this. He only called on them in passing; but since he was, by all reports, a conscientious physician, the care that they received was as good as that given to his wealthy patients.

The others were strangers except for Wain Welling, whom I hadn't seen since Newtown other than for the fleeting encounter in the mist. Like us, Welling must have felt completely out of place at this stodgy gathering. It wouldn't have occurred to Emeric Tromblay to introduce us to his proper guests nor did they expect it. Seeing us standing off to one side, tolerated but ignored, they knew we were Welsh — scorned outsiders in our own country as far as money and society were concerned.

I was accustomed to this. As the son of an impoverished widow, I was an outsider in the London social and financial worlds except when my status as Sherlock Holmes's assistant gained entry for me on any level up to the very highest. When this occurred, a genuine though grudging respect was accorded to me — not for what I was but for what I could do. Its measure was the urgency with which a wealthy or titled personage needed Sherlock Holmes's help.

The extremely capable Wain Welling possessed a similar status. If his master needed him for anything at all, he was available. Otherwise, he stood to one side, observing the proceedings like the outsider he was and taking no part in them unless specifically invited to do so. His slightly bemused expression suggested that he found all of this deliciously entertaining.

It was Madryn who felt his subservient status the most acutely. He was not only a poet but an impecunious poet. He also was a Welsh poet performing before an English audience that would have looked down its collective noses at him even if he hadn't been conspicuously accepting charity from an English patron.

Wain Welling came over to join us. "Are you making any progress with Welsh?" he asked me.

"Cadair ydy hwn, this is a chair," I said. "But I haven't yet learned how to sit down."

He laughed merrily. "There's a Welsh proverb, 'Dyfal donc a dyrr y garreg,' constant tapping will break the stone. You must keep at it."

"I shall. But I can't avoid the feeling that the Welsh language is full of words that were not intended to be spoken."

Laughing again, he led us over to one of the bookshelves and took down a small volume entitled, *A Collection of Welsh Travels and Memoirs of Wales,* by one John Torbuch. It had been published in 1749.

He turned pages until he found the passage he sought. Then he read: "'That which we admir'd most of all amongst them was the *virginity* of their language, not deflower'd by the mixture of any other dialect: the purity of *Latin* was debauch'd by the *Vandals,* and was hunn'd into corruption by that barbarous people; but the sincerity of the *British* remains inviolable. 'Tis a tongue (it seems) not made for every mouth; as appears by an instance of one in our company, who having got a *Welsh polysyllable* into his throat, was almost choak'd with *consonants,* had we not, by clapping him on the back, made him *disgorge* a guttural or two, and so sav'd him.' You will note that he refers to Welsh as the British language, which of course it is — it antedates by centuries the crude tongue we now call English." He glanced across the room. "Who is the gentleman with the Vicar?"

"An old friend of his." I turned to Madryn. "What was his name? Something about a cudgel."

"Batt," Madryn said. "His ancestor was a cudgel maker."

"That was it. Haggart Batt. He's a horse dealer."

"He sounds like an odd friend for the Vicar to have," Welling said. "I wouldn't have expected it of the Reverend."

"I think they were in school together," I said. "The man certainly seems well-educated, and I hear that he plays a wicked game of chess."

"Ah — that explains it!" Welling said. "Anyone who'll play chess with the Vicar is an old friend. I wonder how educated Mr. Batt is with horses. I have one I would like to sell to him."

"If he's a genuine horse dealer, he'll give you every opportunity to do so, but be careful. He may sell several to you while you're trying." I felt confident that Sherlock Holmes would act his role to perfection.

We were joined presently by two harpists, the brothers Roberts, who came from a famous family of Newtown harpists. They had performed before Queen Victoria and had been invited to appear before King Edward and Queen Alexandra during their majesties' forthcoming visit to the Elan Valley. They called themselves Royal Welsh Harpists and viewed their own social standing as somewhat higher than that of Tromblay's English guests whom they were about to honour with their performance. They did difficult pennillion singing, the singing of accompaniments to their harp music, and they scarcely condescended to speak to Madryn, a poor poet who recited without musical support.

We Welsh, including the harpists, ate at a separate table in the vast dining room, along with several servants. The harpists performed — magnificently. They even made me think of getting myself a Welsh harp to accompany Sherlock Holmes on his violin. I wondered how he would react to the suggestion; then I decided I knew how he would react, and I didn't mention it to him.

I told Madryn that I could admire a poet without envy, but I admired and deeply envied the harpists, and I would like to be able to play.

He said, "One of the Welsh Triads declares that there are three things every man should have in his home — a virtuous wife, a cushion on his chair, and a well-tuned harp."

"What are the Welsh Triads?" I asked.

"Commentaries on a variety of subjects — history, mythology, literature, folklore, almost anything. They are always arranged in groups of three."

"Now I remember," I said. "Borrow mentions the good wife of the Triad."

Madryn nodded. "'She is modest, void of deceit, and obedient. Quick of hand, quick of eye, and quick of understanding. Her person shapely, her manners agreeable, and her heart innocent. Loving her husband, loving peace, and loving God.' The Triads can form long lists."

When his turn came, he recited his Welsh tribute to Eleanor Tromblay with evident feeling and sincerity. Emeric Tromblay's reaction was unexpected — at least by me. He sat wiping his eyes, and when Madryn finished, he asked him to repeat it.

After dinner, Welling disappeared with Mr. Haggart Batt, the horse dealer. They were gone for some time. However acrimoniously they may have debated the virtues of Welling's horse, they were talking in friendly fashion when they finally returned. Welling came over to us smiling.

"He certainly is a knowledgeable horse dealer," he told me.

"Did you sell him your horse?"

"He laughed the moment he saw it, but he may have sold me one. I'll take it if it's as described, and I think he knows horses well enough to be honest about them. That makes him a most unusual dealer."

We spent the remainder of the evening watching Emeric Tromblay's more favoured guests talk and laugh with each other. I studied them one after the other while Madryn told me all that he could remember about each of them.

There was Cedric Hodson, an immense man who weighed some twenty stone. The tailor who made his suit surely had called in a tentmaker to assist him. He had grizzled hair and a tallowy complexion, a palsy in his hands, and a stumbling waddle for a walk. His appearance epitomized a lifetime of dissipation, and Madryn thought him morally capable of any kind of iniquity. Fortunately his ruined body imposed severe limitations on his evil actions.

"But he might organize and make plans," I suggested.

"Yes," Madryn agreed. "He might do that."

Langdon Ellward was the opposite — tall, lean, and as tense as a wound spring. It was difficult to imagine him taking time to plan anything at all. He was the warrior who leaped into his saddle and flung himself on the enemy. He passed through life without posing a single question or entertaining a doubt. He kept his own pack of hounds, and he had introduced fox hunting into that part of Wales. He couldn't sit still for two minutes at a time. He kept leaping to his feet and striding back and forth. His conversation was largely concerned with horses and hounds, and he and Haggart Batt had much to say to each other.

Nolan Ivatt, a handsome, dignified, greying old man, gave most of his attention to the ladies. I couldn't see that he favoured one over the others. George Masset, a younger man, equally handsome, distributed his attentions among the younger women present. Since it was a dull party, I refrained from drawing conclusions about the behaviour of either.

There were four men who formed a group around Emeric Tromblay and spent most of the evening talking with each other. They seemed to be summarily disposing of one weighty matter after another. I made a list of their names — Ernest Lumbard, Keith Brady, Randolph Bargh, and Henry Armstead. I very much regretted my back-of-the-room status that made it impossible for me to overhear a word they were saying.

As an old friend of the vicar, Mr. Haggart Batt joined them whenever he chose and took part in their conversation. I sincerely hoped that he was collecting a few items of useful information, because the only thing I could credit to an evening's diligent observation was the fact that Emeric Tromblay was able to weep during a poetic tribute to his dead wife. I couldn't say whether this represented deep feeling or skill in acting.

As for the guests, if one of them was organizing a monstrous conspiracy that stretched tentacles throughout Wales and into England, I had no clue at all as to which one it was. I sincerely hoped that none of them was involved. We had enough suspects to deal with already.

I had no opportunity for a confidential word with Sherlock Holmes until just before we departed. I managed to stand beside him while the horses were being brought around, and he said quietly, "Emeric Tromblay numbers a prime collection of potential villains among his acquaintances, does he not? Did you find one that you favour above the others?"

"No, sir," I said. "I couldn't think of a single reason why any of them would want to murder Glyn Huws."

He looked at me searchingly. "When you have solved that riddle, Porter, you will have solved our case."

16

WE LEFT TROMBLAY HALL LONG AFTER MIDNIGHT. When we reached Pentrederwydd, we found Charles Evans, the neighbour of Jac and Gwen Parry, waiting for us. He had been waiting for hours. He spoke with Madryn in Welsh, and Madryn translated for me.

"He talked with Jac Parry, and Jac let something slip. He said his house guests were leaving on Monday."

"Did he say where they were going?" I asked.

"They're going to visit around Wales, meaning a number of places. They'll go first to Aberystwyth by train."

"I've been wanting to see Aberystwyth," I said.

"Are you thinking of trying to follow them? We'd be rather conspicuous boarding the same train with them at Groesffordd Halt, wouldn't we?"

"True enough. Now that Parry knows both of us, he might refuse to believe a coincidence like that. My idea was to go to Aberystwyth tomorrow, a day ahead of them, and follow them when they arrive."

I tried to express my appreciation to Charles Evans, but he responded with a shrug and unceremoniously set out on his long walk home. He was a friend of the murdered Glyn Huws, and he wanted to help.

On Sunday morning I sent Sherlock Holmes a note by way of Dafi, and he came to see us at once. "There is only one train on Sunday, an early one, and you have missed it," he said. "The train that reaches Groesffordd shortly before five tomorrow morning will have you in Aberystwyth at six-twenty. You must take that one and hope that our subjects decide to travel at a more reasonable hour. I recommend a commercial hotel rather than one accommodating tourists. Try the Lion Royal or the Talbot. As soon as you are settled, leave a note for me — Haggart Batt — with a tobacconist named Meredith in Great Darkgate Street, telling me where I can find you. I'll come as soon as I can."

He gave me no other instructions. For a routine chore such as this one, I needed none. Our task on Monday would be to meet every train until Parry and Griffiths arrived.

Madryn went to chapel with his family. I attended church with Haggart Batt. The Reverend Ezekiel Browne had chosen the Twenty-Third Psalm as the subject for his sermon: "The Lord is my shepherd; I shall not want." He concentrated on the not wanting. The thrust of his message seemed to be that Emeric Tromblay was Pentrederwydd's Good Shepherd, and no one was in want because of his wealth, wisdom, and generosity.

Returning to Madryn's house, I discovered that Sunday was not a day of rest for the Welsh. As soon as we had eaten, the family returned to the chapel, this time for Sunday School. In the evening, there was another service.

I did nothing, thus making certain that one of us would be rested when we reached Aberystwyth. I passed the time by strolling to the edge of the village and finding a patch of shade from which I could enjoy a lovely view of the valley. I saw nothing of interest except for a lone horseman travelling at a gallop toward Groesffordd. The railway halt could not have been his destination because there were no Sunday afternoon trains. He rode extremely well, and his horse, though no beauty with ribbons in its tail, covered the ground with ease. Haggart Batt would have said that it had little show and much substance.

I mentioned this when I saw Madryn again. He nodded. "I saw him. That was Wain Welling — in a hurry, as usual, and on his favourite horse. He is an excellent judge of horses. Tromblay lets him do all the buying except for those he wants to ride himself."

We arrived in Aberystwyth shortly after six-twenty the next morning, engaged a room at the Lion Royal, and set about seeing something of the town before the next train arrived at eleven twenty-five. We walked the length of the sloping

Great Darkgate Street and paused along the way to leave a note for Mr. Haggart Batt with Meredith the tobacconist. Turning back, we strolled along the North Parade where we all but collided with a man who emerged suddenly from a boarding house.

It was Benton Tromblay.

It was a transformed Benton Tromblay. He'd had his hair cut and bought a new suit. It was not a stylish suit — it was ready-made and didn't fit him well — but it was a decided improvement over what we'd seen him wearing in Newtown. He no longer looked like a poorly paid clerk. He had gained weight. There was in fact a smug plushness about him, as though the dinner I had treated him to only a week before had launched him on a series of banquets.

He was as startled as we were, but he was obviously delighted to see us. He wanted to know how much of Wales I'd seen and how long I'd been in Aberystwyth.

"I'm giving a lecture here tomorrow night," he said. "At the university. Can you come?" He'd already taken two passes from his pocket, and he was scribbling his initials in the centre of the woodblock *O*.

We promised to be there. We would be following Rhys Parry and Alban Griffiths from the moment they arrived in Aberystwyth, and they certainly would lead us to Benton's lecture.

We met the eleven twenty-five train; Griffiths and Parry were not on it. That left us free until after two o'clock. We walked back through the town to the beach. A long esplanade, consisting of variously named promenades and terraces and lined most of the way with hotels and boarding houses, stretched along the seafront from the harbour on the south, where the Rheidol and the Ystwyth Rivers entered the sea, to Constitution Hill on the north, a famous tourist attraction reached by the Cliff-Railway. At the approximate midpoint was the Promenade Pier with its entertainment pavilion. Nearby was the bulky building housing the University College of Wales, where Benton Tromblay was to lecture. Like the branch of the University of Wales in Bangor, this one had been established in a former hotel. A short distance to the south were the ruins of Aberystwyth Castle, a twelfth century structure that served as a Royal Mint during the Civil War until it was destroyed by Cromwell's army.

The esplanade offered a sweeping view of Cardigan Bay. It also overlooked a rather untidy beach with a row of bathing machines, a clutter of boats, and a scattering of sedately dressed tourists who seemed intent on avoiding the water. Many of the women wore white dresses and carried parasols. The men could not have been more formally attired if they had been on their way to their offices. University students, men and women, hurried past in their black gowns. The women's hall of residence was at the remote north end of Victoria Promenade near Constitution Hill. Whether or not their brains were being exercised, their feet received daily workouts.

We had left Dafydd Madryn's Wales behind us when we stepped off the train. Aberystwyth was a thriving community, much larger than Newtown and swollen with tourists. English was spoken widely. I felt completely at home there, and I was as pleased to discover that all of my instincts were functioning properly as I was exasperated to find that I needed them.

We strolled slowly along the Marine Terrace just above the beach. There were benches positioned at regular intervals, but few of them were occupied. The tide was out, and the holiday- makers preferred to sit on the sand or the bath rocks. These rocks were strange formations visible at low tide at either end of the beach. Hundreds or thousands of years of tidal action had traced peculiar patterns on them, and they looked almost like living substances. We seated ourselves on a bench for a time, and then we resumed our strolling, talking of nothing in particular except what we saw. Suddenly my instincts sounded an alarm. We were being followed.

It was a small, untidy-looking man wearing a bowler. Either he was sleeping in his suit or he owned only one and gave very little care to it. He almost trod on our heels in his effort to overhear what we were saying.

I said to Madryn, "Dafydd, I have an errand to take care of. Why don't you sit down at one of the outside tables by that tavern and order each of us a pint of cwrw. I'll join you shortly."

Madryn nodded and strode away. I turned in the opposite direction and found a group of tourists to hide myself behind. The little man stood looking after Madryn for a moment. Then he turned with a puzzled frown, squinted about to see where I had vanished to, shrugged eloquently, and walked at a brisk pace toward one of the boarding houses fronting on the sea.

I followed him. I was already angry because the case seemed to be going nowhere, and I resented having an outsider prying into my work. I acted almost without thinking. I entered the boarding house as though I belonged there and hurried up the stairs behind him. Fortunately he didn't look back. I followed him all the way to the top of the house, which I reached just in time to see him closing the door on a room numbered 18. It was a rear room. Across the hall were two doors numbered 17 and 19.

I went downstairs and sought out the landlady. "I'm looking for a room with a sea view," I told her. "What do you have available?"

Room 19 was available. Fervent negotiation was necessary before she would permit me to take it without meals. I insisted because the food would have been wasted. I certainly couldn't eat at the same table or even in the same room with the little man who had been following me. I settled the matter by paying for a week in advance and giving my name as Edward Gatward and my permanent residence as London.

Madryn was appalled about the money when I told him what I had done. The tariff of a room with a sea view in a popular watering place was something entirely outside his experience.

"Never mind," I said. "Better to waste a little money than to miss an opportunity. Mr. Holmes will readily forgive the first but never the second. Finish your beer. It's time for us to go to the station."

Griffiths and Parry finally arrived on the five forty-five train and strolled through Aberystwyth with all of the aplomb of a pair of veteran tourists, each carrying a small valise. They went directly to the Marine Terrace, where they paused at the railing along the beach to admire the sea view. Madryn and I hung back, content to watch them from a distant vantage point on Terrace Road.

A few minutes later, a small, untidy man wearing a bowler hurried toward them. He took up a position at the railing a short distance away and began to edge closer. I watched with fascination. When they walked on, the little man followed them. Madryn and I trailled after the three of them, walking on the opposite side of the street and close to the buildings.

I said to Madryn, "I wonder if he understands Welsh."

"He acts as though he understands whatever they're speaking."

"In London, they were speaking Welsh."

Griffiths and Parry were looking for an address. They found it and entered one of a row of small hotels. The little man made a note and hurried away. We watched him enter the boarding house where I had already engaged a room. Then we returned to the tavern with the outside tables, selected chairs from which we could keep an eye on both establishments, and ordered more beer.

Madryn complained bitterly that while he waited for me before, he'd asked for beer in Welsh and the waiter pretended not to understand him. "In the middle of Wales, a waiter who doesn't understand Welsh!" he said incredulously. He tried again with the same result.

"Probably he's German and never serves anyone but English tourists," I said. "The Saeson, the English, are the source of his income, so he closes his ears to the Cymry, the Welsh. Did I get that right?"

Madryn nodded glumly.

"Would you like to try an experiment?" I asked.

"What do I have to do?"

"Give me a lesson in Welsh."

It was an experiment he'd long intended to make but not under the circumstances I suggested. We rehearsed it while we finished our beer. Then we walked back to Terrace Road keeping close to the buildings, entered the Marine Terrace as though just arriving, and walked slowly along the beach with Madryn carefully pronouncing Welsh words for me and I — carelessly, I fear — repeating them.

It took the little man with the bowler less than two minutes to sight us, put his hat on, and reach the street. He came scurrying towards us and dogged our footsteps all the way to Constitution Hill and back. We paid no attention to him until I deemed the experiment a complete success and decided to terminate it. Then it was impossible to get rid of him. He followed us everywhere we went as long as we were together. Finally I sent Madryn back to the tavern and I turned in the opposite direction. When I looked again, the little man was plodding back to his boarding house.

"So he isn't trying to follow either of us," I mused. "He's only interested in eavesdropping when the two of us are together." That seemed exceedingly strange. I rejoined Madryn, and we sat sipping beer and looking out at the lovely tranquillity of Cardigan Bay. Aberystwyth was a most unlikely setting for a festering conspiracy. Women students in their black gowns walked past in groups, carrying books and chatting gaily, headed south toward the university or north toward their hall of residence. In contrast, the relaxing holiday-makers seemed to be plodding their humourless ways through lives burdened with harsh complexities.

I said to Madryn, "Have you ever attended a university?"

He shook his head.

"But you are obviously well-educated. How did you manage it?"

"Didn't Mr. Saunders tell you? When I was a child, for ten years I was a hired companion to Benton Tromblay. I went to school with him — he had a private tutor — I played with him, I even fought with him, which no one minded as long as I let him win. Emeric Tromblay took a liking to me. He always has treated me with great kindness."

"Then your early education was just as good as Benton's," I said.

"Much better," Madryn said. "He merely attended the classes; I studied and learned. He had an excellent tutor who took a special interest in me because I was a good student." He sighed. "But it ruined me as a Welsh poet."

"You're probably better educated than most of these students," I told him.

He shook his head. "Only in my early education. Since then, my learning has been unsystematic. It has blank spaces. The most important thing that a university provides is system. A haphazard education has gaps that get filled in haphazardly — if at all."

I had the impression that the gaps in his education were being dealt with very competently, and I would have told him so if Alban Griffiths and Rhys Parry hadn't emerged from their hotel at that moment. I followed their progress along the promenade while pretending to admire the beauties of Cardigan Bay, and I asked Madryn, who was facing in the opposite direction, to watch for the small man with the bowler.

"Here he is," Madryn said.

"That," I announced quietly, "is weird. How did he know that they were coming? He couldn't possibly see them from that boarding house. Anyway, his room faces the rear."

"Perhaps he's a wizard," Madryn suggested.

I turned and looked at him. "You're serious."

"Of course."

"In addition to the Tylwyth Têg, or fairies, and the corpse candles, and the prognosticating owls, and the Celtic gods, Wales also has wizards?"

"Of course it does."

"We'll have to go into this later," I said. "Mr. Holmes isn't going to believe it."

Alban Griffiths and Rhys Parry had passed us. The little man with the bowler was following them closely but learning nothing at all because they strolled along without talking. They seemed to be headed for the Promenade Pier or the castle.

Madryn got to his feet. "Shall we follow them?"

"I just thought of another experiment," I said.

We walked over to the railing above the beach, stood there for a moment, and then started after the others. Madryn resumed my language lesson. As we reached the little man's — and my — boarding house, the door opened and a boy of twelve or thirteen came hurrying out. He saw us at once, caught up with us, and followed on our heels.

He was more persistent than the man had been. He followed me for half an hour after Madryn left me. I was following the little man with the bowler, who was closely following Alban Griffiths and Rhys Parry. Finally the boy gave up, and I was able to rejoin Madryn.

I was wishing fervently that Sherlock Holmes would arrive. Whether my action in engaging a room in the little man's boarding house had been brilliant or stupid, I clearly had started more rabbits than I had hounds, and I didn't know what to do next.

Sherlock Holmes came on the last train, which arrived at nine thirty-five. I wasn't aware of that until the next morning. Madryn slept in the room we had engaged at the Lion Royal; I stayed at the boarding house and tried to peep out unnoticed any time I heard sounds that suggested activity across the hall. I got very little sleep, and Madryn awakened me early to tell me that Sherlock Holmes had arrived and wanted to see me. The three of us took breakfast together at the Lion Royal.

I asked Sherlock Holmes if there had been any progress.

"There are a few small indications of it," he said. "I interviewed Cadan Morgan before I left. He can't remember when he first encountered the Rebeccas.

He thinks it may have been as early as April—which would have been some time before Glyn Huws was murdered. He saw them as recently as several nights ago. They never speak to him. In fact, they seem to pay him no attention at all.

"Also, I've heard from London. The person who lectured on Robert Owen at Y Llew Du on June 5th was a retired school teacher. A group of interested citizens invited him, he says. They took him to dinner after the lecture. He'd never met any of them before, and he knew no one in the audience. He has never heard of the Robert Owen Study League—from which I conclude that the London lecture was a rehearsal like the excursion to the Petticoat Lane Market. Have you turned up anything of interest in Aberystwyth?"

"Benton Tromblay is here," I announced dramatically.

"Of course he is," Sherlock Holmes said. "Since Alban Griffiths and Rhys Parry are here, surely you expected to find Benton as well. Did he give you passes to his lecture?"

He wanted to examine them. He studied them for a moment with his lens and then held them up to the light. "They seem to be identical to the others I have seen," he announced.

"Did you expect to find them changed?" I asked.

"I had no expectation. The fact that they continue to use the same format suggests several points of interest. What have the boy and Rhys Parry been doing?"

"Behaving like tourists," I said. "They're doing nothing at all, but we have to queue up to watch them do it."

My tale of the untidy little man with the bowler and his boy confederate was a genuine surprise to him. He made me repeat it, and then he questioned me closely about it.

"The little man has second sight," I said finally. "He knows the moment Dafydd and I turn the corner onto the promenade or the moment Alban Griffiths and Rhys Parry pop out of their hotel. Dafydd says he's a wizard, which I understand is a common occupation in Wales."

Sherlock Holmes shook his head. "No, Porter. We will not admit second sight or wizards until we've ruled out first sight. Did you say that he occupies a back room?"

"With a magnificent view of a mews or whatever is behind the building," I said. "If you're thinking he does it with mirrors, you can forget that. There are no gaps between the buildings along that stretch of the esplanade."

Sherlock Holmes smiled. Then he laughed heartily. "You've done a splendid piece of work, Porter. Your taking the room across the hall was a masterstroke. You reacted to an unexpected situation with audacity and resourcefulness. I especially appreciate the way you persuaded the landlady to let you have the room without meals. The transaction was completely unnecessary, mind you, but since you've paid a week's tariff, we'll find some kind of use for the room. You deserve a reward. Have you been to the top of Constitution Hill yet?"

"I haven't had time," I said. "Ever since we arrived — "

"To be sure. As soon as the Cliff-Railway opens — at nine o'clock, isn't it? — I want you and Dafydd to make the trip to the top and see whatever is to be seen there. I'll wait for you in your room at the boarding house."

Luna Park, at the top of Constitution Hill, was an extension playground for Aberystwyth's tourists. It enabled them to leave town for the day without going anywhere. The park offered several interesting diversions, and there were magnificent views of Cardigan Bay and its background of mountains. The man who sold tickets to the Cliff-Railway called it the best viewpoint on the entire west coast of Wales.

The Cliff-Railway was a funicular railway employing ballast tanks of water. The weight of the water in the car at the top caused it to descend and pull the car at the bottom up the incline. Then the ballast tank on the car at the bottom was emptied, that on the car at the top was filled, and the process was repeated. There also were tea-rooms, a ballroom, a bandstand, a Camera Obscura, and other diversions.

After enjoying the spectacular views in all directions, we went to see the much more spectacular views promised from the Camera Obscura. They were indeed spectacular. The instrument used a lens and mirror to project pictures down onto a horizontal mirror placed on a table so that spectators could enjoy them close at hand. The images had their natural colour, and as the lens rotated it showed the sweep of the bay and Aberystwyth's buildings and streets, with people walking and horse-drawn conveyances in motion. I'd been enjoying these views for several minutes when the device seemed to move on the heels of a man who was strolling along the esplanade, and I suddenly received a staggering flash of illumination.

Our antagonist with the bowler was using a Camera Obscura for his spying, and *that* was why Sherlock Holmes had sent me to Constitution Hill. As he did so often, he had instantly inferred what was happening, but he wanted me to figure it out for myself. There was no way that our subject in the rear room could have spied on people walking near the beach without a Camera Obscura or some equivalent.

When we went outside again, I looked down on the roofs of the buildings along the promenade, calculated the exact position of my boarding house — and saw the cupola on the roof that housed the lens and mirror.

I pointed it out to Madryn, who was sceptical. We left at once, and the Cliff-Railway returned us to the end of the promenade. We hurried back to the boarding house, keeping close to the buildings. The cupola didn't raise the little man's prying lens far enough above the peak of the roof for his instrument to view people walking along the near side of the street. We climbed the stairway cautiously, made certain that the door of number 18 was closed, and burst in on Sherlock Holmes.

My face must have been expressive.

"Now you understand," he said, laughing again. "A knowledge of recent history would have been helpful to you. The Camera Obscura was originally located in the grounds of Aberystwyth Castle. It was moved to the top of the cliff when the Cliff- Railway was built. Obviously someone in this building liked the notion well enough to build his own. Is there evidence on the roof?"

"A cupola," I said. "It is rectangularly shaped, perhaps to make it look like a tall chimney, but the top is unlike any chimney I've ever seen. It should be easy to find out who owns the building."

"The owner may know nothing about it," Sherlock Holmes said. "The name of the person who installed the device might not help us, either, since it obviously has been there for some time. We need to know who is operating it right now."

"The little man with the bowler," I said impatiently.

"No, Porter. He is only an errand boy. The person in charge is pointing at people who appear in his mirror and saying, 'Find out what these two are talking about.' And the little man — or, when he is already occupied, the boy — hurries out to eavesdrop on the persons indicated. There is someone in that room you haven't seen — someone who doesn't go out at all. Food is taken in to him. Our problem is to find out who he is."

The previous day I had tried several experiments that worked well. Sherlock Holmes congratulated me on them. Now he wanted to try one of his own.

First he disguised Madryn, taking enormous pains to render him unrecognizable and attiring him in a splendid waistcoat he had brought for that purpose. He insisted on rehearsing Madryn several times in the role he was to play. Then Sherlock Holmes and I departed.

On Alexandra Street, near the railway station, we found the headquarters of a messenger service. Sherlock Holmes engaged its manager in conversation with the result that both of us donned messenger uniforms in a back room. He removed the beard he wore as Haggard Batt, and we affixed false moustaches to ourselves. Several large packages — containing nothing but our clothing — were prepared for us.

We returned to my boarding house carrying the packages, clumped noisily up the stairs, and beat a tattoo on the door of number 18.

"Delivery!" Sherlock Holmes bellowed.

The untidy little man — without his bowler — opened the door. Carrying my load of packages, I immediately pushed past him into the room. Sherlock Holmes balanced his own packages against the door frame and produced a receipt book.

"Sign here," he said cheerfully. "Number eighteen, that's you."

"But that isn't my name," the little man protested indignantly.

"Ain't you room eighteen?" Sherlock Holmes demanded.

"I'm room eighteen, but I am *not* Edward Gatward, and I have *not* ordered anything," the little man said angrily.

Responding to this cue, Madryn opened the door across the hall. "Gatward? I'm Gatward. Those must be my packages."

We got the muddle straightened out. Of course someone had mistakenly written room 18 instead of room 19 on the packages and the delivery slip. Sherlock Holmes apologized; the little man was appeased enough to help me pick up a package I had dropped deliberately. I thanked him, affecting the cringing voice of a severely intimidated messenger. We withdrew and carried our packages across the hall — where, as soon as we had closed the door, we opened them and dressed in our own clothing, packing our uniforms into the boxes.

The experiment was an overwhelming success. While Sherlock Holmes and the little man argued, I was able to perform a brief but thorough inspection of the entire room. In the far corner, a man sat before a small round table with his gaze fixed intently on the table top. His right arm was heavily bandaged.

It was Kyle Connor.

17

SHERLOCK HOLMES SUGGESTED AN EARLY LUNCH. Walking close to the buildings and out of the range of Kyle Connor's Camera Obscura, we went in a roundabout way to King Street and a small tavern that he had discovered. There he was greeted like an old friend by the elderly waiter, a short, heavy-set, white-haired man whose limp was so severe that I wondered how he managed to carry a tray of tankards without spilling their contents. Sherlock Holmes introduced us and ordered bread, cheese, and beer, using the Welsh words "bara a chaws a chwrw," which startled me.

When the waiter, whose name was Dylan Williams, had served us — without spilling a drop — Sherlock Holmes said to him, "Would you help us settle an argument, Dylan? Porter, your notebook, please. Show Mr. Williams your sketch of the coracle."

I found the sketch and laid the notebook open on the table in front of the waiter, who took one glance at it, nodded, and said, "Afon Dyfrdwy — the River Dee."

"I never saw a coracle from the Afon Dyfrdwy before," Sherlock Holmes said. "I couldn't place it. It vaguely resembles those of the Afon Teifi, but the sides are more indented, and the ends — "

The waiter shook his head. "Na, na. The Teifi coracle — " With his finger, he drew another outline around the one I had sketched, showing one end more rounded and the other with an indentation. In his eyes, at least, there was no similarity at all.

The three of us thanked him, and he limped away.

"Mr. Williams worked for many years as a coracle fisherman on the Towy," Sherlock Holmes told us. "He knows coracles. Where there is a tradition of coracle fishing, each river has its own unique design based upon hundreds of years of experience. A deep, slow-moving river requires a craft with different characteristics from those that would be useful in a shallow river with a swift current, for example. Do you see the significance of that?"

"Not really," I said. "The requirements for a lake should be different from those of any of the rivers."

"No doubt that is true, but the fact wouldn't weigh heavily with an experienced coracle man who needed a craft to use for a very short time on a lake. He would build the kind of coracle he was familiar with. The important point is that the coracles of each river have a distinctive design, and the coracle we found, which certainly was built somewhere near Llyn Tŷ-mawr, is instantly recognizable as a coracle from the River Dee. Therefore its builder must have had considerable experience with coracles on the Dee. Does that direct your attention to anyone?"

I shook my head. Sherlock Holmes repeated the question for Madryn, who was looking totally bewildered.

"Come, Porter," Sherlock Holmes said irritably. "It is a simple exercise in reverse logic. You have the necessary data — you gave them to me yourself. All you have to do is take them for your starting point and reason backward. I've advised you often enough to train your mind to analyze chains of evidence in either direction. What do you know about Rhys Parry?"

"He was born in Bangor," I protested. "That's on the Menai Strait, and surely not even the Welsh use those cockle-shell boats on branches of the ocean. There may be a river there, but if I understand you correctly, its coracles would have a different design from the River Dee coracle we found. Of course, Parry could have left Bangor at an early age and learned to make coracles somewhere else."

"No, no," Sherlock Holmes said, shaking his head impatiently. "You've missed the point completely. According to your report, Parry spoke disparagingly about Bangor and its university. A genuine native of that city would be proud of both. Therefore I infer that the Bangor on the Menai Strait is not his native city. But Wales has more than one community named Bangor. There is also a village called Bangor-is-y-coed, 'Enclosure in the wood.' It requires only a small exercise in logic to conclude that Parry absent-mindedly started to say Bangor-is-y-coed when you asked him where he was born and then thought better of it, mentioning only the 'Bangor.' Or perhaps the natives of Bangor-is-y-coed call it Bangor, and it suited his purpose when his audience at the tavern drew the wrong conclusion."

I had never heard of Bangor-is-y-coed. "Where is it?" I asked.

"In north-eastern Wales, just south of Wrexham. It is sometimes called Bangor on Dee — because, of course, it is on the River Dee."

"Then Rhys Parry was the gunman who attacked Kyle Connor?"

"That's the balance of probability. The coracle the gunman built and used certainly matches those of the Dee. Parry probably is a native of that region. These facts are highly suggestive, but don't forget that we are still dealing in conjectures."

"His clogs also match those of one of the men who killed Glyn Huws."

"That also is suggestive. It furnishes us with another conjecture — that Rhys Parry is the person called upon whenever violence is required — but no exercise in logic could make Parry the organizing genius of a conspiracy that touches all of Wales. We can't complete the equation without certain knowledge of where his orders come from."

"Not from Kyle Connor," I said regretfully, "since Parry tried to kill him."

"Not unless the members of the conspiracy are squabbling among themselves — which ultimately will work to our advantage if it is true. Now I must make arrangements for another experiment."

Characteristically, he set about that without letting me know what he was doing. His instructions to Madryn and me were to pay no further attention to Kyle Connor and his agents but to keep out of the range of his Camera Obscura as much as possible. We were to resume following Alban Griffiths and Rhys Parry that afternoon and attend Benton Tromblay's lecture only if they attended it. If they did attend, I was to keep my eyes on them throughout the lecture and note everything that they did.

I amended this to give Madryn a free afternoon to enjoy Aberystwyth. He had never visited the town before, and I was certain that I would be less conspicuous if I followed Griffiths and Parry alone.

They continued to behave like tourists, and my afternoon was so uneventful that it became boring. They wandered through all of Aberystwyth's streets. They rode the Cliff-Railway to the top of Constitution Hill. I prudently delayed my own ascent until the next trip — and found them ready to leave. They'd had no time to do more than briefly admire the view. I managed to find a seat at the rear of the car and descend with them.

They each paid tuppence to visit the Promenade Pier, but all that they did there was make a quick stroll to the end and back. Trailing after them, I didn't feel that I'd had my tuppence worth. They walked leisurely through the castle ruins and then followed Great Darkgate Street to the centre of the town. From there, they led me back to the esplanade. I joined Madryn at the tavern we had patronized, and the two of us watched Griffiths and Parry return to their hotel.

Madryn said, "I don't feel that I'm helping you."

"It has been that kind of an afternoon. I haven't accomplished much myself. If they go out again before evening, I'll let you follow them."

They must have eaten dinner at their hotel. They didn't reappear until shortly before eight, and they had to walk briskly in order to reach the university in time for the lecture.

The former hotel that housed the Aberystwyth branch of the University College of Wales looked ponderously dull on the outside. On the inside, the main hall had the accents of a Gothic palace: pointed arches, fancy balustrades, and overhanging balconies, all strikingly decorated in tones of white and gold. Doors at the rear opened into the main lecture hall, where there was a platform at one end, a sloping floor with low steps that the benches were set on, and bay windows at the back with, appropriately enough, a beautiful view of the bay.

An appearance at the University College of Wales fulfilled an ambition that Benton Tromblay may not have known he had. It was little more than a week since we'd heard him lecture in Newtown, but when he rose to deliver his address at Aberystwyth—poised, confident—it was evident that his transformation involved more than the new suit and regular meals. He was no longer a failure in life, an Oxford graduate condemned to labour as a poorly paid clerk. He was a speaker who could command and hold and instruct an audience, even at a university.

We arrived just before the lecture was scheduled to begin, and the room was almost filled. Madryn and I sat in the rear; Griffiths and Parry were seated three rows in front of us. I kept my attention on them, but I also glanced about to see what sort of persons had been attracted to a lecture on Robert Owen in a university town. In Newtown, it had been the workers who attended, many of them unemployed textile workers. It was impossible to characterize the Aberystwyth audience, but it did seem like an improbable mixture for a serious lecture on any subject. Among the three hundred or so people present, there were students and faculty members of the university in their gowns; there were flamboyant species and subspecies of the genus tourist; there was a scattering of ordinary people of all ages, including a number of young men who appeared to be farm-hands on an evening out. These latter were looking about curiously as though they had never been in a university before, and I wondered if they knew what they were letting themselves in for. I also wondered how they obtained their passes.

I didn't know whether Sherlock Holmes was a member of the audience in one of his superb disguises or whether he was waiting outside. He had decided to follow Griffiths and Parry himself after the lecture to make certain that they didn't slip away again. In any case, I failed to recognize him.

The elderly chairman, a university faculty member, entered with Benton, who also wore a gown. As a graduate of Oxford, Benton certainly was entitled to do so — but he was wearing the long gown of a scholar, which contradicted all that I had heard about his university career, and the chairman introduced him as a visiting scholar from Oxford. Perhaps Benton felt that he merited the long gown because he *now* was a scholar. There was polite applause, mostly from the students, when he arose to speak.

He had chosen as his subject Robert Owen's views on the evils of the manufacturing system. Owen considered manual labour to be the source of all wealth and of national prosperity, and this was not a concept I would have selected for presentation to an audience largely composed of wealthy tourists, university students, and professors, none of whom would be likely to exhibit much enthusiasm for a celebration of the value of manual labour.

They listened politely, however, while Benton elaborated Robert Owen's conclusions. Owen had thought that a means must be found so that the whole population could participate in the benefits derived from the increased productive power resulting from the use of machinery. Unemployment resulted from some defect in the mode of distributing the enormous increases of capital that the use of machines provided. In order to correct this, he thought it essential to change the standard of value from gold and silver to human labour. The value of the human labour in every article of produce or manufacture could easily be ascertained to determine its exchangeable value. Human labour would thus acquire its natural or intrinsic value, which would increase as science increased human production.

I listened as attentively as I could, wondering as I had in Newtown what the ideas of Robert Owen could possibly have to do with our two murders and a conspiracy that extended throughout Wales. This, along with the necessity for keeping my eyes on Griffiths and Parry, provided sufficient distraction to make me occasionally lose the thread of Benton's argument. I was not the only one who lost it. When Benton began to expound the effect of the new system on agriculture, one of the husky young farm-hands leaped to his feet and shouted, "Twll dy dîn, y diawl bach!"

It came like a thunderclap. The audience had been listening with quiet politeness. Suddenly that raucous shout rang out. Benton was swinging into an explanation of how a society without money operated. He cut off in mid-sentence and watched the scene that suddenly developed in front of him with open mouth. At least thirty young farm-hands were scattered throughout the audience, and all of them leaped to their feet.

I muttered to Madryn, "What did he say?"

Madryn muttered back, "It wasn't polite."

Polite or not, it was repeated by the other farm-hands with elaboration. As they worked their way toward aisles they continued to shout, and they began to throw things. Large darts whistled through the air. One plopped onto the speaker's table. Another smacked Benton squarely in the forehead and stuck there. I felt a twinge of alarm until he angrily pulled it off and tossed it aside. The darts were made of chicken feathers stuck into slices of potato. They made a spectacular but somewhat inaccurate flight. Several struck people seated in the first rows of the audience, one effectively sticking to a man's bald head.

For a few startled moments, I forgot my primary assignment. Then I turned my attention back to

Griffiths and Parry. They sat quietly throughout the disturbance. They didn't even bother to look around.

The hoots and shouts continued. The young farm-hands finally fired off the last of their darts and made a rush for an exit. They stampeded from the room, and the silence that followed their departure was as stunned as that which had greeted their first out-burst.

Benton Tromblay's poise was magnificent. He brushed several darts from the table, stepped down into the audience to make certain that a woman had not been injured — she'd been struck in the face by a dart when she turned to see what was causing the disturbance — and returned to the table to apologize to the audience.

"Throughout Robert Owen's life," he said, "attempts were made to silence him. Attempts are still being made to keep his ideas from the public. The attempts always fail. Thanks to your generous patience, I still have an audience, and Robert Owen's economics remains the subject unfolding before us."

The audience applauded.

A worthy person at the rear of the room had dashed out to fetch the police when the disturbance first broke out. The result was one highly confused constable who now came charging down the aisle. Benton Tromblay ignored him and began presenting Robert Owen's discussion of the ideas of Malthus. Malthus was correct, Owen thought, in saying that the population of the world adapted itself to the quantity of food available but sadly in error in not considering how much more food an intelligent and industrious people could create than would be produced from the same soil by one that was ignorant and ill-governed.

The constable listened in stark bewilderment for a moment, looked around at the attentive audience, lifted his hands despairingly, and trudged back up the aisle.

There were no more disturbances. Benton Tromblay brought his address to a conclusion by returning to a subject he had touched upon in Newtown: Owen's notion that prosperity was the direct result of high wages. When wages were low, all classes suffered, but more particularly those connected with manufacturing, because an employee's wages must first be used for food and rent. If there was nothing left over, no manufactured goods could be bought. Ignorance, overwork, low wages, and unemployment for the lower classes caused all classes to suffer, none more than the employers who paid those low wages.

The applause was generous, but none of it came from Alban Griffiths and Rhys Parry. They got to their feet the moment the lecture was finished and made a hurried departure. Madryn and I waited until the audience had thinned out before we went to the front of the room to congratulate Benton Tromblay. He gave us passes for his next lecture on the following night.

We returned to the Lion Royal to wait for Sherlock Holmes. He came in shortly after midnight, settled himself in his own inimitably comfortable fashion in one of the room's atrociously uncomfortable chairs, and lit his pipe.

"Where did they go?" I asked him.

"They went back to their hotel," he said. "Actually, they went to a meeting, just as they did in London and probably in Newtown. In this case, the others attending the meeting are also staying at their hotel, and the meeting was held in the room of one of them. I listened for a time at the door, but they spoke so quietly I could make out very little that was said. It is interesting that neither 'Griffiths' nor 'Parry' appears in the hotel's register. The others at the meeting will also be using assumed names, so I made no attempt to identify them."

"How did you manage to see the register?" I asked.

"A little money, judiciously expended, can accomplish wonders. Hotels don't pay their night clerks lavishly, and what I was doing harmed no one — as long as the persons I was interested in didn't know about it."

"Benton Tromblay gives another lecture tomorrow night — tonight, I mean."

"I know," Sherlock Holmes said. "Then he goes to Barmouth for two lectures."

"Do you want us to attend tonight's lecture? Benton gave us passes."

"I have something else for you to do. I'll take your passes, though I don't really need them. I am able to manufacture as many as I want."

"You packed the house with those farm-hands!" I exclaimed.

He chuckled. "Any engraver can produce a wood block *O* to specifications, and Benton's initials are easily forged. How did Griffiths and Parry react?"

"They did nothing at all. They didn't even look around to see what was happening."

"Really? They made no attempt to silence the disturbance?"

"None. They were completely unconcerned about it."

"That's highly significant," Sherlock Holmes said. "Obviously the meetings have nothing to do with their own business, and they are only attending them as a blind. I don't often have two experiments in the same day produce such striking results."

"Why is it significant that the meetings have nothing to do with their own business?" I asked.

He smiled. "It's also significant that Benton Tromblay's schedule is taking him to some of the most popular Welsh resort areas — from Aberystwyth he goes to Barmouth and then north to Harlech — and these should be the most unlikely places in Wales for lectures about Robert Owen. The contingent of university students and professors saved him last night. At least they have an academic interest in Robert Owen. It will be interesting to see what happens at Barmouth."

I began to feel sorry for Benton Tromblay. "Do you plan to arrange more disturbances?" I asked.

"No, but I wouldn't be surprised if one occurs spontaneously."

"What is significant about Benton lecturing at resorts?"

"If you wanted to hold a series of secret meetings with people who must come long distances from all over Wales, would you hold them in Pentrederwydd?"

"Even one stranger would cause an upheaval of curiosity in Pentrederwydd," I said.

"Precisely. Newtown, a much larger place, would be better, but those who visit Newtown usually do so for an evident reason — business, for example. A group of visitors who came repeatedly but had no business to conduct would soon arouse the curiosity of everyone who observed them. But a stranger who does nothing at all — or a dozen such strangers — are ignored in Aberystwyth, because the town has thousands of strangers all summer long who come here for precisely that reason — to spend their holidays doing nothing. The conspirators have only to pretend that they are holiday-makers, and no one could possibly imagine anything suspicious about them. This business is extremely well-planned, Porter."

"I've noticed that," I said, "and I doubt that Rhys Parry could have thought of it, let alone managed it."

Sherlock Holmes nodded thoughtfully. "The man we are seeking not only has far-reaching designs, but he has the patience to let them develop slowly over a long span of time. If he hadn't been so unwise as to turn to murder, his conspiracy would have gone unnoticed for years and his power continued to increase, and that would have been catastrophic for both Wales and England."

"But who is he?" I asked.

He smiled. "His identity is still a matter of conjecture. There is one thing that can be said for certain: This is no mere wholesaler in crime-for-profit that we have to deal with. His imagination is boundless, and he aims so high that one hesitates to guess his target."

I had known Sherlock Holmes too long to be taken in by this kind of talk. I said resentfully, "Conjecture or not, you know who he is."

"Yes, Porter. He has labelled himself, and I have read the label. Our problem is no longer one of identification but of finding evidence that will convict him of two murders — for I am convinced, now, that there were two. If we can do that, his conspiracy will quickly wither. I don't yet know how it is to be accomplished. If the opportunity arises, we may be able to take him by surprise and provoke a rash act. It will be a near thing, though. He is as poised, and as cool, and as ruthless as any criminal I have ever encountered."

This confirmed my own conclusions: Emeric Tromblay had labelled himself palpably. He was the only person with a motive for murdering his wife. He was the only person who stood to profit from the death of Glyn Huws. Both were obstacles to his marriage to Meleri Huws. Perhaps he wouldn't murder for the control of one more farm, but neither would he refuse one if it came with a beautiful heiress. He would be much too sly to deal directly with the likes of a Rhys Parry, however. Someone else at Tromblay Hall would have taken care of that for him — but certainly not Wain Welling, his chief support in other matters. Welling was Welsh and wouldn't be in sympathy with an arranged murder of a popular Welsh farmer who was also his friend.

But Tromblay assuredly had labelled himself. What eluded me were his links with the conspiracy that Sherlock Holmes described and with the Robert Owen Study League. Links there had to be, and until I determined what they were, our case would continue to mystify me.

"I have another job for you, Porter," Sherlock Holmes said. "It will be the most tedious thing I have ever asked you to do and physically exhausting as well. I've held off in the hope that I could develop this case without it, but the further I proceed, the more critically essential it becomes."

"I'll do my best," I said.

"Of course you will. You always do, and your best is never less than adequate and often excellent. I want you to return to Pentrederwydd on the morning train. It leaves at seven-fifteen. I will become Mr. Gatward and take over your room at the boarding house. There are several more things we urgently need to know about Kyle Connor."

"What about Dafydd?" I asked.

"He will return with you, of course. You couldn't function in Pentrederwydd without him. Another man will also accompany you. His name is Carl Prowse. He is a geologist who specializes in locating mineral deposits.

"You may remember that in London you mentioned two reasons why Emeric Tromblay might want to marry Meleri Huws. One was to acquire her farm. The other was to acquire her person. I suggested that there might be a third."

"You didn't tell me what it was," I said.

"I thought you would discover it for yourself. What if Emeric Tromblay had reason to believe that the Huws farm is immensely more valuable than it appears? Supposing he had found evidence there of valuable mineral deposits? Tromblay already owns substantial holdings in mines, but the mines of mid-Wales have notoriously short productive lives. In order to remain profitable, a mining company must continually open new works as the old ones become exhausted. If Tromblay had even a mild suspicion that there is a mining potential at Meini Mawr, he would attempt to acquire it at once."

Madryn was shaking his head. "There isn't any. Those valleys have been explored for minerals over and over."

"So the records say," Sherlock Holmes said. "But minerals are found all across mid-Wales, and there is evidence of prehistoric mining almost as far east as Newtown. Immensely rich deposits of lead occur north of Llanidloes, which is not very far from Pentrederwydd. The Van Mine, the most productive lead mine in Britain, is there. Experts may hold that there is no ore around Pentrederwydd, but one promising lode of galena would count more than all of the expert opinion in Britain. So I have asked Mr. Prowse to make a careful search for evidence of mineral deposits at Meini Mawr. He also is to look for signs of prospecting."

My function would be to assist Prowse with this search. Madryn's task would be much more complicated. First he was to find quarters for us where we could function as inconspicuously as possible. Then he was to make certain that no one interfered with us.

"It isn't necessary to tell Meleri Huws what we are doing," Sherlock Holmes said to him. "It should suffice to let her know that we are looking for important evidence concerning her father's murder. The problem is how that can be done without arousing the curiosity of the entire valley. Perhaps she could tell both her employees and her neighbours that she is having the farm's boundaries resurveyed."

Madryn got to his feet. "I'll arrange something with her. If we're to take the first train tomorrow, it's time that we went to bed."

"One moment, Dafydd," Sherlock Holmes said. "I have a special task for you. I want you to find out what Meleri Huws is hiding. She could give us vital information about the death of her father if she would."

Madryn shook his head. "I don't believe that."

"If Porter reported her conversation accurately, I'm certain that she could. A young lady with her attractions who protests so vehemently that she will never marry must have been severely disappointed in love. That disappointment may have something to do with her father's death. Try and find out about it."

Madryn shook his head again. "She loved her father," he said stubbornly. "There is nothing she wants more than to see his murderers punished. If she knew anything at all, she would tell us."

Sherlock Holmes smiled patiently. "Porter described her as being excited when he showed her that two men in clogs killed her father. Is that correct?"

"'Exultant' would be a better word," I said. "Perhaps even 'ecstatic.' It went far beyond excitement."

"Exhilarated?"

"That, too," I said. "Perhaps all three."

"Didn't that strike you as a strange reaction?" Sherlock Holmes asked Madryn.

"I was excited myself," Madryn said. "I'd thought it would be impossible to find any clues at all."

"Were you exultant, ecstatic, or exhilarated?"

"Well — no."

"But Meleri Huws was, and there can be only one explanation. She thought she knew who the murderer was — and the person she suspected never wears clogs and certainly wouldn't have brought a witness with him. She was elated to learn that she was wrong. She knows something, Dafydd. Try and find out what it is."

18

SHERLOCK HOLMES AND CARL PROWSE MET US AT the Aberystwyth station. The geologist was a wiry middle-aged man whose face was as browned and wrinkled from the sun as any farm-hand's. I knew at first glance that a tramp through the Welsh mountains with him would have no resemblance to a holiday outing.

Prowse, Madryn, and I boarded the train and settled ourselves for a ride of almost two hours, and during the entire journey, the geologist didn't volunteer half a dozen words. This was further intimation of the ordeal I was facing. Prowse and I would be living together on an isolated farmstead — with hosts who could speak nothing but Welsh — and I might die of loneliness.

At Y Llew Côch, Madryn hired three ponies. We stopped at his home in Pentrederwydd, approaching it by the path that looped above the village, and I changed to the new walking boots that I had left there and also borrowed two of Madryn's books in English.

The boots got far more use than the books. I wore them — not from dawn to dusk, but from dark to dark, because we were up each morning before the dawn. I did almost no reading because our hosts, who were named Hugh and Menna Thomas, could not offer us candles to read by. I had thought that rushlights — which were made by drawing a peeled rush through melted fat — were prehistoric, but in rural Wales, where they were called canhwyllau brwyn, they were still in use in impoverished homes in that year 1904. It was actually a mark of prosperity among the poor to be able to afford a few rushlights. In order to prepare them, the farmer and his wife had to have a little fat to melt. Rushlights burned for no more than fifteen or twenty minutes, which gave our hosts a choice between using up their entire season's supply in a few nights or retiring early. They chose to retire early, and so did we.

Madryn made all of the arrangements for us, and neither Prowse nor I had any idea of what he told our hosts. He must have impressed upon them that no one was to know we were staying there. They certainly didn't mention it to anyone, and since we left the farmstead before dawn and returned after dark, there was no reason for an outsider to connect us with that isolated place.

Originally the farmhouse had been a tŷ-un-nos, a one-night house, so-called because it was built in one night. According to tradition, a house built between sunset and sunrise became freehold — along with a plot of land to be determined by how far the builder could throw an axe from the door. The law, Madryn said, required that it escape detection by the land's owner for twelve years, but popular rumour omitted this last clause. Although the custom had almost died out, many tiny farmsteads owed their origins to it. Friends would gather after dark, quickly raise a shelter of turf, stones, and earth, and there it would be, happily occupied, when the sun rose. These one-night houses were sometimes called "morning surprises," which they must have been to the landowner.

With the passage of time, the shelter was gradually modified into a more substantial dwelling. This had happened with the house that Hugh and Menna Thomas occupied. It was built of stone with a thatch roof in the form called tŷ-a-siambr, house and chamber. It contained only two tiny rooms, bedroom and living-room. The living-room had a fireplace, which was used for cooking, and so did double duty as a kitchen. At one end of the house was a storeroom with an outside entrance. A lean-to shed at the rear housed a skinny cow and a very broken-down horse. Chickens were chased into the storeroom at night. The loft, where Prowse and I slept on piles of straw, was reached by a ladder through an opening in the living-room ceiling. The ladder was taken down when we were not in residence.

This poverty-stricken farmstead, with its bit of almost worthless land, was located far up the mountain above Meini Mawr. Hugh and Menna Thomas were tenants, which meant that they engaged in an unending struggle to scrape together the small amount of rent money they must pay regularly to avoid eviction. They looked infinitely old, but probably they were in their fifties. Their harsh existence, with its constant strain and struggle to accumulate cash money for rent, to counter bad luck and bad weather and bad prices, to simply survive, was wearing them away in the same manner that granite boulders are worn away, but in a weary procession of seasons rather than centuries. They faced their narrow, confining lives with unquenchable good humour, and their week's labour never left them too tired to make the long walk to church and home three times on Sunday so they could thank God no matter what the week had brought. Hugh Thomas reminded me of Mairwen Madryn's Uncle Tomos.

That first day Madryn brought cheese and several loaves of bread for us so that we wouldn't have to go without lunch. He made arrangements for Menna Thomas to feed us well each morning and each night. Her scrawny hens couldn't even produce eggs in the necessary quantity, and meat was extremely scarce on every impoverished Welsh farm because anything with a market value had to be sold in order to raise the rent money. Madryn returned the following day with bacon and cuts of beef and mutton to vary our diet from the inevitable chicken, which was all that Menna Thomas could have offered us.

At first I regretted not asking him to bring candles, but I quickly gave up any idea of reading. When we returned to the farm at night, I was too tired for any activity except eating and sleeping.

Our host and hostess were elated to have us there. As with Mairwen's aunt and uncle, who were being paid to board horses for Haggart Batt, a cash income, however small, made an enormous difference to them.

Menna Thomas served meals in two sittings — one for Prowse and me, and the other, after we had eaten and ascended to our loft, for herself and her husband. On the second night, I decided after supper to enjoy the cool mountain air. The coolness quickly began to feel frigid, and I returned to the house in time to catch a glimpse of the meal our hosts were eating. It consisted of something called flummery, a watery food made from oatmeal, a few pieces of potato, and a little buttermilk. The meat that Menna had prepared deliciously, the bread, the cheese — these were only for the guests. I spoke angrily to Madryn when he stopped by the next morning. He spoke to our hosts. After that, they took their meals with us and enjoyed the largess that Madryn had provided.

Our work had to be done on foot, and it would have caused talk if it became known that the destitute Hugh Thomas had acquired two new ponies. A passerby couldn't help noticing them —

the tiny farmstead had no stable — so Madryn returned them to Y Llew Côch.

Prowse and I went to work immediately. He showed me specimens of galena — lead ore — explained what he wanted me to look for, and we began a systematic search of the mountainside. Working meant walking. I walked from the time we left the tiny house in darkness until we returned to it in darkness, and then I walked more miles in my sleep. I walked from Wednesday to Saturday, paying meticulous attention to outcrops and configurations of rocks as well as springs and water courses, all of them objects I'd never previously bothered to look at twice. My only respite came when I discovered erosion that had bared an underlying stratum. It was permissible to sit down and study that with care.

On Sunday we returned to Madryn's house in Pentrederwydd, that being a less conspicuous place to spend our enforced day of leisure. If we had tried to work on a Sunday, there was a genuine danger that anyone who caught sight of us would walk for miles out of astonished curiosity just to see who the Sabbath-breakers were and what they were doing.

My new shoes were quickly broken in, and when we returned to Pentrederwydd on Sunday, I looked up Ifan Vaughan to tell him truthfully that they were the most comfortable shoes I'd ever owned. I ordered a pair of clogs made to the same measure on the off-chance that I could learn something from wearing them.

Our hosts were pathetically grateful to us, and their efforts to make us comfortable were untiring. Each hot afternoon, Menna Thomas walked the two, three, or four miles to wherever we were, bringing us a cool drink called shot that she made with buttermilk and oatcake. Whenever the interminable tramping up and down and across the mountainside tired me, I could look up and see the tireless Hugh Thomas at work. He had no wagon. I saw him plodding beside his old horse as it dragged a wooden sledge loaded with the bit of hay he had managed to borrow from the next farmstead. Such grain as he was able to grow would be cut with a scythe or sickle and threshed by hand with a flail. Menna coaxed as much milk as she could from the cow and tirelessly thumped a decrepit wooden churn to produce a tiny amount of butter. This, along with a dressed chicken when she had one to spare and wool stockings if she had any knitted, she carried for miles to whatever town was holding a market and tried to sell for rent money. After a few minutes of watching our hosts at their patient labours, I would square my shoulders and return to my work.

If I looked in the other direction, down into the valley, I saw a model, modern farm with Meleri Huws demonstrating her determination that it remain so. She rode about tirelessly, keeping her farm-hands occupied, working along with them, supervising everything. The buildings were extensive and well-kept. The farm animals looked healthy. Her sheep roamed the upper mountain slopes on either side of the valley, and cattle grazed on the lower levels. There was a windmill that pumped water for the house and even a small water-mill. Meini Mawr could grind its own grain and also that of neighbouring farms.

Whatever explanation Madryn had given to Meleri, she must have spoken sternly to her employees, because they ignored us completely. They rarely came near us, and when they did, they studiously avoided looking in our direction. Only the sheep demonstrated any interest in us. I quickly learned to approach them cautiously. A sudden movement made them bolt.

The taciturn Prowse was untiring. I suspected that he would have enjoyed picking apart the geology of that mountain the way a vulture picks over the bones of carrion it has found. Unfortunately for him, he had our own urgent problem to deal with, but I saw him examining things that couldn't possibly have had anything to do with the land's potential mineral wealth and making notes on them. He wore a perpetually blank expression on his face, and because he rarely spoke, his thoughts remained his own secret. If I found something I wanted him to examine, I marked it with a willow wand and tucked a handkerchief into my hat. The next time he chanced to look in my direction, he would see the handkerchief and come to scrutinize my discovery. *Then* he talked in great detail, trying to make me understand what I was supposed to be looking for and how idiotically I had misinterpreted what I saw. He was calm and matter-of-fact about it, spoke quickly, and hurried back to his own territory.

By the time we returned to work after our enforced Sunday holiday, I had resigned myself to wearily searching every inch of the mountains on both sides of the valley and finding nothing. It was the wrong place to be looking for traces of mineralization. Prowse said as much the day we arrived. The mining country was further south, around Llanidloes, or further west. I had to will myself to examine each new outcrop, to pick over each clutter of rock that I encountered, to prod the source of every trickling spring, to scrutinize watercourses and patterns of erosion as alertly as though I expected to strike gold at any moment. I had in fact asked Prowse about the chances of finding gold, with a bit of silver or copper, instead of lead, and he snorted disdainfully. I couldn't understand why. There were rich gold mines some twenty-five miles west of us, around Dolgellau, and Welsh red gold was famous.

I would have much preferred to sit on the mountainside watching Meleri Huws — in a man's clothing — riding about her farm in the valley far below while

I tried to think of the evidence she might be concealing concerning her father's murder. Twice during our search, Meini Mawr had a visitor. I was much too distant to recognize the rider, but the highly distinctive horse was familiar to me. It was the same splendid animal I had seen outside the Church of St. Peter, Pentrederwydd, when Emeric Tromblay brought wild flowers to his wife's tomb. He was making a neighbourly call, or courting Meleri in his own stiffly formal manner, or both. Once he met her at the end of the valley, probably by chance, and the two of them rode back to the farm together. Neither of his visits lasted more than half an hour. I had the impression that the well-brought-up daughter of Glyn Huws was receiving him with the same polite coolness she had accorded to his son.

When we returned to work on Monday morning, the Thomas' cow was sick. Both Hugh and Menna were devastated. The possible loss of a child could not have affected them more severely. The cow was a member of the family. It also was the principal prop in their struggle for survival. Hugh walked off somewhere to get help, was gone for hours, and returned alone. Their despair deepened. Menna prepared food for us that evening, but neither of them joined us. They were too worried to eat.

Late that night, the help came. I was awakened by a familiar voice — Wain Welling's. He and Hugh talked in Welsh while they worked on the cow. Prowse grumbled and tossed; I listened carefully and tried to make out what was happening. After an hour or so I fell asleep.

In the morning, the cow was better.

It was on that Tuesday, when our futile search had occupied us for almost a week, that I pushed a wand into the ground one more time, tucked my handkerchief into my hat, and continued on down the slope. Half an hour later, Prowse came striding toward me.

"What is it this time?" he asked. The words sounded sarcastic, but his voice was flat and expressionless.

I led him back to the marker, pointed, and stepped aside.

A depression like a misshapen wrinkle creased the mountainside. Water seeped from it, formed a small pool, and spilled over in a dribble that collected in a larger pool a few feet down the slope. The larger pool was drained by a tiny, trickling stream that probably flowed freely after a rain.

Prowse reached into the water and began to collect dull-looking, stone-like masses. "This is it," he announced.

I had noticed two peculiarities about them. They were grey in appearance with clusters of cube-like protrusions, and they seemed extremely heavy. A characteristic of lead ore was that it fractured into a multitude of rectangular blocks when struck. A scattering of such small fragments beside the spring suggested that someone had made the test.

Prowse moved on down the slope, stooping frequently and collecting more specimens. Finally he turned to me. "Do you know where Mr. Holmes is?" He was one of the few people in Wales who knew Sherlock Holmes by his real name.

I shook my head.

"Your friend Madryn may know," he said. "We must send a message at once. You may as well start for Pentrederwydd now. While you're gone, I'll sketch a map."

"It is galena, isn't it?" I asked.

He nodded. "Probably with a small percentage of silver. It'll have to be assayed to determine how much."

"Does that mean there's a lode here?"

He snorted. "Certainly not. There's no source at all for these specimens. Someone salted them here within the past year. I think I know where they came from."

He dismissed me with a nod and took out his notebook and a compass. I'd trudged only about ten steps when he halted me with a shout. I turned.

He gestured at the spring. His voice was expressionless, as always. "You surprised me," he said. "You were seeing everything that wasn't, so I expected you to walk past anything that was."

He returned his attention to his notebook, and I resumed my long walk to Pentrederwydd.

I found Madryn at home. By coincidence, Mr. Haggart Batt had returned the previous day from the south of Wales. He left immediately for Newtown with his horses to sell them at the fair — this was the last Tuesday of the month — but Madryn thought that he had returned. He hadn't planned to stay any longer than it took him to dispose of his horses. Dafi dashed off to the vicarage with a message for him, and he came at once. He had only two horses left, but he borrowed two more from the vicar, and we rode to Meini Mawr. We climbed on foot to the place on the mountainside where Carl Prowse calmly sat waiting for us.

Prowse displayed the specimens. "This is an unlikely place to be finding galena," he said. "There's no outcropping at all and no evidence of an underlying stratum that could account for it. A knowledgeable person would have done his salting elsewhere."

Sherlock Holmes studied the peculiar crease from which the water emerged. "A layman might consider this an excellent place to look for mineral specimens," he observed.

"Perhaps so," Prowse conceded. "If a layman did the salting, that might account for it."

"Just take enough samples for assaying. Leave the rest as they are. We don't want anyone to suspect that the secret has been discovered."

Prowse's snort demonstrated what he thought of the secret. He picked up a few specimens, and then he and Sherlock Holmes returned to the valley for the horses while Madryn and I walked back to the tiny farm to pick up my unread books and a few items that Prowse had left there. Hugh and Menna Thomas were genuinely sorry we were leaving and not merely for the loss of the room and board money that Madryn was paying them. We had been mute company for them — companions who shared their lonely existence and who worked almost as hard as they did. Probably they would have understood no other kind.

I felt that they had taught me a valued lesson in forbearance, and in the loft I left them a gold sovereign, a fortune to that impoverished couple, along with a message that I insisted on writing myself although it strained my knowledge of Welsh to the utmost: Diolch yn fawr, thank you very much. I wondered how long it would be before they found it.

We also were leaving them with a full larder. "At least they'll be able to continue eating well for a few days," I remarked to Madryn.

He shook his head. "They'll try to sell the meat. They always need money for rent."

When we reached Pentrederwydd, Madryn went on to Groesffordd with Prowse to put him on the evening train to London and bring back his horse. Sherlock Holmes and I retired to my loft above Madryn's stable to confer.

He perched on the three-legged chair and touched the tips of his fingers together. "We are making progress," he announced. "*Now* we know why Emeric Tromblay wanted to buy Meini Mawr and why he is courting Meleri Huws. He hopes to bolster his failing mine dividends with a rich new strike. Of course he carefully refrained from letting either Meleri or her father know about the galena specimens, and he would not be so foolish as to call in a geologist to appraise a mineral find on land he doesn't yet own."

"Unfeeling kind of fish, isn't he?" I said disgustedly. "To court a girl merely because — "

"Don't rush to conclusions, Porter. The fact that Meleri is young and beautiful as well as the supposed owner of a potentially rich mining property no doubt doubles the attractiveness of a second marriage for him. His greed might be severely tested if she were hideous and middle-aged. At least we know why he wanted Meini Mawr."

In my mind, it left us with a much more difficult problem. Who placed the ore specimens there and why? Who perpetrated this fraud? The person who salted the specimens must have pointed them out to Tromblay. Tromblay certainly didn't wander about Glyn Huws's farm on foot and make the discovery himself. Probably he wouldn't recognize galena specimens as such unless someone brought them to his attention. Was it a prank? It would be the sadistic kind of joke a humorist might enjoy playing on a greedy millionaire. If not, then we had to ask ourselves who stood to profit from Emeric Tromblay's buying Meini Mawr — or from his marrying Meleri Huws.

"Glyn Huws is the only person who could have profited from selling it," I observed. "Tromblay would have offered him a very good price in his eagerness to acquire a new mine."

Sherlock Holmes shook his head. "That won't do, Porter. Glyn Huws wouldn't have sold Meini Mawr to Tromblay for any price. We also must fit his murder into the equation. Every time I sound these waters, they are deeper and more murky."

"Did you find anything of interest in the south?" I asked.

"Too much," he said gloomily. "Every Friendly Society I investigated has arranged to sponsor meetings in connection with the Robert Owen Study League. But that isn't the worst news. There is enormous unemployment and unrest there, and the entire south of Wales is in the throes of religious mania. I attended several of the services. The congregations wept and groaned and shouted and sang and performed contortions. Nonconformist ministers are overwhelmed with conversions at every service. Publicans are threatened with bankruptcy because so many reformed sinners have taken the pledge. Drunkenness has become such a rarity that in some communities Saturday nights are a second Sabbath. It's even claimed that pit ponies have stopped working in the mines because the miners refuse to swear at them, and the ponies can't understand orders given without profanity. That madness is headed north, Porter — towards us."

"What does it have to do with our case?"

"I don't know," Sherlock Holmes said soberly. "Perhaps nothing — now. But I fear that the author of a conspiracy that already extends from one end of Wales to the other will be clever enough to turn it to his advantage. I have another difficult job for you, Porter. We've been neglecting Tromblay Hall. I want to know everything about it that you can find out — by any means that occurs to you."

When Madryn returned, Sherlock Holmes explained my new assignment to him, and he went off to find a lodging place for me. That night he guided me on a difficult hike over the mountain to another tiny farmstead. My new hosts, Lewys and Blodwen Beddard, looked nothing like Hugh and Menna Thomas — he was tall and gaunt, and his wife was tiny — but they were spiritual replicas. Life was weathering them in the same harsh manner.

This time I made certain that we took our meals together and that they ate well as long as I was there. I arose before dawn the next morning when they did, shared a hearty breakfast with them, and then went outside for my first view of the new valley that was spread out before me. It was much broader than the valley of Meini Mawr and much more prosperous looking. Its wealthy owner didn't have to consider the practicality and potential return of an investment. He could indulge his whims.

The valley's centrepiece was Tromblay Hall. I sprawled on a bed of fresh straw in a shed with the door partially closed so that no chance passerby would have his curiosity aroused by my odd posture, and with a telescope Sherlock Holmes had procured for me, I began to familiarize myself with the comings and goings of the Hall's inhabitants.

After dark that night, I made my way down the mountain along a route I had spent the day memorizing. I prowled the Hall's ornamental gardens, crouched near the house in an attempt to eavesdrop — I could hear nothing at all in the vast rooms beyond the elaborately leaded windows — and satisfied myself that the only way an outsider could penetrate farther was with the help of a servant.

Finally I turned away, defeated. On my cautious retreat through Emeric Tromblay's park, I encountered a poacher. My silent approach took him completely by surprise. He was at work on a trap, and I almost fell over him.

I was surprised myself, and both of us were momentarily panic-stricken. I thought I had stumbled into one of Tromblay's employees; he thought an employee had stumbled into him. It took each of us an instant to realize that the other's business was as illicit as his own.

I said politely, "Good evening."

"Evening," he answered.

"Do you speak English?"

"Some."

From my pocket I took a flask of beer that Blodwen Beddard had presented to me. I removed the cork and passed it to the poacher. He took a long swig and passed it back.

I said, "I'm staying with Lewys and Blodwen Beddard. Do you know their place?"

"Yes."

"Stop by and see me tomorrow. Ask for Iori. I have work for you that will be more profitable than poaching."

"When tomorrow?"

"When you can manage it. I'll be there."

I spent another day with the telescope, and by the time my poacher appeared, I had learned a number of things about the Hall's inhabitants. For one, Wain Welling played the same role at Tromblay Hall that Meleri Huws played on her own farm. Each morning and each afternoon he rode about the valley inspecting, supervising, working with the farm-hands. Dafydd Madryn had said that Welling was too busy to dabble in a conspiracy, and I believed him. He supervised Tromblay Hall and its adjacent farms, he kept the records on Tromblay's far-flung holdings, he travelled widely for Tromblay — and in his free time he doctored sick cows for poor farmers who weren't able to pay a wizard. Wizards were benign witches who practiced both human and veterinary medicine and countered spells placed by evil witches. They were extremely popular, Madryn said, but not as popular as Welling, who was far more effective, never refused his help to poor farmers when he could possibly find a moment to visit them, and never charged for his services.

Emeric Tromblay was rarely seen outside the Hall except when he took his daily ride, and on both those days he rode toward Pentrederwydd or Meini Mawr and quickly passed beyond the range of my telescope. I felt certain that his apparent lack of interest in his property was deceptive. I knew too little about agriculture to form an expert judgement, but obviously the Tromblay farms were very well-managed, and Welling didn't deserve all of the credit for that. Tromblay had known whom to hire and which employees could be relied upon.

My poacher arrived late in afternoon — a wiry little man in ragged clothing. He gave his name as Con Davey. I already knew one thing about him. He was neither a tenant nor employee of Tromblay. Tromblay was astonishingly lenient to poachers the first time they were caught — provided that they were not tenants or employees. Poaching by a tenant or an employee would have been a betrayal of trust. Tenants were evicted at once; employees were summarily dismissed. The stranger was held until identified, all of his particulars were entered into a poaching ledger, he was given a stern warning, and released.

But woe unto him if he were taken a second time. Tromblay would insist on the most severe penalty the law allowed. The days when squires set crippling man traps or spring guns with trip wires for poachers were many years in the past, but the law could deal with poachers harshly when the landowner insisted. Considering the chronic shortage of meat in the diets of poor farmers, it seemed surprising to me that there were not more poachers. Some farmers never tasted meat at all except for parts like the head that couldn't be sold.

Con Davey had a small holding on the other side of the mountain, or so he said. His farm was so impoverished that poaching was the only way he could live. He did it expertly; he had to.

"How did you happen to learn English?" I asked.

"My wife is English," he said.

We were fellow outlaws, and I decided to trust him. "Did you know Glyn Huws?"

He nodded.

"Would you like to see his murderer punished?"

"I would like a hand in that myself," he said softly.

"Two men were hired to do it," I said. "I know who one of them is. I'm trying to find out who hired them. Are you willing to help me? I'll pay you well."

He tossed his head scornfully. "I don't need pay for that."

"I'm being paid for it," I said, "and I want to hang Glyn Huws's murderer just as badly as you do. So you may as well be paid. First I want to know everything you can tell me about Tromblay Hall."

We talked for an hour, and he told me what he could, but he knew almost nothing about what went on inside the Hall. He rarely went near it.

"I know one of the maids," he said finally. "Elen Edwards, her name is. She's my wife's friend. She'll know all about the Hall."

We prowled the grounds of Tromblay Hall together that night, but I learned nothing more than I already knew. The maid was what I needed, and I asked Con Davey to arrange an interview for me.

It took him three days to do it. He couldn't simply walk up to the Hall and ask to see her. He had to have a message smuggled to her, then meet her himself and explain what was wanted, and finally arrange a time and place where she could meet with me.

The interview with Elen Edwards was the strangest I had ever conducted. We met after dark in an unlighted shed some distance from the Hall. Con Davey mounted guard outside; the maid, a respectable, middle-aged woman, was frightened out of her wits to be meeting a strange man under such circumstances.

I spoke quietly, trying to reassure her. I was searching for evidence concerning the murder of Glyn Huws. I meant no harm to any innocent person. There was reason to suspect that a man who sometimes visited the Hall was involved.

As we talked, she became more relaxed, and I questioned her at length about the Hall and the master's guests.

"Can you remember the day that Glyn Huws was murdered?" I asked finally.

"I remember it well," she said, "though we didn't hear about it until the day after it happened. That was a busy time."

"Were there guests at the Hall when Mr. Huws was murdered?"

"Oh, yes. They came the day before and left the day afterward."

"Wasn't it unusual to be having guests then? Your master was still in mourning, wasn't he?"

"These were business guests," she said.

I would have given ten pounds for a glimpse of her face. "Are you certain you're remembering the right day?"

"Oh, yes. We hadn't had guests since the mistress died. But the master had business with those men, so they came. Then he was called away. There was a mine accident."

"He left, leaving his guests?"

"Yes. He left in a great hurry. He'd finished his business with them anyway, but he told them they might as well stay and enjoy themselves."

"And they did?"

"Oh, yes."

The guests didn't seem promising. Even if one of them had arranged the mine accident, he couldn't have known that his host would leave at once and the guests would be left to their own devices.

"Did anything else interesting happen?"

She couldn't remember anything.

"Were there any other callers at the time Glyn Huws was murdered?"

She thought for a moment. "Rhys Parry came."

"Do you know Rhys Parry?" I exclaimed.

"He's staying with his cousin, Jac Parry. Jac's wife Gwen is my cousin."

"Do you know him well?"

"No. Just to speak to him."

"When did he come to the Hall?"

"It was the day after Mr. Huws was murdered."

"Did he come to see Mr. Tromblay?"

"Oh, no. The master was away. Anyway, the likes of him wouldn't be calling on Mr. Tromblay."

"Or Mr. Welling?"

"No. Mr. Welling was away, too. He left before the master did."

"Whom did Rhys Parry come to see?"

"One of the guests, I suppose, since the master and Mr. Welling were away."

I took a deep breath. "Which guest?"

"I don't know," she said.

"Did Rhys Parry come to the door and ask to see one of the guests?"

"I don't know what he asked or who he spoke to. I saw him coming up the drive and later I saw him talking with someone in the garden."

"Who?"

"I didn't notice."

"Who were the guests?"

"Mr. Lumbard and Mr. Armstead," she said. "And that solicitor."

"What solicitor?"

"Mr. Saunders," she said. "The one from Newtown."

19

I HAD THE GIDDY IMPRESSION THAT OUR ENTIRE case had suddenly exploded in my face. I thanked Elen Edwards and rewarded her generously. Con Davey guided me back to the farmstead and had to be persuaded to accept a reward. He kept assuring me that every Welshman in those mountains wanted to see the murderer of Glyn Huws caught and punished.

Sherlock Holmes needed this information immediately, but I knew better than to attempt the mountain paths at night without a guide. Davey volunteered to take me himself. He said, with a shrug, that it was only a few miles out of his way. We left at once.

As I walked, I examined the shreds of our case one by one and attempted to reassemble them. I could find no place for the two new facts I had gathered: Arthur Saunders's casual hob-nobbing as a house guest and business associate with the man he called a fiend in human form; and Rhys Parry, who certainly had murdered Glyn Huws and attempted the murder of Kyle Connor, calmly strolling up the drive to Tromblay Hall the day after Huws's murder to confer — with whom? Tromblay had left the day before. Saunders was the only one present who had any known connection with the case.

I arrived at the Madryn home shortly before dawn, exhausted, discouraged, angry. Our case still seemed to be in shreds. I ruthlessly aroused Madryn, asked him to send a note to Mr. Batt the moment anyone was likely to be awake at the vicarage, and wearily climbed to my bed in the loft.

I expected to be aroused myself the moment Sherlock Holmes received my message, but when I awoke it was mid-morning, rain was rattling against my window, and he had not appeared. Dafi brought hot water as soon as he realized that I was awake. He gave me a written reply from the vicar's housekeeper. Mr. Batt was not expected back until the next morning.

I made my way blearily down the ladder and hurried through the rain to the warm comfort of Mairwen Madryn's kitchen where she was already preparing a late breakfast for me. Then I returned to my loft and spent the remainder of the day, except for meals, in trying once more to piece the shreds into something resembling a case. It proved impossible. Madryn looked in on me, caught my mood with one glance, and went away. The rain continued and intensified.

During our evening meal, Madryn talked gloomily of his attempt to extract information from Meleri Huws concerning her father's death. "I discussed everyone in the valley with her," he said. "She doesn't believe anyone could have done it except two strangers who wore clogs."

"Why would strangers want to kill him?" I asked.

"She said perhaps it was someone he'd had a disagreement with at one of the markets. What do you think?"

"I think Sherlock Holmes is right. She's concealing something."

Madryn nodded despondently. "If she weren't, she'd have a much better story than that."

The Madryn family had received a bidding letter, an invitation to festivities accompanying a wedding, and they talked about it while we ate. The letter was in Welsh, of course, but when Madryn saw that I was interested, he translated it for me. It read, "We intend to enter the Matrimonial State on Friday, the 22nd of July next, and we are encouraged by our friends to make a BIDDING on the occasion on the same day, at the Boar's Head, situated in Groesffordd, when and where the favour of your good company is humbly solicited, and whatever donation you may be pleased to confer on us then, will be thankfully received, warmly acknowledged, and cheerfully repaid whenever called for on a similar occasion."

The bidding feast was held just before the wedding. Gifts of money were welcome, but people also brought furniture and household items to be lent to the couple until they could buy their own —

or until there was a wedding in the lender's family that required their return. The discussion of this novel and charming custom diverted me from my own despondency for almost half an hour.

The next morning it was still raining. Sherlock Holmes came early. He perched on the three-legged chair and listened quietly with a look of intense concentration on his hawk-like face while I recited the maid's testimony as precisely as I could remember it.

When I finished, he asked, "Are you convinced that she had the date correct?"

"Yes, sir. Very little has been happening at Tromblay Hall since Eleanor Tromblay died, and Glyn Huws's death was an event that shocked everyone. It was a day she would remember. Where is our case now? If Arthur Saunders is the sinister intellect behind your conspiracy, and he certainly meets every qualification, the slick way he bamboozled us into chasing after Evan Evans in London is awesome to contemplate. It must have been Bryn Huws who insisted that the two of them consult Sherlock Holmes, and Saunders felt that he had to assent. Then he contrived that rigmarole with Evans to draw our attention away from the murders."

Sherlock Holmes was shaking his head emphatically. "No, Porter. You are handling evidence the way a blacksmith deals with iron — beating it into shape to make it fit. The maid's testimony doesn't support this soaring deduction of yours."

He got out his pipe, lit it, and sent a smoke ring whirling. The draughty air of the loft tore it apart immediately.

I took a deep breath and started over. "Rhys Parry went to see Saunders the day after the murder and report that the deed had been done —"

Sherlock Holmes shook his head again. "Why would he do that? The day after the murder, everyone in this part of Wales knew that the deed had been done."

"Or to collect his payment."

Sherlock Holmes blew another smoke ring and watched thoughtfully while the draught shredded it the way our case had been shredded. "The maid was unable to tell you who Parry talked with."

"Who else could it have been? Ernest Lumbard and Henry Armstead were there. From what I saw of them at Emeric Tromblay's Saturday, I wouldn't suspect either of them of organizing anything more complicated than a game of baccarat. What was your impression?"

"That appearances can be deceiving, especially if the person observed has a natural bent for deceit. You are overlooking the most obvious deduction. Why would Rhys Parry be calling to see one of the *guests?* We have no evidence that he knew who they were or even that Tromblay had guests."

"Wain Welling had been away for at least three days. Madryn says he was in Cardiff. Parry wouldn't nave called to see him. And Tromblay left the day before because of the mine accident."

"It's unlikely that Parry would have known about the mine accident," Sherlock Holmes said.

"Then Parry called to see Tromblay, not knowing that he wasn't at home?"

"That would be a more credible interpretation than the one you were beating into place. Of course, there are other possibilities."

I remembered my own thought that Tromblay would be too sly to have direct dealings with Rhys Parry. Whoever handled that for him would be the person Parry called to see. I resolved to make inquiries about the English butler.

Tromblay had sent Welling to Cardiff, and that seemed significant. He wanted him as far from the scene as possible when Glyn Huws was murdered. He also removed himself from the scene. Had there really been a mine accident? That was another point that had to be investigated.

"I thought I'd turned up a valuable witness," I said dejectedly.

"You did much more than that," Sherlock Holmes said. "You found an invaluable witness. This is the first clue we've had that connects Rhys Parry directly with Tromblay Hall. Now we can look for more witnesses — one of whom may be Arthur Saunders. We'll take the next train to Newtown and ask him about this. I am as intrigued as you are to know what sort of business our worthy solicitor was conducting with the fiend of Tromblay Hall at the time of Glyn Huws's murder."

We splashed through the rain to Groesffordd Halt and took the afternoon train to Newtown. We were able to talk freely because we had the compartment to ourselves. After removing Haggart Batt's beard and carefully pocketing it, Sherlock Holmes told me of a potentially valuable witness that Rabby had found for him. "She may be able to identify our arch-criminal for us," he said. "If she can, we'll have a case."

"Who is she?" I asked.

"A woman who knew him many years ago."

"After I tramped for miles over the Welsh mountains, I suppose Rabby found this important witness in London at Y Llew Du. Is she Welsh?"

"She's English, and Radbert found her in Southwark."

He had several more items of information for me. For one, Kyle Connor had returned home. One of his first actions had been to communicate with the vicarage and invite Haggart Batt to a game of chess. They laboured a long evening over the chess board, battling to a draw. Connor now was able to conceal evidence of his bullet wound under his shirt. He hadn't mentioned his absence from home.

Sherlock Holmes still had no clue as to what Connor had been attempting to do in Aberystwyth, but he had turned up a few items of information about the untidy little man in the bowler. His name was Garat Sibley, and he was a friend of the owner of the official Camera Obscura. There were local rumours that when the device had been located on the grounds of Aberystwyth Castle, Sibley made private use of it in order to admire young ladies in bathing costume. He probably had his own instrument built when the official one was moved to the top of Constitution Hill. He was a relative of the building's owner and lived there permanently.

"When Connor arrived, he engaged room seventeen, the one next door to your room nineteen. Somehow he must have learned about Sibley's Camera Obscura, and he persuaded Sibley to allow him the use of it. Perhaps he threatened to expose him. There would be a minor scandal if it became known that Sibley was secretly ogling women on the beach."

"What did he expect to find out by sending Sibley to eavesdrop on us?" I asked.

"At the first favourable opportunity, I intend to ask him that."

Another item of information concerned the ore samples that Carl Prowse had taken to London. They were genuine even if their location was not. As Prowse had predicted, they contained lead and a small amount of silver. They were distinctive enough for him to identify the mid-Wales mine they had come from. It was the West Van Mine, near Llanidloes, and its owner was Emeric Tromblay.

We were ceremoniously though damply greeted by Humphrey the Bear when we descended the stairs at Newtown station through the continuing rain. We rode the Bear Bus to the hotel and went directly to the proprietor's office. Mr. Breese, as erect and gracious as a sovereign conferring the hospitality of his court, welcomed us as though we were old and valued customers.

"We have confidential business with Mr. Arthur Saunders," Sherlock Holmes said. "We require a comfortable room where we can meet him, and we are in need of someone who can take a message to him."

Mr. Breese conveyed the impression that he had never been surprised in his life and that such requests were a daily routine with him. He bowed and murmured, "Of course."

Sherlock Holmes had written the message on the train. He handed it to Mr. Breese in a sealed envelope. "This is to be placed in the hands of Mr. Saunders and no one else. If he is not at his office, the messenger should try to learn where he is and take it to him if he can be found."

Mr. Breese bowed again. He took the message and went out. He returned a moment later, escorted us to a comfortable room, and asked whether we would require refreshment while we waited.

"Cwrw da," I suggested.

Mr. Breese received this request with either a smile or a grimace. This became the subject of an argument between Sherlock Holmes and myself. He insisted that Mr. Breese had pulled a face because of the peculiarities of my Welsh pronunciation. I considered that unkind, especially when we learned afterwards that Mr. Breese did not speak Welsh. Sherlock Holmes maintained that persons unfamiliar with a language nevertheless learn to recognize a bad accent intuitively when they hear it spoken frequently. I argued that in Wales, even an innkeeper who couldn't speak Welsh was accustomed to accepting any or every variant of the pronunciation of cwrw da. Mr. Breese proved that by bringing the beer.

When he returned with it, I asked, "Is it from Sam Powell's brewery?"

"No," he said. "This is Worthington's beer — Burton-brewed."

I professed astonishment. "English beer — in a Welsh hotel? Cwrw Cymru yw'r gorau, Welsh beer is the best." It was a phrase Madryn had taught me.

Mr. Breese smiled or grimaced again. "This is very good beer," he said. "I'll bring Mr. Saunders to you myself as soon as he arrives."

We drank the beer and waited. Almost an hour went by, and its passage was measured off relentlessly by the quarter-hour chimings of the town clock. Finally there was a discreet tap on the door. Mr. Breese opened it, nodded and smiled, and stepped aside for Arthur Saunders, who was closely followed by Bryn Huws. Our two clients marched into the room and faced us expectantly. The pompous solicitor was as ornately dressed as he had been in London despite rain and mud spatters; Bryn Huws was in work clothing, and the unpleasant odour of his tannery announced him before Mr. Breese did.

"Would there be anything else?" Mr. Breese asked.

"Mwy o gwrw da," I said. "More good beer. Enough for four."

Mr. Breese smiled. "It is good beer, isn't it?"

The door closed after him. Bryn Huws blurted, "What have you found out?"

Sherlock Holmes said soberly, "You might as well know how our case stands. We have identified Glyn Huws's murderer. Unfortunately, there is very little evidence, and it may never be possible to convict him."

Arthur Saunders dropped into a chair. Bryn Huws remained standing.

"Who is it?" Huws demanded.

"It is a man named Rhys Parry."

The two exchanged glances. "I don't know him," Saunders said. "Bryn?"

Huws shook his head. "I've never heard of him."

"He comes originally from the village of Bangor-is-y-coed," Sherlock Holmes said. "He was a coracle fisherman until he went to work in a mine near Llanidloes. For the past several months he seems to have occupied himself with his own affairs. His clogs match prints found at the murder scene."

"Meleri told me that Mr. Jones found two pairs of clogprints at Llangelyn," Saunders said.

"So he did," Sherlock Holmes said. "Rhys Parry had a companion."

"Do you know who the companion was?"

"I know who he probably was — a boy of sixteen who came from London shortly before Glyn Huws's murder. He is known there as Alban Griffiths. Parry has been his mentor and constant companion. The boy's clogs match the other set of prints — they were virtually new clogs — and I found a newly-minted florin where he had been standing. A coin of that description is an oddity in rural Wales. I assume that he brought it with him, and I know that he bought new clogs when he arrived here. This is indication enough that he accompanied Parry. I have no evidence at all that he actually took part in the murder."

"Incredible!" Saunders murmured. "You are wizards — both of you! Then — it wasn't Emeric Tromblay? But why would this stranger want to murder Glyn? Was he hired to do so?"

"Hired — or ordered."

"He worked in a mine near Llanidloes," Saunders said slowly. "Was it a mine owned by Emeric Tromblay?"

"It was," Sherlock Holmes said. "It is called the West Van Mine."

"Ah!" Saunders exclaimed, and Bryn Huws exploded in Welsh. "But must we leave the crime unpunished?" Saunders demanded.

Mr. Breese tapped lightly on the door and brought in cwrw da for four. When he had closed the door again, Bryn Huws seized a tankard and drained it in one long draught. Then he sank into a chair.

"There's much that can be done," Sherlock Holmes said, "and we are doing it. We came to see you because you may have important information for us. The day Glyn Huws was murdered, you were a guest at Tromblay Hall."

"I was. Two of my clients were conducting business negotiations with Tromblay, and they insisted that I accompany them. He is a hard nut in business dealings, and they wanted all the support they could muster." He smiled wryly. "They needed it."

"What was the business?" Sherlock Holmes asked.

"The purchase of a piece of property in Llanfair Caereinion."

"Did you complete the negotiations?"

"We did not. Tromblay was called away by a mishap at one of the mines he has an interest in. He promised to return the next day and settle the matter, but the accident proved to be more serious than he'd thought. He was away for several days, and of course we didn't wait for him. I personally think he had no intention of selling the property. He takes an inordinate pride in his skill as a negotiator, and he will spend a day or two discussing terms just for the pleasure of negotiating."

"It is extremely important to establish the exact sequence of events on the day Glyn Huws was murdered," Sherlock Holmes said. "When did you arrive at Tromblay Hall?"

"Late the previous afternoon," Saunders said.

"And — when did you start the negotiations?"

"Not until after dinner and then in a very casual, almost leisurely way. Tromblay was pretending it was merely a house party. That was why I thought he had no intention of selling the property."

"Those negotiations interest me. Who were your two clients?"

"Ernest Lumbard and Henry Armstead," Saunders said.

"With yourself in support, of course. Did Emeric Tromblay have Wain Welling in support?"

"Welling wasn't there. Tromblay had sent him somewhere on business. Tromblay wouldn't have allowed him to take part in a property sale anyway. Welling is very good at management, but he has no background in appraisals, and Tromblay wouldn't trust anyone but himself in the buying or selling of property."

"Then you had a casual discussion the night of your arrival. When did the serious negotiations begin?"

"Immediately after breakfast the next morning."

"With no progress?"

"Progress on only a few minor points. Word of the mining accident came just before noon. Tromblay left at once, telling us he hoped to be back before noon the next day, and we could complete the negotiations then."

"But he didn't return. And you tired of waiting for him and left — when?"

"The next afternoon."

"Then on the day Glyn Huws was murdered, Tromblay had sent Welling away on business — "

"He left a day or two before I arrived," Saunders said.

"Emeric Tromblay was called away just before noon. Late that afternoon, Glyn Huws was murdered. When did you hear about it?"

"The next morning. When my clients left for home, shortly after noon, I went directly to Meini Mawr to be of what help I could to Meleri."

"There was a caller at Tromblay Hall the morning after Glyn Huws was murdered. Do you remember anything about him?"

Saunders's face went blank. "Are you sure? I don't remember one."

"A rough-looking man with reddish hair and beard."

Saunders shook his head. "No. I didn't see him.

"Perhaps he came to see one of your clients. Would you ask whether either of them remembers him?"

"I'll ask, but I'm certain that he didn't see them," Saunders said confidently. "The three of us spent virtually the entire morning in the billiard room. We couldn't blame Tromblay for being called away by a mining accident, but it was already evident that he had no intention of selling the property, and our only concern was to make a polite departure."

Sherlock Holmes turned to me. "Have you any questions, Porter?"

I could think of nothing further to ask about Emeric Tromblay's strange house party, but it did occur to me that our clients might know something about the local activities of the Robert Owen Study League. "Do you know what Benton Tromblay is doing?" I asked.

"Of course," Saunders said. "I ought to. I'm paying him."

I was too startled to say anything. Sherlock Holmes asked calmly, "Are you a member of the Robert Owen Study League?"

"I'm its solicitor. I assisted with its organization, and I'm handling its funds until permanent officers are chosen. Benton is receiving two pounds a week for lecturing on Robert Owen at meetings around Wales. His travelling expenses are reimbursed. It isn't a lavish salary, but it's considerably more than he was paid by the Royal Welsh Warehouse, and he's living much better. He'd gained weight the last time I saw him."

"What is the Robert Owen Study League?" Sherlock Holmes asked.

"It's an organization established by a group of local citizens who have long thought that Robert Owen has been shamefully neglected in his native town. Its purpose is exactly what the name implies — to disseminate Robert Owen's ideas and to encourage their study. Money to finance its activities has been raised by subscription. The first project decided on was the lecture series. This will be the fulcrum for an attempt to organize local chapters throughout Wales and eventually in England. In fact, the organizing meeting will be held a week from this coming Friday. July 15th."

"Where will it be held?" Sherlock Holmes asked.

"At Devil's Bridge."

"Is there a place to meet there?"

"It will be an outdoor meeting. We'll use a tent pavilion — to protect people from the sun or the rain as the case may be. In Wales, we always prepare for rain."

"Will you be attending?" Sherlock Holmes asked.

"Certainly. I'm the group's solicitor."

"And you?" he asked Bryn Huws.

"I don't need any theories about work," Huws said sourly. "I am too busy doing it."

"Exactly where will this meeting take place at Devil's Bridge?"

Arthur Saunders neither knew nor cared. The arrangements were none of his responsibility. Several of the organization's sponsors would accompany him, and a guide would be provided for them.

"How much money was raised for the Robert Owen Study League?" Sherlock Holmes asked.

Saunders frowned. "Do you have a reason for asking?"

"I do. The organization may be connected with the murder of Glyn Huws."

"That's preposterous!"

Bryn Huws sent a scrutinizing look at Sherlock Holmes. "Tell him what he wants to know," he said to Saunders. "If his reason turns out to be preposterous, then nothing more need be said about it."

"Two thousand pounds was subscribed," Saunders said reluctantly.

Sherlock Holmes raised his eyebrows. "A handsome sum. Are there arrangements to raise more money later?"

"That hasn't been discussed. By the time more money is needed, there will be permanent officers, and the finances will be none of my concern."

"Who subscribed the money?"

Saunders said stiffly, "That's confidential."

"Of course," Sherlock Holmes said. "We'll see that it remains so."

"I don't have it memorized."

"Then kindly send us a copy. I must have the list of sponsors and the amount that each contributed. We'll wait here for it."

The two Welshmen left. Sherlock Holmes said to me, "Whatever inspired you to ask them about Benton Tromblay?"

"I thought they might know something about the Robert Owen Study League's activities in New-town."

"Astonishing! Your discussions with Madryn about the Tylwyth Têg, and wizards, and corpse candles, and Celtic gods must be affecting your thinking. I hope you took note of the fact that the Robert Owen Study League continues to hold its meetings at places where crowds of tourists are to be found. Devil's Bridge is one of the most popular scenic attractions in Wales — and justly so. I want you and Madryn to go there tomorrow and learn what you can in advance of this meeting."

"Are you coming back to Pentrederwydd with me?"

"No. There are matters that need my attention here. You'll have to return alone on the next train, which — if our client doesn't dawdle — will be shortly before five."

Mr. Saunders didn't dawdle. He rushed the information to us, and it arrived in a sealed envelope brought by a thoroughly wet messenger. While I rewarded the messenger with a shilling in compensation for his drenching, Sherlock Holmes ripped open the envelope. He glanced down the list of names and pursed his lips thoughtfully.

When the messenger had left, he handed the paper to me without comment. The names were arranged in a column with an amount of money set opposite each one. None of them was familiar to me except the one at the bottom of the list. That entry read:

"Mr. Kyle Connor .... £1,000."

20

THE JUNCTURE OF THE RHEIDOL AND THE MYNACH Rivers occurs in wild country twelve miles west of Aberystwyth. The Mynach, after rushing through a series of cauldrons gouged out of solid rock by its swirling waters, plunges down a rocky chasm in cascades that form a three hundred foot drop. The turbulent Rheidol, in its approach from the north, has carved its own twisting chasm for several miles before the two meet, including a spectacular fall. The combined flow continues westward to meet the sea at Aberystwyth. The two rivers offer some of the most awe-inspiring scenery to be found anywhere in Britain.

Devil's Bridge, called by the Welsh Pont y Gŵr Drŵg, Bridge of the Evil Man — in order to avoid mentioning the Devil by name — or Pont y Mynach, the Monk's Bridge, spans the Mynach at the point where its falls begin. Since the bridge has several names, it is only fitting that there should be three Devil's Bridges. The lowest of the three, the original Bridge of the Evil Man, is an old stone structure of the Middle Ages, probably built by monks from Strata Florida Abbey some ten miles to the south.

The name is thought to have originated in later times among superstitious peasants who refused to believe that mere humans could build a bridge over such an awful chasm. Since the bridge was there, they thought the Devil must have built it. This gave rise to the folk-tale about the woman who discovered that her cow had somehow made its way to the other side. While she was wondering how to recover it, the Devil appeared and offered to build a bridge for her — on the condition that he could have the first living creature to cross it. She accepted; he quickly built the bridge. Then she cheated him by rolling a loaf of bread across. Her small dog pursued it, the Devil acknowledged himself bested, and she retrieved her cow. The Devil's Bridge remained.

Above the still-intact medieval bridge is a stone bridge dating from the eighteenth century; above that bridge is a modern iron bridge.

These untamed surroundings seemed an odd setting for an organizational meeting of the Robert Owen Study League; but Devil's Bridge had been an immensely popular tourist attraction for decades, and it was easily reached from Aberystwyth in slightly more than an hour by the narrow-gauge railway that ran several trains daily. Neither conspirators nor those attending the meeting of the League were likely to attract much attention. A regiment could have lost itself in the crowds of tourists at Devil's Bridge or the wild land surrounding it.

George Borrow arrived there in 1854 after a two-day walk in the rain. Dafydd Madryn and I also arrived there in the rain along with a trainload of tourists. The tourists hurried down the steep hill from the station toward the Hafod Arms Hotel and other establishments offering refreshment and shelter. This rain had continued steadily for several days. With that forewarning, they had dressed themselves in an amazing variety of mackintoshes and waterproofs, but they were going to get drenched regardless. After a heavy rain to swell the rivers, these were extremely damp scenic wonders.

Madryn and I trudged in the opposite direction. Gareth Vaughan, the brother of Pentrederwydd's boot and clogmaker, had a small farm in the neighbourhood, and we carried a letter to him from Ifan. Gareth was a thinner, shorter edition of his brother. He greeted us with warm friendliness and immediately made us welcome. He put Ifan's letter aside to read later — or perhaps, as Madryn suggested, until he could find someone to read it to him — and he gave us permission to sleep in his barn loft as long as we wanted to stay. Madryn arranged with Gareth's wife, Olwen, to prepare meals for us whenever we required them, after which we set out to enjoy Devil's Bridge with the tourists and at the same time spy out the place where the Robert Owen Study League would hold its meeting.

That first afternoon we climbed down to view the cauldrons below the bridges, and then we made the very wet descent to the foot of the Mynach falls and the long, tiring, exceedingly sloppy and slippery climb back up. Even in the rain, the scenic wonders were wonderful, and the Mynach, in spate from the prolonged downpour, had the long descent of its cascades transformed into an almost continuous, spectacular drop.

We made our way back to the road and the various establishments offering refreshments, climbed the hill to the railway station with the crowd of tourists hurrying to catch the last train back to Aberystwyth, and then returned to Gareth Vaughan's farm, where Olwen Vaughan had supper waiting for us.

That evening we sought the nearest tavern in the hope of picking up useful information from local gossip. Madryn translated what he overheard, and I quickly learned that gossip among the natives at Devil's Bridge was no more interesting than gossip at Pentrederwydd. I was suggesting that we make a wet retreat to Vaughan's farm and hope for better luck another day when there was an outburst of laughter from a group at a nearby table. Madryn nudged me and cocked his head to hear better.

"They're talking about someone named Einir Jones," he whispered finally. "He has a reputation like that of Cadan Morgan in Pentrederwydd."

"Does he also work in his uncle's tavern?" I asked.

"His brother's," Madryn said. "Einir claims to have seen some Rebeccas last night. All of his friends think that's hilarious."

"Was last night the first time he saw them?"

"They're talking as though it was. They attribute it to more drink than usual, but Einir was sober enough to count the Rebeccas, which is what seems so funny to them. He counted them several times, and he always got the same number. There were seven of them."

"I suppose that proves he was drunk," I said. "How could he see to count anything on a black, rainy night?"

"There were buildings nearby and a bit of light from the windows. His friends are joking that he must have counted the horses' legs and divided by four. It proves — "

"It proves that our case has moved to Devil's Bridge," I said. "Tomorrow we must go to work in earnest."

Because Arthur Saunders hadn't known the exact place where the Robert Owen Study League was to meet, our task was to find it. Sherlock Holmes considered it imperative that we know the site long enough in advance to reconnoitre it carefully. His plan depended on this.

For four days we tramped or rode — on borrowed horses — throughout the neighbourhood, ranging as far south as the evocative ruins of the Strata Florida Abbey, which in the thirteenth and fourteenth centuries was the political and religious centre of Wales, and as far north as the village of Ponterwyd, the Bridge of Erwyd. Every time we crossed the Devil's Bridge, I paused at the parapet to stare down into the narrow abyss that the river had carved and gaze hypnotically at the turbulent waters that thundered through the cauldrons far below. With each additional day of rain, their turbulence increased.

Despite the area's popularity with tourists, the local farmers had small profit from that trade, and many of them resented it. Madryn thought it wise to give them the impression that both of us were Welsh. He conducted our inquiries, and there was nothing left for me to do but follow him about and wait for him to tell me afterward what was said.

We accomplished very little. An army brigade could have vanished into the country around Devil's Bridge without leaving a trace. If the Robert Owen Study League wished to meet in secret, it couldn't have selected a better location.

A mile north of Devil's Bridge was the lovely little church of Ysbyty Cynfyn. A short distance west of it lay the deep chasm through which the Rheidol flowed, spanned by the famous Parson's Bridge. The roar of water could be heard long before the chasm was reached. Madryn and I descended the precipitous, slippery, zigzagging path into its depths and stood on the bridge looking down at the violently rushing river. The rain had swollen the Rheidol, also, and it pounded with foaming fury in its swirling rampage through the weirdly carved, rocky bed. The parson for whom the bridge was named had used it as a short cut to the church. He rode out from Aberystwyth to conduct services and left his horse on the west side of the Rheidol, continuing on foot across the bridge and up the steep, meandering path that led out of the chasm to the church.

As at Devil's Bridge, the relentless water had a hypnotic effect on me. I shouted to Madryn above the incessant roar, "Did anyone ever fall in here?"

"I never heard of it," he shouted back. "Anyway, the water is usually much lower."

Now it was in spate, and any human or animal that tumbled into that twisting, rushing torrent would be pounded to a pulp against the rocks.

A short distance north of the bridge was a structure that looked like a stone factory building with the rusting remnant of a large wheel. This seemed like a most unlikely and inaccessible place to locate an industry, but at one time there had been a productive lead mine here. Now it was abandoned as no longer profitable.

We returned to the church, which strongly reminded me of the ruins of St. Celyn's church at Llangelyn. It was a place of worship such as Llangelyn might have become if the good saint nadn't chosen a location so remote and inaccessible. The Ysbyty Cynfyn church also stood within the remains of a circle of standing stones on a site whose religious function dated far back into pagan times. Five of the stones survived and had been incorporated into the stone wall that surrounded the churchyard.

While I meditated the possible fate of St. Celyn's church in kindlier surroundings, Madryn went about the churchyard reading Welsh messages on the tombstones. He returned to me shaking his head.

"So many young men," he said. "Such a terrible thing for men to be dying young and in such numbers."

"What killed them?" I asked.

"This is mining country. You saw the old mine. There are many of them near Devil's Bridge. One way or another, mining is killing work." He gestured at the tombstones. No further evidence seemed necessary. Each represented a family tragedy that left parents, a wife, and children in mourning.

We began again with a well-thought-out search, floundered about for an entire day, and succeeded only in getting ourselves lost for several hours. In desperation, because the meeting was now only four days off, we tried a much simpler approach. We called on the farmers of the neighbourhood, introduced ourselves as Robert Owen Study League members who had arrived early for the meeting, and observed the response. The first six had never heard of the organization and wanted nothing to do with it or with us. The next had heard something from one of his neighbours; the neighbour had heard something from his neighbour; and in this roundabout manner we arrived back at Devil's Bridge. On the north side of the bridge, in an open space high on a hill above the Mynach, we found the pavilion awaiting erection — a thick pile of folded canvas with poles laid nearby.

When we returned to Gareth Vaughan's farm, Sherlock Holmes was waiting for us. He had stopped off in Pentrederwydd and commissioned Con Davey to arrange a meeting with Elen Edwards. "She brought another servant with her," he said. "One Gwynora Howell. I now know who Rhys Parry was talking with at Tromblay Hall the day after Glyn Huws's murder. It was an ostler named Elgan Bowen. Parry visits him frequently."

"Does it mean anything?" I asked.

"I'm certain that it does, but I'm not yet prepared to say what."

"Perhaps Bowen receives Parry's reports and delivers orders to him."

"That is one way to read this riddle — one of several."

He wanted to see the site of the meeting at once. He moved about the hilltop with long strides, pointing his nose like a bloodhound in pursuit of a fugitive, his face taut with worry and concentration. The plan he had formulated offered our only hope of bringing the case to a quick conclusion, he said, and its success depended on our knowing the ground perfectly.

"There must be more to it than this, " he said finally. "The League's members will gather here. They'll hold another of their innocuous meetings, transact their business, and leave. Then — as has happened in every instance I have been able to investigate — a few members of the audience will forgather somewhere nearby to conduct their own very private meeting. In the past they've met in taverns, or hotel rooms, or private homes. None of those are available here, but assuredly they will meet. It is absolutely essential that we find out where."

We nosed our way down pathways from the hilltop, investigated pleasant glades, circled clearings, pushed through groves of trees. Finally Madryn found it: a second, much smaller pavilion awaiting erection in a concealed hollow. Sherlock Holmes paced around it in widening circles, clucking his tongue thoughtfully.

He was like a Field Marshal studying the ground while he plotted strategy and tactics for a major engagement — placing infantry here, the light brigade there, meditating the timing of the great counterstroke that would change the course of the battle. I'd never seen him so intensely serious. By the time he finished, I was ready to believe that the tide of history could be turned by what we accomplished here.

"The witness I mentioned is staying at the Hafod Arms Hotel," he said. "I brought her here myself. She seems sprightly enough despite her seventy-six years, but I want to impose as little physical strain on her as possible. There are certain to be sentries posted on every approach. I expect to avoid them by reaching our places of concealment before they arrive. You and Dafydd will be attending the meeting, so you may have difficulties."

He kept us searching until both Madryn and I were familiar with the surrounding ground and prepared for any contingency. Finally he pronounced himself satisfied and gave us our instructions.

That night the three of us went to a tavern in the little village of Pontrhydygroes, Bridge of the Ford Crossing, where Einir Jones worked. When he brought us our cwrw, Sherlock Holmes asked him, "Have you seen any more Rebeccas?"

Einir drew back angrily. He understood very little English, but his friends had been poking fun at him about the Rebeccas in both languages. Sherlock Holmes asked Madryn to explain to him in Welsh that we, also, had seen the Rebeccas — riders who obviously were men dressed as women.

Einir Jones darted anxious glances about the room. Then he leaned forward, spoke in a whisper, and hurried away. Madryn translated, "He sees them every night. But now when he sees them, he leaves the road — and he no longer takes the trouble to count them."

"Interesting," Sherlock Holmes mused.

"Are there reports of Rebeccas from all over Wales?" I asked him.

"There have been sightings of Rebeccas in several places where the Robert Owen Study League was holding a meeting. Probably the reports would be more widespread if people weren't so reticent on that subject. The same was true sixty years ago. People who spoke out about something that didn't concern them found their own property smashed."

"What possible connection could the Rebeccas have with the Robert Owen Study League?" I demanded. I tried to imagine a link between the rather stodgy respectability of an Arthur Saunders and his fellow citizens of Newtown and night riders wearing dresses. I failed utterly.

Sherlock Holmes tapped his fingers together and remarked, "This is a complicated case."

"I've noticed," I said.

He looked at me with a smile. "Never forget this, Porter. 'Complicated' doesn't necessarily mean 'difficult.' Our case is complicated only because it contains so many disparate elements. They are easily understood by concentrating on the main facts and remembering that the same mind is responsible for all of them. The larger crimes are always the most simple, and this is the largest crime I have ever encountered."

We rode back to Devil's Bridge and stopped at the Hafod Arms Hotel, where Sherlock Holmes introduced us to a charming little grey-haired woman named Liza Williams. I gave this key witness my utmost attention. She seemed to be equally interested in me.

"Mr. Holmes told me your grandfather was Welsh," she said.

"Yes. He worked on a canal boat that brought slates to Paddington, and he decided to stay in London."

"My husband was a drover," she said. "He brought Welsh cattle to England. He was a handsome devil, always bent on a good time, but there was no evil in him. He wasn't the *Diafol* Mr. Holmes has told me about, the man who murders. But my husband wasn't much good at anything but droving — except for talk. In English or Welsh he could talk a brush out of its bristles. He was a great one for stories." She sighed. "He was a great one for Welsh history, too. I thought all of that was done with long ago."

"Some stories keep repeating themselves," Sherlock Holmes said. "Are you comfortable here?"

"Very much so. Do you know — I've never been in Wales before. I've never been farther from London than Greenwich. After all the talk about Wales that I listened to from my husband for more than thirty years, it's a strange feeling to look around me and think that this was what he was talking about."

"We'll call for you in the morning and take you to see the place," Sherlock Holmes said.

"Very well. As I told you, I don't give a fig for your conspiracy, but when it's a question of murder, I quite agree that something must be done."

"It's a question of two murders," Sherlock Holmes said. "Without your help, there certainly will be more."

"I still find that difficult to believe, but I'll do the best I can."

The next day the rain continued. We paid another visit to the meeting places and reviewed our plans, and then we took Liza Williams to see the hollow where she was to perform such a critically important role. Wrapped in a flapping waterproof, she climbed about as agilely as I did. When I congratulated her, she exclaimed, "Gammon! My husband couldn't hold a job, and I had to char all my life to support my family. After climbing those steep stairs in London, Welsh hills are nothing."

We took her back to the hotel. Sherlock Holmes went off on an errand of his own, and since there was little that we could do in the heavy rain, Madryn and I returned to our loft. We tried to pass the time by expanding my Welsh vocabulary — "Ceffyl ydy hwn, this is a horse. Gwely ydy hwn, this is a bed." I was too worried about the weather to concentrate. If the heavy rain continued, it would make severe difficulties for us on the morrow.

By evening it had diminished to a drizzle, and the next day dawned cloudy but rainless. The clouds soon blew off to the east. The sun was shining brilliantly, and Sherlock Holmes and Liza Williams had already sought their hiding place near the hollow, when Madryn and I walked down to Devil's Bridge and paused to look again into the chasm. The roaring, swirling torrent looked more swollen each time I saw it. It fascinated and terrified me as it foamed and pounded and tossed from one rocky cauldron to another, attacking them with relentless fury, before it vanished under the bridge to take its dramatic plunge to the valley floor.

We walked on across the bridge and followed the road up the hill. The large pavilion tent on the hilltop was invisible from the road, but there already was a smiling attendant at the path that led up to it, waiting to greet supporters of the Robert Owen Study League. A quarter of a mile farther along the road we passed another path without seeming to notice it. It led in the direction of the meeting place in the hidden hollow, and the sentries posted there sat on a rock behind a clump of bushes, almost — but not quite — concealed.

Many of those attending the meeting of the Robert Owen Study League arrived on the first tourist train of the day, gave themselves the thrill of climbing down into the chasm for a close look at the churning waters, and then, perspiring and satiated with scenic wonders, moved on to the pavilion on the hill. Madryn and I turned back to join them, and we were among the first arrivals. Our forged passes were not challenged. We took seats in the rear of the tent where we could watch later arrivals struggling up the last steep lap of the path to the hilltop.

The pavilion was already half-filled when a sturdy Welsh pony heaved into view. Its rider presented a remarkable profile to us — large head, well-developed arms and shoulders, emaciated legs. It was Kyle Connor. Gerwyn Pugh, the elderly husband of Connor's housekeeper, was leading the pony, and two farm-hands, one on either side, were swearing at it in English. Probably this was the only English they knew. When they reached the pavilion, they lifted Connor down from the pony and got him seated. Then they led the pony to one side and settled themselves to wait.

Connor had already seen Madryn and me. He waved to us. Then he motioned us to join him. His arrival had been so conspicuous that it seemed silly to pretend not to notice him. When we reached him, he adroitly separated us, placing Madryn on one side and me on the other.

"I had no idea that you two were interested in Robert Owen," he said.

"It's Benton Tromblay we're interested in," I told him. "Dafydd grew up with him, in a manner of speaking, and I met him in Newtown. The real surprise is in meeting you here."

"It was an excuse for a short trip," he said with a shrug. "I don't get away from home very often." He managed to keep his face completely innocent.

I leaned toward him and said quietly, "In Newtown last week, I chanced to meet several of the men responsible for the Robert Owen Study League, and they told me something about the League's history. I was astonished to learn that you are its most important financial backer."

He glanced about cautiously. Then he leaned forward and spoke almost in a whisper. "It's too good a joke not to tell. Can you keep it to yourselves?"

"Of course," I said.

"Personally, I think all of Robert Owen is balderdash. I can't understand how such an impractical person was able to make himself a business success. I wouldn't contribute a farthing to advance the study of such nonsense. I got involved as a favour to a friend. It wasn't my money that I donated — it was his."

I waited expectantly.

"It was Emeric Tromblay's money," Connor went on softly. "He heard that the League would hire Benton as a lecturer if it raised enough money. He wanted to get him out of the Royal Welsh Warehouse — he loathes the Pryce-Jones family — and he thought travelling about and making himself known to audiences all over Wales would be excellent experience for him. He expects him to stand for Parliament in a few years and depose Col. Edward Pryce-Jones. But of course Emeric couldn't donate money in his own name to such a project, so he asked me to help him out. And since I'm now the League's most important donor, thanks to his money, I had to come to this stupid meeting just to maintain appearances." He sighed. "It all comes of helping a friend. I'll tell you something even funnier. Emeric is coming, too."

"Emeric Tromblay is coming here?"

He nodded. "He's never heard Benton lecture. He wants to find out if he's as good as people say. He'll disguise himself, of course. I've always been curious as to how he would look with whiskers. I wonder what style of beard he'll choose."

"Benton really is a very good speaker," I said. "We heard him in Newtown and again in Aberystwyth. He knows his subject thoroughly."

Connor ignored my reference to Aberystwyth. He turned to study a group of newcomers. "Look for a beard," he said. "Emeric certainly will use a beard. How else could he disguise himself?"

"Where did he get his pass?" I asked.

"From me. I asked for one for a friend. They'd have given me a hundred if they thought I wanted them." He turned and looked at me levelly. "Where did *you* get passes?"

"We got ours from Benton," I said.

He nodded and turned to look at another group of new-comers. "There he is!" he exclaimed suddenly. "Emeric Tromblay — at a meeting of the Robert Owen Study League! Who would have believed it! He looks moth-eaten."

"Moth-eaten" was not quite the correct term. I would have described the bristling monstrosity of a beard that filled Emeric Tromblay's face as untidy and excessive. He seated himself and looked about curiously until he saw us watching him. Then he stiffened self-consciously and fixed his attention on the empty speakers' table.

The speakers arrived a few minutes later, Benton Tromblay amongst them. The meeting began, and it was the dullest two and a half hours I have ever been condemned to sit through. Benton Tromblay brightened the occasion for twenty minutes or so with an exposition of the importance of Robert Owen's ideas and a devastating blast at those who considered Owen an impractical dreamer. All of Owen's major ideas, he said — and he ticked them off — had been tried out and found successful by Owen himself before he advocated their widespread use. Benton spoke very effectively, and he actually awakened that drowsy audience for a few minutes. Then we all went back to sleep while Arthur Saunders presented a charter and an initial slate of officers for our approval, introduced the organization's new chairman of its new directors, helped that confused gentleman to answer several highly technical questions asked by another gentleman who sounded like an unsuccessful candidate, reminded the audience that the directors would be meeting with local committees all over Wales during the next several months, and adjourned the meeting.

I'd expected Emeric Tromblay to sneak away the moment Benton finished speaking, but he sat patiently through the entire meeting. Probably he feared to make himself conspicuous by leaving early, but he was the first person out of the tent when the meeting was over. Kyle Connor had aptly expressed his own opinion of the affair by drifting off to sleep during the presentation of the charter. I woke him when Arthur Saunders pronounced the adjournment, and Madryn went for his pony. The two of us helped the farm-hands get him mounted again. Then we excused ourselves, telling him that we wanted a word with Benton Tromblay before we left. Gerwyn Pugh led the pony away, and the farm-hands marched silently on either side of it. No profanity was necessary to propel it *down* the hill. It walked with alacrity. Probably it had found the meeting as boring as we did. We went to the table at the front of the tent where the new directors, Benton among them, were surrounded by well-wishers and critics. I caught Benton's eye and waved, and then Madryn and I made an ostentatious departure.

We started down the path toward the road, took a carefully planned wrong turning, circled widely, and then, with extreme caution, we followed the route Sherlock Holmes had selected for us. We managed to avoid three separate sentry posts and reach our assigned vantage point without incident.

Because of the favourable turn in the weather, the pavilion in the hollow had not been erected. Instead, a large tarpaulin was spread on the ground. There were no chairs. A few men stood about talking quietly. Others joined them until eventually there were more than thirty. When a signal sounded nearby — the cry of an owl — they took their places on the tarpaulin as though they were arranging themselves for some kind of ceremonial game.

I kept my eyes fixed on the path, eagerly awaiting the arrival of our arch-villain. Finally I saw a group of men approaching. Emeric Tromblay was not among them. Neither was Kyle Connor. First came Rhys Parry and behind him the fair-haired Alban Griffiths. The others followed closely. The newcomers filed to one side or the other and found places for themselves on the tarpaulin. A hushed, expectant silence settled over the hollow, and then, slowly, all of them removed their hats and sank to their knees.

The music began, which startled me because I hadn't seen any musicians. The sounds were peculiar. The instruments were more so — two each of types that were entirely new to me. I learned later that they were crŵths, a small harp played with a bow, and pibgorns, a reed instrument with a tone that resembled that of an oboe. Both of them had been obsolete for a century or more.

The procession they led arrived from an unexpected direction. I found myself looking down onto the backs of two attendants attired smartly in doublets and short breeches, cloaks, and tall boots. Their broad-brimmed hats were rakishly topped with long feathers. Following them with measured, majestical stride came the king.

I gasped and looked again. The King! The thought struck me squarely and almost toppled me. "Not Edward VII!" I exclaimed to myself. "Surely there's no place in this case for royalty!"

The stately, crowned figure swept on with regal stride, purple robes flowing. Two more attendants followed, attired like the first two. Those waiting in the hollow kept their eyes averted while the procession moved past them. It was not until the robed figure took his place at the head of the gathering that I was able to see him in profile.

Then the picture snapped sharply into focus. He looked nothing like Edward VII. There was no paunch and no beard.

It was Wain Welling.

The four attendants backed away respectfully, removed their hats, and sank to their knees. Welling began to speak in Welsh. His resonant voice carried perfectly. Madryn whispered a translation of his opening sentence in which he told those assembled there that they held the future of Wales within their grasp, to shape it or destroy it.

That was the moment Sherlock Holmes chose to impose his own plan on the battlefield. Liza Williams entered the hollow with a puzzled sentry trailing after her. She had been instructed to say in Welsh to anyone who tried to stop her, "I have an urgent private message for the Prince." The sentry's orders didn't cover that kind of contingency. He permitted her to pass, but he followed closely after her to make certain that she actually did have a message.

In her old-fashioned clothing she looked like an incongruously thin Queen Victoria as she marched up to the perplexed Welling, made a low curtsy, and handed him an envelope. Behind her, the sentry sank to his knees. The others continued to kneel. Madryn and I moved closer to the hollow during the disturbance that Liza Williams and the sentry made. On the opposite side, Sherlock Holmes did the same. By the time Welling finally turned his attention to the envelope and ripped it open, we were in position to see and hear everything.

He glanced at the paper, read it, then read it again. When he had finished, he gazed at Liza Williams open-mouthed.

She spoke to him in English. "Don't you know me, Harry? Liza Williams. I lived next door to you in Southwark when you were a child. Surely you remember me — I've known you all your life. It seems funny hearing an English boy like you speaking Welsh. My husband taught you well, didn't he?" She turned to the assembly. "Why are you silly people kneeling to a plain Englishman like Harry Smith?"

Rhys Parry got to his feet. He advanced several steps. Alban Griffiths brushed past him and went to Welling's side. Parry said, "Harry Smith? An Englishman?" He made the word sound like something foul.

"She's lying," Alban Griffiths said.

"I speak the truth," Liza Williams said. "This man who calls himself Welling and pretends to be a prince is plain Harry Smith. He grew up next door to me in Southwark — that's across the Thames from London. He used to play with my children. He lived there from the time he was born until he got married and moved to the next street. Of course he's an Englishman. I knew his parents for years — there was no better Englishman anywhere than his father, Dick Smith. I attended Harry's wedding. When his wife died giving birth, I helped him find a Welsh family willing to look after his son so he could go to Wales and seek his fortune. From the way you silly people are kneeling to him, he must have found it." She turned to Alban Griffiths. "This is his son. He looks just like his mother, who was a sweet, pretty girl and as English as his father is. He was called Alban Griffiths by the people who raised him, but his real name is Bertie Smith. He was named after Prince Albert, and I attended his christening."

Rhys Parry said again, "Harry Smith? An Englishman?"

Harry Smith — alias Wain Welling — acted with startling quickness. He tossed aside the paper Liza Williams had handed him, slipped out of his robes and crown, and grabbed his son's hand. The two of them dashed away toward the road. Rhys Parry stared after them, momentarily stunned. Then he sprinted in pursuit with a howl of rage. Sherlock Holmes, Madryn, and I burst from our cover on opposite sides of the hollow and followed them, leaving the kneeling assembly looking after us with blank astonishment on every face.

The chase was not a long one. Welling and the boy pounded down the hill to the bridge, dodging among the throngs of tourists. In the center of the span, Welling turned and looked back. Rhys Parry had drawn a knife. A short distance behind him, Sherlock Holmes, no longer disguised as Haggart Batt, was closing on Parry with long strides. He had a revolver in his hand. Madryn and I followed closely.

Welling shouted something into the boy's ear. The two of them deftly mounted the bridge's parapet and leaped into the abyss below. Parry reached the spot an instant too late. His howl of rage was drowned in the roar of the water as he stared down at the foaming, raging torrent that already had whirled Welling and his son out of sight. Then, as Sherlock

Holmes closed to within a stride of him, he vaulted the parapet and disappeared.

Madryn and I arrived a moment later. I caught only a fleeting glimpse of Parry at the bottom of the chasm as the stream's churning fury seized his body. Probably there were screams and shouts of horror from the tourists below and also from those in the valley beyond who had seen the bodies of Welling and the boy carried by the foaming cataract on its long plunge, but they were lost in the torrent's incessant thunder.

Sherlock Holmes resignedly pocketed his revolver. He signalled with a nod of his head, and we hurried back up the hill toward the hollow to make certain that Liza Williams was receiving no discourtesy from the late prince's subjects.

"I'm sorry about Alban Griffiths," he said regretfully when we were far enough from the bridge to make ourselves heard. "He was young. I had hoped that he could find a new life for himself."

Madryn was still too stunned to speak. "You were right, Dafydd," I told him. "You said the old Celtic gods would inflict a terrible vengeance on those who profaned St. Celyn's church." I asked Sherlock Holmes, "Is the case finished?"

"Completely," he said. "We can report to our clients and go home."

21

We had clients I wasn't aware of. After we took Liza Williams back to her room at the Hafod Arms, Sherlock Holmes led me to another private room, where he knocked three times on the door and then twice. When the door opened, he quickly drew me inside.

There were three men in the room. One I had met several times previously when he called upon Sherlock Holmes for assistance in confidential state matters: Arthur Balfour, who in that year 1904 was the Tory Prime Minister, tall, urbanely handsome, impeccably dressed even in Wild Wales. The second, whom I hadn't met before, was a younger man — small, tense, ruggedly good looking: David Lloyd George, Liberal M.P. from north-west Wales, the dynamic symbol of a new age. The presence of these natural enemies on a joint errand signified the extraordinary nature of the case we'd been investigating.

The third man was a plump, elderly major-general — a very major, major-general in his own way of thinking. He sprang forward as we entered and confronted Sherlock Holmes with a tirade. He wanted to call in his troops immediately and put this nuisance in its proper perspective.

Sherlock Holmes had no patience at all with fulminating major-generals. He spoke forcefully to

Arthur Balfour. "The British Government shouldn't be making war-like postures in Wales unless it wants war."

Balfour smiled. "I take it that the matter is under control."

"Entirely," Sherlock Holmes said. "Wain Welling has committed suicide."

Balfour turned to the general. "When Mr. Holmes assumes the task of quelling a rebellion, the army becomes redundant. Take your headquarters back to Cardiff.

The general sputtered objections. Eventually he had to concede that a strategic withdrawal was no disgrace when there was no enemy, but he was still sputtering when he left.

Arthur Balfour, who always sat as though he would have preferred to be lying down, unhinged himself slowly, pushed himself to his feet, and shook my hand. "It's a pleasure to see you again, Porter. I understand that you've been living with the natives and learning Welsh. No sacrifice too great for your work, eh?"

This last was a gibe at David Lloyd George, who scowled angrily at him but said nothing.

"Have you met my distinguished colleague, Porter?" Balfour asked. He introduced us. "You'll have to excuse him," he added. "He's in a foul mood. Nothing is supposed to happen in *his* Wales without his knowledge and consent, and yet a full-blown revolution came very close to hatching here after years of incubation, and he had no inkling of it. Sit down, both of you. Tell us about it." He sank back restfully into his chair.

Lloyd George was incapable of appearing languid. He bounded out of his. "I want the whole story," he announced petulantly.

"No, you don't," Arthur Balfour told him. "No politician ever wants the *whole* story — or needs it. We want enough to understand what the fuss was about and not a jot more. Please proceed, Sherlock."

Lloyd George seated himself again. I took the nearest chair; Sherlock Holmes selected the most uncomfortable seat in the room to make himself comfortable in, thoughtfully pointed the tips of his fingers together, and began. "Some forty years ago, in Southwark, the parents of a child named Harry Smith lived next door to a former Welsh drover, Robyn Williams, and his English wife. Williams was a born story-teller who loved Welsh history and folklore. He told his tales to the children of the neighbourhood — about dragons and warriors and Welsh fairies; about the immortal Welsh poets and King Arthur and the great princes, Llewelyn the Great and the tragic Llewelyn the Last; and especially about Owen Glendower, who came so close to establishing an independent Wales. The other children were highly entertained, but young Harry Smith was enraptured. He began to learn Welsh from Williams. Perhaps he dreamed, as small boys will, of someday going to Wales and becoming a Welsh prince and the instrument of revenge for the lost Owen Glendower and the tragic last Llewelyn.

"Probably nothing more would have happened if he hadn't experienced a tragedy of his own. His young wife died. In his grief, he broke away from his past life and went to Wales. There he shared the trauma of an exploited people and revived his dream." He turned to me. "Have you deciphered his label, Porter?"

"The 'Wain' was meant to stand for 'Owain,' Owen Glendower's name in Welsh, wasn't it?" I asked. "Was he pretending that he was a descendant?"

"That was only the half of it. 'Welling' derives from 'Llewelyn.' He pretended to be a direct descendant of Owen Glendower and also of the two Llewelyns and thus a true prince of Wales. Fraudulent genealogies occur often in history. Owen Glendower himself claimed descent from the Llewelyns, but Glendower was a nobleman from birth and a descendant of the Welsh nobility through both of his parents. For someone to claim a nonexistent throne on the basis of a fictitious family tree is unexpected in the twentieth century.

"Welling lived in Wales for more than fifteen years, and he thoroughly made himself a Welshman. The Welsh language must have been easy for him, perhaps because he learned so much Welsh as a child. He attracted the attention of a wealthy man and in time became his trusted assistant. He travelled throughout Wales looking after his employer's affairs, and this enabled him to meet large numbers of people and recruit them to his cause. Slowly and quietly he built an enormous following, and from it he chose his principal henchmen with great care.

"Wales has suffered tragically at the hands of its English overlords, and it isn't surprising that the Welsh people responded to the appeal of this new leader who claimed to be a genuine Welsh prince. Smith, now Welling, had a gift for inspiring loyalty and trust. He laboured tirelessly to help the downtrodden without any apparent thought of reward, and everywhere he went he gained new followers. He also had a genius for organizing and planning. Most important of all, he had patience. The great coup in which all of Wales would rise in revolt under his leadership was still years in the future. He was building well, and he was content with his progress. He considered it inevitable that England would involve itself in war or some related turmoil during the next decade or two, and he planned to strike at a nation that was already weakened.

"As the number of his followers continued to increase, he knew that sooner or later the British Government must become aware of his burgeoning plot. He prepared for that with ingenuity and a remarkable foresight. Probably the plan was suggested by his proximity to Newtown, where controversy over Robert Owen still simmers. Working through followers, he created a completely innocuous conspiracy as a facade to conceal his real one. Investigators seeking evidence of his secret meetings and his bold plan to overturn England's hold on Wales, were to find, in every instance, an innocent Robert Owen Study League, sponsored by well-meaning and respectable citizens whose only offence was naïvety and idealism.

"The Study League was designed to conceal Welling's plot at every point, and he already had begun to use its meetings as cover for the meetings of his followers. He also was employing elaborate and seemingly unnecessary subterfuge to pass documents or messages. Eventually such precautions would be necessary, and by that time these procedures would have become second nature to his followers through years of practice.

"In the meantime, Welling's son, who was being raised by a Welsh family in Southwark, was growing up. He'd received a thorough Welsh upbringing, and his foster parents even changed his name from the English Albert — or Bertie — to the Welsh Alban. Now he was sixteen and old enough to take his place at his father's side. Welling brought him to Wales, gave him a mentor and bodyguard, a man named Rhys Parry, and began his education as a Welsh prince. The present round of meetings was designed to introduce Welling's son to his followers as the heir of the true Prince of Wales. Rhys Parry and the boy have been attending the Robert Owen lectures all over Wales and then meeting with local conspirators, who probably knelt and swore fealty to the son as they already had to the father.

"All was going well for Welling and would have continued to do so had he not attempted to advance his fortunes by murder."

"Murder?" Lloyd George exclaimed. He bounded to his feet again. "He doesn't seem to have encountered any opposition at all. Why would he commit murder?"

"There were in fact two murders, both very capably planned. The authorities accepted the first as a natural death, and the second left them completely mystified. The murders brought about Welling's downfall nonetheless because they put me on his trail. Welling had a criminal's interest in crime — no doubt he studied police news with care in search of pointers by which his followers could avoid the police. He knew me by reputation, and he feared that I might cause problems for him with an investigation at this critical stage of his conspiracy. When he suspected that two citizens of Newtown were about to ask me to look into the murders, he took elaborate precautions. The result was the opposite of what he intended. It directed my attention to his conspiracy. When I arrived in Wales, I concentrated my efforts on that and left the murders to Porter."

Arthur Balfour turned to me with interest. "Did you solve the murders, Porter?"

"Mr. Holmes solved them," I said. "All I did was fetch and carry."

"Were the murders part of the conspiracy?" Balfour asked.

"Only indirectly," Sherlock Holmes said. "I won't describe them here. There is no need to sully the deliberations of statesmen with matters that are more properly the concern of a police court." His eyes were twinkling, and I saw Arthur Balfour suppress a smile.

Lloyd George missed it completely. He seated himself again and said, "Never mind the murders. Tell us what went wrong with the conspiracy. It was developing nicely. Welling's followers accepted him as a prince of Wales. He was even able to commit murder successfully. Why did he suddenly decide to kill himself?"

"Because I administered two shocks to him. I confronted him with a woman out of his English past, and the paper she handed to him indicated that a deadly danger was about to overwhelm him. He knew that the game was up. He also knew that his duped followers all across Wales would soon be at his throat."

I was supposed to listen quietly to such demonstrations, but I couldn't restrain myself. "What was the paper about?" I asked.

Sherlock Holmes turned to me with a smile. "It was a copy of an exhumation order for Eleanor Tromblay."

"Emeric Tromblay would never consent to such a thing!" I protested.

"He wasn't asked. A copy was delivered to Welling, but there was no original. My object was to shock him into a demonstration of his guilt. He'd safely committed a murder without arousing a shadow of suspicion, and that paper suddenly cut the ground from under him. Proof of arsenic in Eleanor Tromblay's body would have constituted an enormous danger to him. According to the maid, he visited her regularly during her illness. He even had the tender compassion to talk with her and feed her himself at meal time. The authorities would far more readily suspect him than Emeric Tromblay. An exhumation order was as dangerous to him as a loaded revolver pointed at his head.

"I gave him no time to speculate on the genuineness of the paper. Before he could fully comprehend what was happening, a former friend out of his long-buried past suddenly announced his true identity. In that instant, his conspiracy was destroyed. The moment his devoutly patriotic followers comprehended who he really was — *the moment he was revealed to them as an Englishman* — he lost everything. They were certain to feel enraged and defrauded. A renegade Englishman, a mere nobody, had pretended to be a true prince of Wales — and they had believed him!"

"Didn't he make any effort at all to refute her?" Balfour asked.

"No, because he knew that both he and his scheme were finished. Once his real identity was known, a dozen or a hundred witnesses could be brought from London. His son also was known to many people there who could give evidence as to his true identity.

"Not only was his conspiracy destroyed, but he was in grave physical danger. Rhys Parry, for example, had followed him blindly and even committed murder for him because he accepted Welling as a genuine Welsh prince who would lead his people against the hated English for the ultimate glory of Wales. When Parry learned that the supposed prince was only an English adventurer, he was furious. Have no doubt that he drew his knife with murderous intent."

"But he jumped with Welling!" I protested.

"No, Porter, he did not. The moment Welling jumped, Parry was left to face the consequences of his own crimes. He knew that he, too, was finished — but never again would he do anything at all in concert with Welling. He jumped alone."

He turned to the two statesmen. "That's the end of the story, gentlemen. With its leader gone, Welling's conspiracy will quickly wither. No follower will care to admit that he had anything to do with a plot concocted by a masquerading Englishman. The Robert Owen Study League will continue to offer lectures while its money lasts, but there will be no further meetings of Welling's conspirators in conjunction with it."

"Splendid!" Arthur Balfour said. He turned to me. "What is your view of all of this, Porter?"

"I am wondering whether we did the right thing," I said. "Welling was a villain, but I've been living with the Welsh people, and I can't understand why they didn't revolt years ago. When I think of the farmers selling the little meat and butter they have because they can't afford to eat it, and the graves of the miners who died young because of the terrible conditions they work under, I'm convinced that a revolution is long overdue. I would like to sentence every member of Parliament and the House of Lords to eat a typical Welsh dinner three nights a week: flummery with a few pieces of potato washed down by half a pint of buttermilk."

Lloyd George sprang to his feet and seized my hand. "You've lost him, Mr. Prime Minister!" he exclaimed gleefully to Balfour. "This is one young man who'll never cast a Tory vote. Britain is full of them — as you will learn at the next general election!"

Arthur Balfour took no offence. He'd been considered a radical himself when he was young — though never so much so as to abandon his own privileged life for some equivalent of flummery and buttermilk. He smiled kindly and thanked Sherlock Holmes and me for a job well done. David Lloyd George added his own thanks, and we took our leave of them.

Sherlock Holmes led me down one flight of stairs where he knocked on another door. I expected

Arthur Saunders to open it for us. Instead, it was Kyle Connor.

He wheeled his chair around and burst into laughter. "Come in, come in, gentlemen. Please be seated. So Haggart Batt was a bearded Sherlock Holmes." He laughed again. "No wonder the horse dealer was such a formidable chess player." He turned to me. "And who are you when you're not disguised as Iori Jones?"

"Just plain Edward Jones," I said, "but you may call me Porter."

"Don't tell me that you're a genuine Londoner and a solicitor's clerk!"

"A Londoner but not a clerk. I work for Mr. Holmes."

"So! No wonder you're extraordinarily well informed." He turned to Sherlock Holmes. "I heard what happened. I'm most grateful to you—but I also envy you. I wish I could have done it myself."

"I thought a comparison of notes would be beneficial to both of us," Sherlock Holmes said. "Just to begin with, who are you when you're not disguised as Kyle Connor?"

Connor burst into laughter. "But that's my name! My mother was Welsh; my father was an Irishman who settled here. I left Wales at an early age and worked up and down North and South America as an engineer and became successful and moderately rich.

"In South America I had a good friend named Wyn Davies. He died of a fever while building a railway there, poor chap. He was the brother of Glyn Huws's wife. I made a deathbed promise to him that I would visit his sister and return his personal effects to her. Unfortunately, when I finally reached Wales, his sister was recently dead. Glyn Huws was left with a young baby, Meleri. He was as fine a man as I have ever met, and we became close friends.

"Through all of my wanderings down through the years we continued to correspond and meet when we could. Then I suffered my unfortunate accident. I returned to England — to London and then Shrewsbury and eventually to Wales. I had no family of my own, and Glyn was a brother to me. He visited me as often as he could while I lived in Shrewsbury. What he told me about local events sounded alarming. He didn't understand what was happening, but he knew instinctively that something was wrong, and he was worried about Meleri. When Tynewydd became available, I decided to move to Wales and give him whatever support I could. He could visit me there easily, and he did so, several times a week.

"But there was little he could tell me, and my other visitors — the vicar, the doctor, Emeric Tromblay's guests — knew even less about what was happening. Then Eleanor Tromblay died, and Glyn felt certain there was something wrong with her death. His worries about Meleri increased.

"He told me about his appointment with Welling— Welling claimed to know something about Emeric Tromblay and Meleri—and when he was murdered, I immediately concluded that Welling was responsible. I also knew that the authorities would take no action without evidence, and there was none, so I kept the information to myself. I suppose that needlessly complicated your own problems in investigating Glyn's death."

"Not really," Sherlock Holmes said. "The background of Glyn Huws's death was apparent from the beginning, and Welling's connection with it emerged early in the investigation. As you discovered yourself, the problem was in finding evidence."

"If I'd known who you were, I would have told you at once, but I thought both you and Porter were Welling's henchmen. When I no longer had Glyn to talk with, I was completely helpless. I couldn't find out anything at all. I sat there like a fat, ugly spider waiting for someone or something to come to my web, and no one or nothing did.

"Finally I sent for friends to help me. They stayed in Llanidloes and nosed around to see what they could find out—as Englishmen in Wales, they found out very little — but they did happen onto the resurrection of the Rebeccas, which intrigued me no end. I determined to learn what I could about that. I swam across the lake at night to meet my friends, and I joined them in night rides in an attempt to identify the Rebeccas. In time I might have succeeded, but the Rebeccas identified me first and suspected me of constituting a danger to Welling's plans, which I certainly would have been if I'd known how to go about it. So they took action."

"Then you knew that Welling was responsible for the attempt to assassinate you," Sherlock Holmes said.

Connor nodded. "In a way, it was flattering. He thought me so much more dangerous than I was. It was a confounded nuisance, though. I understand that you fired several times at Parry. I was under water at the time and not counting, and my friends thought you were shooting at me. They were unarmed, and they feared that we were outnumbered as well. We left in a great hurry. There's nothing more I can tell you. I'm glad it's finished."

"How did you happen to meet Garat Sibley?"

Connor laughed heartily. "I met him two years ago on a trip to Aberystwyth. He showed me his Camera Obscura then, and I thought it a bit of a joke. But Aberystwyth seemed as good a place as any to convalesce from the bullet wound, so I telegraphed, and Sibley reserved the room for me. It was a nuisance getting myself carried up to the top storey of that boarding house, but once I was there, I was very comfortable. On the day I arrived, I looked out of the window and saw two men whom I recognized as Rebeccas. I decided to put the Camera Obscura to practical use — first with the Rebeccas, then with

Porter and Dafydd Madryn, and finally with Rhys Parry and his young friend."

"What did you learn?" Sherlock Holmes asked.

"Nothing. Not a blessed thing. Parry and his friend rarely talked. All I got from Porter and Madryn were language lessons, and the Rebeccas never returned to the seafront after that one sighting. But watching the Camera Obscura helped me to pass the time. Tell me — what *was* the idea with the Rebeccas?"

"Welling was reaching back into history to make use of every weapon available to him, just as he made ceremonial use of those antique instruments, the crŵth and the pibgorn. His object was to ally himself with Wales's illustrious past. At the crucial moment in his revolt, he would have revived the legend about Owen Glendower sleeping with his army in a mountain cave and finally awakening during some great crisis to fall upon the enemies of Wales. He intended to present himself as the reincarnated Glendower, of course.

"The criminal often is a hero in Wales because he aligns himself against authority and especially against English authority. The Rebeccas were immensely popular for their revolt against oppressive road tolls. Welling wanted to create the impression that this legendary force had joined in his own battle against injustice. From what we know of him, I suspect that there also was another object. The Rebeccas had a darker side — unprincipled men made use of them for private vendettas and to silence their critics. Welling would have employed them in the same way the moment his cause developed opposition. For the present, their only function was to frequent the neighbourhood where the Robert Owen Study League and Welling's conspirators were meeting and to make themselves as conspicuous as possible. They took action against you only because Welling considered you a threat."

"I see," Connor said. "I thank you for your help. You may have saved my life, and bringing Welling to justice certainly saved my sanity." He added with a laugh, "That doesn't mean that I'll be merciful the next time we play chess, which I hope will be soon."

"I hope so, too," Sherlock Holmes said. "By the way, you really were of immense help in my pursuit of Welling. The ruthless action he took against you added considerably to my understanding of his character."

We exchanged another round of compliments and took our leave of him.

"He seems extremely capable," I observed.

"He's a brilliant man," Sherlock Holmes said. "He must have been an excellent engineer. Were it not for his unfortunate disability, he might have battled Welling on equal terms. We have two more clients to report to, Porter. I want to see them together, so I told Arthur Saunders we would meet him and Bryn Huws in Newtown."

"I thought perhaps you'd want to report to Emeric Tromblay. I was looking forward to telling him that I have no interest in working for him."

"He does have a vacancy," Sherlock Holmes said. He looked at me with a half-smile. "Perhaps you should consider it."

"No, thank you. I know better than to try to fill Wain Welling's shoes. I could climb a mountain at night to see a sick cow, but I wouldn't have any idea of how to cure it."

"Welling was extremely capable. His energy was astonishing. He was able to work so effectively for Tromblay and still find time for his monstrous conspiracy. How tirelessly he laboured for so many years!"

"He was playing for high stakes," I said.

"Do you know, Porter, if he'd avoided his delusions of grandeur, he easily could have got himself elected to Parliament. He could have teamed with Lloyd George and accomplished something really worthwhile for the Welsh people. This tragedy cuts more ways than would seem possible."

Madryn was waiting patiently for us. "Here is Dafydd," Sherlock Holmes said. "If we hurry, we can catch the last train to Aberystwyth."

We stopped for a day at Pentrederwydd to collect belongings left there and to take leave of our friends. In Newtown, Humphrey the Bear's Bear Bus delivered us ceremonially to the hotel where we asked

Mr. Breese to send a message to Arthur Saunders. This time Saunders didn't keep us waiting. He and Bryn Huws arrived promptly. Mr. Breese brought cwrw da for all of us, swept the room with a smile as he left, and discreetly closed the door. Bryn Huws leaped to his feet. "We heard that Wain Welling killed himself," he said. "Then it wasn't Tromblay?"

Sherlock Holmes shook his head. "You might as well sit down," he told him. "I'll make my report as brief as possible, but it was a complicated case." Huws sank back into his chair.

"You engaged us to investigate the murders," Sherlock Holmes said. "While doing so, we discovered that Wain Welling was not Welsh, but an English adventurer, and that he had contrived a serious plot against His Majesty's Government. I've delivered my report on that conspiracy to the proper authorities. I mention it to you only because the murders grew out of it.

"Welling had one fatal weakness as a revolutionist. He wasn't wealthy. His devoted followers were contributing enough money to run his organization in a modest way, but eventually he would need an army and weapons. He knew that he couldn't mount a revolt against the British Government in this century without an enormous amount of money. He also knew that wealth attracts wealth. In a revolution, the wealthy, who have the most to lose, will calculate the odds with care before they back either side. A threadbare revolution would be doomed from the start, so Welling needed huge quantities of money. He may have sought employment with Emeric Tromblay years ago in the expectation of someday usurping his fortune. That was what he was trying to do now, and it destroyed him.

"The plan he contrived is credible only for a man totally without moral principles. Welling believed the end justified any means. He had long been Meleri Huws's lover — "

Bryn Huws leaped to his feet again. "That can't be true!"

"Meleri Huws admired men who could do things," Sherlock Holmes said soberly. "She laughed at the pathetically inept Benton Tromblay, but she was vulnerable to a man like Welling, who was superbly competent in almost anything. She was patriotic, and Welling posed as the quintessence of the patriotic Welshman, engaged in a tireless struggle to free his country from England. Finally, he presented himself to her as a true prince of Wales. She was to be his princess. How could she resist that? In comparison, being mistress of Tromblay Hall held no attraction at all for her.

"If Welling had courted Meleri in the usual way and asked Glyn Huws for his daughter's hand, he would have gladly consented. He liked and admired Welling. But first Welling needed money — Emeric Tromblay's money. The plan he contrived to obtain it was a simple one, but only a totally unprincipled man would have thought of it.

"Meleri Huws was to marry Emeric Tromblay — having insisted beforehand that Tromblay make her his heir in place of the unfortunate Benton. A short time after they were married, Tromblay would die — from an accident or an unexpected illness. After a suitable period of mourning, the young widow would marry Wain Welling, giving him control of Tromblay's fortune, and Welling would have the financial power for his revolution.

"Welling's first step was to convince Tromblay that Glyn Huws's farm was immensely valuable. Welling salted ore specimens at Meini Mawr and then told Tromblay that he had accidentally found something that looked interesting and took him to see the place. Tromblay, alert to the possibility of acquiring a valuable mining property for the mere cost of a farm, sent samples to be assayed and told Welling to keep his discovery a secret. Then he tried to buy Meini Mawr. As Welling anticipated, Glyn Huws refused to sell.

"The next step was to remove a major obstacle to the plot, Tromblay's wife. It was Welling who administered increasing amounts of arsenic to Eleanor Tromblay. Letty Howell, the servant who nursed Eleanor Tromblay during her fatal illness, has testified that he had ample opportunity.

"Tromblay was genuinely fond of his wife, but he is a practical man. He thought she died of a natural illness. Fate willed it, but fate certainly didn't intend him to be a recluse. He considered himself a young man with many years to live. When Welling suggested that he acquire the Huws farm by marrying Meleri, he thought it an excellent idea. The girl was highly attractive and so was her property."

Bryn Huws muttered something in Welsh.

"But there was one more obstacle," Sherlock Holmes went on. "Glyn Huws would never permit his daughter to marry Emeric Tromblay — so Glyn Huws had to die. Rhys Parry and Welling's son kept an appointment that Welling had made with Glyn under the pretense of having something important to tell him about his daughter and Tromblay. Welling took the precaution of arranging the appointment at a time when he would be in Cardiff on business."

"How did you find all that out?" Bryn Huws demanded.

"By collecting every available scrap of evidence and forming my own deductions. Meleri Huws supplied several important clues unknowingly. She is a genuine heroine in this tale. She refused to submit to Welling's nefarious plans. Despite the attraction he held for her, she'd had glimpses of his true character, and she greatly feared he had murdered her father. Nothing less than that could explain the joy with which she reacted to Mr. Jones's discovery that her father was murdered by two men in clogs who had waited to ambush him. She mistakenly thought this discovery proved her lover's innocence.

"But when she saw Welling again, he was more insistent than ever that she marry Emeric Tromblay.

She ordered him from her presence a second time, but he was confident that eventually she would yield. He encouraged Tromblay to press his suit, and Tromblay continued to make polite calls at Meini Mawr. And that set the stage for the final drama. I was able to confront Welling with evidence of his crimes and also of his past, and he chose suicide. Perhaps Meleri played an inadvertent role in that dénouement. Welling knew that she would scorn him the moment she realized he was English.

"You gentlemen have been guilty of serious misjudgement concerning one person in this case. Emeric Tromblay was in no way the monster his Welsh neighbours and tenants thought him. That was an image created by Welling, who slyly managed to take credit himself for Tromblay's many commendable charities and actually manoeuvred his employer into reprehensible actions such as evictions — usually by making false allegations against tenants — so he could dramatically come to the victims' rescue. As you certainly are aware, the Welsh are a close-knit group. A kind act toward one of the victims gained Welling a legion of followers among friends and relatives who admired him without reservation for the way he appeared to outwit his monstrous employer."

Sherlock Holmes took out his watch. "And now, gentlemen — your case is finished, and the Bear Bus is waiting for us."

"It is well-finished," Bryn Huws said. "Liwyraf dial, dial Duw, the most complete vengeance is the vengeance of God."

We took our leave of them. Outside the inn, the aristocratic-looking Humphrey the Bear waited with his Bear Bus to assist us in boarding. In addition to my knapsack, I was carrying a package. Sherlock Holmes had paid no attention to it on the train from Pentrederwydd, but now he looked at it curiously.

"It's my walking shoes and the pair of clogs Ifan Vaughan made for me," I explained.

"Pray tell me what use you intend to make of clogs in London."

"I'll wear them once a week," I said. "Every Sunday afternoon I'm going to Y Llew Du to drink cwrw da. I must keep in touch with the culture of my ancestors. If I extend my researches to other Welsh taverns, and drink enough cwrw da, I may even be able to convince myself that I'm descended from Owen Glendower or the Llewelyns. What would it feel like to be a true prince of Wales?"

The Bear Bus was getting underway. Sherlock Holmes made no comment. The prospect of feeling like a prince didn't interest him.

"What will happen to the religious fervour you told me about?" I asked.

"It's still there," he said indifferently. "It will have to run its course, but at least there is no longer a Wain Welling waiting to exploit it."

"I'm still wondering whether we did the right thing," I said. "The Welsh people need a genuine hero."

"Welling's revolution wouldn't have helped the Welsh people," Sherlock Holmes said. "They would have exchanged an indifferent master for a ruthless one. Welling's object was not to free them but to enslave them anew to his own glorification. And what kind of prince would his son have made after watching his father murder his way to the throne? But Welling's revolution was foredoomed to failure. It would have made a battleground of Wales, bringing only misery and destruction in its wake. The same was true of Owen Glendower's revolution — it left Wales devastated — but that's an aspect that the Welsh prefer not to dwell on. Violence begets violence, Porter. The people of this beautiful land must find a way to prosperity and happiness without destroying themselves and their country.

"Let's turn our thoughts to brighter things. I had a telegram from Radbert yesterday. He has a surprise waiting for us. Not another mouse, I hope. You must see him as soon as you arrive."

Sherlock Holmes planned to travel south instead of east. His objective was the south coast of Wales and the island of Flat Holm, a place he had long wanted to visit. He didn't explain why, but a guidebook provided ample clues. Not only did the island possess its own murderous history — among other things, a force of marauding Danes had once been marooned on it to starve — but the murderers of Thomas à Becket were supposed to be buried there.

He lit his pipe. I leaned back and reflected on Mrs. Hudson's probable reaction if she caught me wearing iron-soled clogs in her house. The Bear Bus bounced its way toward Newtown Station.

Envoi

A Study in Scarlet, THE FIRST SHERLOCK Holmes story, was published more than a hundred years ago. Because of the considerable lapse of time since the Great Detective was ranging through gas-lit London, a new Sherlock Holmes novel must be researched and written as historical fiction as well as mystery fiction. The contemporary author will find it helpful to visit the locations he is about to describe — I consider it essential — but that is only the beginning. For a *Glendower Conspiracy,* the author must evoke the London, the Newtown, the Wales of 1904. These exist in pieces — sometimes very small pieces — in a million books and public records and photographs and postcards and letters, and the search takes one to libraries and museums and private collections and the reminiscences of the elderly. It sometimes seems that the one essential small piece that the author needs is the one that is impossible to find.

I am deeply indebted to two classes of authors who have written in vivid detail concerning life in Britain during the first decade of this century. One group, consisting of writers such as Ford Maddox Hueffer — who later called himself Ford Maddox Ford — James Douglas, E. V. Lucas, Edward Thomas, and W. H. Davies, described their own contemporary world. The other group, with writers such as Thomas Burke and C. H. Rolph, experienced the first decade of this century as children and described it later in reminiscences. It would be impossible to faithfully recreate Edwardian England without drawing upon the invaluable material left for us by these and other writers.

A third resource consists of descriptions of various parts of Britain in the writings of travelers or travel writers and in contemporary guides such as those of Baedeker. Again the useful material may exist only in very small pieces, for descriptions of places seen in passing are likely to be limited to a sentence here, a paragraph there, nothing in several other books. Where it is found, however, it is sometimes pure gold. For example, my description of Yr Hen Dafarn, the Old Tavern in Pentrederwydd, is based upon Hissy's *A Leisurely Tour in England,* published in 1913, and is actually a description of the tavern *Aleppo Merchant* in Carno, a village only a few miles from the site of the fictitious Pentrederwydd.

Historical fiction is a blending of the historical and the fictitious. Many of the characters of this novel were real. Robert Owen was as described throughout (but the Robert Owen Study League is my invention). So were Owen Glendower, Arthur Balfour, and David Lloyd George. Mr. H.E. Breese really was the proprietor of the Bear Hotel, Newtown, in 1904. Information about Mr. Breese and the hotel came from an interview Maurice Richards conducted with Mr. Breese's daughter-in-law, Mrs.

Leslie Breese, aged 77 at the time of the interview. A real Humphrey the Bear drove a real Bear Bus, a popular conveyance at that time. Humphrey's real name was Humphrey Thomas, and his local fame was sufficient to cause his photograph to be included on a postcard with three other popular Newtown characters." Mr. Breese's brother, Andrew Breese, was the proprietor of the Unicorn Hotel. Samuel Powell did run a brewery in Newtown, a business founded more than a hundred years ago that has been continued through four generations of Powells. The Pryce-Jones family's Royal Welsh Warehouse flourished until after the First World War and then declined, but its mail-order business is still operating under another owner. Sir Pryce's mother was related to Robert Owen, and his son, Col. Edward Pryce-Jones, succeeded his father as M.P. for the Montgomeryshire Boroughs. Members of the Roberts family of Newtown were famous harpists who performed before Queen Victoria and in 1904 — shortly after the time this novel closed — for King Edward VII and Queen Alexandra during their majesties' visit to Wales. Mr. Philip Snowden did lecture on "Co-operation: Its relation to other reforms," in Newtown in February, 1904. Many small farmers of this period did have to sell their meat, butter, and eggs for rent money rather than eat them. The backdrop for this novel, including Newtown, Devil's Bridge, Aberystwyth, and London, is as accurate as the author's research and the generous interest of persons in England and Wales could make it.

On the other hand, the book's central characters, including St. Celyn, are fictitious, as are the places Groesffordd, Pentrederwydd, Tromblay Hall, Llangelyn, Tynewydd, Llyn Tŷ-mawr, Meini Mawr, and their valleys — and also including 221 Baker Street! I have pulled apart the map of Wales west of Newtown and inserted a small fictional region where much of the story's action takes place.

Probably few readers are aware of the delicate balance between history and fiction that the historical novel demands. I was not fully aware of it myself until Maurice Richards found for me this notice in the January 26, 1904, issue of the *Montgomeryshire Express:*

PUBLIC HALL, NEWTOWN
ONE NIGHT ONLY
Wednesday 23rd March
CHARLES FROHMAN presents the LYCEUM THEATRE SUCCESS
WILLIAM GILLETTE'S CELEBRATED PLAY
In Four Acts — entitled —
SHERLOCK HOLMES
(By William Gillette and A. Conan Doyle)
Front seats 3/-, 2/- Admission 1/-
Doors open 7.30; Curtain 7.45
Early Door at 7 o'clock, 3d extra.
Carriages at 10.20
Plan of Hall and Seats at Phillips' Music Salon

In *The Glendower Conspiracy,* Porter Jones arrived in Newtown on June 13, 1904. On that same day, Sherlock Holmes traveled a few miles past Newtown to the fictional Groesffordd, where he collected the horses waiting for him and went on to meet his "old friend," the fictional vicar of the fictional village of Pentrederwydd. But what is fictitious and what is real? Less than three months earlier, the Sherlock Holmes drama was performed in Newtown's Public Hall showing Sherlock Holmes as a character in a play. That performance was real — it is history. My novel shows Sherlock Holmes as a real person investigating a real mystery in the immediate vicinity of Newtown. That is fiction.

I was tempted to make reference to the play; but, as Sherlock Holmes would have quickly pointed out, this would not do. In the novel, Sherlock Holmes is and remains real, and no fictions, dramatic or otherwise, are to be admitted.

In July, 1986, with my daughter, Donna Emerson, as chauffeur, I ranged widely through southern and mid-Wales, from Cardiff and St. Fagans in the south to Snowdonia in the north, from Aberystwyth in the west to Newtown in the east, in search of clues as to what Sherlock Holmes might have been doing in Wales. We visited Devil's Bridge and Parson's Bridge. At the Ysbyty Cynfyn church we met its vicar, the Reverend Alexander Clark, who invited us to tea, discussed the history of Wales and of the Devil's Bridge area with us, and introduced us to his 92-year-old cousin, Mr. David Edward Davies, with whom I taped an interview about Wales in the early twentieth century. Mr. Davies worked on farms from youth until retirement, and he described that life in vivid detail — including the prank the young farm hands delighted in playing at the theatre in Aberystwyth. They threw darts fashioned of chicken feathers and potato slices at the performers. After almost three quarters of a century, he was still gleeful about the way the potato slices stuck to the performers' faces. I felt a genuine regret that the scope of the novel didn't permit more extensive use of Mr. Davies's recollections.

In Newtown we visited Robert Owen's grave and the Robert Owen Museum, and there I found the clues I was looking for.

This novel owes its existence to the assistance of a great many people, many of whom gave it with friendly cheerfulness and without the faintest notion that it was an author they were helping. I am pleased to thank these anonymous benefactors again. Among them were the friendly and knowledgeable attendants at the Welsh Folk Museum in St. Fagans, a magnificent indoor and outdoor museum that provided a memorable introduction to Welsh history. One of its exhibits featured coracles from the various Welsh rivers, and the display of the different designs side by side was illuminating. Like Porter Jones, I sketched them. Across England and Wales, a host of shopkeepers, museum attendants, bed and breakfast and hotel operators, and total strangers who were met in likely or unlikely places made their own unique contributions unawares.

The personnel at the National Library of Wales, in Aberystwyth, were extremely gracious in dealing with a confused foreigner.

Miss Norma Morrison, a graduate of the University College of Wales in Aberystwyth, kindly furnished information and photographs.

John Davidson, secretary of the Robert Owen Museum in Newtown, kept the museum open for us long after its scheduled closing, plied me with a quantity of material that later proved invaluable, and did me the greatest favor received during my travels by giving me an introduction to the Newtown historian, Maurice Richards.

Not all of the assistance came from Britain. Mineralogist Allen Cichanski, of Eastern Michigan University, provided information about prospecting for galena and reviewed a draft of the chapter where that occurs.

Lt. Col. Mervyn D. Lemon, a British liaison officer stationed in the United States, kindly read the entire manuscript and helped to clarify my understanding of a number of points where English language and living differ from U.S. traditions. In England, Sir John Winnifrith, former Director General of Britain's National Trust, did the same and provided both historical and editorial guidance.

Maurice Richards, the historian whose name appears on the dedication page, is a tireless perfectionist whose temperament matches my own. As an example of his response to the dozens of questions I sent his way, when I asked whether there had been any kind of memorial plaque on Robert Owen's birthplace in Newtown in 1904, he answered, "No plaque there then, but I have seen a picture, which I think has been reproduced in Podmore's *Life of Robert Owen,* which shows the inscription **BIRTHPLACE OF ROBERT OWEN, PHILANTHROPIST** in large black capitals on the ledge below the top windows. . . . I am fairly certain that it was there in 1904 for two reasons: (1) it was probably put there at the time the tomb and library memorials were erected in 1902-03, and (2) Podmore's book was published about 1906." When I asked him whether John Torbuch's *A Collection of Welsh Travels. . . .*, which I quoted from a source that only vaguely identified it, was an actual publication or a manuscript, he looked for it in the National Library of Wales on his next visit and was able to inform me that there were published editions of 1742, 1743, 1749, and 1759. When I raised questions about Cwrt-Plâs-yn-dre, Owen Glendower's Parliament House in Newtown, he went there and photographed it and sent copies of the photos. In response to my queries about Mr.

Breese, he interviewed Mr. Breese's daughter-in-law. He even recruited a Newtown task force to search for items of information that I needed. Mrs. Pam Clayton and Mrs. Jean Williams, both veterans of Mr. Richards's projects in local history, rendered valuable assistance, and Mr. Tony Clayton made it possible for the trains to run on time throughout the novel by turning up a 1904 Bradshaw — the volume of railway schedules that was one of Sherlock Holmes's favorite publications. Mr. Richards also interviewed Mr. Trevor Powell, a direct descendant of Sam Powell, the brewery owner. Mr. Powell kindly furnished information about beer in Newtown at the beginning of this century, making it possible for the hotels in this novel to serve the brands they actually did serve in 1904.

Enormous difficulties are encountered when one attempts to write about a distant place visited only briefly, and the accuracy of this book in numerous small as well as several large details is due to Mr. Richards's magnanimity. He also gave me lessons in Welsh by mail, but it would be unfair to hold him responsible for my halting progress.

Douglas Morgan, of Cardiff, served as a meticulous and highly literate final proof reader for the manuscript, deftly culling an inevitable small crop of errors everyone else had overlooked.

Finally, no historical backdrop would have made this book possible without a Sherlock Holmes to place in front of it. *The Glendower Conspiracy* is one more tribute to Arthur Conan Doyle's immortal creation.

Lloyd Biggle, Jr.
Ypsilanti, March, 1990

BOOKS BY LLOYD BIGGLE, JR.

MYSTERIES

The Quallsford Inheritance, A Memoir of Sherlock Holmes
Interface for Murder
The Glendower Conspiracy, A Memoir of Sherlock Holmes

SCIENCE FICTION NOVELS

The Angry Espers
All the Colors of Darkness
The Fury Out of Time
Watchers of the Dark
The Still, Small Voice of Trumpets
The World Menders
The Light That Never Was
Monument
This Darkening Universe
Silence is Deadly
The Whirligig of Time
(with T. L. Sherred) *Alien Main*

SCIENCE FICTION SHORT STORIES

The Rule of the Door, and Other Fanciful Regulations
The Metallic Muse
A Galaxy of Strangers
(as editor) *Nebula Award Stories Seven*

OTHER BOOKS IN THE BROWN BAG MYSTERY SERIES FROM COUNCIL OAK:

THE MARK TWAIN MURDERS
by Edith Skom

ISBN 0-933031-17-3

A killer is loose in the library at Midwestern University and the entire English faculty is under suspicion. Beth Austin, a member of the faculty, has exhumed some curious facts about an award-winning student paper. Facts suggesting plagiarism. Suddenly the student is discovered dead and Beth herself becomes a moving target.

THE CHINESE OXYMORON
by Veronica S. Pierce

ISBN 0-933031-29-7

Minikin Small has inherited a townhouse in Manhattan when a man is murdered in her foyer. Suddenly she's plunged into the center of an international intrigue. Dashing through the streets of New York carrying a priceless violin, she finds herself eluding hit men, foreign spies and the police while she sorts out the bad guys from the good guys in this fast-paced mystery thriller.

THE FAST-DEATH FACTOR
by Virginia Crosby

ISBN 0-933031-30-3

Campus politics prove lethal for the controversial president of Tipton College, who is found dead following a faculty reception. An analysis shows that the instrument was a water-bloom toxin stolen from the biology lab, but which of the several plausible murderers is the real one? The president's neglected wife, a disgruntled faculty member, an ambitious administrator? Or is it the lovely dean of the college, Anne Parker-Brown?